Blood and Bone

A Dream Walker Novel

Michelle Miles

This is a work of fiction. All characters, organizations and events portrayed in this novel are either products of the author's imagination or used fictitiously.

BLOOD AND BONE

Cover Design by Erin Dameron-Hill

Copyright © 2020 Michelle Miles
Dusty Tome Publishing

All rights reserved. The author has provided this book for personal use only. This book or any portion thereof may not be reproduced or used in any manner whatsoever without the express written permission of the publisher except for the use of brief quotations in a book review.

ISBN: 978-1-7343068-5-9

*Whosoever possesses this Holy Lance and
understands the powers it serves,
holds in his hand the destiny of the world for good or evil.
—Legend of the Holy Lance*

*Put on the full armor of God,
so that you can take your stand
against the devil's schemes.
—Ephesians 6:11*

Dedication

For my husband, who continues to believe in me and this series.

Chapter 1

Somerset, England, Late September 2038 A.D.

AT FIVE YEARS OLD, I was called a demon child. I dream walked my foster mother's younger sister by accident. Ruby's dreams were erratic and scary and I didn't understand them. Naturally, she thought I was a freak. She'd come to visit and spent the night with us and, well, she wasn't the most upstanding young adult on the planet. She drank, smoke, cussed, had a boyfriend named Ricky who rode a Harley. They were both part of a motorcycle gang. They both enjoyed the use of recreational hallucinogens.

Ruby and Ricky were quite a pair.

As a curious five-year-old, I caught her stealing my foster mother's wallet to support her habits and her boyfriend. She smacked me hard and threatened me within an inch of my life if I told her sister.

I tattled anyway and got in trouble for telling lies. But when my foster mother found her wallet empty and her credit card gone after her sister disappeared, she apologized. I remember the conversation as clear as if it happened yesterday.

"She called me a name, Mama. And she hit me."

"She shouldn't have done that." She patted me on the hand to reassure me. "You went into her mind, didn't you?"

I nodded. "I didn't mean to."

As she often did, she pursued her lips in thought. Worry flickered in her eyes. "People don't understand what you can do, Anna. It scares them."

"Like it scared you?"

"Yes, like that. You mustn't do it without permission. You must learn control. Can you do that for me?"

As a child, I gave an emphatic nod. "Yes, Mama."

I did manage to control my dream walking—by never doing it again. At least until that fateful day in Dallas.

I never saw Ruby again. If she returned, my mother kept her far, far away from me.

Funny the things you remember. Only now as an adult did I understand Ruby's completely fucked up mind. I forgot a lot about my childhood until I flipped through the pages of the journal I found in my old room at my uncle's manor. I spent late nights reading it and remembering with fondness the woman who raised me the first thirteen years of my life. I missed her.

I hadn't thought of her again until recently. My life changed dramatically when, at thirteen, my uncle found me and brought me to England. I spent five years in England with Edward and his tutors. During that time, I corresponded with her but somewhere along the way, her letters and emails stopped coming. When I returned to Dallas, I searched for her only to discover she had moved. Forwarding address unknown.

One thing was for sure. I wasn't a demon child. I was a demon killer.

Demons called me a demon-seer. Archangels called me the Keeper of the Holy Relics.

Back in June, my life was turned upside down by the archangels and the Fallen, a band of fallen angels led by Lucifer intent on hunting down human souls to build his dark army. They both wanted me to do a job for them—find the five Holy Relics. A job I reluctantly agreed to take. I went after the Horn of Gabriel because my archenemy and fallen angel, Azriel, gave it to Mammon the Prince of Greed.

I lived with regret and guilt on a constant basis. I regretted a lot about the decisions I made over the last several months. The biggest regret was dream walking a patient at the hospital where I worked. Her name was Emma. We were friends once. That's when my life utterly derailed, when I met Azriel, and, in a weird twist of fate, Kincade Harrison.

Two thorns in my side.

And, of course, there was the messenger angel, Joachim. He was another prickly thorn. I was cursed with thorns.

Gideon's fist crashed against my cheekbone, the pain exploding across my face bringing me back to the present. I should focus on my training instead of reminiscing.

My head snapped back and my teeth clinked together with a sickening snap. I refused to go down. I retaliated with a left hook which missed his face. I caught nothing but air. His right fist landed in my ribs and pushed the wind out of my lungs. I doubled over, coughing. He jabbed me in the back of the head with his elbow. Stars burst into my vision. I collapsed to my hands and knees, staring down at the gray workout mat while trying to catch my breath.

My uncle's idea of training stunk.

"Too slow, chickadee."

There was a sneer in Gideon's voice. He got a sick kind of joy out of beating the shit out of me. I flopped over, resting my forearms on my drawn-up knees. Peering at him, I squinted against the harsh fluorescent light as a drop of sweat slipped into my open eye. The salt stung.

He grinned at me, his lips stretching over his teeth. A dimple pierced his left cheek. Beads of perspiration dotted his forehead. He flexed his fingers in his fingerless gloves.

"Being that slow will get you killed."

Gideon was hired by my uncle, Edward, to kick my ass and teach me to fight and defend myself. The old man didn't like the way I rescued him from Hell.

"Step aside, Gid, it's my turn."

Gilli cracked her knuckles and licked her lips in anticipation. She was his twin. I called them the Wonder Twins. She had a matching dimple, the same brown eyes, the same brown hair and was as pretty as her brother. She relished kicking my ass, too.

I held up my hands in surrender. "I think I need a break."

"No breaks." And it was punctuated with the slamming of the door.

I peered around Gilli and Gideon to see my uncle standing inside the workout room. The one he made for me in one of the outer buildings on his estate in Cannington, a small village in Somerset, England.

"You trying to kill me, old man?" I climbed to my feet and stalked across the room to snatch up my water bottle.

"You don't have time to rest," Edward said, his voice hard.

"Ah, give her a break, Eddie. She's worked hard this week."

I suppressed a snicker. Every time I heard Gideon call my uncle Eddie, it took all my strength not to burst out laughing. He was about as far from an Eddie as he could get. An upper-class Englishman, he always wore a designer three-piece suit. His jaw was set in a straight stubborn line as his dark blue eyes assessed me from across the room. His black hair had nary a strand out of place.

Gideon snatched his towel off the floor and wiped the two beads of sweat off his face. Seriously, I hated him. Why couldn't he sweat like the rest of us? Sweat dampened my hair, neck and back.

"Time is of the essence," Edward said in that clipped British accent.

I rolled my eyes.

"You should be out searching," he continued.

I pinpointed him with my best glare. "You're the one who wanted me here to train. You said I fought like a girl. You said I couldn't cut it if I found myself up against a truly dangerous enemy."

I ditched Kincade in Hong Kong and headed to Somerset not long after finding the Horn of Gabriel and handing it over to Darius, the warrior angel who'd been helping me. I still had a pang of guilt for leaving without saying goodbye the day before his release from the hospital. Add that to the long list of regrets. I should have stuck around to at least make sure he got out okay. But I didn't because, deep down, I was a coward. Keeping people at arm's length was kind of my thing.

Kincade's insistence on helping me find the other relics bugged me. I realized he could track me down in England. I expected him to. It wasn't like I tried to disappear. There was only one place to go—the only home I had. But he hadn't made an appearance. A little piece of me was disappointed.

A thin smile crossed Edward's face. But it wasn't a friendly smile. It was that smile that said I was in deep trouble. "Will you two excuse us for a moment, please?"

Aw, crap.

Gilli and Gideon grabbed their stuff and headed for the door. It banged closed. The sound of the overhead lights buzzing was deafening in the silence. We stared each other down. I didn't budge as I took a sip of water.

"Well?" I said.

"It's time for you to start searching for the Spear of Destiny," Edward said.

"I told you I would."

As I said it, the denial hit me hard and fast like one of Gideon's punches to the face. The pain and shame flamed through my cheeks and I refused to look at him. Even Edward knew my inner denial but said nothing.

The memory of Isobel Marques burned in my mind. She came to me in Hong Kong with a warning about the Spear of Destiny. I didn't forget what she said.

Your path has been foretold. If you alter it, if you change the direction of your destiny…then…you will most certainly die.

Thanks for that, lady.

I used the excuse to train at Edward's sprawling estate to avoid searching. But I couldn't escape my fate.

"You must leave here, Anna," he said. "You must search for the next relic."

What if I didn't want to? I realized I didn't have a choice but hiding here in the countryside seemed like a much better plan. Here I didn't have to worry about demons chasing me. Or Azriel popping in to torment me. With Edward around, he used some sort of mind power that kept Azriel out of my dreams and I managed to sleep. I enjoyed the best rest I had in a long while these last few months.

Joachim hadn't even showed up to taunt me about my progress.

Here, I was Anna. I was chickadee to Gideon. I was Anna to Gilli and Edward and the servants. I was Miss Walker to Kincade. I wasn't Keeper of the Holy Relics.

I wanted to be Anna. Nothing more.

"And you know where to begin," he said.

I did. I still had the envelope with block lettering addressed to me and the postcard of Istanbul with the words *Spear of Destiny* written on the other side. I brought it with me to examine the picture, to try to figure out what the building was and where to begin.

When I received a similar postcard of Hong Kong pointing me to the Horn of Gabriel, it was a clue where to find it. I assumed the postcard of Istanbul was also a clue but I hadn't researched it.

I was too damn scared.

My uncle stood there in his perfect three-piece suit gazing at me as though I were an errant child. As though we hadn't gone to Hell and back together. As though I hadn't saved his life.

"I'm not ready," I said. "I have to finish training with Gideon and Gilli."

"No." His voice was hard and unforgiving. "You've been training with them for three months, Anna. You are ready. And if you aren't, you'll get yourself killed and this is all for naught."

Thanks for the vote of confidence.

"I know what you're doing. You're hiding from your duties. From your fate." He took a step toward me. "But things have not changed, Anna. Your fate is still the same. You *are* the Keeper. You must continue with the quest until all the relics are located."

"And then what, uncle?" I asked. "Then what happens?"

All the lines on his face hardened and his mouth turned into a thin line. I knew what he was going to say before he said it.

"And then we fight for mankind. For all mankind."

Totally not looking forward to that.

He walked from the workout room, his high-polished shoes tapping on the floor as he made his retreat. I was alone now to contemplate my fate. My destiny. I dropped to the floor and rested my head against the wall, closing my eyes and wishing to be somewhere and someone else.

"He's right, you know. It *is* time."

Joachim's voice floated to me. I opened my eyes to see him standing on the other side of the room, leaning casually against the wall with his big forearms crossed as he watched me. His snowy white wings weren't visible, but they were still there. The funny thing about these angels was they all dressed the same. Jeans, T-shirt, boots. Joachim had a face that looked like it'd been chiseled from granite. All hard angles. He had those cold blue eyes and short, cropped black hair and a physique that matched Azriel's. Tall, toned, muscular.

The scent of strawberries and chocolate wafted to me. Joachim's signature scent.

Blowing out a breath, I shoved from the floor and snatched my water bottle. "Are you going to lecture me, too?"

"No." He pushed off the wall and headed for me, stepping too close into my personal space. "You know what you're supposed to do. You belong to us now."

By *us* he meant the archangels. To Michael. I had my own run-in with that angel I wanted to forget. Forgetting was not an option and I didn't like belonging to anyone. "I'm not your property."

Gone was the fun-loving angel—like he'd ever been that—as he snarled. His top lip rolled upward. "You are playing a dangerous game, Annabelle."

I cringed at the use of my given name.

"Best be careful," he added. He turned to leave. He never walked through a door. He usually popped in and out.

"I'm always careful," I called.

He halted long enough to give me a sideways glance over his shoulder, then started walking again.

"Joachim, wait. I want to know about...the warrior angel."

Darius. I couldn't stay his name out loud because it would call him. I wanted to save his name for a rainy day. I summoned him by blowing the Horn of Gabriel. He saved my ass—and my uncle's—when we were trapped in Hell. And because of that, his feathers had started to turn from pure white to black and gray. He was turning into one of the Fallen and it was my fault.

"What about him?" he asked, clearly aware of whom I spoke.

I hesitated, unsure how to proceed. "How...how is he?"

"He is not your concern."

Ouch. That hurt. "Yes, he is. If there's some way I can save him—"

"There is no way. His fate is sealed."

I refused to believe that as I shook my head. "But the spear could—"

"It will not help you."

But I still wasn't convinced. "The staff, then. It can perform miracles. The Staff of Moses could help me save him."

"The spear is your next destiny, Annabelle. See that you get it before the Fallen."

And with that he poofed away. Maybe it was time to pack my bags for Istanbul.

Chapter 2

I LEFT THE WORKOUT ROOM and stepped into the chilly damp air and shivered. The last few months were rainy and cold. I walked across the immaculate lawn to the manor house which had been in the family for centuries. Uncle Edward was actually Edward Walker III. My mother was his baby sister. She left England when she was newly pregnant with me. She arrived in Dallas, Texas, alone and, I imagined, scared. She died the day I was born.

I entered the house through the kitchen and headed to my room. Piers, the butler, intercepted me.

"You have a visitor in the library, Miss Walker."

"Who is it?"

"The gentlemen wouldn't give his name. He mentioned you would know him."

He sniffed derision, annoyed with the visitor. He did the same thing to me when I returned to Walker Manor after a ten-year absence. I had a sneaking suspicion who it was and I did not want to see him.

I sighed and gave a nod as I trudged up the stairs to the library. It was my uncle's favorite room in the house and doubled as his office. I wondered why Piers took the visitor there. Usually we greeted guests in the parlor. I took a deep breath as I pushed open the door to the library and stepped inside.

The smell of old books was the first thing I noticed. An irate Kincade was the second.

Groovy.

My appearance was atrocious. Sweat dampened my workout clothes. Not a lot of people walking around in Fabletics looked good. I wasn't one of them. My thighs were too big and my ass was too round. My hair finally returned to its original shade of black after my skunk stripe fiasco though the white streaks at each temple remained. It was pulled into a pony tail and matted with sweat against the back of my head.

We stared at each other a long silent moment. I shifted from one foot to the other, acutely aware of the form-fitting workout clothes. He no longer sported the cowboy attire he wore the last time I saw him prior to his hospital stay. Gone was the scuffed cowboy boots, the jeans, the button-down shirt. It confirmed my suspicion he wore that back in Dallas to fit in with the culture.

It made me wonder if he was a part of this covert unit for which he claimed he worked.

His missing badge was also of note.

He wore khaki cargo pants, brown lace-up combat boots, a heather-gray three-button Henley conforming to all his upper body muscles. I tried to ignore the veins popping under the skin of his muscular hands and the way the sleeves of his shirt molded to his thick biceps. Before, he was always been dressed in a button-down shirt and sometimes a sport coat. His sandy blond hair was cropped short, like he recently got a military haircut.

Had he been this hot before? I didn't recall.

His green-gold gaze wandered over me from head to toe, taking me in as though he hadn't seen me in a few years. In truth, it was three months. I wondered how long it was going to take Kincade to find me. Guess I had my answer.

"Hello, Miss Walker." He spoke in a calm even tone. I hated when he used that tone.

"Hello, Mr. Harrison." I could fight fire with fire. "I didn't expect to see you here."

"Lie."

Of course, it was a lie. Kincade had some weird internal lie detector. He always sensed when I fibbed.

"You expected me," he added.

"I'm surprised you had the courage to show up here." I wasn't sure why I wanted to needle him.

"Courage, Miss Walker?" He lifted a brow in question. "I don't lack courage. I was here the day after you arrived."

Huh? "Now I believe that is a lie. My uncle would have told me."

"Would he?"

Doubt edged my conviction. Back in Hong Kong, my uncle made arrangements for me to have an apartment within walking distance of the hospital. I was convinced Uncle Edward was pushing us together. Maybe I was wrong? If Kincade showed up here after I did, why wouldn't my uncle tell me?

"Yes, I believe he would. But it doesn't matter now, does it. You're here. What are you doing here?"

"You have to ask?" He clenched his jaw, holding back the anger. The muscles ticked along the edge and his lips thinned.

I knew why he was there. He was pissed because I left before he was released from the hospital. He insisted on coming with me on my remaining quests under the guise of help. I guess he thought I was helpless.

"There's been another killing and more people ending up in the hospital in a catatonic state," he said.

Ah, so that was it. He wasn't pissed at me after all for not sticking around. Was that disappointment creeping through me? Nah, it couldn't be.

I met Kincade shortly after Emma died. She was the patient I dream walked in the Dallas hospital. In her dream, her guardian angel was dead. Azriel killed her by taking her soul, which also killed her in the real world. Now Kincade was here to see if I had any knowledge about this latest case.

"I haven't dream walked anyone lately." That was the truth. I was too busy getting my ass kicked by Gideon and Gilli every day.

He peered at me as if trying to decide if I lied or not. He must have been satisfied because he said, "A guardian angel, Ramiel, was killed the same way the other guardian angels were killed."

"And you think Azriel was responsible and I might have seen it in a dream?" I asked.

"Did you?"

I shook my head again. "I assume Ramiel's death also resulted in the death of the person he was guarding?"

"His ward was Rodrigo Marques. Did you know him?"

"No." But the tingle of familiarity trickled through me. Marques? I remembered that name.

"He is your cousin by marriage." Edward spoke as he walked into the library, his long strides eating up the carpet as he made his way to his desk. "Married to Isobel Marques."

Surprise punched me in the gut. I had no idea Isobel was my cousin when she came to see me in Hong Kong. She hadn't mentioned it when she arrived to give me a warning about the Spear of Destiny. I tossed her out like yesterday's garbage, not interested in her warnings. Maybe I should have listened.

"My cousin?"

"She is the daughter of my sister, Tilde."

The family tree came back to me. Edward was the oldest and had three younger sisters. Matilda, or Tilde as Edward affectionately called her, also had a son, Alaric. Josephina was Lexi's mother and had two other children, William and Victoria. I never met any of the other cousins. Annabelle, the youngest and my namesake, was my mother.

Kincade and Edward sized each other up, like two peacocks.

"Mr. Harrison, nice to see you again."

"Is it? You never told Anna I was here three months ago." Angry lines creased his brow.

"I did not. She arrived for training. I intended to make sure she got it and stayed focused." Kincade's anger didn't even fluster Edward. I admired that.

"And you thought I'd distract her from training? I'm sure I could teach her more than those two idiots you have working with her."

"Gideon and Gilli are two of the best self-defense and martial arts teachers in England. I'll thank you to remember that." Edward's tone was snooty. Clearly, Kincade insulted him.

I smirked through my annoyance they talked about me as if I didn't exist. Their verbal volley was entertaining.

Uncle Edward turned to me. "Isobel is in the parlor. I'd like you to come with me while we speak to her. Piers will show Mr. Harrison out."

I opened my mouth to respond but Kincade cut me off.

"I need a minute alone with Miss Walker."

The icy glare Uncle Edward gave him sent chills up my spine. "We have important business to discuss with Isobel. There is no time—"

"A minute," he insisted.

Edward clenched his jaw, gave me a swift glance that said he was not pleased by the interruption or the demand. He gave a stiff nod to Kincade then turned to me.

"Meet me in the parlor when you've finished."

Edward closed the door with a snap on his way out of the library. Silence descended and we stared at each other once again. Kincade clenched his hands into fists, then relaxed them.

"You left."

Was that an accusation or a statement? Those two little words burned through me. I hoped he wouldn't bring it up. I swallowed the sudden lump in my throat.

"My uncle was hounding me to train. I had to—"

"Don't lie to me, damn it. You didn't want to come to England."

Curse his lie detector.

He was right about that. I didn't want to come to England. I came because I wanted as far from Kincade as possible. Something was happening between us and, frankly, I wanted no part of it. I didn't want it to go any farther and I didn't want him hanging around while I searched for the remaining Holy Relics.

I guess I should have picked a better hiding spot. Walker Manor was the first place he looked.

"Why'd you follow me here three months ago?" I asked.

"We had a deal."

"A deal you forced on me."

I had my own agenda. Besides finding the relics, I needed to find a way to save Darius from what was happening to him. From turning Fallen. I couldn't do that with Kincade as my partner.

He took two steps toward me and stopped, standing toe to toe with me. He towered over. I had to crane my neck to look up at him.

Kincade was all wrong for me. He was so not my type. He was the junkyard dog that liked to bark orders. Sure, he saved my ass a couple of times. Sure, I almost got myself killed traveling to Hell to retrieve the Horn of Gabriel. But did that mean he had to become my constant companion?

Heat flushed over me as I remembered the dream where we shared a kiss. I shoved it into to the deep, dark recesses of my mind.

"You need me. Admit it."

My eyes widened as I recalled another dream we shared. Azriel tried to take Kincade's soul, but together we fought him off. When it was over, he said those exact words to me.

My stubborn streak reared. "I told you I didn't need your help."

"You don't have a choice."

"There are always choices, Kincade. Mine is I work alone." I headed for the door. As far as I was concerned our conversation was over.

"Yeah? That's not what your uncle told me."

That stopped me cold. I looked at him over my shoulder. "What do you mean?"

"He told me about Lexi."

How? When? Why? "Why would he tell you about her?"

"When I was here before, he told me she betrayed you. I'm aware of your trip to Hell to retrieve the Horn of Gabriel."

Damn Edward. Why did he have to tell Kincade about that? I handled it. "He had no business telling you about that."

"Well, he did. Azriel can track you. He intends to kill you," Kincade said.

Again, I stared at him, my anger simmering. Why couldn't Edward keep his mouth shut?

"When you leave to search for the Spear of Destiny, I'm going with you whether you want me to or not."

It sounded more like an order or a demand than a request. "No way."

He clenched his jaw, his lips forming a thin line. "Your uncle will back me up on this."

"Azriel can't touch me." The Fallen needed me alive to do their bidding. At least, I hoped so.

"Are you sure about that, sweetheart?"

"Yes." About as sure as anything but even so, he managed to plant a little seed of doubt along with the irritation of him calling me sweetheart.

"I'm coming with you."

This was definitely a battle I wasn't going to win. I threw up my hands. "Fine. You win."

"Glad you see it my way." He plopped down in one of the chairs, leaning back as though he intended to stay a while.

"What are you doing?"

"If I leave now, you'll find a way to go without me. I'm staying."

Infuriating man. I huffed out a breath. "Do what you want. I have a meeting."

I stormed out of the library, down the stairs, and to the parlor where my uncle waited for me to make an appearance. When I entered, I halted. My uncle was seated across from Isobel Marques.

The last time I saw her, I slammed my apartment door in her face after she came to warn me about the spear. Today, she wore a business suit with a long statement necklace in crystal and pearls. Her appearance was perfect without a hair out of place. While mine, on the other hand, was reminiscent of something the cat dragged in from the back porch.

"Ah, Anna at last."

I stepped close to Uncle Edward and dropped my voice so only he could hear. "We need to talk about Kincade."

"Later," he said. "Anna, I believe you've met your cousin, Isobel."

"We met briefly," I said, then, as an afterthought, "in Hong Kong."

"Yes, when you slammed the door in my face. I remember." There was no mistaking her haughty tone or her annoyance.

Edward poured tea and handed me a cup. I was used to having Earl Grey but I still preferred coffee.

"Did you follow me from Hong Kong?" I asked. "I mean, it makes sense. Everyone else has followed me here from Hong Kong. I'm starting to think I'm popular."

"Anna." Edward's voice held a tone of warning. He never appreciated my sarcasm.

"I've come to help you," she said.

"Why do people think I'm some helpless waif? I don't need anyone's help. And anyway, if you're my cousin, then why didn't you say so when you came to my apartment?"

"Anna—" Edward began.

"Secrecy was vital. I told no one I was there," Isobel broke in. "I needed you to trust me. You didn't."

"And you think I will now? Not a chance, sister."

"You're being unreasonable," Edward said. "You need to listen to what she has to say."

"Why?" I took a sip of tea. "Why should I?"

"Because my husband, Rodrigo Marques, was murdered by Azriel when he tried to recover the Spear of Destiny." Her voice wavered as she said it.

Heat trickled over me. I blinked, shoving down the shock. Tears glistened in her eyes.

"I'm sorry for your loss," I said and meant it.

"You should sit down, Anna." Edward waved me toward a chair. "We have a lot to discuss."

Isobel hadn't moved from her seat. My uncle took the wing-backed chair—the same one he sat in when I first came back to Walker Manor. I took the chair opposite my uncle and to the left of Isobel. He poured a cup of tea and handed it to her. Then he poured another one for himself.

Isobel sniffed, holding back her emotions as she took the tea from Edward. She was upset by the news her husband was dead and I had sympathy for her. I did. But I wondered why Edward sent someone else to search for the Spear of Destiny.

"I'm all ears," I said.

"You've been away for a long time," Edward said. "I never lost hope you would return, however, I had to make other arrangements."

"And those other arrangements were sending someone else after one of the relics?" I asked.

"My husband was a dream walker," Isobel said.

"He was sent by Michael," Edward said. "To help find the Holy Relics."

"Wait a second." I put up a hand, trying to make my brain comprehend what they were saying. "Back up. You mean Michael already sent people looking for the relics?"

"At the time, you were not a viable option," Edward said. "You left England. You had no idea who or what you were.

And we had no idea when you would return. I needed a contingency plan."

"Your contingency plan was…what?"

His lips thinned in annoyance. "I had to find someone else to search for the relics. I couldn't allow Lucifer's band of Fallen to find them first. I had to take action, so I begged an audience with Michael and asked for help."

I turned to Isobel. "What does this have to do with you?"

"Rodrigo was a powerful dream walker," she said. "A lot like you."

"Meaning?" I asked.

"Meaning there are other's like us, Anna. He could control dreams and people in the dreams," my uncle replied. "He was willing to search for the relics. He along with a few others Michael appointed. In my arrogance, I thought no harm would come to them. I trusted them far too much, I suppose."

I wasn't sure my uncle trusted me, even though I was the designated Keeper.

Isobel picked up the story. "Rodrigo went after the Spear of Destiny. He received a tip it was somewhere in Berlin. But when he arrived, he realized it was a trap. The spear was never in Berlin. Azriel and his minions were. They tortured him before killing him." Her voice cracked. Sadness creased her face as she fought to hold back the tears.

I frowned, a pang of sorrow hitting me for Isobel's loss. While I was busy being a pain in the ass and refusing to help my uncle, Rodrigo was looking for the spear. I imagined the horrors Azriel inflicted on Rodrigo. He was sadistic on his best day. As his guardian, Ramiel, would have tried to protect him and faced off with the fallen angel. I wondered if Isobel and Edward were aware of the death of his guardian angel or if only Kincade knew.

"As soon as I heard about his death, I recalled the others and told them to cease searching for the relics. Around that same time, you finally surfaced in America when Azriel found you," Edward said.

"Rodrigo, God rest him, told him there was another dream walker," Isobel said. "One destined to find the Holy Relics."

"How do you know this?" I asked.

"He came to me…" Her voice cracked. She cleared it and tried again. "He came to me in a dream before he was killed. He told me he was sorry he wasn't strong enough to resist the torture. He told Azriel about you."

"But not how to find me," I said.

"No," Edward agreed. "However, Azriel is Fallen with a dream walking ability. He used that to find you when you tapped into that girl's dream in the hospital. It was like a homing beacon for him."

A chill skittered over me, raising gooseflesh on my arms. Dream walking Emma in the hospital in Dallas was the first time I used those abilities in years. Turns out, it was my downfall. The catalyst that set everything into motion from meeting Kincade to returning here to England.

Azriel was dangerous but now I understood *how* dangerous. He was able to walk into dreams, kill guardian angels, steal human souls. He also murdered Ben, my boyfriend, in cold blood in front of me. I still hadn't gotten over that.

"How did Rodrigo know about me?" I posed the question to both of them, looking between them.

Isobel shifted in her seat. My uncle cleared his throat.

"Anna, everyone in the Walker clan knows about you."

"Why didn't I know about me?" The heat of anger pulsed through me again. I had no idea who I was until I got a visit from Azriel and then Joachim all in the span of less than twenty-four hours. A great day, that one.

"We've been through that."

Yeah, yeah. It was to protect me. I sighed.

Why should I expect a different answer? My uncle was never the most forthcoming with information. I figured shit out for myself. I felt like I was flailing around like a crazy person with no direction. The only help I got was the mysterious envelopes with the postcards inside giving me clues where to search for the relics. I had no idea who sent the envelopes.

"Our lead was a falsehood. We don't know where to look for the spear," Isobel said, getting the conversation back on track.

But I did. "I think I have an idea."

"How?" Edward jumped on that the second the words were out of my mouth.

"I got a postcard of a place in Istanbul. Another clue. Like the one I received of Hong Kong."

I expected my uncle to give me crap about that but he merely nodded. "Start there then. Isobel will join."

"What? No way."

I already had a tag-a-long with Kincade. I didn't need her, too. Besides, the last cousin who joined me on a search, betrayed me and left me for dead. That bitch, Lexi, was working with Azriel the whole time to obtain the Horn of Gabriel first and give to the Fallen.

And yet when I saw her later in the depths of Hell, she regretted her decision. I made it my mission to rescue her so she could redeem herself. I hadn't shared that particular plan with Edward.

"She's going," Edward said. "We will not debate this."

Gaw, I was so sick of everyone telling me what to do. This was my quest, not theirs. I was in charge, wasn't I?

"Do I need to remind you about what happened with Lexi, old man?"

His eyes narrowed, unhappy with his nickname. "You do not."

"I'm going alone."

"With all due respect, Anna, I lived in Istanbul for a few years. I believe I could help you," Isobel said.

I didn't want to budge but this was an argument I wasn't going to win. I peered at her. "Can I trust you?"

"I will give you my word I won't betray you," she said.

"I trusted her husband with finding the spear, Anna," Edward said. "I'd trust her with the same task as well as my life."

If Edward trusted her with his life, then I probably should, too. I sighed.

"All right."

"I will have my private jet take you to the city," Edward said. "You leave within the hour."

He already planned the trip, the bastard. I should have known.

"I have a few things to pack. I'm staying in the village. I'll meet back here before then." Isobel placed her teacup on the nearby table and left the parlor.

I didn't move from my seat. Neither did Uncle Edward.

"What's this about Kincade?" he demanded.

"Why did you tell him about Lexi?" I countered.

"Why didn't you tell me about Ben?"

I winced. I never told my uncle about Ben because we built our own little cocoon between the two of us. I was safe with Ben. I never told him about my ability, nor had I intended to use it again until I saw Emma in the hospital. I was reluctant to get too close to him because I wasn't sure how to explain my weirdness or my fractured family.

"How could I? He had no idea about my abilities. And besides, you and I weren't exactly on speaking terms since I left England."

Thoughtful consideration crossed his face. "I'm sorry for your loss."

Hot tears pricked my eyes. I hadn't expected him to say that. Ben was taken from me in the most cruel and vicious manner. I still grieved over his death and hadn't come to terms with it. I replayed that day in my head over and over wondering if I could have saved his life.

"Azriel would have killed him anyway," Edward said, as though reading my thoughts. "There was nothing you could have done to save him."

"Yes, there was." My voice wobbled with unshed tears. "I should have agreed to find the horn before he could get to Ben."

"No, Anna." He shook his head slowly. "Azriel used Ben to coerce you and it worked. Even if he hadn't killed him then, he would have found another way to use Ben against you."

Silenced stretched between us as I pondered his words. He was right. Even if I had agreed right away to search for the horn, eventually Azriel would have used Ben anyway to coerce me into doing more of his dirty work. There was no going back in time to change things.

"I told Kincade about Lexi because he needed to know," he said then.

I frowned. "He doesn't need to know anything about me or what I'm doing."

"He does if he's going to accompany you."

I stared at him in disbelief. "You knew about that?"

"I was the one who suggested it." He leaned forward, his cool blue eyes meeting mine. "When he showed up here before, he was livid you'd left Hong Kong without him. You shouldn't have done that."

"I don't need a babysitter."

"Azriel is dangerous. You don't understand how risky this is, I think."

I scowled.

"Wipe that look off your face, Anna. It's for your own good."

Bah. What did he know about my own good?

"But he's so…so…" Annoying. Frustrating. Infuriating. I huffed out a breath and leaned back in the cushions of the chair. "He's waiting in the library."

"Good. He will accompany you and Isobel to Istanbul. You need his help. The Fallen will use whatever means necessary to coerce you into helping them."

"That's not news. They've been dogging my ass since Hong Kong."

"There are others as well. More dangerous than the Fallen."

"*More* dangerous? How can that be?"

"The spear has a long history. It has passed through the hands of some of history's most influential and malevolent rulers. Including Adolf Hitler."

I snorted. "Right. Are you going to send Indiana Jones after it, too?"

"This is not a joke." He didn't bother to hide his glare. "The Neo-Nazis have taken up where Hitler left off. They will stop at nothing to claim the Holy Relics. Especially the Spear of Destiny because whoever possesses it will hold the world's destiny in his hand. It is nothing to be trifled with."

"I get it." Did he think I was dumb? I totally understood how important the relics were. I recovered the Horn of Gabriel, used it to summon Darius.

Darius. Another loose end.

"You may *get it*, Anna, but you do not yet understand the magnitude of this mission. It's far more important than finding the Horn of Gabriel. The Neo-Nazis run the Knights of the Holy Lance. They are mercenaries willing to do anything—lie, cheat, steal and kill—for whatever they're after. What makes you certain the spear is in Istanbul?"

"I'm not," I admitted. "The postcard I received in Hong Kong was of Istanbul with the picture of an ancient palace on the front. It's the best shot we have."

"It had the location written in the same hand as the first postcard?" he asked.

I nodded. "The same block handwriting with Spear of Destiny written on the back. I haven't researched the city yet. Isobel will probably know where it is."

"Be careful, Anna. I trust Isobel, however, I fear she is on a quest for revenge."

I intended to take his warning to heart.

He stood. "You have a bag to pack, I presume?"

I nodded and pushed out of the chair. I headed off to my room to pack clothes and my arsenal of knives, daggers and other sharp objects.

Good times were ahead.

Chapter 3

I HEADED UP THE STAIRS, pretending Kincade wasn't still in the library. He must have heard me coming because he popped into the hallway and followed me to my room.

"What do you think you're doing?"

"Not letting you out of my sight," he said. "You're not ditching me again."

I halted and turned to him. "Listen, bucko." I punched him in the chest with my forefinger. It was like poking a solid wall of muscle. I tried hard to ignore how awesome that was. "I don't need a chaperon. You're not coming into my room."

"I'll wait outside in the hall."

I frowned. I wasn't going to get my way. I spun and stomped to my room, slamming the door. I did that a lot when I was a teen and my uncle made me angry. My room was my solace. It was the only place I called home. The only place I truly felt safe since leaving Texas. Here, my dreams were quiet. Here, Azriel couldn't reach me.

I grabbed my duffle and shoved clothes inside. As I passed the mirror, I got a good look at myself and realized I still wore the sweaty workout clothes. Yuck. Luckily, my room had an ensuite and I headed off to clean up. After my shower, I exited to the bedroom with a towel wrapped around me and stopped short.

On the floor was an envelope like the others I received. I bent to pick it up. My name was written in that same block lettering. I glanced at the door, wondering how the envelope got there. How could someone sneak past Kincade to leave it? There was no way he'd allow that.

I cracked the door wide enough to poke my head out. I glanced up and down the hallway but the only person lurking there was Kincade. Surprise etched his face at my sudden appearance. In a towel, no less. I didn't miss his assessment of my attire.

"You all right?" he asked.

"Did someone come in here?"

He shook his head. "No. Why?"

"No reason." I shut the door with a snap and leaned against it, thinking. Whoever kept leaving me these messages was super sneaky.

I flipped open the flap, pulled out a piece of plain white paper and stared down at the familiar block lettering. *Station 211 Antarctica.*

What was Station 211 and what did it have to do with the spear? I wondered if Antarctica was in lieu of Istanbul or if it would lead me on a wild goose chase. If I followed this lead, would I find the spear or something else? I slipped the note back into the envelope and put it along with the one of Istanbul in my duffle.

I dressed in my typical uniform of black cargo pants, shirt and pink combat boots. I pulled my still damp hair into a high ponytail. The jade-handled dagger went into the holder at my waist. I acquired it in Hong Kong from a woman named Li Mei as a gift. It killed demons by turning them to ash. I packed the rest of the daggers.

When I opened the door, Kincade was still there only now he had a duffle at his feet. He had enough time to pack a duffle? He leaned against the wall like he had all day to hang out in the hallway. The guy's uber preparation annoyed me.

I glared at him with a scowl.

"Something wrong?" he asked.

"No."

"Lie."

I hated when he did that. "Yeah, it is."

I brushed past him and headed down the stairs. He snatched his bag and followed. I was aware of every footstep landing on every step behind me. He was close. Too close. So close I was uncomfortable.

At the bottom, I reeled on him. We stood toe to toe but he towered over me. Even so, I met his gaze and we glared at each other. Or rather I glared. Amusement creased the lines around his mouth.

"You're in my personal space," I said.

"On the contrary, Miss Walker, you're in mine."

He was probably right but I was never one to admit defeat. His gaze moved down to my lips and back up again to my eyes.

"You have the most unusual eye color."

I flushed and spun around. My purple eye color was courtesy of my mother. I stomped toward the door, Kincade still on my tail.

"I saw the portraits in the hallway including your mother's, Annabelle."

That infuriated me. His invasion of my personal space was enough, I didn't need him nosing around our family portraits, too. I rounded on him, flung out my free hand and gave him a mighty shove. He hadn't expected the violent response and stumbled back a step.

"Don't you speak to me about my mother, ever."

He held up his free hand in surrender. "Sorry, sweetheart."

"And don't call me that."

I flung back around and hurried to the door. My mother died because of me. I didn't need that reminder. Kincade snooping around my uncle's house bothered me. I disliked it a lot.

Outside, the limo was parked in the drive ready to take us to the airport where my uncle had his private jet gassed and ready to go. The rain turned from a drizzle to a sprinkle. Isobel and Edward waited for us. My uncle stood under a large black umbrella, impatience creasing his face.

"What kept you?" he asked.

"I had to shower and change. Doubt anyone would want me in the car stinking."

I handed my duffle to the driver, Raul, who put it in the trunk with Isobel's. Raul tried to take Kincade's next, but he shook his head and gave him a warning glare. The driver backed off, not willing to fight him.

"Isobel Marques, this is Kincade Harrison. He'll be accompanying both of you on your trip," Edward said.

"Marques?" Kincade repeated. One eyebrow rose to his hairline in recognition.

"Yes. Nice to meet you."

As they shook hands, Kincade glanced my way. No doubt thinking of Rodrigo and Ramiel. He probably wanted to question her about their deaths. I shook my head. Now wasn't the time.

"You best be on your way." Edward motioned us into the car.

"Uncle, a word?"

I waved him to the back of the limo where the trunk remained open to talk to him in private before we left. Kincade continued to stand like a sentry holding his duffle and eyeing us as we spoke. Rain dotted his hair and shoulders. I stepped next to Edward under the umbrella and kept my voice low.

"Before I leave, I need you to see these." I pulled both envelopes out of my bag and showed him Istanbul and Antarctica.

He examined them for a long silent moment. His brows drew together in question. He gave me a sideways glance. "What does it mean?"

I shrugged. "I received this one in Hong Kong." I pointed to Istanbul then pointed to the note about Station 211. "And this one here today. Minutes ago. Can you research Station 211 for me?"

He nodded. "Of course. I'll let you know what I find." He took the Station 211 note and slipped it back into the envelope. He handed it back to me.

I waved him off. "Do me a favor? Hang on to these for me."

"Why?"

I didn't have the answer but something niggled at the back of my mind. Maybe an inherent mistrust of Isobel I wasn't aware of. Or the fact Kincade was so determined to go along with me. I lifted a shoulder in a half shrug. "A gut feeling. When I need them, I'll contact you."

"All right. Be careful, Anna."

"I will." I glanced at Kincade. He gave me the side-eye and chunked his duffle with an audible thud into the car before ducking inside. "I have my watch dog."

I bid my uncle farewell and climbed in the backseat, taking the bench with my back to the driver across from Isobel and Kincade. He stretched out his long legs, folded his massive forearms over his chest, leaned his head back, and promptly went to sleep.

Isobel studied a walking map of the city. Each of us tried to ignore the other. Not a pleasant car ride.

"Is the story about your husband true?" I asked.

Her gaze lifted to mine. She folded the map with precise movements, sliding her fingers down each crease and placing it on the seat between her and Kincade.

"My husband died trying to do *your* job. If you hadn't been a self-centered bitch caring about no one but yourself, he'd still be alive."

Her vehement tone took me aback. I didn't like where it was going. "I'm not self-centered."

Was I? A nagging doubt crept into my mind making me re-evaluate my character.

"You are. All you care about is yourself and what happens to you. Do you even realize the consequences of your actions? I know what you did with the horn." She pressed her lips together in distaste.

Dumbfounded, I stared at her. How did she know about that? I told Joachim and the archangel Michael.

And Edward.

And, okay, Kincade, too. I couldn't remember.

Still, it wasn't like they were gossips.

I stole a glance at Kincade, hoping he'd intervene but he continued to feign sleep.

"And what did I do with the horn?" I folded my arms, defensive. She had to be guessing.

"You gave it to that warrior angel." When I remained silent, a triumphant smile parted her lips. "Ramiel told me before he died."

Wait a minute. How could he? Ramiel died protecting Isobel's husband. I narrowed my eyes at her, about to call her out for her lies.

But Kincade cracked an eye at the mention of the angel's name. "You knew him?"

"Of course, I did. He was a Watcher. Cast out because he chose to help my husband in a quest *she* was supposed to undertake."

"A Watcher?" My brow furrowed.

I recalled hearing that term once before from Kincade. He told me the Watchers were a clean-up crew, that they removed dead demons. He said they weren't on the police department payroll, that they were more of a subcontractor. Now I wondered who they were exactly and how Isobel knew about them.

He didn't react to her statement that Ramiel was a Watcher. He merely stared, stony-faced, at her. I couldn't read his expression even if I wanted to.

"Azriel killed him as he killed my husband before Anna resurfaced in England."

"I didn't know about any of the Holy Relics until Azriel found me," I said, defensive.

"Yes and because of you, Rodrigo and his guardian angel were murdered."

She said it as she gazed out the car window, ignoring me. There was no mistaking the vehemence in her tone. She blamed me for her husband's death. I cut a glance at Kincade, remembering Azriel calling him *gardien*. His hard-angled face registered no emotion whatsoever.

"You don't like me, do you?" I asked.

She turned her heated glare on me. "No. I think you're a spoiled brat Edward coddles. You aren't experienced enough to be on the hunt for the Holy Relics. You don't deserve to be Keeper."

Resentment, anger, annoyance filtered through her words. I wanted to shrink into the seat. Instead, I stared right back at her.

"I didn't ask for any of this. I don't *want* any of this. But I'm in this and either you're going to help me or hinder me. If the former, great. If the latter, get the fuck out of the car."

Astonishment rounded her eyes before she quickly recovered. Kincade's head swiveled in my direction a little stupefied I spoke to her that way. I didn't care. I was sick of her shit.

She opened her mouth to reply when the limo lurched forward with a sudden jerk as it came to an abrupt halt, tires squealing. Isobel's map flew off the seat and fluttered to land at our feet as she gripped the edge of the upholstery and her seatbelt locked. Kincade's duffle slid across the expanse of floor and halted with a thud next to me. I craned my neck to see, but the combination of tinted windows and rain sluicing down the glass in rivulets made it difficult.

The driver honked several times but whatever blocked the roadway didn't move because we didn't move. He cursed under his breath before shoving open the car door and getting out.

"Where's he going?"

Isobel's question was a rhetorical one because I didn't know the answer either. I unsnapped my seatbelt and reached for the car door. Kincade's hand clamped around my wrist.

"Stay here." He shoved open the door and slid out, unfolding his tall frame with a catlike grace.

As soon as he closed the door, I reached for the handle.

"Are you sure that's a good idea?" Isobel asked.

We stared at each other a long minute. "I'm going."

No, I didn't particularly think it was a good idea but I intended to do it anyway. I stepped out of the limo as the rain slowed to a fine mist. The second I saw him I knew there was going to be trouble. Azriel stood in the middle of the road, his wings hidden from view. He was flanked by two demons.

They smelled like death and rot and pure evil. But Raul, the driver, an ordinary human, wouldn't know that. The demons hid behind a glamour that made them look human. Behind them, a black van with blacked out windows was sideways in the road.

Please. Like they traveled in that. They could pretty much flash anywhere they wanted. Well, Azriel could. Maybe not the demons.

I moved to stand next to Kincade.

"I told you to stay put."

"I'm not good at following directions."

"No kidding."

Azriel had that lethal wolf-grin on his face when he saw me. The one I was all too familiar with. Like seeing me was the best present he'd had all day.

"Isn't this a delightful surprise? Both of you here, together. How are you, *chéri*?"

"Let us pass, Azriel."

His lips thinned. "Now, now. Don't be like that." He made a move toward me.

Kincade stepped between us. Rage emanated off him in waves.

"I could kill you right here," he said.

"I doubt you could. Where is your fancy demon gun?" Azriel's gaze flickered over him to prove his point.

My eyes widened. Azriel was right. He wasn't carrying it.

"I don't need a gun to kill you." His hands fisted, the knuckles leaching of color.

"You think so?"

The van doors opened. Demons poured out. Another car screeched to a halt. I glanced back to see more demons pouring out of a second van behind us.

"It's an ambush," I said.

"It doesn't have to be. All I want is you, Anna. I've missed you, my pet," Azriel said.

Kincade swore the most creative string of expletives jammed together. If it was under any other circumstances, I might have giggled.

"You'll have to go through me if you want her," he said.

For the second time that day, I flushed. White hot heat pulsed over me in a way I never expected to feel around Kincade. If I was the swooning type, I'd have swooned. But since I wasn't, I unsheathed my dagger.

Azriel's faced turned dark and terrifying. "So be it."

He lifted his arms from his sides in a gesture that beckoned the demons to do his bidding. They swarmed toward us. Isobel shouted something incoherent and dove back into the limo. Raul was no idiot. He got back behind the wheel and revved the motor. Kincade gave me a shove toward the car.

"Get in."

"No. I'm staying and fighting." I had new skills I wanted to try.

He growled annoyance and gave me another shove. This time forceful enough to make me stumble toward the open door. I fell forward and bashed my shin against edge of the door frame. I fumbled with the dagger until I got it back into the holder.

Clearly annoyed with my failure to comply to his satisfaction, he said through gritted teeth, "Get. In."

Isobel shouted at the driver to *go, go, go*. I scrambled into the car as it lurched forward, Kincade right behind me. He shoved me aside, his hands working the zipper on his duffle. He pulled out two guns then used the butt of one to smash a hole in the glass of the back window. I watched in horrified fascination as he shot the demons one after another, the high-pitched whine followed by the flash of his demon guns. He never missed.

Raul floored it as he headed straight for the van parked in the middle of the road. I wasn't exactly sure what his plan was because it was clear to me, and maybe even Kincade since he cursed again, he couldn't drive through them.

The car jolted to a halt so hard the back end came up off the ground. I slammed against the back of the seat behind Raul. Isobel and Kincade went flying and landed in a heap on either side of me.

"What was that?" I asked. I tried to turn around to look at the driver.

"Don't," Kincade warned. "He's dead and you don't want to see it."

Even Isobel heeded his warning. She cowered against the seat, keeping her head down. "How are we going to get out this?" she asked.

"I'm working on it." He handed me one of his guns.

"What am I supposed to do with this?" I said.

"Kill demons." He broke out the window with the butt of his other gun and flung open the door, using it as a shield as he fired off round after round.

I was more of a knife girl, but the gun would do in a pinch. I slid to the opposite side and pushed open the door, intending to take aim at the demons behind us. As soon as the door opened, a demon charged inside and grabbed me around the throat.

That's what I got for opening the door without looking first.

The gun jumbled in my hands. I dropped it and fumbled for the dagger at my waist all the while gasping for breath. Seconds later, a high-pitched whine followed by a flash of light and demon guts exploded all over me and Isobel, who was still huddling on the seat next to me. She squealed with disgust but this was nothing new for me.

Thanks, Kincade.

"For the love of God, woman!"

He was back in the car, reaching across me and Isobel for the door. He slammed it shut and locked it before more demons got in. He grabbed my arm and dragged me over to him. Away from the dead stinky demon that now resided on the floorboard.

"This is couture." She indicated her once pristine pantsuit now covered in smelly black gunk.

"*Was* couture," I countered. "Now it's trash."

She gave me a thin-lipped glare in response.

The car was surrounded by demons, clawing and trying to get in. An attempt made easier by the broken back window and the broken door window courtesy of Kincade. A few were starting to break through. Kincade and I shot them as they tried, leaving gory dead demons in the openings.

"We can't hold them off forever."

As soon as the words were out of my mouth, Azriel flashed inside the back of the car. There was nothing more uncomfortable than having the fallen angel take up the rest of the space in the limo. He lunged for Kincade, catching him off guard and knocking the gun out of his hand with one swift motion. Before I could react, he placed his hand over Kincade's heart. I froze and sucked in a sharp breath as Kincade was rendered immobile. Azriel gave me a wolf grin. A second later they were gone in a flash.

As soon as they disappeared, the demons ceased their attack and scurried away. I kicked open the nearest door and scrambled out of the limo, the gun and Isobel forgotten. Azriel stood still holding his hand on Kincade's chest smiling that smile. Two demons flanked Kincade, each one holding him in place.

"Let him go." My hands clenched into fists.

"You think it's that easy?" Azriel asked. "That I'll release him because you say so?" He stared at me with those black, hate-filled eyes and shook his head. "All you had to do was come with me. Join me. You still refuse to help me, so now you force my hand. I'll release him when you bring me the Spear of Destiny."

Blackmail. I met Kincade's gaze but his eyes were empty. He didn't blink. It appeared he didn't even breathe. Azriel had a powerful hold on him with his demon magic.

"If you try to cross me, I take a little piece of your man here."

My stomach lurched. Azriel had killed three people that way. He took their souls, stealing their lives. The thought of him doing that to Kincade made me sick.

"I'll take bits and pieces of his soul until he belongs to me. Then I'll have enough to turn him into a demon lord," he continued. "Now that you understand what's at stake, perhaps you'll be more willing to do what I ask instead of disobeying me as you did before."

The horrifying dream I had with Azriel trying to take Kincade's soul came back in a flood. Almost as though my dream predicted it. Remembering shook me to the core, but I managed to remain calm, cool.

I snorted derision. "Disobeying you?"

He glanced over to one of his demons. "Let's give her a parting gift. Shall we?"

Azriel released his hold on Kincade. As soon as he did, Kincade struggled against the demons. Their claws bit into his arms with an audible hiss. He made eye contact with me and the weirdest thing happened. His voice exploded in my head.

Don't do it. Don't give him the spear. No matter what. And don't come after me.

My gaze flew to him, meeting his. My heart pounded a wild beat. He had a stern look on his face. How the hell could he speak into my mind?

The two demons hustled Kincade into the van while Azriel flashed one last smile. All but one followed him. The last one used a rocket launcher aimed at the limo. I spun toward the car to shout a warning—Isobel had exited and stood next to it—but it was too late. The car exploded into a fiery ball. I had time to leap out of the way, land on the concrete and roll to the side of the road. Shrapnel and debris flew everywhere.

Tires squealed as Azriel and company sped away taking Kincade with them. I glanced up. Taillights faded through the haze of smoke and orange flames. My arms stung with pain. Gravel stuck to my abrasions. Blood seeped through the cuts and scrapes. The instant I saw blood, the pain sharpened.

I hobbled-ran toward the limo engulfed in flames looking for any survivors. I scanned the area, too, in the hopes Isobel made it out. But no. She was nowhere in sight. They were both dead. Kincade was captured. I was left on the side of the road covered in demon guts, fear and horror chugging through me, wondering how the hell I was going to make it back to my uncle. I bit my bottom lip to keep from crying in despair and grief.

Everything hurt. I dropped to a sitting position, my skinned arms resting on my knees. The car burned into nothing but a hollowed-out shell.

Tears filled my eyes. I liked to think it was from the smoke but it wasn't. I failed again. But none of us were prepared for an attack from Azriel and company.

I couldn't stomach the thought of Azriel killing Kincade. Nor could I imagine what it would be like for him. Azriel had it wrong. Kincade wasn't my boyfriend. We were barely friends. He saved my ass a few times but that didn't make us a couple. Azriel kidnapped him because he knew he it would affect me, like killing Ben would affect me. He could force my hand and make me do what he wanted me to do—give him the spear.

I hated him for that.

I didn't understand how Kincade was able to speak into my mind. In that one instant when his eyes met mine, it was as though we were connected over the distance in a way we had never been connected before. Kincade was different because he had this innate ability to detect when I lied. I suspected he wasn't a cop and the covert division of the Dallas PD he claimed to be a part of was fabricated.

Who, or rather what, was he?

He was dead wrong if he thought I wasn't coming after him. I wasn't going to leave him to whatever fate Azriel decided. If had to trade the spear for his life, so be it.

My arsenal of knives was in the trunk. They were probably melted metal by now. At least I still had the jade-handled one on my waist. I hadn't been able to pull it out of the holder when I was attacked.

Sitting there crying like a baby wasn't going to help matters. I picked myself up, brushed dirt from my pants and started a long hobbling walk back up the road.

The explosion had to have been heard for miles, but Walker Manor was in a relatively remote location. It wasn't likely first responders would arrive anytime soon. I halted, turned to look behind me. Black smoke curled toward the sky. The air shifted around me. The temperature dropped from chilly and damp to downright frigid and damp. I shivered, gooseflesh dancing up my arms and down my back. A bright iridescent veil came down around the dead demons and the burning car. A flash of light and *poof* it was all gone. No burning car. No dead demons. No nothing. All trace of the carnage was wiped away.

I stood there dumbfounded wondering if my eyes played tricks on me.

A man emerged from the veil almost as if appearing out of thin air. He reminded me of Kincade as he approached—tall, overly muscled and hugely intimidating. He had broad shoulders and was dressed the way as Kincade—boots, cargo pants, Henley, gun holster on one hip. His approach alarmed me. I wanted to sprint away but my body hurt so bad. He halted in front of me, regarding me with a critical eye, disgusted by the demon guts all over me.

"What happened here?" he asked.

I was still a little shell-shocked and didn't answer with my normal flippant reply. Sarcasm would be lost on this fella. "Demon attack."

"And you're the lone survivor?"

"Yes. No," I quickly corrected. "My friend was taken." I didn't know what else to call Kincade.

"Who's your friend?"

"His name is Kincade."

His eyes widened, then narrowed. "Who are you?"

"Anna Walker."

He stared at me, mute, for what seemed an eternity but was merely a few heartbeats.

"The Keeper of the Holy Relics?" he asked finally.

"Yep, you got her."

"You need to come with me."

I opened my mouth to object but he waved his hand and suddenly, there was nothing but darkness.

Chapter 4

"SHE'S COMING AROUND."

The voice was dark, deep and succulent. Like something out of a dream. Was I in a dream? The last thing I remembered was standing on the road talking to a guy who stepped out of the veil. A broad-shouldered guy who not only knew who I was, but also Kincade.

I blinked my eyes open and stared up into a garish bright light, wondering where the hell I was. I squinted against the blinding light and pushed to a sitting position. The bright light turned out to be nothing but a lamp over the chaise I was on. After I got the dots out of my eyes, I glanced around the room.

It was an ultra-modern windowless office with an oversized desk on one side. Bookshelves lined the wall behind it. On the other side, where I was, a chaise along with a couple of chairs, a glass coffee table with brass legs, and a liquor cart with a decanter full of some amber liquid I hoped was ten-thousand-dollar whisky. The monochromatic gray and white and gray decorating scheme left a lot to be desired.

The abrasions on my arms were cleaned and bandaged. However, I still wore the stinky clothes with demon guts all over them.

Not exactly how I wanted to make a first impression on whoever stood near me.

"Hello, Miss Walker." That voice again.

It was painful to turn my head but I managed and was greeted by the most drop-dead gorgeous man I'd ever seen leaning against the edge of the metal and glass desk. He was positively drool-worthy with wavy black hair and the greenest eyes I'd ever seen on anyone in my life. I wished like hell I was not wearing smelly clothes, I'd done my hair and put on some mascara and lipstick, even though I didn't own lipstick.

"Hey," I croaked. Such a terrible opening line but my neck was stiff. I rubbed the back of it and tried to examine the room without looking like I was examining the room.

"You are safe here, I assure you," he said and smiled showing perfect white teeth. "My name is Sebastian. The man who brought you is Decker."

He motioned to the other side of the room. Decker stood in front of the door, arms folded over his massive chest, a blank expression on his face. It was impossible to read him, like trying to read wallpaper.

"Where is here?"

"Ah, that I can't tell you. Not exactly. I apologize for having you brought here under such mysterious circumstances, but Decker thought it would be better if you didn't have the location of our headquarters," Sebastian said.

I glanced at Decker but not even a muscle ticked in his impassive face. He continued to stare at me with sharp black eyes.

I continued to rub the back of my neck. "Why am I here, exactly?"

Sebastian moved to stand in front of me. He was close enough now I could smell the clean scent of his aftershave. "You mentioned Kincade was taken. I need to know everything you can tell me."

I licked my dry lips. "Not much to tell. We were ambushed by Azriel—"

"Azriel? The high lord?" he asked.

I nodded. In the realm of Hell, I learned Azriel was a high lord, so that wasn't a surprise. I wasn't sure why I was surprised this guy was aware of him, too. Azriel got around.

"Go on," he said.

"He attacked Kincade, put a hand over his heart and told me to bring him the Spear of Destiny if I wanted him to live," I said. "So, yeah, I'd like to get on that."

"You can't possibly think that's a good idea?" This from Decker who broke his chilly silence and moved to stand next to Sebastian.

He was as tall as Kincade and, like Kincade, sucked all the oxygen out of the room. I didn't sense the same from Sebastian, though. He appeared much more subdued.

"You got a better idea?" I gave him a pointed look.

"I had hoped he hadn't been taken. Kincade is lost to us. We can't free him now." Sebastian's tone was hopeless.

I blinked, the sudden bright flare of anger searing through me. "You're giving up on him just like that?"

"You cannot give Azriel the spear, Miss Walker," he said.

I'd be the judge of that. Not this guy. "But Azriel will kill him."

Take his soul like he took poor Emma's and Ben's. I couldn't allow the same fate to befall Kincade. I had to take action. I was going after Azriel to save Kincade and that was final.

"Then so be it," Sebastian said.

"*So be it?*" I couldn't believe this guy.

My gut twisted into a knot as I glanced between him and Decker. Sebastian didn't bother to hide his sorrow at having lost Kincade. Decker, though, clenched his fists. His veins and muscles flexed along the back of his hand and through his arm under the form-fitting three-quarter sleeve.

"She doesn't understand," Decker said. He gave Sebastian a heated glare. "She doesn't know about us."

"And she shouldn't. We understand the rules as well as Kincade." Sebastian turned away and started for the door. "Come, Miss Walker. It's time for you to go."

"Already? I just got here," I said.

"I received the information I needed. If Azriel took him, then nothing is left for us to do." He waved toward the door.

But Decker stepped between me and Sebastian, reminding me a lot of when Kincade stepped between me and Azriel. He puffed up his chest. If he was a rooster, his crest would come up, too.

"You should tell her. She's the Keeper. She deserves to have the truth."

"We are not supposed to interfere," Sebastian replied.

"I don't give a fuck. Tell her."

"Language, Decker." Sebastian's brows drew together, his forehead creasing.

They stared each other down. I stood, mute, waiting for them to finish their silent pissing match. Finally, Sebastian blew out a breath and released his hand from the door.

"You have no idea who we are?" he asked, looking at me.

I shook my head.

"We are the Watchers, Miss Walker."

I stared at him, eyes wide and round as I struggled to comprehend what that meant. Back in Dallas, when Ben was killed and Kincade dragged me away from the apartment, he called for backup. But it couldn't have been police backup. It must have been the Watchers. The Watchers were the ones that removed the dead demons from human sight as they did when Azriel took Kincade.

Isobel also mentioned Ramiel was a Watcher. Dots started to connect.

"She doesn't understand what that means, Sebastian." Frustration edged Decker's tone.

Sebastian glared at him. "I can't tell her everything and I won't. Telling her who we are is more than enough." He waved me toward the door. "Now, come. I will return you to your uncle's estate."

I started to take a step but Decker put his hand on my arm, giving my elbow a gentle squeeze. "I'll take her."

Sebastian nodded and stepped away from the door. He moved to the other side of the room and sat behind the desk. Decker propelled me forward and out the door. He closed it with a snap behind us, then turned to me in the hallway.

"You don't like leaving Kincade behind, do you?" he asked, point blank.

"No, would you?"

"No." He paused, his dark eyes studying me. "So, I'm going to help you."

Oh, for the love of Pete. Why did everyone want to help me? "I don't need any—"

"Can it. If you want Kincade back alive, then you need my help."

"Oh, really?" I lifted an eyebrow in question. "Why does everyone think I'm some helpless woman?"

"I don't." He scrutinized me with apparent disdain. "And judging by your clothes and your stench, you aren't."

I flushed, embarrassed. "That was Kincade's fault."

"I'm not surprised."

He took me by the arm again and led me down the hallway. It was a long gray corridor with gray carpet and even gray lighting. It was probably the drabbest place I'd ever seen.

"Listen, Sebastian didn't tell you everything because he's afraid of the consequences. I'm not. But we're not going to talk about this anymore until we're away from this place."

"Where is this place anyway?"

"London."

London? They'd transported me all the way to *London*? Who were these Watchers? At the end of the hallway was an elevator. He punched the down button. When the doors swished open, he turned to me.

"Sorry about this."

He waved his hand across my face and blackness immediately consumed me.

I woke up what seemed like seconds later slumped in one of the chairs in the garden outside my uncle's manor. My uncle sat in the chair opposite me calmly drinking a cup of tea while Decker paced the length of the flagstone in front of the table and chairs. The two envelopes rested on the table next to him. One held the postcard of Istanbul. The other had the note of Station 211.

"Ah, she's awake," Uncle Edward said. "Good."

Decker halted mid-pace. "About time."

My head hurt. I put a hand to my forehead and rubbed. "What happened? How did we get here?"

"Decker has a talent for getting places quickly. I'm aware Isobel and Raul are dead. Tell me what happened." He said it with a stoic deadpan tone.

Edward poured a cup of Earl Grey and pushed it my direction. I frowned, wishing it was something stronger.

"Did you even shed a tear over their deaths?"

"I grieved sufficiently in the time you were gone, Anna. I was also rather relieved to see you made it out alive. Now tell me."

I groaned, so not wanting to relive that horror but I wasn't getting out of the retelling. I told him how we were ambushed by Azriel, how the Fallen captured Kincade and was trying to blackmail me. I also told him about meeting Decker and Sebastian.

Edward didn't hide his surprise as he turned to Decker. "You took her to headquarters?"

"She saw what happened to Kincade. I thought there was a chance Sebastian would go after him if he talked to her," he said.

"But he didn't want to?"

"No. The meeting lasted five minutes."

Edward met my gaze. "What information do you have about them?" He indicated Decker, like he was some kind of weird species I'd never seen before.

Decker reminded me a lot of Kincade in demeanor and mannerisms. Decker was darker and more brooding, though, which was strange because Kincade was pretty dark and brooding himself.

"Sebastian mentioned the Watchers," I said with a shrug. "Nothing else."

That wasn't entirely true. Kincade mentioned them once before back in Dallas after my life exploded. He was tight-lipped on more detail. I examined Decker's reaction to my response to see if he had the same lie detection ability as Kincade. He didn't appear to.

Edward took a sip of tea. "I see." He glanced back at the big man. "And you told her nothing else?"

"Sebastian didn't want to tell her anything. He couldn't wait to get her out of there."

"You brought her here. Why?" Edward placed the teacup in the saucer and sat back, his hands folded in his lap as he gave Decker an inquisitive glance.

I waited in anticipation for Decker's answer. Edward had more knowledge about the Watchers than I did. He forced Decker to talk to him. He had a way with people.

"Because who she is."

I sighed. Every time a third party was in the room with me and my uncle, they talked about me as if I wasn't there. It was damned annoying.

Decker cut me a glance before looking at my uncle again. "I brought her here so we could both tell her."

Edward gave him a slow nod as contemplation flickered over his face. I could see the wheels turning in his head. He was trying to decide if he wanted to tell me. Decker wanted Sebastian to tell me everything, for whatever reason.

"Kincaid and Decker are part of the Brotherhood of Watchers."

He said it like I was supposed to know who the Brotherhood of Watchers were. "And?"

He sighed, as if he couldn't believe I was so dense. I waited while he didn't bother to hide his disappointment.

"Do you remember nothing I taught you?" Edward said. "In the early Middle Ages, a band of knights swore an oath to protect those making the pilgrimage to the Holy Land. They were known as—"

"Knights Templar?" Disbelief hitched my voice. "You're telling this Brotherhood of Watchers are the Knights Templar?" I wanted to laugh.

He frowned. "No, if you'll let me finish. There is more to the story of the Knights Templar. The Brotherhood of Watchers was tasked with protecting the knights from supreme evil when they went into battle."

"Which they were called upon frequently," Decker interjected.

I nodded. I had a working knowledge of history. "The Crusades and all."

Decker picked up the story here. "The Brotherhood of Watchers formed to keep the dark forces from taking over. A few of the Holy Relics were entrusted to the Templars and the only way to keep Lucifer and his band of Fallen away from them was to make sure they were well protected."

I gaped. "Are you telling me the Watchers were sent here as guardians?"

"Yes," Edward said. "Sent here to protect humans but most notably the Knights Templar."

"But that's not the end of the story, Edward," Decker said, though it wasn't a question. He gave my uncle a pointed look.

Edward shifted in his seat. "The Brotherhood of Watchers are divine."

"Divine?" I continued to stared at him.

If Edward was saying the Brotherhood of Watchers were divine, then Decker, Sebastian and Kincade were…angels. The revelation was another layer of truth peeled back from the shadows. I started to understand more and more about what I was into and that terrified me.

Now I understood why Azriel called Kincade *gardien*. He wasn't *my* guardian as I previously thought. He was *humanity's* guardian. Kincade was sent to watch over and protect us all.

"You're telling me the Brotherhood of Watchers are angels."

"Yes," Edward said. "But of a higher order than your everyday guardian angels."

I wanted to snicker at his term *everyday guardian angels* but didn't. Learning this about Kincade and this Brotherhood gave me a better grasp of who and what they were and where they fit in the hierarchy. But I still had questions.

My brows drew together. "So, if they are guardian angels, why were the Templars wiped out in the 1300s?"

"We are forbidden to interfere in the natural order and affairs of the human race," Decker said. "Our mission is to destroy Fallen and protect humans from them. When the Templars were attacked at Acre in 1291 and fled the city, we could no longer protect them from their human enemy."

"But what happened to the Holy Relics they were guarding?" I almost said hoarding but refrained.

"History suggests the remaining Templars escaped to Cypress to rest and regroup. They may have stashed some of the treasure and relics in the caves, but there is no trace of that in any history or record book. Ultimately, everything was lost," Edward said. "Likely the relics, as well as the treasure, were scattered around the world."

I thought of Kincade when we first met. I suspected from that moment he wasn't a cop like he pretended to be. But why pretend he was part of a covert department in the Dallas Police that didn't exist? Was he trying that hard to blend in with humans?

I thought back to that day in Hong Kong when I stood on the street and saw, for the first time, the guardian angels protecting humans from demons. I saw them but hadn't understood what I was seeing. Now I did. I also understood why Azriel was killing them. He wanted them dead and out of the way so he could easily take the human's souls. But why? That was an answer I still didn't have yet.

"I thought you were a cleanup crew," I said.

"There have been some instances where we've cleaned up dead demons," he said. "At the road and your apartment."

Finally! I had confirmation. When Kincade called for backup, he called Decker and company.

"You were in Dallas that night," I said.

"I was. My brother tends to leave a path of destruction in his wake."

I stared at him. "Your brother?"

He nodded. "Yes. Kincade is my brother."

My breath halted, as though all the air was sucked from my lungs. I tried to imagine the two of them as young boys fighting over toys but I couldn't envision a clear picture in my head. Were they created or born? At least I had one question answered, though.

"That's why you want to help me. Why you want to rescue him."

He nodded. "Sebastian is not willing to risk anything for another Watcher if we're lost to evil."

"There have been more?"

"In the past, yes," he said. "That's the price to ensure humans are safe from evil."

What I saw in Hong Kong and what information I had on the Fallen scratched the surface. This was more than finding the relics. I was in over my head and in so deep, I'd never claw my way out. All that talk about me being the key to the coming war wasn't talk. It was truth. I was blind to it, but my eyes were opened when I dream walked Emma and met Azriel for the first time. An awakening flared to life inside me.

I pinpointed my uncle with my gaze. "Did you know about Kincade? That he was a Watcher?"

"I did."

He didn't even try to hide it and that shocked me. "Why didn't you tell me?"

"I was curious to see how things would play out. He's taken an interest in you."

That was unsettling. "Why?"

"You'll have to ask him yourself," Decker said. "As soon as we find him."

"To do that I'll have to give Azriel the Spear of Destiny," I said.

My uncle took another sip of his tea. "Decker, could I have a moment alone with my niece?"

He nodded, then walked a good distance away, taking an interest in a hybrid rosebush.

"You can't give Azriel the spear," Edward said.

"If that's how I save Kincade, then that's what I'm going to do."

Even if the world burned. Even if Fallen angels reigned. No matter what, I had to go after Kincade.

The thought startled me deep to my core. Why the hell did I have such a deep response for this man I hardly knew?

Edward gave me a contemplative look I couldn't quite read. I thought maybe he was going to tell me I was out of my mind but he didn't. He reached into his jacket pocket and pulled out a piece of paper, unfolding it on the table. It was a map of Antarctica.

"I found information about Station 211," he said. "The Germans claimed land along the Prime Meridian on the south pole. They built a secret bunker to store all sorts of artifacts—priceless paintings, sculptures, jewels, and…the holy relics they managed to find. Hitler was somewhat of a fanatic on finding these Christian relics."

"All stolen. What does this have to do with the spear?"

"During World War II, Hitler sent Heinrich Himmler to take the spear, or the Holy Lance as it's also called, to a secret bunker named Station 211. After the war, a German U-boat submariner came forward and admitted the spear and other items were there. The Germans recovered several items in 1946. It was thought the Holy Lance was one of the relics recovered and put on a cargo ship headed back to Germany. However, a tropical storm pushed the cargo ship off course and it wrecked in Jamaica. One man was appointed to protect the spear with his life and take it to Berlin."

"But that didn't happen, did it?" I asked.

"From what I could find, he died under mysterious circumstances and the spear disappeared again. There was mention of it in a German communique it was still in Antarctica. As you're aware, Rodrigo was killed in Berlin trying to recover it," Edward said.

"Because he was lured there," I reminded him.

"I found this in Isobel's effects she left here." He pulled another piece of paper out of his other pocket and handed it to me.

I unfolded it and read the careful script. It was a note from Rodrigo to Isobel. *Information suggests spear can alter the destiny of the world as well as the one who wields it. Tell Edward. He needs to know.*

She got that information from Rodrigo. She tracked me down in Hong Kong to warn me holding the spear could alter my destiny. I chewed on my bottom lip, considering how this affected me. I glanced up from the paper at Edward's grim face.

"That's how she knew."

"She did. I'm still not sure how she found you in Hong Kong. She never told me. The Holy Lance is a dangerous relic, Anna." Concern lined his face.

"You sound worried."

"I am." He clenched his jaw, as though he wanted to say more but was afraid to voice it.

He was worried for a specific reason and didn't want to say. I wasn't sure why. I let it go for now. Eventually, I would find out the truth.

I knew what Station 211 was now but it didn't answer another question. "What's the connection to Istanbul? And why did the second note appear with Station 211 on it?"

"That I can't answer. Unless whoever sent the second one wanted you to know the history."

"Or it somehow ended up back in Antarctica."

"I don't think it ever left Antarctica," he said. "Azriel didn't retrieve it because he's blackmailing you for it."

"You think it never left Station 211 on a U-boat," I said.

"Correct," he said, again with a nod.

I was kind of proud of myself. Like I'd figured out all the right answers to the pop quiz. I folded Rodrigo's letter and slid it across the table to my uncle.

"So now what? If I can't give Azriel the spear, how am I going to save Kincade?"

"Perhaps there is a way we can get Kincade back safe with us without giving Azriel the spear."

"How?" I asked.

He shook his head. "Decker brought you to me for a reason. The Watchers and our family of dream walkers have long had an understanding. Sebastian wasn't willing to go after Kincade because of consequences. Consequences with which I have never agreed. I intend to help you as well."

I blinked surprise. "Why haven't you shared that information with me before?"

"It wasn't relevant. It is now." He waved Decker back over who rejoined us.

Decker took the seat between us. "You done with your sidebar?"

That sounded oddly like Kincade. I gave him the side eye. I didn't doubt for a moment they were related.

"Private family business." Edward gave him a thin-lipped smile. "If we're going to find Kincade alive, then we need to give Azriel what he wants. Anna received a clue that leads us to Antarctica to search for the spear."

Decker lifted a brow. "The south pole?"

"You think we should start there?" I asked.

"I do. I think there's a greater chance of finding the spear there instead of Istanbul."

"Great," Decker said, less than enthusiastic. "When do we leave?"

"Anna and I will head to Antarctica. You will find out where Azriel is holding him," Edward said.

They stared at each other in another silent pissing match. My uncle wasn't likely to back down. If Decker was anything like Kincade, he wouldn't simply agree.

"You think I'll be able to find him?" he asked.

"You know more about Kincade and his history with Azriel than either of us. You'd know where he'd take him. And likely it'll be someplace only you can get to," Edward said.

"All right. I'll go back to headquarters and see what I can find." He pushed from the table, his chair scraping along the stone. "Once I do, then what?"

"We will meet in Punta Arenas in three days," Edward said.

Decker shifted from one foot to the other. I wasn't sure he liked the plan or not. Edward didn't care either way. He glanced between the two of us.

"Be careful."

"We will," Edward said. "Piers will show you out."

As if on cue, Piers showed up in the garden with an expectant look on his face. How did Edward do that? It was clearly his super power and I wished I had it. Decker gave me one more long lingering look I couldn't read and wasn't sure what to make of before he followed the butler out of the garden.

"We'll need cold weather gear if we're going to trek across the south pole," Edward said. "I'll gather that. You'll want to bring whatever items you need."

I assumed he meant my favorite dagger and any other weapon I might want. "When do we leave?"

"It will take me the rest of the day collect them items we need, so we'll leave at first light." He rose and gathered the papers from the table, folding them each and sticking them back into his pocket. "This will be a dangerous mission. I hope you're prepared for that."

"I'm ready for anything."

"Good. And Anna? You might want to clean up before we leave." He wagged a finger at me.

I guess I was used to the stench because I forgot I still wore the demon gut-encrusted clothes.

"Will do."

"And you'll want to take care of these." He pushed the envelopes my direction.

I took them, cradling them against my chest as if they were precious love notes. I was so glad I had the forethought to leave them with my uncle. Otherwise, they'd be nothing but charred bits of paper.

We both headed inside to prepare for the journey ahead. The last trip we made together ended up in Hell. And we nearly died at the hands of Mammon, Azriel and several thousand minions.

We were going from extreme heat to extreme cold. Everything I did with my uncle was extreme. I wasn't sure I looked forward to it.

Chapter 5

I SHOWERED AND LOCATED clean clothes and another duffle. My knives were gone. All I had left was the jade-handled one. I decided to keep it on my person at all times. I couldn't afford to lose this one.

I went downstairs after packing to find Edward but he'd left the manor. I made my way to the library in search of the family history book. With my uncle out of the manor, I could finally poke around without interruption. I expected the doors to be locked but they opened when I twisted the knob. Our family history book rested on Edward's desk, which was odd to me because in the past it was always locked away. Unless he wanted me to find it. I sat in the chair and took my time flipping through the book. Along with the drawing of the Horn of Gabriel I had already seen, there were drawings of each relic I was tasked with finding.

The Spear of Destiny looked how I expected. The drawing depicted a long point covered in what appeared to be a sheet of gold. At the bottom, a shaft for the missing staff. I couldn't tell much from the drawing other than the shape. From the time period it was forged, it had to be made of iron but I'd have to see more than a drawing to figure that out.

Above the drawing, a fragment of scripture was written in a careful hand.

But one of the soldiers with a spear pierced his side, and forthwith came there out blood and water. John 19:34

Below the drawing, another bit of scripture.

And again another scripture saith, They shall look on him whom they pierced. John 19:37

Staring at the scripture and the drawing gave me a sense of...what? Not fear exactly. It was surreal, awe-inspiring and sacred. I had a difficult time putting it into words.

I flipped the page to the Staff of Moses. It was nothing more than a tall, gnarled walking stick. A note was written out beside the drawing.

Passed down from generation to generation in possession of the Judean kings. When the First Temple was destroyed and the Jews were exiled, it disappeared from the land.

The staff would be my next relic to locate, so I filed away the information about the First Temple in the back of my mind for future reference.

On the next page, the Holy Grail, which was nothing more than a plain carpenter's cup. Nothing fancy. No jewels. According to the written text, the grail would grant anyone immortal life. I traced the outline of the cup with my forefinger.

And finally, on the last page, the Ark of the Covenant. Instead of a drawing, a picture of a piece of artwork was pasted to the page. The large box-like structure encrusted with gold had two long poles on either side and two kneeling angels on the lid leaning forward, the tips of their wings touching. Several men dressed in what appeared to be ancient world attire carried the ark in front of them. I turned the page and saw a different picture. This one had a similar box-like structure under some type of covering sitting on a wooden platform to keep it from touching the ground.

I stared at the two pictures for the longest time before I finally closed the book, leaned back and pinched the bridge of my nose between my thumb and forefinger.

How was I going to find all these relics on my own?

You are not alone.

I bolted straight up, my eyes popping open and my heart racing as I glanced around the empty library. There was no one there, but I was certain I heard a voice.

I shoved from the desk and hurried from the room, closing the door behind me. I leaned against the door, taking in deep breaths trying to calm my ragged nerves and racing heart.

"Miss Walker, are you quite well?"

At the sound of Piers' voice, I nearly leapt out of my skin. I yelped as I turned to face him. "I'm...fine. Just tired I think."

"Shall I have your evening meal brought up to you?"

"Yes, please. Thank you."

I hurried to my room, scrubbed the dirt from my face. Piers made good on his promise and had dinner brought up to me. As I ate, I pulled out the two cards to study them. Istanbul and Station 211 both had the same exact handwriting. Perfect. Blocky. Definitely written in some type of chisel point black marker. The depression at the tops and bottoms of certain letters was typical of handwritten notes. Not that I was an expert. I certainly wasn't, but I'd studied the cards enough.

I couldn't for the life of me figure out the connection between the two. Maybe it would be obvious when we arrived at Station 211, a thought I didn't relish. I didn't do well in cold climates, which was why I returned to Texas. The cold English weather was hard on my skin, plus I hated to be cold in general.

My uncle mentioned the Neo-Nazis continued Hitler's work. If that were the case, I wondered if they knew the possible location of the spear was Antarctica.

Before I headed off to bed, I went in search of my uncle again but he still had not returned. Piers didn't know where he'd gone, only that he said he needed to prepare for our trip. With nothing left to do, I went to bed.

The following morning, packed and ready, I met Edward downstairs. He had another driver waiting next to a black sedan with blacked out windows. No limo this time. With his stony exterior in place, he didn't appear too broken up about the death of Raul or Isobel.

He was on his cell as I approached and waved me inside the car. I tossed my duffle in the trunk and got in the back. He joined me a few minutes later with his soft-sided briefcase, still on the phone speaking to someone in French. He consulted his watch, replied in French, and then hung up.

"What do you know about Marrakesh?" he asked.

I shrugged. "It's in Morocco."

He gave me a straight-faced expression. "We're going to meet with a friend of mine named Rafiq Al-Ashab. He's a merchant in the square, Jemaa el-Fna."

"I thought we were going to Antarctica?" I asked.

"We are but Rafiq has information he can give me. His business deals with trading and selling antiquities. He also knows a good bit about Holy Relics as well as the people who tend to deal in them." He reached into his briefcase and brought out a manila folder. He handed it to me.

Inside was a copy of a page from a book with the drawing of the spear.

"This is in the family history book," I said.

"Yes. That, along with the other artifacts, were drawn by Edward I. I told you about the Knights of the Holy Lance. When they stashed the lance and other artifacts in Antarctica, they made an extensive catalogue of all the items they kept in the bunker. A few photographs exist."

"You have access to these, I assume?"

"I do not. But Rafiq does."

How did a merchant in Marrakesh have access to Christian artifacts held by the Germans stored in Antarctica? My head might explode with all the crazy surrounding these Holy Relics.

"And so...what does that mean for us?" I asked.

"It means if the spear is there, Rafiq will be able to give us more information about who has it and who controls Station 211."

"And you trust him?"

"As much as I can."

That didn't sound promising. I had about a million other questions. And the more I thought about it, the more I felt like I was living a page out of an action adventure novel. I handed him back the folder.

"What about Raul and Isobel?" I asked.

"What about them?" He tucked the folder back in the briefcase.

"Aren't you upset about their deaths?"

"Death is a part of life, Anna. Just as it's a part of hunting for the Holy Relics. Isobel understood the risks, too. I grieved for both her and Raul in my own way," he said.

Not that I thought my uncle was an unemotional robot, but it was weird he didn't show more sadness. I wondered how he would react should something happen to me.

"I guess nobody gets out of this alive, huh?"

"No." His voice held a tone of finality as he gazed out the window.

I wondered what was going on inside his head. The rest of the car ride was in silence as we pulled into the airport parking lot. Uncle had a private jet and that meant he employed his own pilot and paid for the hangar, too. I hated admitting I thought that was pretty awesome.

We boarded the plane and were airborne moments later. Edward selected a seat away from me which gave me time to think about Kincade and what I was going to do. Once I had the spear, then what? I didn't want to contact Azriel. He always found me one way or another.

"How long is the flight?" I asked.

"Three hours. Rest, Anna. I have more arrangements to make for our visit." He dialed his phone and stuck it up to his ear.

With nothing else to do, I leaned my head back and closed my eyes, drifting to sleep.

It seemed as though I had just closed my eyes when Edward shook me awake.

"Time to go."

I grabbed my bag and followed him off the plane. A black limo waited for us at the airport with a driver standing guard looking like Secret Service. Complete with shades, ear piece and that *don't fuck with me* stance. He was big, balding and looked awfully mean.

As we neared, he opened the back door. I tried to make eye contact, but his sunglasses were too dark to see through.

He gave Edward a casual nod. "Mr. Walker."

I granted him a bright smile and greeted him with a chipper, "Hi!"

"Miss Walker." He wasn't impressed with my exuberance. I slid in the back and he closed the door behind me.

"He's a friendly one," I said.

Edward waved me off. He was already on the phone, speaking French and then quickly hung up. "We have an appointment with Rafiq."

I liked he got right down to business. "Where are we meeting him?"

"At his shop in the souk. You'll need to leave your weapon here."

I didn't like the sound of that. I scowled at both leaving my weapon and the ominous nature of this little meeting. Edward didn't elaborate and I didn't press him for more information. He'd likely tell all once we arrived.

A short drive later, the chauffeur opened the door. I was surprised by the clamor and mish-mash of odors accosting my nose as I stepped out into the oppressive heat.

Jemaa el-Fna was the main square. Cries of merchants created a cacophony as we pushed through pungent people. Henna artists painted arms, legs, and other body parts. Palm readers told tourists their fortune. A dentist—if he could be called that—was doing molar extractions in the center of the square.

If someone wanted to rip out my molars with no anesthesia, I might have to stab them in the face.

Vibrant color exploded everywhere. My eyes didn't know where to look. Foreign spices and other odors tinged the air. Some pleasant. Some not so pleasant. A loud mixture of noise filled the air from wandering minstrels, a real live snake charmer, folk-singers, magicians, and vegetable vendors hawking their wares. Their carts popped out of every available crevice—even alleyways.

We passed shop after shop of everything one could imagine. The experience was vastly different than the one I had in Hong Kong's shopping district. It couldn't even compare. This completely overwhelmed the senses and left me with a desire to get lost for a day instead of following my uncle to wherever he was headed.

The streets were a maze. I stuck close to my uncle for fear I'd lose him. I had doubts I would find my out way even if I wanted to. I was at the mercy of my uncle who led me zigzagging through the shops with merchants encouraging us to view and purchase their goods. Edward gave them all a firm refusal, never letting them persuade him differently.

At last, we reached Rafiq. Edward entered a tiny shop featuring nothing but trinkets and junk. Brass ewers, pots, silver platters, cups, bowls, statues, jewelry. All stuffed in shelves and display cases and made from either hammered brass or silver. Some were quite old and covered in dust. Others appeared as though they were finished yesterday.

"Ah, my old friend Edward Walker."

Rafiq Al-Ashab spoke with a thick French accent. He was a tall thin man wearing a tunic and khaki pants. His hair was close cropped to his head due to his balding. He wore glasses and had a thick mustache under his crooked nose.

"And this must be your niece." His dark eyes met mine and I nodded in greeting.

"Yes, this is Anna."

What exactly did Edward tell this Rafiq character? He scrutinized me carefully.

"She is not what I expected, Edward. So much prettier than you." He barked a jolly laugh. "Come with me so we may talk in private." He turned to one of the other shop workers and said something in French. Then waved us behind the counter with a good-natured grin.

I didn't like this one bit, but I was a suspicious sort. I fell in step behind my uncle and Rafiq as he led us through a red velvet curtain into a back office. Shelves lined every wall crammed full of more items. Vases, relics, artifacts, statues, rocks, jewels, cups, trivets. Anything and everything imaginable. All covered in dust. Looking at the place made my nose itch.

A small meeting table with four chairs was in the center of the room. Rafiq motioned us to the chairs and Edward and I sat. The merchant went to a nearby filing cabinet, opened a drawer and flipped through the files until he found the one he wanted. He pulled the folder out and dropped it on the table in the center before taking his seat.

"You mentioned the Holy Lance," he began. "This is all I know."

Edward slid the folder to him and flipped it open. I leaned toward him to get a peek at the contents. Inside were several color pictures. One was of a long spear shaped object with gold wrapped around the center. The photograph was similar to the drawing from the page in the family history book.

"Edward, I should caution you. Going after the spear is nothing to be taken lightly," he said.

"I'm aware."

He flipped the picture. Behind it was a yellowed newspaper clipping about the Knights of the Holy Lance dated two years ago. The bold headline read *Knights of the Holy Lance Search for Fabled Artifact Heats Up.*

He paged through more of the folder. There were more drawings of the spear but in different shapes and sizes. One was much smaller. Another drawing was a rendering of the crucifixion with Longinus piercing Jesus in the side. None of these images were things I hadn't seen before. I was familiar with the story of the crucifixion and subsequent rising. I never expected to be looking for the actual artifact.

"The Knights of the Holy Lance have their own agenda and want the spear for themselves," the merchant said.

"I assumed," Edward replied. He closed the folder. "What can you tell me about Station 211?"

"Nothing but a myth, *oui?*" he asked.

"I have information that says otherwise," I countered.

Rafiq gave me a look that said women should be seen and not heard. He turned back to my uncle. "I found nothing in the file about Station 211."

"Because you think it doesn't exist or because you don't want to tell me?" Edward asked.

The merchant pressed his lips together in a thin line. "The rumor was the spear made its way from Germany to Antarctica. It remained there for a number of years until it was loaded onto a U-Boat headed back to Europe."

"The story was true?" I asked.

Again, he cut me a glance before answering my question to Edward.

"The U-Boat never arrived. It sank in the Caribbean off the shores of Jamaica."

"That is not new information," Edward said. "Tell me some new information."

He hesitated as he chose his words. "All right, *mon amie*, I will tell you what I know but I have no evidence to back it up."

"Why not?"

"Because it is unwritten family history."

Family history. I related to that. I cut a glance at my uncle. He nodded for him to continue.

"My grandfather was a jeweler who often went to the royal palace in Marrakesh. He learned of the meeting between representatives from France and Germany to discuss the question of Jews in the country and made a point to visit the princess that day. He overheard the king tell the representatives the Jews were all Moroccan citizens."

"To protect them?" Edward asked.

"*Oui*. They also discussed the spear. The Holy Lance, as they called it.

"Rumors circulated that Hitler found it in Austria in 1938 and first took it to Nuremberg. My grandfather came to believe they transported the Holy Lance from there to the secret bunker, Station 211, where they stored other relics and art. He became obsessed with learning about it. He wrote extensive notes but he never left Morocco to search for it.

"After my grandfather died, my father found his notes and started his own search."

Rafiq rose and went back to the filing cabinet. He reached into a drawer and pulled out another folder. He handed a black and white photo to Edward. In it, a group of men smiling into the camera. The man in the middle resembled Rafiq.

"In 1965, my father took up the quest and led his own expedition to Station 211 to find the spear. I was a young boy when he left. He wrote me to say he found it along with a copy," the merchant said. "This is the last photo I have of my father."

"How did he know the spear was a copy?" I interjected.

Rafiq gave me a curious glance. "My father became an expert in the spear after researching it for so many years. He knew what to look for."

It wasn't a great answer, but I guess I'd take it.

"It's rumored several copies of the spear appear around the world," Edward pointed out in his best schooling voice. It took a lot of self-control not to roll my eyes.

"Yes. My father took the spear and sailed back to Morocco. However, on the way, the ship was attacked by pirates and sank in the Atlantic. I never saw him again."

Silence stretched between us until finally Edward said, "I'm so sorry." He handed him back the photo.

"I thought the ship wrecked near Jamaica," I pointed out.

"Misinformation no doubt," my uncle said. "Please continue, Rafiq."

The memory still haunted the merchant but he collected himself to continue the story. "The Germans recovered the wreckage near a small unnamed island, but they found no cargo," he said. "Around 1972, a man was found along the shores of Venezuela, dehydrated and delirious. He kept chattering about some holy artifact he had in his possession which he'd lost. He died a week later from what appeared to be radiation sickness."

"Radiation sickness?" Edward repeated. "How is that possible?"

"It is unknown," he said.

"What happened to the spear?" I asked.

Rafiq shook his head indicating he didn't know.

"Someone found it," Edward said. "And perhaps somehow it made its way back to Antarctica."

"And the copy to Istanbul?" I asked.

"Or the other way around," Edward said with a nod. "We must explore both places."

Great. At least I had answer as to what the two mysterious clues meant. Whoever sent them must realize there were two. The spear could be in either city. Edward was right. We had to go to both which was a thought I didn't relish at all.

"If you're going to Antarctica…" Rafiq paused and drummed his fingers along the closed folder. "You'll need this."

"What is it?"

"Before my father went on his expedition, he made copies of all his notes. They include a map, blueprints of the building and other information that may help you." He pushed the folder to Edward.

"Thank you, Rafiq. How can I repay you?" Edward asked.

"Repay me by finding the spear."

As he said it, he glanced at me for the first time during the whole conversation. The back of my neck tingled. He gave me a small nod as if to say he understood who and what I was.

Edward reached into his back pocket and brought out a slim wallet. He slipped several dirhams out and handed them over. "For your trouble."

Rafiq waved it away. "I cannot, Edward. I gave you information freely."

But Edward shoved the money at him anyway. "I must insist. If we make it back with the spear—"

"Don't you mean *when?*" I interrupted.

He cut me a glance then nodded. "When we make it back with the spear, I will make sure to communicate it to you. Your father will not have lost his life for nothing."

"I hope not, *mon amie*. I certainly hope not."

After we bid Rafiq farewell, Edward had one thing on his mind—getting back to the airport. He wasn't interested in spending more time in the souk. He was all business and no fun time.

We pushed our way through the crowd. Edward once again refused every merchant plea with a firm no. When I hesitated a few times, he gave me the evil eye. He didn't have to say anything to convey my urge to shop was his displeasure.

I had to keep up because I couldn't find my way out even if I wanted. But his long legs and his ability to weave through crowds left me in his dust.

I halted, scanning the mob of people trying to find his dark head bobbing in the sea of strangers but had no luck. Once Edward realized I wasn't behind him anymore, he would come back for me. He'd be angry and glare at me and then we'd go on our merry way.

That's what I thought until I saw Azriel.

Damn.

He stood in the middle of the frenzy of people. So casual shoppers went around him as though they didn't dare push past him. We made eye contact. He gave me that sardonic grin and I wanted to punch him. Here I was without my weapon. I left my dagger in my duffle loaded in the car.

Without taking his eyes off me, Azriel stepped into an alleyway. He motioned for me to follow him. Even though I probably shouldn't, I did. I wasn't that stupid but today I had this nagging feeling that wouldn't go away. I was powerless to resist.

It was that gut thing. I had to listen to it.

I hurried past the masses and into the alleyway. Normally, people were everywhere. Merchants calling hawking their wares and customers clamoring to buy. But this alley was different. It was quiet.

And empty except for Azriel and two demons standing on either side of Kincade.

The second I laid eyes on Kincade my stomach twisted. Azriel stood between us like a barrier, his wings fully visible. Kincade's face was bruised. His left eye was nearly swollen shut. His clothes were dirty. His hands were bound in front of him with rough rope. He looked pissed off…at me. His voice exploded in my head like before.

I told you to not to come after me, damn it, Anna.

I told you I don't follow instructions, I retorted. It was worth noting he used my first name and didn't call me Miss Walker. *Besides, Azriel brought me to you.*

"You don't listen well, do you, *chéri?*"

See? Even Azriel understood that about me. "What do you want?"

"What I asked you for. The spear is not in Marrakesh, is it?"

Did he know that or was that a leading question? I wasn't going to tell him. "That's none of your business. I'm the one charged with finding it."

He took a step back, halting directly in front of Kincade. I took a step forward, trying to close the gap. I had no plan. I had no idea what I was going to do. Azriel was more powerful than me. Kincade was defenseless but the demons were dumbasses. If I had my dagger, I might have a chance.

How was I going to get Kincade away from the fallen angel?

"You disobeyed me. You do not take me seriously," Azriel said.

"Oh, I do. Believe me, I do." I couldn't tell him I had discovered the spear was in two places—a copy and the real deal.

"You will bring me the spear as soon as possible."

The back of my neck tingled. I stared at him, mute.

Get out of here, Anna, Kincade said in my head.

I met Kincade's gaze. His face showed no emotion whatsoever. I couldn't read anything in his eyes, either.

"Or what?" I lifted my chin and challenged Azriel.

"Or this."

He flattened his hand on Kincade's chest, never breaking eye contact with me. Kincade pitched forward. That he didn't scream didn't bother me. But the gut-wrenching growl he emitted did. It was a deep guttural sound I would never forget. It made my blood turn to ice. He strained to contain his pain and probably his rage. The cords on his neck stood at attention and his face turned a deep shade of red.

"Fighting me will not help your case," he said to Kincade, and then to me, "Or yours, Anna."

I wanted to rush him but couldn't move. I wasn't sure if Azriel had some hold on me or what but I was definitely not moving.

"Let him go!"

Heavy footsteps halted behind me and I suspected Edward had finally caught up. I didn't turn around. I didn't dare take my eyes off Azriel and Kincade for a second.

When he removed his palm, white mist circled upward, coiling in a lazy spiral before it turned black, reminding me so much of the day he killed Ben. Azriel held his palm flat and the smoke floated into his hand. He closed his fingers around it and smiled. Kincade sagged between the two demons holding him.

Finally able to move, I took a step toward him, fists at my side ready to charge. My whole body quaked with fear and anger. Edward's hand landed on my shoulder. He pulled me back. Seeing what Azriel did to Kincade shook me to the core.

"A piece of his soul now belongs to me. Every time you disobey me, I will take another piece. Every time you ignore my commands, I will take another piece. Every time you refuse to do as I say—"

"Yeah, yeah. You take another piece. I get it."

My fright was covered by the sarcasm in my voice. I didn't need him to spell it out. Azriel was taking Kincade's soul and slowly killing him. Sweat dotted his forehead. Anger and defiance lined his face. He may be livid for not listening to him, but he still wasn't going down without a fight.

"Now that you understand, perhaps you will be more willing to do what I wish," Azriel said.

"I was willing before. I still am. Let him go, Azriel. He has nothing to do with this fight or you or me."

"Let him go? You think I would release him that easily? For now, he belongs to me. Bring the spear and you can have him back."

They were gone in the blink of an eye, leaving behind nothing but the murmur of the souk behind us. I stared at the vacated spot, blinking and trying to decide what to do next.

"Come away, Anna." Edward's soft voice floated over me.

I turned to look at him. The compassion in his face nearly made me come undone. I managed to hold it together when all I wanted to do was crumble to my knees and cry like a baby. I wasn't a crier either. I was stronger than that. But I watched Azriel kill Ben the same way he was trying to kill Kincade. As it did then, helplessness eroded away my confidence.

"Let's go," Edward said.

He started out of the alleyway and wove his way through the crowd. This time much slower so I could keep up with him.

As we made our way through the souk, a merchant stepped in front of me with a handful of scarves. I shook my head at him and tried to push past him, but he was a persistent little bugger. He shoved more scarves in my face, spouting his fee. He thought I was an American sucker out on a shopping spree. He thought wrong.

And since I was in a piss-poor mood, I couldn't control my fist landing against his face with a loud pop and a crack. Blood spurted out of his nose. He stumbled backward and roared. The next thing I knew, I was surrounded by shouting, angry men.

"Bloody hell, Anna!"

Uncle Edward grabbed my arm and dragged me away from the roar of the mob but they insisted on following. Yeah, punching the merchant wasn't the best idea. Edward was on the phone speaking quickly into it but his voice was drowned out by the din. He shoved hard me into the back of the car and told the driver to go.

My knuckles were red and swollen and hurt like hell but it was worth it. I had no doubt I broke the bastard's nose.

"What the hell were you thinking?" Edward said.

"He wouldn't stop harassing me with his damn scarves."

"Anna..." He blew out my name on an exasperated breath. "You can't go around punching people in other countries."

"He had it coming." I sucked on my swollen knuckles, not caring one bit about the merchant with the busted nose.

Edward huffed. "This isn't America."

"I know where I am, uncle," I said.

He gave me a disgusted look and then reached for my hand. He examined my swollen knuckles. The skin had split in a couple of places. "You need ice on this."

"I'm fine." I pulled my hand away and dropped it in my lap, trying to ignore the throbbing as I turned my attention out the window to sulk.

"What are we going to do about Kincade?" I asked, my voice hollow.

"We'll get him back."

But first we had to find the spear.

The car came to a halt outside the airport.

"So where are we going?" I asked.

"Antarctica first. If you can't detect the spear there, then Istanbul."

Great. I couldn't wait to freeze my ass off.

Chapter 6

MY UNCLE DID AMAZING THINGS with little resources. In a matter of hours, he had organized our entire expedition to Antarctica with a detailed itinerary. We flew from London into Punta Arenas, Chile, the southernmost city on the tip of South America. From there, we met a guy my uncle knew and loaded up a plane full of cold-weather gear. Several backpacks were full of supplies that included everything one would want or need when trekking across the frozen tundra. One large duffle included binoculars, flashlight, medical kit, extra socks, hats, gloves, scarves, long johns in assorted sizes.

All I brought was my jade-handled dagger stuck in my boot. Talk about being unprepared. When we landed in Punta Arenas, we stopped for the night at a hotel to rest before the final leg. That morning, I dressed ready to freeze.

"I took the liberty of packing a few extra things for you," my uncle said, as though he anticipated my lack of forethought and preparedness.

"Thanks," I muttered.

As I stood on the tarmac watching them load, a man sauntered toward us. Decker arrived carrying a backpack slung over one shoulder. As he approached, he gave us a jaunty wave like we were about to leave for the best vacation ever.

"How'd you get here?" I asked.

He gaped at me as though I lost my mind. "On a plane. Same as you."

Before I could reply, Edward interjected. "Good, you're here. We can use the help."

"Any leads on Kincade?"

"No. Azriel is hiding him all too well," Decker replied.

I chewed my lower lip, wondering if I should tell him about seeing Kincade in Marrakesh. I wasn't sure how he would react when I told him Azriel intended to take a piece of his soul every time I "disobeyed" him.

"We should go. We have a long journey ahead." Edward motioned for us to board the plane.

If we didn't find the spear at Station 211, out next stop would be Istanbul.

Punta Arenas was cold and raining reminding me of late fall in Texas. I shivered thinking about hiking across the frozen land. I was already geared up wearing my subzero parka, hat, gloves, scarf, and boots. The boots Edward managed to find in my signature pink. I didn't want to freeze to death which, in my mind, was a real possibility.

But my uncle was prepared. He had enough survival gear for three people that included MREs, flashlights, water bottles with filters. I glanced at Decker who was as ready as ever for the trip in a bright yellow hooded parka, boots and cold weather pants. My uncle looked rather stylish in what appeared to be designer parka, scarf, hat and gloves. Where did he find this stuff?

We boarded the plane and took off. Once we were in the air, Edward moved to the seat next to me. He pulled out the folder Rafiq gave him and opened it.

"This is a floorplan of Station 211." He handed it to me. "That should help us navigate the place when we arrive."

I peered down at the shrunken blueprint. The text identifiers for each room were in German. I turned it to and fro, trying to make sense of it.

"I don't see how this will help us," I said.

"It gives us an idea of the layout."

"How will we know this Station 211?" I asked.

"Aerial photographs show an opening in the rock face big enough for a 747 to enter. We'll be able to identify it easily I should think." He pulled out a photograph to show me.

The opening appeared small to me. It was hard to tell from the picture.

Next, he pulled out the map of Antarctica. "This shows where the station is hidden on the continent. It won't be easy to get to."

As I examined the documents, Edward got up and moved to the back of the plane. When he returned, he exchanged the papers in my hands for a parachute. I stared down at it for a long silent moment. My stomach churned acid as he handed one to Decker.

"Are you expecting a tragedy?" I asked, trying not to sound alarmed. My uncle put away the papers and the folder and retrieved his own parachute.

"We'll be doing a static line jump over the target area," Edward said. "It will save us the time from trekking across the continent in the bloody cold."

My ears perked. "What does a static line jump mean?"

"You said she wouldn't go for it," Decker said to Edward, then to me, "We'll be jumping out of the plane."

My mouth went bone dry. What the fuck was happening here? "You said nothing about that to me." My tone was short of accusatory.

"I anticipated your reaction," Edward said. "Time is of the essence, Anna. Jumping is the most efficient means. After they drop our gear, we will follow."

I stared at him, trying to decide if I wanted to freak out or not.

"Relax, kid," Decker said. "It's only five hundred feet AGL. The static line attaches to your D-Bag. It will inflate as soon as you leave the plane."

"D-Bag? AGL?"

"Deployment bag and above ground level. Do try to keep up, Anna," Edward said. "And he's right. As soon as you leave the plane, the chute will open. Maintain a stable body position as you descend."

"How do I do that?" Panic laced my voice.

"Don't flail around," Decker said, deadpan.

That didn't sound like good advice at all. I flashed him a disgruntled look and he chuckled.

"When the chute levels out and you start to land, bring your knees up to your chest and slide into the landing. Easy," he said.

"For *you* maybe."

"We'll be with you every step of the way," Edward said. "Nothing could possibly go wrong."

I snorted. Famous last words.

A sense of foreboding washed over me. My stomach knotted. If the spear was there, I'd be able to sense it. Edward knew that as much as I did. And if it wasn't, this little trek was all for nothing.

I tried not to think of all the bad things that might happen but there were a lot of unknowns. Edward had the map and floorplan from Rafiq, so finding the station wasn't a problem. Would it be guarded? Was it still manned? I gripped the arm of the seat as we made our descent and glanced out the window. Below us was nothing but icebergs and frigid water and a frozen wasteland. My uncle moved from his seat. He squeezed my shoulder as he went by.

"Time to jump," he said.

At the door, there was no hesitation. Two men stood at the ready. With the nod from one, my uncle was connected to the line and jumped as if he'd done it all his life. It was odd how much I learned about him the longer we hung out together.

My turn was next. I pulled on my goggles and tightened my hood around my face trying hard not to freak out because all I wanted to do was freak out. Decker gave me a reassuring pat on the back and two thumbs up. I was far from confident. I closed my eyes and took a deep breath. The guy attached my line. Before I exhaled, he shoved me out the plane.

I stiffened as I free fell hurtling toward the earth. Time slowed down as the wind beat against me and the landscape was a white blur. I heard nothing but my ragged breathing and the whoosh of a gust of air. The chute opened seconds after exiting the plane and, as Decker said, leveled out. A few seconds later, the ground approached at a rapid pace slowed a little by the chute. My brain was clear enough to pull my knees up to my chest. I slid into a snowbank and landed face first. At least the landing was soft.

Decker was at my side to help me to my feet.

"Not bad for a first time."

"I hope it's the last time," I groaned.

I shoved out of the harness, glad to be on solid ground.

My uncle was ready to go with his backpack on waiting at the pile of gear. He waved us over and was all business. He pulled out the map, fumbling with the brittle paper in his oversized gloved fingers and fighting the wind. Decker and I stood on either side of him and peered over his shoulders.

"According to Rafiq's map, Station 211 is about three and a half kilometers in that direction." He pointed east.

I nodded understanding and we headed that way, my uncle in the lead. Decker and I fell in step behind him. I didn't expect any sort of small talk. It was damned cold but at least my feet were warm and dry. Decker, though, wanted to chat.

"Tell me, Anna. How did you meet Kincade?"

Odd question. We weren't dating or anything. "Long story." My voice was muffled behind the layer of scarf and hood.

"We have plenty of time."

"What's it to you?" I asked.

"Watchers typically don't interact with others," he said.

"You're interacting with me," I pointed out.

His expression was hidden behind his ski mask. "Point taken. I find it interesting my brother and you are well acquainted."

"I wouldn't go that far," I said. "We barely know each other."

"Is that so?"

Amusement and disbelief in the sound of his voice made me look at him. He gazed at me with humor in his eyes. At least, I guessed it was humor. All that was visible were his eyes and not the rest of his face.

"What does that mean?"

"It means you're special."

I snorted. "Yeah, sure. Special."

My uncle used to tell me I was special when he insisted on grueling studies without a break.

I told him about meeting Kincade for the first time at All Saints Hospital where I worked as a phlebotomist, that Azriel was our common denominator, and how he'd managed to save my ass a couple of times when I needed him. I didn't tell him about Ben or Emma or Thomas. Mostly I didn't want to talk about it. Especially about Ben. The pain was still too raw for me to voice it. I thought about him almost every single day.

"So why are you so interested?" I asked.

"As a Watcher, we have certain rules that cannot be broken or we face severe consequences," he said.

"Are you saying Kincade broke those rules?"

"Hard to say," he said. "It's why I asked how you met."

I had the distinct feeling Decker wasn't telling me everything and that unnerved me. I cut him a glance, trying to decide if I wanted to push it or not. He was a lot like Kincade but was a little softer around the edges. Kincade was all hard angles with a tough exterior and didn't let me get away with shit. Decker was different. While he had a similar harsh exterior, he didn't give me nearly as much crap as his brother.

I found that intriguing.

"He's been tracking Azriel for a long time," he said.

"How long?"

Decker cut me a glance. "A *long* time."

I wondered what that meant as I chewed my lower lip. He sounded ominous.

"We're close," my uncle announced. He paused to pull out a pair of binoculars and peer through them. He handed them to me, pointing to the ridge in the distance. "Look."

The opening ahead was like the one in aerial photograph. I handed Decker the binoculars so he could take a look.

"We should arrive soon," he said.

One couldn't measure time on Antarctica by the sun setting or rising. Here, it was daylight twenty-four hours. How much longer was soon? I resisted whining, *are we there yet?*

We continued on our way but the closer we got, the more uneasy I felt. I sensed demons before I saw them, but with ninety-percent of my face covered and the bitter cold air, I couldn't smell anything. I wasn't sure demons were near, but something wasn't right.

Next to me, Decker stuck his hand deep into the pocket of his parka and pulled out a gun. It was similar to the one Kincade carried.

"You sense it, too?" I asked.

He nodded. His sharp and assessing eyes squinted against the blinding brightness as he scanned the white desolation. He was too cool to wear goggles. My uncle continued his quick pace ahead of us, completely oblivious to our concerns.

The movement was ahead of us before I could react. It was as if the landscape had come alive and suddenly, we were surrounded by men with guns. My uncle came to a jarring halt. Decker concealed his gun in a lightning quick move and put his hands up in surrender, as did I.

A tall man approached us. It was hard to tell anything about him because he was dressed totally in white from head to toe and blended in quite well with the landscape. All the men surrounding us did. We were foolish to think we'd make it to the opening undetected. He halted in front of my uncle and spoke in German.

Edward didn't respond. The man gave me and Decker a cursory glance, spoke in German, then returned his attention back to my uncle who still did not respond. The leader stepped toward him and they squared off, facing each other toe to toe. He spoke again and this time Edward did respond but since I didn't speak German, I had no idea what they said to each other.

Edward glanced at me and Decker but I couldn't read his expression. He turned back to the leader, gave him a smile and spit at his feet.

Crap.

One of the henchmen smacked Edward in the side of the head with the butt of his gun and he went down. A black hood went over my face, blocking out everything. All I heard was my own breath. Someone grabbed my hands and tied my wrists together, then gave a yank on the rope and forced me to walk. I stumbled forward.

I was pretty sure we were screwed.

Chapter 7

I WAS PUSHED AND SHOVED and led blind through the foreign hallways. I strained my ears to listen, to catch any sort of hint where we were going. Footsteps echoed through what I imagined was a tunnel. The floor sloped and we descended. The scrape of a door opening—metal?—and closing.

The temperature warmed and I assumed we'd made it to some interior place. It sounded like less footsteps which made me think they'd split us up. Another door opened and closed and someone shoved me down into a chair.

Whoever it was unbound my hands and helped themselves to unzipping my parka. I struggled but was rewarded with a smack in the side of the head. I didn't know how many were in the room with me. It could be two or twelve. Meaty fingers wrapped around my wrist and the other assailant got my left arm out of my parka, then shoved up my sleeve.

I didn't like where this was going.

The next thing I felt was a prick. They'd injected me with something.

As hard as I tried, I couldn't stay alert and soon passed out.

I stood on the snowy hill. The opening in the side of the mountain was in the distance. I somehow made it out of the bunker. I wasn't sure how that was possible when moments ago I was marched inside. I was not dressed for the extreme cold temperatures and, oddly, wasn't cold.

A figure crested the ridge. I squinted against the twenty-four-hour sun for a better look, shading my eyes with my hand. The gait was that of a woman. A woman carrying a semi-automatic machine gun.

Pointed right at me.

She paused, aimed and fired.

I sprinted down the hill away from her. Bullets pounded into the ground around me, missing me. On purpose? She wasn't ready to kill me yet?

I tripped and stumbled downhill, rolling to a stop, covered in ice and snow. Despite that, I still wasn't cold. I scrambled to my feet, trying to catch my breath. She crested the ridge and halted, holding the gun down at her side.

"You can run, Anna, but you can't get away." Her words were laced with a thick German accent.

Who was this chick?

She pointed the gun at me again and I took off running in a zig-zag toward…what, I had no idea. There weren't exactly places to hide in the frozen tundra.

I glanced back over my shoulder to give her one more look and collided with a solid wall of muscle. Hands gripped my upper arms hard and steadied me. Demon. A feral smile plastered his ugly face. Two sharp-tipped horns protruded from his forehead.

I took a mental inventory and realized I didn't have my jade-handled dagger. It was missing from my belt and wasn't in my boot, where I stashed it before. Did someone take it from me?

He spun me around, pulled me to him and wrapped his arms around me, holding me next to him as the woman approached, gun swinging at her side.

"Bring her," she said.

The demon picked me up like a sack of potatoes and threw me over his shoulder. We walked a short distance to a metal bunker sticking out of the snow. The demon kicked open the door.

The interior was dimly lit and musty. Like the place was closed up for a long time. He put me in a chair and stood guard behind me to make sure I didn't try to escape. We waited as she shed her cold-weather gear, then turned to face me with a contemplative look on her face.

She was tall, blonde, blue-eyed, gorgeous. Her lips were full and red. She had classic features with high-cheekbones and reminded me of a super model.

"Your traveling companions. Who are they?" she asked.

I pressed my lips together, refusing to answer.

She backhanded me so hard I tasted blood. "Tell me."

"Fuck you," I said.

She hit me again. This time on the other side of the face.

"You give me no choice."

She remained standing in front of me. I bravely met her gaze. She used some kind of mind power to keep me from looking away. A burning sensation went through my mind and the vision of Decker and Edward burst through it. I couldn't stop it even if I wanted to. I scrambled to erect those mental walls Edward taught me, but it was too late. She had what she needed from me. She had their identities.

"Edward Walker and the other is Decker. Explain to me what the three of you are doing here."

I refused to answer. She poked at my mind again but this time I was ready for her.

"Clever." She smiled. "You learn quickly."

She circled me with a feral look in her eyes like a wild animal ready to pounce on her prey. "If you won't willingly tell me why you are here, I will be forced to take more drastic measures." She halted in front of me and bent so we were eye to eye. "Measures you will not enjoy."

I didn't want to tell her anything despite her threats of torture. The real question was, could I handle it? I was kind of a wimp. So probably not. Still, I had to do something.

I nodded for her to come closer. One thing Gideon and Gilli taught me was how to get out of a jam like this.

She moved close enough for me to see pale gold flecks in the irises of her eyes. I cocked a smile seconds before I reared back and head-butted her hard. Our skulls bashed together with a sickening crack and, for a second, stars danced in my vision. I shook it off, though, trying to regain my composure while she reeled back with a screech. She landed on her butt, her head in her hands.

They hadn't bothered to tie me to the chair. I bolted out of it, kicking it back into the demon standing behind me. He grunted but his reaction time was slow enough to give me time to dive past the woman on the floor to the small kitchenette. I grabbed a knife and flung it at the demon. It went end over end and found its mark in the center of his chest.

Dude. Like that only worked in movies. I was glad it did now.

The woman on the floor clamped a hand around my ankle and yanked. My mistake. I stood way too close to her. I went down, landing hard on my back. It knocked the wind out of me. As I gasped for breath I looked up into the face of my attacker.

"Night, night, bitch."

She flashed a grin before she punched me in the face.

I blacked out again.

And woke up in another chair with a hood on my head. Like before when I was brought inside initially. My sleeve still pushed up to my elbow.

I expected my body to be in serious pain but it wasn't. My face should be throbbing from where she punched me. It wasn't. I realized what happened. They gave me some type of sleep aid to make me fall asleep so the woman could dream walk me as a form of interrogation and torture. That's why she was able to probe my mind so easily. Why I didn't experience the bitter cold when I was outside in the elements. Why I was able to knife the demon with accuracy.

Why did I feel when I head-butted her and when she punched me? It was a mystery.

Someone whipped the hood off my head.

I was in a sparse room with three unfamiliar men. Instantly, the demon death and rot stench hit me. I glanced between the three of them trying to decide which one it was or if they were all demons.

White walls, gray metal chairs. One door. No windows. The man in the middle was the one who spoke in German to Edward—I recognized his voice—but I didn't scent demon on him or the others when we were outside. He shed his coat and now wore a drab olive-green uniform with shiny black boots smoking a cigarette. The other two were armed guards standing at attention with automatic weapons at the ready. If they were demons, they were hiding behind some type of glamour. I had no clue where Decker and Edward were and that bothered me.

I took a quick mental inventory. The dagger was still in my boot which gave me some relief. At the moment, I couldn't reach it.

"Good evening, Fräulein Anna." He took a long drag of his cigarette and blew the smoke toward me.

I refused to cough on it. I held my breath and pinned him with my best fuck off glare.

"Your resistance to Sofia is quite admirable."

I wasn't a total idiot. I put the pieces together and figured out Sofia was the one who dream walked me. Why? Did she know who and what I was? Or was it merely happenstance?

"How did you and your companions find this place?" he asked.

It hacked me off she was able to probe my mind and discover our identities. Sarcasm was my first defense.

"Google Maps."

Rage flickered across his face at my flippant response before he gave a sideways nod. One of his henchmen stepped forward. He slapped my face, fingers spread, between chin and earlobe making my ear ring.

So that's how it was going to go.

I was sure Kincade wouldn't be popping up to save my ass this time.

"Care you change your answer, *fräulein?*"

Not really but I was going to have to, wasn't I? "I read about it on Wikipedia."

Again, he was not amused. He took one final puff of his cigarette, dropped it on the floor and crushed it with the toe of his boot. He stepped to the door and pulled it open.

The woman who chased me down with the machine gun and subsequently smacked me around entered. Her appearance was the same as in the dream but no gun this time. She was dressed in all black. Her blonde hair hung in waves over her shoulders.

"Hey, Barbie," I greeted.

Sofia didn't care for the nickname one bit. She scowled, full lips turning into a grimace.

Pissing people off was totally my thing.

"She doesn't wish to cooperate," the leader said.

"Then perhaps we give her a reason," she replied.

She waved at one of the guys. He stepped back into my line of vision with a syringe. They were going to put me out again to allow her to dream walk me. It had to be the only way she was able to do it—the subject had to be asleep.

Joke was on her. I had the ability to do it without my victim being asleep. At least, I hoped so. I hadn't done it without touching the subject but now was my chance to give it a try. I focused on her face, memorizing every line, every eyelash, every crease, every detail. My eyes fluttered closed and I was in her mind a second later, pushing through the shadows of her memories and fire and brimstone reminding me a whole lot of my trip to Hell.

Odd, that.

And I didn't like it one bit.

I pushed further into her mind until I found her psyche. She shrieked when she saw me. A sort of high-pitched shrill noise that grated on my nerves. I reached her in an instant, my hand wrapping around her throat.

"You can't control me," I said.

She kicked my shin. My hand tightened on her throat, fingers pressing into her larynx. Her eyes widened as she stilled.

"Who are you?" she whispered, eyes wide and round as she stared at me.

"I'd like to know the same about you. You can dream walk?"

"I-I can enter people's minds, yes. When they sleep. Only when they sleep. Not like this. Not like you." Genuine fear lilted her voice.

Imagine that. Barbie was scared of me. So, she understood what it was but not what it was called. Interesting. Had she been trained to do it?

"Y-you can..." she paused, licked her lips, "...control it?"

"Yes."

My link with her was broken. I found myself on the ground looking up into the butt of a gun that had no doubt smacked the back of my head behind the ear because it throbbed like a son of a bitch. Sofia was curled in a ball against the far wall coughing, a hand print on her throat. I did that in real life, too, not just in the dream. She was dangerous, but I was deadly.

"Take her to the holding cell," the leader ordered.

He knelt next to Sofia, concern etching his face. His lips moved but I couldn't hear him. She nodded, her hand at her throat where I nearly choked her.

One of the guards hauled me to my feet, his fingers biting into the flesh of my upper arm like a vice grip. He gave me a shove, forcing me to walk. We exited the room. He walked me down a long shadowy hallway to another door where the leader opened it. They pushed me inside the room.

Chains and manacles were on the wall. They were all too happy to put me into them. Wrists and ankles both.

My heart rammed hard in my chest, the pain in my head forgotten. Bile rose to the back of my throat as one of the guards put a metal contraption on my head resembling a medieval torture device. The cap was a metal frame that hugged my skull while circular electrodes rested against each temple, the center of my forehead and the base of my skull. The leader flipped a switch and the thing hummed. A warm sensation went through my scalp. I was paralyzed. I suspected he was about to conduct an intense mind fuck on me.

"I'll give you another chance to tell me why you're here." He lit a new cigarette, puffing the smoke my direction.

I gave him a hint who I was by conducting my little parlor trick on Sofia. He understood my ability to manipulate others' minds with mine, so he was going to damage my greatest weapon.

I was screwed.

I watched him puff on that damn cigarette, watching his eyes and his mouth. I saw a blip of red flicker through his eyes, changing the color briefly. My senses instantly went on high alert. I inhaled, sniffing the air but there was nothing demon-related on him, which told me the others in the room were the demons. I was absolutely certain a demon was behind his eyes, though.

Perhaps the cold, dry air worked as a suppressor of sorts. I had to admit my sinuses were jacked up and it was difficult to breathe. If only I could wield my dagger.

I wondered who he truly was underneath that human exterior. Azriel's scent wasn't like demons—he carried the sharp tang of cinnamon. When Joachim visited me, his decadent fragrance was chocolate and strawberries. I got nothing tickling my olfactory senses with this guy.

"The more you resist, the more uncomfortable it will be for you."

He gave a nod to the dude at the switch who nudged it up a bit. The pulsing sensation increased tenfold through my head. It made my eyes hurt. I winced and closed them, trying to control the pain.

More smoke circled me as he moved a step closer.

"You are playing with fire, *fräulein*. Tell me what I wish to know and you will not experience further pain. Refuse to tell me and I dig into that brain of yours to find out what makes it work. That is how I discovered Sofia, after all."

My eyes popped open, my mind racing with questions. What did he do to her? Did he turn her into a dream walker? And if so, how? Why?

"I will give you time to reconsider."

The guard shut off the machine but left the metal skull cap on my head. The leader waved the guards to follow him. They left the room, flicking off the light and leaving me in the dark as the door scraped closed.

Chapter 8

I DOZED OFF AND DREAMED.

Kincade stood across from me, his massive forearms crossed as he glowered with those green-gold eyes. Like he was super pissed. And he probably was. He didn't want me to come after him and I deliberately ignored that command.

We were back in his high-rise apartment in Dallas. I'd been there once the day Ben was murdered, when Kincade scraped me off the floor and took me away from the grisly scene. He gave me ten-thousand-dollar whisky and I gave him shit.

The dream was oddly different with a great amount of detail. That wasn't the unusual part. I often dream walked details of places I had never been. But this…this dream wasn't my own. I wasn't in control and that gave me pause.

"What the fuck, Anna? I told you not to come after me."

"I know what you told me."

"You don't listen to me." He paced the length of the pristine living room from end to end, the backdrop of a nighttime downtown Dallas behind him.

"I don't listen to anyone," I pointed out. "Besides, was I supposed to leave you in Azriel's hands?"

"Yes."

"He's dangerous."

"I know what he's capable of." He halted and pinpointed me with his gaze. A gaze that made gooseflesh burst across my exposed arms. "More than anyone. I've been hunting him for longer than you've been alive. Do yourself a favor, Anna. Don't come after me."

"Why?" I demanded. "He wants the spear. If I don't give it to him, he'll take your soul."

He raked his hand through his hair, making it stand on end. "I know what he wants and he won't get it. This is an opportunity for me. I'm finally face to face with him."

I blinked, surprised. "What do you intend to do? Arrest him?" He wasn't a cop so that idea seemed absurd.

I witnessed one of the heinous murders Azriel committed while trying to lure me out of hiding. It had worked, too. Kincade showed up at the hospital where I worked, masquerading as a homicide cop.

"Let me worry about that," he said.

I didn't like that answer. "I'm not leaving you with him."

His gaze softened as he looked at me. My heart double-timed in my chest. He stepped toward me. My mouth went bone dry. I had a dream before where he'd kissed me like he wanted me. My hands clenched. I wasn't sure I wanted that again. Or did I?

"He won't take my soul."

"You don't know that. You can't know that." I flexed my fingers. I was no good at this emotional stuff.

Azriel took Ben's life from me—and his soul—and I worried he'd do the same to Kincade to punish me when I failed to produce the spear.

He cracked a rare smile. "Trust me."

Trust him? I snorted. "You're his prisoner. How do you intend—"

I didn't realize he had moved so close to me until he put a finger over my lips to silence me. "Don't worry."

He dropped his hand almost as quickly as he touched me. But my lips still burned in the wake of his touch. We stared at each other a long silent moment. Indecision and maybe a little regret flashed in his eyes, as though he realized he hadn't meant to touch me.

Dream walking was weird like that. I could touch, feel, think, move. It was almost as though it was happening in the waking world.

"I know where you are," he said then. "I'll send help."

My brows drew together as I peered at him. "How the hell do you know where I am?"

He grinned again. "My brother told me."

And then I woke up.

I was still in the manacles in the dark room. Still alone. Kincade couldn't send help to us. We were stuck here and we were screwed. I was pretty sure the German dude had more torture planned for me before this was all over.

The door cracked open and I sucked in a sharp breath. A slash of light came into the room from the hallway as a hulking form slipped inside the room.

"Anna?"

It was Decker.

"Here," I said.

He flipped on the light. His face was black and blue. Like someone had used it for a punching bag. He shoved the door closed with a snick and took two giant steps across the room where he used a lock pick to release my wrists and ankles. He removed the thing on my head and chunked it on the floor.

"How did you escape? And where's my uncle?"

"Trade secret," he said. "I'm not sure where they're keeping him. I didn't find him on this floor."

"On this floor?" I asked.

"Yeah. As near as I can tell, we're in the bunker several feet underground. The Germans built several levels that go farther down."

"We have to find him," I said.

"We will, but first we need to make it out of here unseen. There are cameras in the hallway."

"How do you propose to do that? Wait a second. How did you get in here without getting caught?" I examined him with narrowed eyes for some sign of super power ability.

He reached for my hand and pulled me close, pressing our bodies together. "Another trade secret."

A sudden dizziness swept through me and I swayed on my feet. He wrapped an arm around me and turned toward the door.

"It'll pass in a second."

"What will?" My mind was foggy and I couldn't think straight.

He pulled open the door and stepped into the hallway. "Stick close to me or this won't work."

"What won't work?" I demanded but my tongue was the size of an elephant and I sounded like I developed a speech impediment.

One second we stepped out of the doorway, the next we flashed to the end of the hall to the elevator. It dinged and we stepped on, the doors whooshing closed.

Kincade's super power was the ability to tell when I lied. I started to understand Decker's super power was the ability to flash from one place to another. And that ability made me sick to my stomach not unlike when Darius, the warrior angel, flashed me from one place to the next. With Decker, it was different and I was violently ill.

I fell to my knees in the elevator and heaved. Luckily, my stomach was empty and nothing came up. My head was full of lead. My vision blurred. My stomach knotted. I curled into the fetal position on the floor of the elevator.

I never had a lot of luck in elevators.

"I forget how fragile the human body is," he said. "Sorry about that. I would have put you out like before but I need you awake."

"Before?" I croaked.

"When I met you on the road."

In England, he meant. When he appeared after cleaning up the dead demons.

I sucked in a deep breath, trying to make the disgusting sensation go away. All the while, I was acutely aware of the elevator descending down, down, down into the bowels of the bunker.

We stopped and the doors opened. Decker peeled me off the floor, setting me upright. I wobbled, using his big body to stabilize my feet.

"You all right?" he asked, his hands on my shoulders to steady me.

"I think so."

"We have to do it again."

"Do what again?"

He pulled me to him, his arms wrapping around me in a big hug. "Sorry about this."

We moved into the hallway. My stomach remained in the elevator. My head pounded a wicked tattoo as we came to a jarring halt. He released me. I crumbled to the cold hard ground. My hands fisted powdery snow and crumbles of ice.

"We're safe here. No cameras."

He walked around me, his booted feet crunching on ice and snow. "The sickness should pass soon. We'll wait here until it does."

I didn't care where here was but I was grateful for the cold under my body even though I shivered. It calmed the violent illness coursing through me.

"What did you...do to me?"

"Hard to explain." He stopped moving and leaned against a nearby wall, crossing his ankles as if he had all day to hang out with me.

I lifted my head to peer up at him through blurry eyes. "Try me."

"Watchers are all unique," he said. "We all have different...abilities."

I nodded understanding, suspecting as much. He confirmed it.

"I can teleport."

Teleport, huh? I resisted the urge to ask if he was part mutant. I put my head in my hands and rubbed the temples, trying to make the throbbing cease.

"And it makes me ill."

"Yes. Your body isn't designed for that but it was the only way to avoid the cameras. They're everywhere." He paused, looking me over, indecision in his eyes. Like he couldn't decide if he wanted to tell me more or not. Then he added, "I can also turn invisible."

I dropped my hands. That was certainly handy. "You can?"

He demonstrated. Now you see him. Now you don't. I had to admit that was a cool trick.

"I suspect the invisibility coupled with the teleportation did a number on you," he said. "Again, sorry about that."

"What about Edward?" I croaked.

"We'll find him. He has all the maps on him. We need him."

"That doesn't do us much good," I said. "How do you intend to find him?"

"I'm working on it."

I glanced around and realized we were on the edge of an ice cave. I shoved to my feet. "Where is this place?"

"Basement of the bunker, I think."

"Or another chamber under the bunker. I don't remember seeing this on the blueprints."

I took a tentative step forward, my boots crunching on the icy snow. Still without my parka, I shivered. Decker unzipped his and handed it to me.

"What about you?" I asked.

"You need it more than me. I have enough layers. I'll be good."

Grateful, I took it and slipped my arms in. It was still warm from his body heat. "Can I ask you a question about your…kind?"

"Yeah."

I chewed my lower lip, wondering how exactly to ask him. It was probably better if I didn't beat around the bush. "Can Watchers dream walk?"

He considered me a long quiet moment, his face devoid of all emotion which reminded me a lot of Kincade. "Why do you ask?"

"I have a feeling."

"Which is?"

The verbal volley also reminded me a lot of Kincade. "Before you showed up, I had a…dream. Kincade was there. But I wasn't dream walking him."

He lifted one dark eyebrow. "What do you mean?"

"I think he was...dream walking me."

Decker clenched his jaw so hard, the muscles ticked along the edge.

I knew it.

"It's a possibility." He pointed toward the cave and changed the subject. "Let's see where this leads."

Fine. I'd let that go but I was going to question him later on the subject.

We moved deeper into the manmade ice cave's narrow walkway. Numerous man hours must have gone into carving this thing underground. It opened up into a sizable cavern. To the right and left along the walls were chambers encased in ice. I stepped to one of them and peered through what appeared to be thick glass but was actually a thick sheet of ice. Behind the ice was a decomposing body.

Gross.

A tingling sensation started at the base of my neck and skittered down my spine. Revulsion rippled through me. I'd seen dead bodies before but nothing this sinister. Why would whoever our host was keep decomposing bodies behind a wall of ice?

Decker stepped next to me. We exchanged a look of disgust. We moved to the next chamber. Another body but this one less decomposed. The next one had another body but this one appeared as though she were merely sleeping. Several more chambers with dead women. I counted twelve in all.

It was the creepiest thing I'd ever seen.

"What is this place?" My whispered voice shook.

"Look at her head." He pointed.

I peered closer. Her head was turned slightly to one side. A faint scar in the shape of a circle was on her temple and forehead.

"That thing that was on your head—"

"Yeah."

I knew what he was getting at and I also suspected what it meant. That German dude was conducting some kind of experiment. The sick bastard.

Wait a second...

I took a step back to the previous chamber and took another look at the decomposing bodies. They all appeared to be women. I hadn't noticed it before. Long hair. High cheekbones. Delicate features. The women who were not decomposing all had the same circular scars on their foreheads and temples.

I clutched my elbows and shivered with the horror. Try as I might, I couldn't look away.

When I was in Sofia's head, I saw all sorts of weird shit. Death and destruction. Hellfire. And before that when we were in the strange bunker when she tried to interrogate me, there was a demon. But I hadn't seen any demons since our arrival. Only the one in the dream I managed to knife.

I suspected the German dude poked around in Sofia's head to make her what she was. She hadn't a clue what a dream walker was yet she had the ability. Though not like me. Not while the subject was still semi-conscious. She stepped into my mind and found our identities when I was less guarded. She'd never do that to me again.

"He did it to her," I whispered.

"He did what to whom?"

Decker didn't know what I was thinking because he wasn't in my head. I had to explain. "The German leader. He made her that way."

"Anna, you're not making sense."

I gripped his wrist and shook his arm, frustrated I couldn't communicate what I wanted to say. "A woman named Sofia dream walked me to interrogate and torture me. But she didn't know it was called dream walking. All she grasped was she had the ability to enter people's minds when they slept. *He* did that to her. He made her that way with that…that…metal hat thing."

The dawning of understanding entered Decker's eyes. He looked from me to the corpse and gave a slow nod. "He created her. These must be his failed attempts."

"Damn straight he did. If there's one, there's another. I have to find out how many more he created. I have to stop him."

I charged back the way we'd come, intending to find this German leader dude and kick some ass. I didn't have a clue how to stop him from doing whatever he was doing, but I had to find a way. I couldn't let more innocent women die or be twisted into a super dream walker.

"Anna, wait." Decker caught up to me and pulled me to a stop. "That's not our mission."

"Fuck the mission, Decker. He's killing innocent women." I pointed back to the macabre chamber. "And he's somehow managed to create a woman who can dream walk."

"Charging back up there to confront him isn't going to solve anything. If anything, you'll get yourself killed. Let's find Edward and regroup and then figure out a game plan. Okay?"

That made a lot of sense. I blew out a breath. "Okay."

"Let's go back this way. There might be another way out or at least another way back into the bunker."

Decker had a point. I didn't like it but he was right. German dude wanted to tamper with my brain. If he caught me again, there was no telling what he'd end up doing to me. If he fucked with my head, what would that do to me? Would it turn me into a vegetable?

"Fair enough."

I followed him back through the tomb, averting my eyes from all the dead women in various states of decomposition. It was hard not to look. We finally made it past them and into another chamber.

We both halted. My mouth dropped open.

On the other side of a frozen lake was the Spear of Destiny.

Chapter 9

"HOLY SHIT." My breath plumed white.

"What is that?"

The spear was exactly like the picture Rafiq gave my uncle and a lot like the drawing in the family history book. All that remained of the spear was the tip. Like in both the picture and the drawing, gold wrapped around the center. It rested on a small pedestal which sat on a large icy outcropping across a frozen lake.

"It's the Spear of Destiny."

"Are you sure?"

"My uncle had pictures. It looks exactly like it."

The only way I was would know for sure was touching it. When I did, if the history flashed through my mind, I would know for sure it was authentic. I was gifted with that as one of my special abilities as Keeper of the Holy Relics.

Unfortunately, there was no way across the frozen lake.

I took a tentative step forward and placed the toe of my boot on the edge of the ice. As I put weight on the ice, a cracking sound immediately followed. Decker grabbed my arm and yanked me backward.

"What the hell do you think you're doing?"

"I have to get across."

"The ice is too thin. It'll never hold you." He pointed down at the crack.

I dropped to my knees for a closer look. He was right. The ice was paper thin and transparent with a new hairline fracture. Below was clear blue water. Stepping on the ice would indeed make it break. I'd fall into the cold water with no way out and either drown or die of hypothermia.

Neither of those deaths sounded appealing.

"It's a booby trap," I said.

"Oh, you think?"

I cut him a sideways glance as I rose. "Funny."

Overhead, the ceiling of the cavern soared high above us. The thick glacier had a blue tint. There was no way to rig some type of harness and swing across. And besides, we hadn't exactly come prepared for that type of thing. All we had were our wits.

I examined the chamber and noted tiny ledges from floor all the way around the lake to the icy outcropping. My mind translated them to handholds and footholds. I unzipped the parka and slipped it off, handing it to Decker.

"I have an idea."

"You can't climb across the wall." He must have read my body language all too well.

"Such a Negative Nancy," I said.

He scowled. "Those handholds are too narrow."

But I was agile and thin and fairly certain I could do it. "I can make it."

"Anna…"

"I have to try, Decker." Kincade's life hinged on the spear and I wasn't leaving without it.

"At least let me teleport you."

My stomach churned at the thought. I shook my head. "I don't want to puke again."

He gave me a scowl of annoyance. "Fine, then, don't fall."

I gave him a thin-lipped smile. "Thanks for the advice."

I took a cleansing breath and stepped on the first tiny ledge about four inches off the thin ice. It was barely wide enough for the toe of my boot. I reached for the ledge at eye level and dug my fingernails into the ice. It didn't exactly give me the leverage I needed but it made me feel better.

I pulled my other foot up and flattened my legs and ankles against the wall as I inched down. I was over the ice now. I was aware Decker was behind me but damn if I couldn't even hear him breathe. Likely he held his breath as I made my way along the wall ever so slowly.

So painfully slowly.

And my fingers were turning to numb from the cold.

"How far am I?" I asked.

My right foot slipped off the ledge. Decker sucked in a sharp intake of breath as I got my foot back on the ledge. The muscles in my thighs and arms trembled from the shear exertion.

"Not far. Keep going."

Creeping along that icy wall seemed like an eternity. My hands and fingers were numb. My nose started to run and my eyes watered from the cold. I lost all the sensation in my face.

"You're almost there, Anna," he said.

Another inch. Two. Three. My extremities were frozen. It was probably a mistake to take off the parka, but the bulky material would be in the way.

"You're there," Decker said. "One step and you'll be on the ground again."

"Thank God."

I inched down off the ledge. First one foot then the next.

I collapsed on the solid ground, my heart racing and pain searing through every muscle in my body. I cupped my hands over my mouth and breathed warm air into them, trying in vain to thaw them out.

"You all right?"

"Yeah," I said, looking up at the ceiling. "Tired."

"Can you move?"

"Give me a second, will ya? That wasn't exactly easy."

I realized then getting back to Decker holding the spear wasn't going to be easy either. And I had no pockets big enough to put it in.

Yeah, I didn't exactly think this through.

I pushed to my feet, my legs shaking. The spear was within reach. This was it. Now or never.

I took another step toward the outcropping on which the holy relic rested. My foot went right through the ice and snow. I over-corrected and stumbled, dragging my foot out of the hole. My arms flailed in a windmill motion as I tried my hardest to keep from falling. It didn't occur to me there would be some type of trap on the other side by the spear. I was a terrible excuse for a treasure hunter.

"Anna!"

I lost balance and toppled toward the ice lake. In the process, my hand smacked the pedestal. The spear tumbled, landed and skittered across the frozen lake coming to a halt in the center. I crashed against the hard ground but managed to fling my arms out to break my fall. The front half of my body landed face down on the icy lake.

I didn't dare move.

"Great." Frustration and anger edged his voice.

"Uh…Decker…now what?"

That was about the time the ice cracked. One little hairline fracture made a spider web from my left hand below making a beeline for the spear. Like when a rock hits a windshield. The ice cracking as it weakened under my weight was deafening.

Fucking great.

"Ah, shit," Decker said.

Today was not my day. Or any day for that matter.

"Hold still a minute," he said.

"Like I have a choice."

He looked around the cavern. No doubt trying to find something to toss me to save my dumb ass.

"Don't worry about me. Grab the spear," I said.

"And let you fall?"

"The spear is more important. You can take it to Edward."

I peered down through the thin ice at the calm blue water below. Where my fate awaited. I glanced back up at the spear across from me. Decker laid down on his stomach and stretched out his arms but he couldn't reach it. Maybe I could give him a boost. My fate was sealed anyway.

I bent my toes back and dug them into the snow for leverage.

"I have an idea," I said.

More cracking ice punctuated my words.

"Stay put," he ordered.

He inched forward, stretching to reach the spear. As he did, the ice cracked under him. We looked at each other. He was ten feet from me. Too far to reach.

"I'll meet you in the middle," I said, joking.

It was almost as though the light bulb went on over his head. "Yes. Do it."

Knowing we didn't have much time, I nodded.

"On three. One…two…"

"Three!" we said together.

I shoved forward the same time he did. Our hands collided, knocking the spear out of the way. It skittered across the ice, spinning like a game of Spin the Bottle. I whimpered. But we'd met each other in the middle. A second later, the ice shattered and down we went.

He tried to grab my hand but missed. We splashed into the crystal blue water. The cold smacked into me and seeped into my bones, stealing my breath. I was never a good swimmer and sank immediately. My arms and legs flailed as I tried to make my way to the surface. Decker wrapped his arms around me and then we were on cold but dry land and I was sick again.

He'd teleported us out.

But now we were cold and wet and freezing our asses off. My teeth chattered.

"N-now what?" I asked.

"Stay here."

Like I had any place else to go. Was he trying to be funny?

He disappeared, leaving me to freeze to death. Hopefully he'd return sooner rather than later. I huddled against the frozen ground, curling into a tight ball trying my damnedest to keep warm, my body quaking in a violent shiver. The spear crossed my mind. I had no idea where it ended up. Likely at the bottom of the icy pool. No way was I going to retrieve it.

Decker appeared in a flash of light. "I found something."

"G-great."

"Someone's sleeping quarters is on the other side of this wall a few feet in. It's warm and dry and there are extra clothes."

"O-okay." My teeth rattled inside my head. Why didn't he look as cold as I felt?

"I have to teleport us." He gave me an apologetic look.

I sighed and nodded. I would be violently ill again. At this point, I didn't care.

"Sorry about this."

He wrapped his arms around me and we took off. A second later, we were in the room. He released me and I crumbled to the floor, too sick to move. The room spun like I tied one on the night before. I felt as though I might pass out any second.

Decker banged what sounded like metal doors and then dropped a woolen blanket over me.

"Here, kid. Change out of your wet clothes and into these dry ones."

The illness subsided long enough for me to see he held out a pair of thermal pants, a shirt, socks, and army fatigues reminiscent of World War II—padded cargo pants and a padded shirt. He turned around while I changed.

How gentlemanly. He moved to the side of the room and fiddled with a thermostat.

I peeled out of my wet clothes and wet boots, leaving them in a heap on the floor, and quickly dressed, then wrapped the blanket around my shoulders. I was already warmer. I placed the dagger on my belt. It gave me comfort it was back where it belonged.

"I'm decent," I said.

Since I was thawing out and more coherent, I took in my surroundings. He was right that it appeared to be someone's sleeping quarters. It was spacious and furnished with good furniture. I assumed this belonged to some high ranking official. Maybe the head German dude himself.

A narrow metal-frame bed was on one side of the room covered with several thick blankets and a pillow. At the foot of the bed, an army-green footlocker. On the other side, a gray metal desk scattered with papers. I seriously thought I'd stepped back in time to the 1940s.

Decker took an interest in the footlocker. It was full of weapons and ammo. He stuck a couple of guns in his waist band and ammo in his pockets like he was ready for the zombie apocalypse. He appeared dry and warm as though he'd never dipped a toe in the chilly water.

"What is this place?" I asked.

"Not sure but we shouldn't hang around too long. I suspect the occupant will be back soon."

"How come you're not wet and freezing?"

"Teleporting helped me dry off," he said as he shouldered a machine gun. "Plus, I'm not human."

Right. There was that. I was sure he had some magical super power that kept him from turning into a popsicle. I wandered over to the desk, clutching the blanket at my shoulders. Several papers had untidy scribble scrawled across them in English, not German. I shoved them around looking for some evidence as to the experiments they performed on the women.

I stopped cold. My stomach dropped to my feet. My hands shook.

"Good God," I whispered.

"What did you find?"

"Knights of the Holy Lance," I said. "They're our host and the German dude is their leader. Heinrich Schneider."

I shoved the paper with his picture over to Decker. He examined it as I shuffled through more papers and came across a thick folder filled with notes from the various experiments. All the victims were women. All of them were between the ages of twenty-five and thirty-five, blonde, blue-eyed, fair skinned.

Hitler's idea of the perfect German.

Off to one side was a crude drawing of a familiar twisted ladder. I'd seen it before but my brain was still fuzzy from the cold and I couldn't figure out what it was. Below the squiggle of the weird ladder were more notes. In his quest to make the perfect German more perfect, he'd killed nearly two dozen women before he succeeded. The twelve in the cavern were his favorite. The ones that had come close but hadn't quite made it to the stage Sofia had.

"Why?" Decker peered over my shoulder reading through the pages as I flipped them.

"I guess it has to do with the Spear of Destiny." I regretted leaving the spear behind in the pool.

"Look, there's more." He pointed to a journal hidden underneath the folder.

I flipped it open. Inside were pictures of the spear similar to the one I'd seen before. They were pasted to the pages like some rudimentary scrapbook. But there were other iterations as well. One noted that the spear was actually in Vienna.

Then I found the motherload.

The plan written in explicit detail.

The Knights of the Holy Lance intended to find the Spear of Destiny to alter the course of the world. They wanted to take over as Hitler had. To eradicate all the "dirty" races including the Jews once again as well as Muslims, Palestinians and anyone deemed not perfect in their eyes.

Schneider called himself Chancellor. He enlisted a doctor to conduct experiments on women to create the super race to control others via their mind. A lot of scientific babble followed after that I couldn't comprehend with the limited brain power I had at the moment. I read most aloud to Decker as he continued searching.

"How did he know about dream walkers?" It was a rhetorical question. One I didn't expect him to answer.

"Perhaps this."

He handed me a piece of paper yellowed with age. It was the ripped-out page from the family history book. The one that was missing. I noticed it the first day I flipped through the book. I ran my finger down the jagged edge of paper sticking out from the binding. That day seemed so long ago now. My heart moved into my throat as I read the all-too familiar handwriting.

It was a detailed description of who and what we were, that we entered minds and controlled dreams. And they wanted that power. Enough to lie, cheat, steal, kill for it.

"Someone betrayed us." I looked up at Decker. "It's the only way he would have known about the dream walkers."

"The text doesn't say what you are. Only what you can do," he pointed out.

It wasn't much of a comfort, but he was right. I turned over the page.

Received page from her. Testing can begin.

A scribbled note mentioned someone—"her" and no name—was manipulated into helping the Knights of the Holy Lance. Or maybe she willingly gave up our secrets in exchange for…what? Money? Power? If she was a true dream walker, would she be able to locate the Holy Relics like me? I had to find out who the traitor was. I had to warn my uncle.

"Schneider figured out how to create us. Not cool," I said. I knew what I had to do then. "I can't let him keep the spear. I have to fish it out of the water."

Decker reached into his back pocket. He held the spear in the palm of his hand. "You mean this?"

I stared at it for a long moment before looking at him. "You found it?"

"The pool wasn't deep. I grabbed it before I got you out." He stretched his hand toward me. "Take it."

I hesitated. If the spear was the real deal, then Kincade would be saved from Azriel. I took a deep breath and reached for the spear.

In Hong Kong, when I located the Horn of Gabriel and touched it for the first time, the history of the relic flashed through my mind, all the way back to the time of its creation. Edward told me I would be able to do that with all the relics.

There was one way to find out if this was the real Spear of Destiny.

I rested my fingertips against the cold metal and waited.

Nothing. Nada. Zilch.

To make sure I wasn't wrong, I picked it up and held the weight in my hand. I still got nothing. This wasn't the real spear.

The real spear was somewhere in Istanbul and this trip to Antarctica was for nothing.

Or had it? I held in my hand a fake spear. One I could use as leverage to save Kincade.

"It isn't the real spear," I said.

"How can you tell?"

"As you have your abilities, I have mine. When I touch the Holy Relics, I see their history in a flash in my mind's eye. I get nothing from this." I closed my hand around it. "It's a fake."

"What now?" he asked.

"I'm taking it. I can use it as a bargaining chip for Kincade's life. Let's find my uncle and get the hell out of here." I slipped it into the front pocket of my shirt.

I needed to tell Edward everything I found about the experiments. He'd know what to do because I sure didn't. I flipped the journal and folder closed and snatched them off the desk.

"What are you doing?"

"These are coming with me, too," I said.

"Anna, if Schneider finds that on you…" He paused for dramatic effect, leaving the implication hanging in the air.

"I don't care. I'm taking it." I clutched the documents to my chest.

I was aware he'd torture me. Maybe kill me. I was also aware this probably wasn't the only copy of his research and notes. If he was smart, he had other copies. Maybe even a digital copy. I assumed he was smart.

"Maybe it will put a halt to the experiments for a little while," I said.

Decker started to reply when we both heard a noise at the door. The handle jiggled and then someone pushed it open. I sucked in a sharp breath. Decker dropped the paper he had in his hand and took a giant step toward me. He grabbed me in a bear hug and teleported us outside, far away from the bunker in the bloody cold again.

I fell to my knees, dry heaving as my stomach revolted. The folder and journal landed in the snow but I was too sick to give a shit.

"You've got to stop doing that," I croaked.

"Do you want to get caught?"

I fought off the bile rising to my throat and swallowed hard. I grabbed a handful of snow and pressed it against my burning forehead as I shook my head. "Not exactly."

I curled to my side, drawing my knees up to my chest waiting for the nausea to pass. It'd take time. Time I didn't have. As I waited, though, I considered my life choices and realized I left my wet boots behind and was currently shoeless.

"We have to find Edward." My voice was raspy as though I smoked cigarettes and drank shots of Jägermeister all night.

"I know we do. Any bright ideas, kid?"

Funny how he called me kid. I was so far removed from being a kid but maybe to him I was still wet behind the ears. I closed my eyes trying to stave off the wave of nausea going through me. "Not really."

And then it occurred to me. Like a duh moment—dream walk Edward and find him that way.

"Give me a second," I said, eyes still closed.

I pushed my mind to connect with my uncle's. We'd trained for this during my stay in England. It took some doing because he was stronger than me, but I found him and he let me in. He was in his typical three-piece suit which suggested he slept.

"Anna, it's not safe here. Leave me."

"I'm not leaving you, uncle, so forget it," I said. "I'm coming after you."

"Schneider is dangerous. He's creating a super race of dream walkers."

"Yes, I had the pleasure of meeting Sofia. I can't figure out how he did it. I found his notes."

"All I can guess is he has a test subject," Edward said. "He found someone to study and replicate or clone."

His comment reminded me of the notes. It merely looked like a drawing of a ladder but now I understood it was a DNA strand. Schneider must have used the DNA of whoever his subject was to try and replicate a dream walker by using brain manipulations and merging the DNA. Uncle Edward and I would have to discuss it later in detail.

"Where are you?" I asked, changing the subject.

"Anna—"

"Tell me, damn it. I'm coming after you if I have to charge in armed and shooting up the place."

He was silent, his lips thinned with that familiar displeasure. I saw it numerous times when he was either disgusted or exasperated with me. "Fine. Somewhere on a lower level. They put a hood over my head. She dream walked me but didn't find out anything from me. I, however, retrieved a wealth of information from her. She didn't care for that."

I winced, embarrassed I was weak and Sofia was able to find out our identities. At least that was all she was able to learn.

Edward, though, was a master at dream walking. He would have pulled out what she was without her knowing. Someday I was going to be able to do that.

"She's powerful but still not as powerful as you," he continued, unaware of the guilt swarming through me. I wanted to preen at the compliment but kept myself in check. "She has the ability to enter dreams but not waking dreams."

This was not new information for me. I nodded. "She paid me a visit, too. How do I find you?"

"I'm not sure, to be honest. I didn't learn the layout as I had a hood over my head."

That did pose a problem.

I, however, was dressed like one of them. Perhaps I could sneak in and find him.

"Sit tight. I'm coming after you," I said.

"Be careful."

At least he didn't try to talk me out of it.

I broke the connection and came back to the real world shivering so hard my teeth rattled.

"We've got to take you back inside before you freeze to death. I refuse to have that on my conscious," Decker said.

"I know…how to find Edward. Can you find me a full uniform?"

His brow wrinkled. "Why?"

"So I can walk the halls without raising suspicions."

It was too bad teleporting and invisibility with Decker made me so violently sick. Otherwise, I'd ask him to use his super power to take me around the complex.

"*That's* your plan?"

"He doesn't know where he is. It's all I got."

Decker was not on board with that idea by the look of annoyance on his face. He didn't say anything, though, as he flashed away in the blink of an eye.

He returned a second later with a coat, hat, gloves, scarf…and my boots. I eagerly put everything on and tried to control the shivering and teeth chattering. It was going to take a while to warm up, though, especially with my feet encased in wet boots. It was better than nothing. I scooped up the folder and journal and cradled them against my chest.

I glanced his direction, wondering if I could handle one last teleport.

"I'll take you to the door," he said as though reading my mind. "After that you're on your own."

I didn't respond as we stared at each other. I willed him to read my mind again with my piercing gaze. Finally, I nodded.

"You want me to teleport you and your uncle when you find him, don't you?"

I grinned, though he couldn't see it behind the scarf. "You got it."

"And how will I know where and when?"

Excellent question. "One of us will signal you."

"And by signal I assume you mean get into my mind."

I nodded again.

He scowled, unhappy with that idea. He ran his hand through his hair, also reminding me of Kincade.

"Fine. I'll wait out here."

I guess the cold didn't bother him as it did me. He didn't even shiver.

"Thanks. I'm ready."

He wrapped his arms around me and away we went.

Chapter 10

DECKER TURNED INVISIBLE as he left me outside the main bunker door. Like he was making a package delivery, he dropped me off and then disappeared while I huddled on the ground trying my damnedest not to dry heave again.

My stomach muscles were getting a work out and I had nothing fun to show for it.

Frigid precious minutes passed as I waited outside for one of the patrol groups to return from their outside shift. I leaned against the bunker wall wishing I had a cigarette to at least look cool instead of like some wallflower waiting for someone to ask her to dance. They approached, giving me a sideways glance as one of them used a badge to open the door.

One of them spoke to me in German. I smiled with my eyes and shrugged my shoulders. I was sure I looked suspicious. I slipped into the building behind them. They didn't give me a second thought as they were too cold and too tired to question me.

At least that worked out in my favor. I followed them inside down a long gray corridor to another set of doors at the end of the hallway. One of them used the same badge to open the door and we all went through.

The doors slid closed behind us, sealing us in and closing out the cold.

This reminded me of the sightless trip I took when we were first captured. I had no doubt we were headed in the same general direction. The floor sloped downward. They took a left turn while I halted at the corner, glancing left and right trying to remember which way they took me. It seemed as though they went right, so I went that way hoping luck was on my side.

I wandered down the long corridor lit by garish fluorescent bulbs buzzing overhead. I took another turn and headed toward an office. Large plate-glass windows lined the top half of the wall giving visitors a view of the interior.

Not an office. This was a laboratory with whitewashed walls and gray floor tile. Upper cabinets went around the entire space. Each table hosted all sorts of test tubes, beakers, equipment, computers. I stared through the window, my heart in my throat. Perhaps this was where they manipulated the DNA to create their super dream walkers.

I walked past the door to the next room. No windows. I paused at the door and tried the handle. It turned with ease. I pushed open the door and walked in like I belonged there.

And stopped short as the door closed behind me. It reminded me of an old hospital ward from the 40s or 50s. Three beds were occupied by women. My stomach twisted into a tight knot as I tried to decide what to do. I took a tentative step toward the woman closest to me. Her eyes were closed. She had two burn marks on either side of her head and in the middle of her forehead. It had to be from the same thing they put on my head. I checked her wrist and found a weak pulse.

The next woman was in the same condition.

The third one was in a semi-conscious state. Her eyes fluttered open as I approached. I halted mid-step by her bedside as she gazed at me with the coldest, bluest eyes I'd ever seen. She stared at me a long moment before her eyes closed again. Her head rolled back and forth on the pillow in a state of semi-consciousness.

She had the same burn marks on her head. Her head lolled to the side. Her hair was shaved from one side of her head. Behind her ear was a long incision that was stitched back together.

What was he doing to these women?

I reached for her, intending to check the pulse in her throat, when her hand flew up and her fingers clamped around my wrist. I nearly jumped out my skin.

I met her gaze and we stared at each other a long moment.

"Are you all right?" I asked.

"Who are you?" she whispered. Her English had a heavy German accent.

"A friend."

"Never seen you before," she said. "I know all the techs."

"I'm new," I said. "And I'm getting you out of here."

Her brows knit in confusion. "Why?"

"Because they're hurting you."

She huffed out a laugh. "They aren't hurting me. I'm here because I want to be here."

Now I was confused. "You volunteered?"

"To become part of something bigger than me, yes."

I eyed the incision. "What did they do to you?"

She released my wrist and reached for the stitches, placing gentle fingertips against the wound. "They gave me power. They told me I would be able to do things. I would be able to help them change the world."

I blinked, trying to understand. Schneider wanted to control the world. What better way than with the Spear of Destiny and an army of dream walkers?

A chill skittered through me, raising gooseflesh despite my clothing layers.

"And you *want* to do that?" I asked.

"Anything for the cause." She dropped her hand to her side.

"The cause to take over the world?" I asked. "To commit genocide?"

"You are clearly not one of us if you think that's what we're doing." Her eyes flashed fire now. "We are the stronger race. We will conquer the weaker and make a better world. I believe in the Chancellor's vision."

So that was the brainwashing crap Heinrich Schneider was doing. Asshole. He was more of a menace than Hitler was, though, because he had figured out how to manipulate DNA strands.

I wanted to ask her another question but she'd passed out. Probably just as well. I stepped back from her bed and made my way out of the room. In the hall, I glanced back at the lab and wondered if I could get inside.

The knob twisted with ease. I pushed open the door. I wondered, though, if it was common practice to leave rooms unlocked. If Schneider had people he trusted the most in Station 211, then it appeared likely. He didn't account for random strangers with a rampant curiosity, though.

It always got me into trouble.

I closed the door behind me and glanced around the room, trying to decide where to look first. I had zero knowledge about DNA labs and doubted I would find anything useful. But it was worth a look around since I was there.

Several glass vials were labeled with a number and a first initial last name. My guess was the test subjects.

And then vials of blood in a cooler caught my eye. I peered through the glass at them all labeled in a precise hand. One in particular stood out.

A WALKER

Hot pinpricks went all over me as I stared at the name in bold print. *My name.* Had Schneider somehow stolen my blood when I was out cold while Sofia dream walked me and kicked my ass? And if he had, how had he managed to manipulate the DNA so fast? It didn't make sense.

Even if he had the best scientists in the world working on his experiments, I didn't want to believe it was my DNA he had. But where else could he have gotten it?

My stomach cramped much like when Decker teleported me. A queasy sickness came over me and I pressed my hand against my ailing abdomen. Did I take it and risk getting caught with it? Or did I leave it and risk the creation of more dream walkers?

I was paralyzed with indecision. My hesitation was going to cost me my life.

Without thinking, I snatched the vial labeled A WALKER and tossed it to the linoleum, expecting it to shatter. It didn't. All it did was bounce a few times across the tile. Growling annoyance because I didn't have time for this shit, I stomped on the vial hard. The glass cracked, the blood spilling in a pool.

I didn't know if that was the one and only sample, but on the off chance, it was, it made me feel better knowing I'd destroyed it.

A blaring alarm sounded throughout the complex.

I bolted toward the door and yanked it open, running out into the hallway. I headed back the way I came. I had to abandon the idea of rescuing Edward to save my own skin. My heart pumped a wild beat as I ran down the hall...and skidded to a halt as two demons stepped out in front of me. I scented them immediately. It was hard to miss their rotting stench.

They lumbered toward me, in no hurry to take me down. I grabbed the jade-handled dagger off my belt and charged, not waiting for them to attack first. I took them out quickly, one after the other, and watched as they turned to nothing more than a dust pile.

With my senses on high alert, I scanned the area and waited for another demon to step out in front of me. Seeing them confirmed my suspicion this Schneider guy was either part demon or possessed by a demon. And I could take him out with my jade-handled dagger.

I sheathed it, intending to take off down the hall and find him to end it all here, now. The leaders of the Knights of the Holy Lance would be wiped out. The experiments would stop and there would be no more super dream walkers.

As I headed toward the end of the hall, a woman stepped out in front of me.

She was tall, lithe, dressed all in black like Sofia. But unlike Sofia she had a mane of glossy black hair cascading over her shoulders. Shadows flickered over her face and I couldn't quite make out her features. She lifted her arms from her side, her black-gloved palms toward the ceiling.

A sharp, stabbing pain went through my mind. I doubled-over, too weak to stand, and collapsed to the floor on my hands and knees. The sharp pain turned into a searing heat flashing through my mind and behind my eyes. I cried out with the all-consuming pain.

She was in my mind. Pushing through my consciousness with nothing more than a thought and blinding me with a bright light that seemed to sear my corneas. Which was weird since the light came from inside my head. I couldn't escape her grip. I tasted blood in the back of my throat. Blood seeped from my nose. My ears were ringing so loud, all other sounds were drowned out.

Decker.

His name floated through my mind and I prayed she couldn't hear it. I hoped he somehow heard my plea in my weakened state and would come for me. My gut clenched. God, it felt like she was turning me inside out. The pain blinded me, burning through my senses.

Oh, God, Decker, please.

The woman's voice drifted into my head. A soft, mellifluous voice that lilted through my mind with the hint of an accent. *Decker. What is Decker?*

Shit.

She didn't understand what Decker meant. I shut off my mind, trying to build those walls as Edward taught me back in England but she was more powerful. Far more powerful. I didn't understand the things she did with merely a thought. I coughed and opened my eyes. Drops of blood dotted the floor.

It felt as though the woman had somehow twisted all my guts in her fist and yanked. I collapsed to the cold floor, coughing up blood. Through hazy eyes, she walked toward me in her shiny black boots with slow, methodical steps. I craned my neck to look up at her but I still couldn't glimpse her features.

Strong arms wrapped around me and scooped me off the floor and then the scene shifted. It was over in a flash. Somehow Decker heard me, flashed to me and teleported me out of there. We were on a snowy embankment. He had me cradled in his arms against his chest.

"What the fuck happened, kid?"

I wished knew.

"Fuck. You're a mess."

He wiped my mouth and nose with the sleeve of his shirt. My eyes were still hazy but I was able to discern a blurry image of him. It was like looking through fog. I was grateful he'd managed to flash me out before she killed me.

"Who was that woman?" he asked.

The sharp tang of blood was still in my mouth. I couldn't form any words. I shook my head to indicate I didn't know. I coughed, sputtered. He turned me over and I spit out a mouthful of blood. The red was a stark contrast against the snowy ground. I shivered. He pulled me back to him, his arms around me in an effort to warm me.

"She was…I don't know who she was." At least I didn't have a mouthful of blood anymore.

The alarm blared in the complex, echoing across the tundra. *Edward.* I unwittingly put Edward in danger. What if the woman went after him next?

"We…have to go back," I said.

"We aren't going anywhere."

"Edward…"

"We have to leave him behind." A hint of sadness edged his voice.

My eyes flew open and I stiffened. "No."

"Anna—"

Leave this place, Anna. You and Decker. They've come for me.

Decker mouth moved but I didn't hear him because Edward's voice burst into my mind drowning him out.

I couldn't imagine what horrors he faced. If that woman got to him…

"I can't leave him here, Decker." I turned toward him, fisting his shirt and looking up to meet his gaze. "He's all the family I have."

Understanding and compassion came into his eyes and he nodded. He understood. Because we were fighting for Kincade's life, too.

"Then let me handle it," he said. "I'm going to do this my way."

I had no idea what that meant but I nodded agreement. "What do you want me to do?"

"Nothing. Stay here. Where it's safe. Out of harm's way."

"But—"

"No. You'll stay."

His voice was firm. He meant business. He shoved the journal into my hands. They were damp, as if he'd stashed them in the snow when he rescued me.

"If you insist."

"I do."

"Decker, one more thing. Demons are inside. I killed two of them."

He gave me a nod. "Understood," he said, then released me.

I crumbled to the ground as he got to his feet. He flashed away, leaving me in the snow with nothing but time on my hands and scary reading material.

Chapter 11

I DIDN'T KNOW WHAT to do with myself. I was too chicken to read through the material in the journal or folder. I wanted to wait until Uncle Edward was with me. Decker was gone thirty seconds when I stood and started to pace. The only thing keeping me on my feet was the adrenaline rushing through my veins. Otherwise, I felt like I'd been hit by a Mack truck.

I left a well-worn path in the snow as I walked back and forth. The gray domed top of the bunker was in the distance. I halted to look at it, wondering if he found my uncle and if my uncle was all right.

An explosion erupted from the bunker, sending a ball of fire upward with a belch of black smoke. The ground rocked beneath my feet as I watched the place burn.

What the hell did Decker do?

A second later, he appeared out of nowhere with my uncle draped over his shoulder. He eased Edward down into the snow.

"What happened? Is he all right?" I dropped to my knees to check on him.

I examined him for signs of the violent illness I experienced when Decker teleported me, but Edward appeared to be fine. That was so not fair. Why did it make me so sick and not him?

"He's fine," Decker said. "I got to him before she could."

"She?" My brows knit with question.

"The woman who attacked you."

Edward groaned. "I'm...all right, Anna. I told you to go."

"I don't follow orders very well," I said, smiling down at him and relieved he was okay.

He pushed to a sitting position and looked me over. Concern etched his face. "What the bloody hell happened to you?"

"I'll tell you later. I think we've worn out our welcome." I nodded toward the burning bunker.

"Sorry about that." Decker didn't sound sorry. "I hope you have an exit plan."

"Always."

Edward lifted his wrist and checked his watch, tapping the black face. Like he was a crime-fighting super hero.

"We can't linger here much longer," Decker said. "I doubt they like my redecorating."

"Patience," Edward said.

My uncle was a man of few words at times. This was one of those times.

"What about Schneider?" I asked. "Did you kill him?"

"No. I left a bomb in my wake to keep them from following right away."

I was disgruntled to learn the chancellor was still alive.

"Decker, since you have that handy trick, can you take us to the eastern shore?" Edward interjected.

"I can."

I frowned. "Do we have to do it that way?"

"If you wish to get caught..." Edward let his words trail off with the unspoken threat.

"Teleporting makes Anna sick," Decker said.

"They know we've escaped. They'll send a search party." Edward scrutinized me with narrowed eyes. "What happened to your eyes? They're bloodshot."

"They are?"

"It looks like a blood vessel popped in them," Decker said. "Likely an after effect of the attack."

"What attack? Who attacked you? Where did you find that folder?" He was full of demands.

In the distance, several men with guns headed our direction in addition to a demon horde that seemed to have been released from the pit of Hell.

"We can discuss all that later. I have much to tell you." I turned back to Decker and said, "Let's do it and get it over with."

He nodded. "I can only take one at a time."

"Take Anna first," Edward said. "I'll wait here."

Decker didn't wait for more instructions. He grabbed me and teleported away to the shore, dropping me off and flashing way again. I crumbled to my hands and knees to allow the sickness to pass. It didn't escape my notice a ship was waiting. Out intended getaway was a ramshackle cruise ship?

Decker was back with Edward. He helped me to my feet. I stumbled once, twice. By the third time, Decker huffed and scooped me up. We all hurried toward the ship and boarded.

"You can put me down now," I said.

Decker released me. It was definitely a cruise ship but nothing like a Carnival. This was more...rustic. The hull featured rust marks and it looked as if it'd seen better days.

"We're getting out of here on this?" I asked.

"Decker, take her to the cabin. I need to speak to the captain."

Proof my uncle knew people anywhere and everywhere. Someday I was going to be able to do that trick.

"We have a cabin?" This was getting weirder all the time.

Decker gave me a gentle nudge and we headed from the deck down a flight of steps. Below, there was a long hallway with several cabins off to the right and left. Decker headed to one and shoved open the door.

The small cabin hosted a built-in bureau for clothes and a narrow bed next to the wall featuring a porthole. The tiny bathroom had a cramped shower, a toilet and a sink. A mirror hung over the sink with a bright light fixture over that. Decker plopped down on the bed, leaning back on the wall and stretching out his long, muscled legs. He folded his arms over his chest and closed his eyes. He was clearly not concerned with me at all.

"What are we supposed to do now?"

"We wait for Edward."

I put the folder and journal on the bureau and shed the coat, hat, gloves and scarf and checked out the bathroom. The face peering back at me in the mirror was unrecognizable. The whites of my eyes were so bloodshot they were red. Indeed, it did look like a blood vessel had popped in each one giving me a terrifying appearance. Blood crusted around my nose. Dried blood was in my hair where my ears also bled.

I was rather disgusted by my appearance and wondered how anyone could look at me. Maybe that was why Uncle Edward ordered Decker to bring me to the cabin. I grabbed a cloth turned on the faucet and washed my face. There wasn't much I could do about my eyes.

I thought back to the woman in black. She was capable of terrifying things I didn't even know were possible. How was she able to get into my mind? What did she do to my innards to make me bleed from nose, ears and mouth? It was fucked up.

I finished cleaning my face and emerged from the bathroom as Edward entered. He pushed the door shut and leaned against it, looking between me and Decker.

"The captain has agreed to take us to Ushuaia."

"Via the Drake Passage?" Decker asked. "Isn't that a little dangerous?"

Edward nodded. "It's notorious for being a bit choppy—"

"A bit?" Decker shook his head at Edward, then said to me, "Brace yourself, kid. We could be in for a bumpy ride."

"Great." Just what I wanted. Motion sickness in my near future.

Concern etched Edward's features. If he was worried about my well-being, he didn't voice it. "I'm sorry we didn't find the spear."

"Me, too," I said with a nod. "We found a fake, though." I pulled it out of my shirt pocket and handed it to him. Edward turned it over in his hands, examining it.

"It looks like the pictures. But it's not the real one?"

"No. I got nothing from it when I touched it."

"Why keep it?"

"Because I can use it as a bargaining chip for Kincade's life."

"I'm not sure that's a good idea," Edward said.

"What am I supposed to do? Hand over the real one?" I asked.

He shook his head. "No."

"Then what?"

Silence stretched between us as Decker and Edward exchanged a look. Instantly my senses went on high alert as an eeriness prickled my skin.

"You're supposed to let him go," Decker said finally.

"Fuck that!" I exploded.

"Anna—"

"Uncle, I owe him. He saved my life more than once. I intend to save his."

"He won't want that. He *doesn't* want that." Decker's tone of voice was casual as he sat on the edge of the bed, his elbows on his knees as he hunched over looking up at me. He was serious.

Frustration and anger raked through me. I pinned him with my heated gaze. "Why did you come if not to help save him? I thought you wanted that."

Guilt flashed over his face before he regained control.

"It was, until…" He paused and huffed out a breath. "It's complicated."

"Complicated? This is not a Facebook status."

"I asked him to help us locate the spear, Anna," Edward said.

"And not Kincade?" I clenched my fists. The vein in the side of my head throbbed. I glanced between the two of them but they were silent, refusing to say anything more.

If they thought I was going to give up trying rescue Kincade from Azriel, they were both dead wrong. Nothing would stop me from my quest to save him. *Nothing.* Even if I had to give up the real spear to do it. I was determined because I owed him that, whether Kincade or Decker or Edward wanted me to do it.

Kincade was there when Azriel murdered Ben and dragged me away from the crime scene. He saved me from Chen and his cronies in Hong Kong. I was aware of what evil Azriel was capable of because I saw it firsthand.

"There are things about the Watchers you don't understand," Edward said.

"I don't care. I'm going after him whether I have help from either of you or not." I snatched the folder off the edge of the bed and handed it to Edward. "We have another pressing issue. This is far more important."

"What is this?" Edward took the folder. He balanced it in the palm of his hand and opened it, skimming the page. I left the ripped-out page from the family history book on top. His eyes widened when he saw it, then met my gaze. "Where did you find this?"

"In Schneider's office," I said. "Someone betrayed us. One of our own as near as I can figure. Look at the note on the back."

He turned it over, read it aloud. "Who is the woman he mentions?"

"I don't know. I discovered more. In the lab, I found a vial of blood in a cooler with the name A WALKER on it. Me, uncle. I think he stole my DNA," I said.

"How?"

I shrugged. "When I was out cold maybe." I pointed to the folder. "He has a drawing of the DNA."

Edward flipped through the pages until he came upon the page with drawing of the double helix. He paused on it a long time, studying it, not saying anything. An eerie sense came over me again. It was never good when Edward was silent.

"He figured out our unique DNA strand. He used it to manipulate brain activity in his test subjects. It must be how he discovered how to make his own dream walkers."

"Yes, I think so," I said with a nod. "And about Schneider. I don't think he's human."

Edward met my level gaze. "You sensed something from him?"

"More like saw it in his eyes. I think he's part demon but I didn't smell demon on him. My guess is he's hiding behind a glamour."

"Schneider did more than you think," Decker said, breaking into the conversation before Edward could reply. I hadn't noticed he'd picked up the journal. "He used the DNA to figure out what test subjects were the most similar. Once he discerned them, he connected their brains to nanobots and implanted them into the neocortex."

Edward and I both stared at Decker as if he'd grown a third head. I missed that in the journal because I was too focused on the page from the family history book. How had Schneider figured out how to connect nanobots to the brain? It was like something out of a science fiction movie featuring a mad scientist.

"Not possible," I said with a shake of my head.

"It is. It's all laid out here." Decker pointed at the page in the book.

"No way he used Anna's DNA for that," Edward said. "We weren't there long enough for him to conduct those intensive experiments. It'd take years and a staff of scientists. I'm sure Schneider has more than one doctor working on the premises."

"Right and let's not forget about the mausoleum we found in the ice cavern," I said. "Those women had been dead for quite some time."

"Whose DNA was it, then?" Decker asked.

A WALKER. The picture of the vial with the name printed on it floated into my mind's eye. I knew of one other A WALKER but she was long dead. I looked at Edward, my gut churning acid. I didn't want to say it out loud.

His face drained of color as though he'd seen a ghost. He met my gaze, his eyes wide and round and glassy.

"I don't believe it." His voice was raspy, soft. I never heard him that way before. Shear, cold terror skittered down my spine. "I *won't* believe it."

I thought of the woman who attacked me back in the bunker. Her glossy black hair over her shoulders. The way she was dressed all in black with shiny black boots. Her face was shadowed, which was strange because the corridor was brightly lit.

Edward was right. That was impossible. I refused to believe it.

"It can't be," I said.

"It can't be what? Do you know who it is?" Decker asked.

"I think it's—" I began.

"No." Edward composed himself quickly by shutting the folder and handing it back to me. It was as though we hadn't even had the conversation. "I think we're all a bit tired. It's a two-day passage to Argentina. I have travel arrangements to make to Istanbul. I suggest we all get some rest."

I glanced at the one bed Decker currently occupied. He tossed aside the journal, shoved to his feet and stretched his arms over his head.

"Are we all bunking up together then?" he asked with a smirk.

"The captain was generous enough to give us each a cabin of our own," Edward said.

"That was nice of him," I said.

"It was. Especially because I paid him double for each one. Anna, this is your cabin. Come, Decker. I'll show you to yours."

They left me alone. I tossed the folder on the bed with the journal and stared at the offending material. I suspected I knew who A WALKER was. In a fit of rage and frustration, I shoved them both off the bed letting them crash to the ground. Papers scattered. The pages in the journal bent at odd angles. Then I shed my clothes and climbed into bed with a yawn.

I'd think about that weird shit tomorrow.

Chapter 12

I AWOKE SOMETIME LATER rested and refreshed. When I opened my eyes, I was disoriented at first as I gazed up at the unfamiliar ceiling from the narrow bed. Several minutes ticked by before I remembered where I was. Thankfully, I had no dreams or if I did, I didn't remember them. And I certainly didn't have anyone busting into my dreams.

I suspected that was because Edward was nearby and he wielded some kind of weird mind magic shit to keep folks out of my head and his.

I stretched then shoved the blankets back and sat up, glancing around the room. A stack of clean clothes resided on top of the bureau. Next to the clothes, the journal and the folder with the pages tidied up. Someone visited me while I slept. Probably Edward.

I got out of bed and snatched up the clothes. A pair of thick pants, long underwear, a thermal undershirt, a button-down flannel shirt, even underwear. On the floor was a pair of pink hiking boots and thermal socks. He thought of everything.

I padded to the tiny bathroom with an armload of clothes and took my first hot shower in what seemed like days. I replayed everything that happened in Antarctica. I couldn't shake the thought it was somehow my mother's blood in that vial back in the lab.

But how could that be?

I was told all my life she died in childbirth. I entered the foster system as an infant. How did Schneider acquire her blood before she died? While she was pregnant with me? And how was her blood preserved for twenty-eight years?

Nothing about this situation made sense.

I also thought of the woman who attacked me with her mind in the corridor outside the lab. Who was she? Why couldn't I see her face? Did she do some sort of weird trick to keep me from seeing exactly who she was? And why would that matter?

Unless she didn't want me to know who she was. But...why?

I stepped out of the shower and toweled off, then wrapped it around me. I peered at my face in the mirror. My eyes were less red. At least I didn't look scary anymore. Still, the red was a strange contrast with my purple eyes which appeared more lavender than the deep purple they usually were.

Despite my rest, fatigue still pressed into me. We'd been traveling nonstop for what seemed like months when in reality a few days had passed. My stomach rumbled, spurring me into action. I dressed and stepped out of the bathroom.

And nearly came out of my skin.

Azriel stood in the room, filling up all the empty space as he leaned against the small dresser. His black wings were spread out behind him, glistening in the pale light of the tiny cabin. He dwarfed everything in the room. I never realized how big and tall he was because we were always in a space that accommodated both of us.

I pressed my hand against my roiling stomach. He granted me that feral smile to which I'd become so accustomed.

"Anna, *mon chéri*, a pleasure to see you."

"What do you want?" I feared his unexpected visit was to tell me he finally killed Kincade.

"I came for the spear. Do you have it?"

I hesitated. I had to play this right. If I told him I had it—the fake—and turned it over to him now, he would likely figure out it was, in fact, a fake. He could hurt Kincade. If I told him the truth and said I didn't have it, he could still hurt Kincade.

"Your silence speaks volumes." He pushed off the bureau.

"I need more time." I started to explain the spear wasn't in Antarctica but stopped myself. What was the point? He likely already had that information and that's why he appeared. His little visit was to taunt me.

"Time is a commodity you do not have, *chéri*."

Anger snapped through me. "You think finding Holy Relics all over the world is *easy*? I'm not a magician, for fuck's sake. I have to actually travel from one place to the next by conventional means. I can't pop in and out wherever I want."

"While that may be true, you leave me no choice."

"For what?" I demanded. Panic rose through me. "What do you intend to do?"

"I warned you before. Every time you disobey me, I will take another piece of his soul."

Before he disappeared, my hand shot out. I clamped my fingers around his wrist, my nails digging into his skin. "Don't you touch him," I said through clenched teeth.

His brows winged upward. "Protective of him, aren't you? How romantic."

My fingers tightened on his wrist. I felt the steady beat of his pulse. He didn't even flinch. "I'll give you want you want but you have to give me time to find it."

"You failed in your search in Antarctica." It wasn't question.

I hated he knew that. "Yes."

"Pity." He glanced down at my hand and then back up at me. "Release me. Or do you wish to go with me?"

"Yes, I want to see Kincade." I couldn't deny the impulse. I needed to see if he was still alive for my peace of mind—that is, if I could achieve peace of mind with him in Azriel's hands.

He laughed. "You want to witness his torture? As you wish."

Before I could answer, we flashed away in the blink of an eye. Unlike flashing with Decker, I didn't get sick to my stomach. It seemed strange I wouldn't have the same symptoms but perhaps traveling with a Fallen was different.

We landed in what appeared to be a dungeon. Where, I had no idea. Somewhere in the distance, the trickle of water echoed through the chamber. The place was dank, dark and dismal. Flickering torches in brackets down the wall lighted the place. We stood inside a cell door that resembled something out of medieval history. An eeriness settled over me as I took in my surroundings.

Kincade was shackled by his wrists to a wall, his head hanging between his shoulders. His clothes were dirty and torn. His hands were limp. His skin was rubbed raw on his wrists underneath the shackles.

I still had my hand wrapped around Azriel's wrist. I released him and went to Kincade, pausing in front of him trying to decide what to do next. I was afraid to touch him. He was in bad shape but still breathing. I wondered how much of his soul Azriel had taken. I whispered his name.

His eyes fluttered open but he didn't respond with any other movement.

"I'm going to get you out of here," I said. "I promise."

He lifted his head with some effort. Torchlight flickered over his bruised face, which was dirty and bloody. Dark circles smudged under his eyes. Fatigue creased the corners. He hung there, listless, as if all the fight had left him, like he was ready to give up. He'd been tortured, no doubt. He wasn't the same man who gave the nurse hell in the hospital back in Hong Kong.

"Don't," was all he said.

The word hung between us and it took me a few seconds to realize what he said. I started to respond but his head dropped down between his shoulders again. I spun to face Azriel.

"What have you done to him?"

"What I said I'd do. Every day you delay bringing me the spear is another day of hell for Kincade." Azriel glanced over him with that wolfish grin that made me hate him all the more. As though he admired his handiwork. "He has a surprisingly high threshold for pain, I do have to admit. It took me some time to break him."

A stabbing pain went through my chest. I bit my lip to keep the whimper I wanted to release contained.

He hasn't broken me yet, the arrogant fuck.

Kincade's voice exploded in my mind and I winced, putting my fingers to my head. Now that sounded like Kincade. Azriel took note of my reaction with one lifted eyebrow though he didn't say anything.

I told you before not to come after me.

I focused on Kincade, but he still had his head down. His snarled response in my head gave me hope he was still in there somewhere and maybe hadn't lost his fight. He was giving the performance of a lifetime to make Azriel think he had beaten him. He deserved an Oscar.

I know what you said, I replied, though I wasn't sure he heard me.

It didn't matter. I was still going to find a way to release him from Azriel's grasp.

I remembered Kincade told me he'd hunted him longer than I'd bee alive. I thought I understood what he was up to. He wanted to lull Azriel into a false sense of power and security. Maybe he was hoarding his strength with the intention of striking when Azriel least expected.

That's exactly what I'm doing.

So, he *had* heard my thoughts.

A grin wanted to erupt on my face but I contained it. Instead, I turned away from Kincade, my hand over my mouth as though I was completely horrified and upset by his appearance.

"Time's up, *chéri.*"

"Fine. Take me back."

"If you insist. But first…"

He paused and moved toward Kincade, forcing me to turn and look at them. Azriel grabbed a handful of hair on the back of his head and jerked upward. Kincade's eyes came open and for a moment, clarity sparked there before he stifled it. Azriel's dark gaze met mine as he opened his free hand and placed it against his chest.

I clenched my fists and gritted my teeth, doing my best to keep my face impassive. I refused to look at Ariel and instead focused on Kincade. His gaze met mine.

Don't watch, Anna. Shut your eyes.

I refused. I kept my eyes on him as Azriel pulled the white light from his chest. Kincade's eyes closed as he pressed his lips together in a thin line. He refused to cry out like he had back in the alley in Marrakesh. But he couldn't control the low guttural growl that rumbled his throat.

Azriel pulled his palm away and closed his fist around the white light. Smiling. All the while smiling.

My hatred for him increased tenfold.

"Another piece is mine," he said. "Next time, your boyfriend may not be so lucky."

"Take me back, damn you, Azriel." I didn't bother to correct him about Kincade not being my boyfriend.

He stepped to me and put his hand on my shoulder. I gave one last glance to Kincade who appeared to have passed out before we flashed back to the cabin.

As soon as we arrived, Uncle Edward jumped to his feet. Decker pulled his gun and aimed at Azriel. Before he could get the shot off, the fallen angel disappeared. Edward pushed Decker's gun down so he wouldn't shoot me. He re-holstered the gun.

"Where have you been?" Edward demanded. "You've been gone more than a day."

Time had moved that quickly while I visited Kincade with Azriel?

"Azriel came to me demanding the spear so I demanded he take me to Kincade."

"You saw him?" Decker asked.

I nodded. "Azriel is torturing him." Again, I left out the part about the fallen angel stealing part of Kincade's soul.

Decker clenched his fists. Rage creased his face. "Bloody bastard."

"Did he hurt you?" Edward asked.

"No."

Edward breathed out a sigh of relief. "Good. He must have taken you to another realm. I couldn't find you."

I was pretty sure I didn't want to know where that was. I was glad my uncle had tried to find me, even though he couldn't.

"We've docked in Ushuaia. I have a charter plane waiting to take us as far as Rio de Janeiro," he said. "We'll rest there for a day while I make arrangements to Istanbul."

"Great." I glanced around. "Where's the journal?"

"I packed it along with the fake spear in my things," Edward said.

I was far from excited about the prospect of getting on another plane and going to yet another city. But I needed and wanted that spear. I needed it for Kincade's life.

Rio reeked like a toilet.

After landing, my uncle had a car waiting for us to take us to the Grand Hyatt. I was looking forward to a hot shower and a bed. I was travel weary.

We checked into the hotel and all went to our separate rooms. Edward managed to secure suites for all three of us with an ocean view. There wasn't much conversation because there didn't need to be. Edward was focused on pulling strings to get us on another plane to somewhere. I was focused on worrying about Kincade. Decker was Decker. He looked pissed from the time we left Argentina to the time we landed.

I wondered what was going on in that head of his. Nothing good, I'd wager.

I pushed open the door to my hotel room which was a luxurious suite with a palatial bathroom, a bedroom with a king size bed and a balcony with a shore view, a gourmet kitchen and a small living area. The place rivaled my apartment in Hong Kong. My uncle spared no expense. It must be nice having an unlimited bank account. As I moved into the room, I was immediately overwhelmed with the smell of chocolate and strawberries. Joachim was there somewhere. I sighed.

"Show yourself," I said to the messenger angel.

He stepped out of the bedroom, wings displayed, wearing his usual garb. Blue jeans, white shirt accentuating every ripple of muscle, black boots. Joachim was dark-haired, tall and good-looking, with wings as white as snow. His icy blue eyes pinpointed me the second I entered the room.

"What's up, angel boy? Haven't seen you in a while. Did you miss me?"

He scowled at my nickname. He'd never been fond of it. "The Spear of Destiny, Annabelle. Do you have it?"

He cut right to the chase. He knew I hadn't found it or he wouldn't be there to needle me.

"I'm fine, thanks. How are you?"

He hadn't bothered to stop scowling. "The spear."

"I don't have it. However, I have a great knock-off if you want that."

He folded his arms across his massive chest. "When you have the spear, you will also hand over the Horn of Gabriel."

I bristled. We had this discussion before. I refused to give it to him so I entrusted the horn with the warrior angel, Darius. He agreed to keep it for me until I was ready to take it back. He was the only one I trusted with the relic. I was afraid if I left it at Edward's manor, Azriel would try to steal it.

"No," I said.

"Annabelle—"

I hated when he called me by my full given name.

"I told you no before. My answer is still the same," I said. "The horn is safe. Once I have the spear, I will make sure it's also safe."

"Do you mean by giving it to the warrior angel who has been poisoned by Hell? Or by giving it to Azriel to save the Watcher's life?" he asked.

I stared at him, shocked he was aware of my plan. But I shouldn't be shocked. These angels knew things before I did sometimes. It was unnerving.

"I'll worry about that."

"Annabelle, you cannot give the Spear of Destiny to Azriel. He will turn it over to Lucifer," he said. "We cannot allow the Dark One to have it. The Spear of Destiny is a relic of formidable power."

Anger boiled through me as I clenched my fists. "Stop telling me what to do."

"Watchers are not allowed to interfere with human affairs. There are consequences if they do," he continued as if I hadn't spoken.

"Oh, yeah? Like what?" I demanded.

Joachim was silent for a moment, his lips pressed together in a thin line as if he didn't want to answer.

"Tell me, damn it," I said through clenched teeth. I heard the spiel before the Watchers would face consequences but I didn't know *what* that was.

"Watchers who decide to forsake the rules and choose one person to help," he paused and gave me another pointed accusatory look, "will be cast out as punishment."

"Cast out?" I furrowed my brow, wanting to make sure I understood exactly what he was telling me.

"Yes, Annabelle. Cast out of the Watchers. Meaning they will lose their place and fall out of favor."

My skin prickled. The back of my throat constricted and I started to swallow the sudden lump that was there. Kincade risked more than I knew to help me and yet he did it anyway.

He told me, back in the hospital in Hong Kong, that he was coming with me whether I liked it or not.

I'm going to make sure that bastard, Azriel, never puts another hand on you. If he does, I'll fucking kill him.

Oh, crap. I understood what his plan was now. Getting captured by Azriel was fortuitous, yet Kincade considered it an opportunity. I chewed my lower lip. I needed to find that spear now more than ever.

"Giving the spear over to Azriel will do Kincade no favors."

I clenched my fists tighter, my nails digging into my palms. "I know what I'm doing with the relics more than you think."

"By going through the motions?" He shook his head. "You have not yet embraced your true power or purpose."

"How can you say that?" My voice hitched at the end, nearing hysteria. "I've done *everything* everyone has asked of me. I've trained. I've been dragged all over the world looking for these relics and this is the thanks I get?"

"You cannot deny the truth, though, can you? While you may have accepted who you are, Annabelle, you have not truly embraced it," Joachim said. "The day will come when you will have to…or die."

"Thanks for that. I'll log that away."

He was less than amused with my sarcasm. "Bring me the spear, Annabelle."

It was the last thing he said to me before he disappeared.

I unclenched my fists. My palms ached. When I glanced down, little crescents were left behind where my nails dug into the skin. No matter what I did, it wasn't good enough. I wasn't fast enough. I wasn't smart enough. Every step I took, every breath I sucked into and out of my lungs, was being monitored by some heavenly creature somewhere.

My shoulders drooped and I expelled the air out of my lungs. I trudged to the bedroom, kicked off my shoes and flopped on the bed face down, staring out at the ocean watching the waves ebb and flow.

I wondered about Darius. The last time we were together was the night in Hong Kong when I handed him the Horn of Gabriel and he whispered my apartment number in my ear. He kissed me on the cheek and disappeared. I wondered how many of his feathers had turned black because of me. I wondered if I would ever see him again.

A knock sounded on the door.

Oh, gaw. I couldn't handle another visitor today. I turned over onto my back and stared up at the ceiling hoping whoever it was would go away. Another knock. This time more forceful.

"Anna, open up." Decker's muffled voice came through the door.

I pushed up and stalked to the door, flinging it open in one fluid motion. He didn't wait for an invitation. He pushed his way inside.

"We need to talk."

"Sure, come on in." I shut the door.

He made his way into the suite to the living area, pacing the short length of the floor. "I need you to tell me everything you remember about the place Kincade was in."

"There's not much to tell."

"Everything, Anna. Details. I need them."

"Why? What are you going to do?" I put my hands on my hips.

He halted mid-step and stared at me. "None of your concern. Now tell me everything you remember."

"It was some sort of dungeon. With torches lining one wall. It was kind of weird. I could hear the trickle of water."

"From where?"

I shrugged. "Somewhere in the distance. I'm not sure what it was. I never saw water. It was pretty dark and depressing. Kincade was shackled to the wall."

He started pacing again, raking his hand through his hair and looking a lot like Kincade in his mannerisms.

"And Kincade? How was he?"

"How do you think?"

He flashed me a glare as he paced.

"His face was black and blue, like he'd been beaten. His wrists were raw and bleeding from the shackles. His clothes were dirty. He had a hole in one of the knees of his jeans." Odd I remembered that. "Like he'd been there a while."

"Is that all you remember?" he asked.

"Yes. Everything. He's not giving up, Decker. Kincade was coherent enough to mind-speak to me."

He halted again and stared at me, eyes wide with shock. "He spoke into your mind?"

"Yeah. So?" I bit my lower lip, wondering why that was so special.

Decker went back to pacing, snapping his fingers and clenching his fists alternatively. "An unexpected development."

"What's the big deal?"

"Nothing," he said in a clipped tone. "Do you remember anything else?"

"Azriel thinks he's broken him but Kincade told me he hasn't."

That stopped him again. I wondered why he kept starting and stopping the pacing. It was making me dizzy. "He was coherent enough to tell you that?"

"In my mind, yes."

"He intends to kill Azriel. I have no doubt," he said.

"I'm the one that wants to kill Azriel and I will if it's the last thing I do. He took my boyfriend from me. He deserves to die."

"Vengeance is not a positive emotion, Anna."

I didn't care. It was all I'd thought about since he took Ben from me. "And yet Kincade intends to kill him, too. I doubt it's because he likes the guy."

"Azriel has been killing guardian angels for some time now. Kincade's job is to retire him."

Retire? I wanted to snort.

I was aware of Azriel's deeds. I witnessed a couple of them. They were images forever burned into my mind.

"What does that mean 'retire'?" I asked.

"I think you know. I will not be going with you to Istanbul," he said.

"Why not?"

"Because I'm going after Kincade myself. I have an idea where to start."

Frustration edged through me. "On the boat, you said he didn't want us coming after him."

"*You*. He doesn't want *you* coming after him, Anna."

I scowled, offended by the way he'd said it. "But—"

"Your uncle was correct in that Azriel has taken him to another realm. A realm that is likely unreachable by conventional means. I will have to find another way."

"I have *no* idea what that means," I said. "How does one travel to another realm by unconventional means?"

"There are ways."

"Take me with you," I demanded.

"No."

"I can handle myself." I pulled the jade-handled dagger from my belt. "This thing will turn demons to dust. I can help you."

"You cannot come with me." He took two steps toward me and put his hands on my shoulders and squeezed. "Stay safe, Anna. You have a far more important job. I'm simply taking Kincade out of the equation so you can focus. I have no doubt you will find the spear."

So that's what this was about. I resented the decision being made for me but I tried to be the bigger person. I swallowed the acid retort I wanted to let fly. Likely Decker would find Kincade before me anyway. Saving him was all that mattered.

"I hope you find Kincade," I said and meant it. "Will I see you both again?"

"I don't think so. He and I will return to our rightful place and I will have my own consequences to face."

Not see Kincade again? That was a punch in the gut. I didn't understand what he meant by any of that and I wasn't sure I should ask.

It sounded to me as though Decker intended to find him before I had a chance to turn over the spear to Azriel to save him. I assumed that was by design. Perhaps a plan concocted by him or uncle or both to keep the spear out of the fallen angel's hands.

I said nothing, though, and merely nodded.

"Perhaps someday our paths will cross again." He released me and started for the door.

"Decker, wait." He stopped, turned to look at me. "Is it true Watchers are cast out if they decide to help a particular human?"

He nodded. "It is." After a long silent moment, he said, "I'm sorry, Anna. I cannot allow him to forsake his position in the Watchers for you."

A stabbing pain went right to my heart. I wasn't good enough for him because I was merely human. I got it. It didn't lessen the sting anymore, though. I pressed a hand against my chest and nodded.

"I get it," I said, though I didn't. Not really.

"Farewell." And then he was gone.

Chapter 13

I WANTED TO THROW a temper tantrum. Why wasn't anything ever simple?

Instead, I stalked back to the bedroom and sat on the edge of the bed, watching the waves glisten in the moonlight. Night had fallen while I visited with Joachim and Decker.

Decker didn't want Kincade to forsake his position—whatever that was—*for me*. It sounded like we had some kind of romantic involvement and we didn't. Far from it. We were nothing but...what? Friends? Not exactly. We were allies. We fought against the same common enemy. He wanted Azriel dead as much as I did.

I didn't want to go to Istanbul any more than I wanted to go to Antarctica. I wanted to go with Decker to help but, apparently, I wasn't good enough for that.

So now I decided to sit here and pout.

A knock sounded on my door.

Was this Grand Central Station or what?

I huffed out a breath and headed for the door, flinging it open. My uncle stood on the other side.

"What?"

"We're leaving."

"Already? We just got here."

"I managed to secure transportation to Lisbon. I have a plane waiting for us but time is of the essence. We have to leave now."

I clenched my jaw as the anger boiled inside me but I didn't say anything. I didn't even have any bags to grab. We'd traveled light from Argentina to Rio. I never did get that hot shower.

"Fine. Let me get my shoes."

I shoved my feet into my pink hiking boots, then slammed the door on my way out and followed him down the corridor to the elevator, wondering if he was aware Decker left. Wondering if he knew Joachim paid me a visit.

"Decker will not be joining us."

I guess that answered that. "I'm aware."

We got in the elevator and the doors whooshed closed. Silence descended around us. I shifted from one foot to the other trying to decide what to say or if to say anything. I wanted to rant and rave to my uncle about the injustice of Decker leaving to rescue Kincade without me but what good would it do? Nothing, that's what.

"You're upset," he said.

"Oh, was it obvious?"

"Anger radiates from you, so, yes, it is quite obvious. Care to tell me why?"

"No."

But I did. I wanted to tell him everything about my conversation with Decker. Not that it would do me any good but maybe I needed to get it off my chest.

"Decker told you why he was leaving."

My uncle enjoyed needling me. "He did."

"And you do not approve?"

The elevator dinged and we exited into the lobby of the hotel. I followed him to the waiting car outside.

"It obviously doesn't matter whether I approve or not."

I slid into the backseat. My uncle tossed in his bag and followed, barking orders at the driver to head to the airport.

"Did you have something to do with it?" I asked. "Is it because I want to give the spear to Azriel in exchange for Kincade's life?"

"I did not have anything to do with Decker's departure. However, I think you have a clear understanding how I feel about you handing over the spear." He punctuated that with a sniff of derision.

"Let's have it out here and now, uncle. You despise the idea. But if it saves his life—"

"The point is moot, Anna." He refused to look at me.

Which set my teeth on edge and the anger boiling even hotter. "Then why insist I tell you why I'm angry if you already know?"

His eyes were sharp and bright. "Why don't you tell me what you're upset about?"

"What does that mean?"

"Come, Anna. You and I can both agree there is some connection between you and Kincade."

This again? Annoyance flashed through me.

"I do not agree. There is no connection between us," I said almost too quickly.

But Edward was having none of it. "He tracked you down in Hong Kong and followed you to England. He came looking for you at the manor. He wanted to find you and you let him. Otherwise, you wouldn't have returned to the most obvious place when you left Hong Kong. He knew you'd return home just as you knew he'd follow you."

"That's absurd." I folded my arms and sat back in the seat, the leather squeaking with my weight.

"Is it?" he asked with that tone of voice that told me he didn't believe me for one second.

"Yes, it is. I left Hong Kong because I didn't want his help looking for the relics. I had no idea he'd follow me. I came because you wanted me to train. And nothing is between us. Never has been. I'm not even sure we're friends."

I punctuated every word with heat. As much as I wanted to deny the truth, I had to face the fact my uncle was right. I wanted away from Kincade to keep him from joining me in my search for the Holy Relics. Or did I? I grappled with that since I left him in that hospital in Hong Kong. I tried to ignore the guilt and couldn't. I returned to the one place that was closest to home I had. I hated my uncle was right. I suspected—hoped, even—Kincade would follow me.

He declined to respond and merely stared ahead.

He didn't believe me. Maybe I didn't believe me, either. I insisted nothing was between us but perhaps I was wrong. Edward told me not so long ago Kincade took an interest in me and that terrified me. How could I even unpack that information? And what exactly did it mean?

I knew so little about the man and now I'd never see him again.

We arrived at the airport. As soon as the car stopped, Edward was out and stalking toward the private jet. I flung open the car door.

As soon as I stepped out of the car, I sensed the demons.

"Edward, wait!"

He halted at my jarring tone and glanced back, anger evident on his face. When he noticed me looking beyond him, he followed my gaze. The demon exited the plane and headed for my uncle at a dead run, poison sword at the ready.

For a second, I froze. Then I grabbed the dagger at my waist and charged. Edward was already in action as two more demons headed for us. He dropped his bag and wielded two daggers I never realized he had. I spun, shoved my dagger into the gut of the one closest to me. Edward was busy with the one that left the plane. I turned my attention to the third one and killed it, turning it to dust. Edward managed to handle the last one by stabbing it in the neck.

We moved back to back, each of us looking around for more demons headed our way.

"Ambush?" I asked.

"Likely," he said, his tone clipped. "I thought getting this charter was too easy. I should have listened to my instinct."

More demons swarmed from the darkness. More than the two of us could handle. I wished Genghis and his buddies would show up to help us, but they were likely busy with their own demons in Hong Kong.

"What now?" I asked.

"We have no choice. We must fight."

Fantastic.

"We're outnumbered," I said. "You realize that."

"I'm aware, Anna."

How the hell were we going to get out of this one? Demons swarmed toward us. My heart rammed hard in my chest as I gripped the dagger in my sweaty palm, ready to do battle.

The demons split like the Red Sea and the woman with sleek black hair dressed in a black catsuit, shiny black boots, black gloves moved through them. It was the same woman I encountered in Antarctica. How had she found me here?

She was tall with a perfect hourglass figure as she moved into the light from the runway. I got a good look at her face for the first time. Her striking face hosted high cheekbones befitting someone of royal blood. Her face looked like it was carved from the most perfect, smoothest marble. She had red, full lips, a long slender neck.

But the thing that struck me the most was the color of her eyes.

Eyes like mine.

Purple eyes.

She was the spitting image of the painting hanging in the gallery in Edward's manor.

Edward stiffened next to me. He had all but stopped breathing as a shiver ran through him with such violence it vibrated through me, too.

Even though my eyes witnessed the truth, my mind refused to believe.

The demons huddled behind her as she took the lead and halted in front of me. We stared each other down, the only sound that of the wind and the planes gearing up for take-off.

She lifted her arms like she had back in the bunker. It took three seconds for the wave to hit me. My knees buckled and down I went. I dropped my dagger. It clattered on the pavement. The illness took over and I dry heaved, then coughed out a mouthful of blood.

She was killing me.

Edward moved to stand between me and her, as if to shield me, but it didn't seem to do any good. Through my hazy eyes, he snatched up the dagger and charged her. I wanted to cry out for him to stop but words wouldn't form. He was on her in a second. She was so focused on me she didn't realized he was there until it was too late. He stabbed her in the shoulder, making her break her concentration.

She shrieked and clutched her shoulder. Blood seeped through her fingers.

I curled into a ball, my knees on my chest. I shivered violently. My teeth chattered.

"Who are you?" she said.

And her voice matched the same mellifluous voice in my head that day.

"Stay back." Edward waved the dagger at her.

"Kill the man. Bring me the girl," she ordered.

"No. I won't let you have her," Edward said.

The demons charged.

I was too weak to move. My uncle produced a glowing sword—I was certain I hallucinated that but I wasn't sure. He fought like a madman. All the while the woman evaded the skirmish and headed right for me.

What the hell was I going to do now? I was unarmed and incapacitated.

She knelt next to me, her purple eyes matching mine locked onto me. My breath caught in my throat.

"Mom?" The word gurgled out in a whisper.

She blinked, question in her gaze. For the briefest second, lucidity flickered through her eyes before they narrowed. She reached for me, placed two fingers on the side of my head.

I have no idea what happened next. All I remembered was a blinding white light as a scream ripped from my lungs.

And then darkness.

Blessed quiet darkness.

When I awoke, I was in bed. The soft mattress and pillow gave me comfort in a world of chaos. But I was blind. I whimpered as fear coursed through me. A tear leaked from the corner of my eyes. *I was blind.* The woman with purple eyes blinded me.

"Shh, rest."

Edward's voice. He placed a cool hand on my forehead, then touched each of my cheeks as if checking for fever.

"You gave me a fright," he said.

"I can't see." Panic laced my voice.

"I've brought someone to help with that," he said.

His hand lifted mine from the bed and placed it in someone else's. Warm. Large. The hands of a warrior.

"Hello, Keeper."

Darius.

I burst into tears.

A door closed. The mattress sighed with his weight. His hand enclosed mine as I sniffled and tried to get my emotions under control. I gripped his hand hard, as though he were a tether keeping me anchored to the here and now.

"What are you doing here?" I asked, my voice quiet in the darkness.

"Your uncle called me. Still getting into trouble, Keeper?" A smile was in his voice.

"I'm glad you came. Where am I? What happened?"

"We are in Rio. I will defer to your uncle to explain what happened because I don't have all the details. I merely came to help."

I couldn't help but wonder how Edward had called Darius. The last interaction we all three had was after Edward and I returned from our trip to Hell, both of us near death. Edward was poisoned by demon swords and I was beaten and almost killed by Azriel. If not for Darius, neither of us would have survived.

His snowy white feathers were slowly turning charcoal gray and black. The penance for rescuing us was he slowly turned into a Fallen. A warrior angel was forbidden into the depths of Hell and yet he came anyway. I wondered how many white feathers remained.

Darius had healing powers. He'd drawn the poison from my uncle's body into his. That was why his feathers turned from white to dark. Michael told me the Staff of Moses would save him. It would have been the next relic on my list, but I'd been tasked with finding the Spear of Destiny first.

"Can you help me?"

He patted my hand. "I will try, Keeper."

He placed his hand over my eyes and kept it there for what seemed like an eternity. I had no idea what he was doing. His fingertips gently pressed against my eyelids while my heart thumped against my chest. When he removed them, my eyesight was nothing more than a gray haze.

The door opened and then snicked closed followed by the steady tap of someone light of foot. My ears tuned to even the slightest movement in the room. My uncle returned. He had the stealth of a mountain lion.

"That is the best I can do."

It was like looking through an opaque veil. I focused on Darius. His form was blurry, but I made out some of his features. Light from the nearby lamp caused his blond hair to shimmer. The strands resembled pure gold. In my shadowy haze, it was clear more of his feathers turned black. I winced.

"Will she recover her eyesight?" Edward asked.

"Hard to say. There was a lot of damage." He rose, the weight gone from the side of the bed. "I did all I could."

"I'm sure it will be enough. Thank you for coming and for helping," Edward said.

My uncle moved into my line of vision as Darius walked toward the door. I didn't want him to go. I wanted him to stay.

Edward had a bandage on one of his forearms from wrist to elbow and a white one across his forehead. It must have been a hell of a battle. I missed it all because I was crippled with pain and then unconscious. Worry lines etched his face.

"I thought she was going to kill you."

"She didn't."

But she wanted to. Those big purple eyes staring back haunted me. Her beautiful familiar face was permanently imprinted in my mind's eye.

"I'd never seen anyone do anything like that before. Who was she?"

"Don't you know?"

He shook his head. Either he didn't believe it or didn't *want* to believe it. But we both saw her.

"She was at Station 211. She's the one who attacked me the same way. If it hadn't been for Decker, she would have killed me. I can't figure out how she tracked me here," I said.

"I don't know how she did either."

He prowled the room, pausing at the window. I guessed we had returned to the same hotel. He was nothing more than a silhouette against a blur of light. Judging by the rigid line of his shoulders and the way he stood staring out at the surf with his hands clasped behind his back, he was bothered by the events.

"Uncle, you know who she is." I pushed to a sitting position in the bed.

"No, I don't." He didn't turn around to respond. His words were quiet, nearly getting lost with the sound of the tide.

But I heard him.

"Yes, you do. *She's alive.*"

He spun and came toward me in two steps. Now that he was closer, the look of horror was clear on his face. One I'd never seen before. Color stained high in his cheeks. "No, Anna. She isn't. She died a long time ago."

"You're in denial. You don't want to believe it. I didn't either. But I saw the vial of blood in the lab with the name A WALKER on it. It had to be her blood. She had to be the one they used to create their dream walkers. Not me."

"No." He spit the word at me with such vehemence, I wanted to shrink back into the bed and hide under the covers.

I wasn't the sort of person to hide under the covers and I never backed down from a fight with my uncle. I sat a little straighter.

"Who else could it be?"

He walked back to the window and blew out a breath.

In my mind, there was no other explanation. That woman was my mother and she'd tried to kill me. I had a suspicion, though, she wasn't the same person who gave birth to me. I refused to believe she would willingly hurt me. When I called her mom, a moment of clarity came into her eyes but quickly vanished.

"That woman is not my sister." Sadness tinged his words.

He wanted to believe, but resisted the idea she was Annabelle Walker, his sister.

I wanted to believe she *had* to be Annabelle Walker, my mother.

She was altered somehow. Schneider poked around in her head until he figured out what made her a dream walker. He'd turned her into a badass who killed with her mind. She told the demons to kill Edward, but I had no recollection after that.

"What happened to me?" I asked.

Edward still stood with his back to me, his hands clasped there, as he looked out. "What do you remember about the attack?"

"Not much. Only that she told them to kill you and bring me to her. And then she lifted her arms and it was like…" I paused, trying to put it into words. "Like someone was shredding my insides."

"You bled from your nose, mouth and eyes." He turned to me but his face was shadowed in the gloom or through my hazy vision. Only that bandage on his arm and head was visible. "It was terrifying."

A chill shifted through me, prickling my skin from head to toe. Few things in this world terrified my uncle. Hearing him say that about how I looked must have fucked him up. It probably would have fucked me up, too, had I seen it.

"She managed to do that to you without touching you, her arms outstretched, looking at you. Everything she did to you she did with her mind. I don't understand how."

But she *had* touched me when she knelt next to me. And when she had, the pain subsided. She controlled what she did.

I twisted the sheet in my fist and bit down hard on my lower lip, trying to keep it from quivering. Tears threatened. We *did* know, though. We read it in the journal. Schneider and his scientist figured out how to get into her mind, how to control her, how to make her into what she was. He exploited her, brainwashed her, made her do things she likely would never do if she hadn't been altered. I was convinced her mine was being controlled and she didn't realize what she was doing.

"When I stabbed her, it distracted her long enough to release her hold on you. I was able to kill some of the demons but I was outnumbered. I couldn't fight them alone. I did the only thing I knew to do."

"You called Darius," I said.

"He got you out, away from her, then came back for me."

"But you got injured."

"Nothing that won't heal."

I peered at the bandage wondering how bad his wound was. My uncle always downplayed his injuries, likely so I wouldn't worry. But I did worry. It wasn't the first scuffle we had with demons. Or the first time he'd been injured by them. Darius had used whatever healing powers he had to remove the demon poison from Edward after our little adventure in Hell. I wondered if he had to do the same again.

"Did you have a...flaming sword?"

He was silent and, because he stood on the other side of the room by the window, I couldn't read his expression. I was almost certain he wielded a flaming sword moments before I passed out.

"How do you feel?" he asked, ignoring my question.

Typical evasion. It was a question he didn't want to answer. Maybe I truly had hallucinated it. "Like I've been hit by a truck. Why didn't you take me to a hospital?"

"No hospitals. Darius was the only option I had."

"What about Istanbul?" I asked.

"You're not strong enough to travel. We'll leave when you are. Rest now. I'll be in the next room."

He started to leave but I had one more burning question to ask. "Uncle, do you think I was sent to Antarctica for a reason?"

"What do you mean?"

"I mean, do you think I was sent to find her instead of the spear?"

He stood so still and so quiet, he looked like a statue. "Is that what you think?"

"I received the two messages from the same person. I think I was meant to find her."

"Rest, Anna." It was the only response he gave me before he left me alone.

Chapter 14

WHEN EDWARD LEFT, I leaned back into the pillows. I blinked in the shadowy darkness, trying to focus on anything in the room. The gray haze was still there but inky blackness crept into the edges of my vision. I whimpered as it slowly overtook the haze, blotting it out and leaving me blind once again.

My eyes were gone. I would never see again. She'd taken that from me and even Darius with all his healing skills couldn't help me. My shoulders slumped into the pillows as my head *thunked* back on the headboard. Without eyesight, I couldn't fight the demons or Azriel. I couldn't save Kincade and I couldn't hunt for the Holy Relics.

Tears leaked from the corners of my eyes as I threw myself a giant pity party. I squeezed them shut and tried to remain positive but there was nothing positive left in me. Evil won. I was defeated.

I drifted off. Restless at first but finally falling into a deep sleep. And then I dreamed of a place that was pulled from a deep memory. The place where I'd met Michael, the archangel. The place with golden lampposts and golden paved streets and a bright light pulling me deeper and deeper into its glow.

A shape formed, blotting out some of the light. It was a man, tall, with huge wings behind him. As he neared, the light diminished and he came into focus. His snowy white wings were threaded with gold feathers. Bigger than Darius's or Joachim's or even Azriel's. There was an inherent strength in his ageless chiseled face that bespoke of power. He had high cheekbones, a thin straight nose, eyes so green they rivaled an emerald, wavy black hair, broad shoulders. He must be an archangel.

He halted, looking at me as though I were a long-lost relative he hadn't seen in years. When he reached for me and hugged me, I didn't draw back. I let him fold me into his arms and squeeze me so tight he nearly crushed the breath out of me. He pulled back and held me at arm's length.

"Anna." He practically beamed with joy as my name rolled off his tongue.

My brows drew together. "You know me?"

"Yes." He smiled, placed his hands on my cheeks, his thumbs grazing my skin in reverence.

"I don't know you." It was a dumb thing to say but it was all I came up with.

His grin broadened. A grin that reached all the way to his dark green eyes.

"Who are you?"

"Close your eyes," he said, ignoring the question.

"But—"

"Please, Anna."

I complied. His thumbs brushed over my eyelids with a gentle touch. It was as though I actually felt his thumbs skimming over my skin, though it was merely a dream. My dreams were like that. I felt everything that happened to me in them.

"Open your eyes now, Anna," he whispered. "And wake."

I did as he said and opened my eyes to the archangel sitting on the edge of my bed with his palms resting on my cheeks. He dropped his hands but remained at my bedside.

He somehow repaired my vision. I glanced around the room, looking at everything. This was no hotel room. It was a bedroom with a balcony that overlooked the sea not unlike the hotel room, but a different view. It had more of an apartment vibe than a hotel. There was no television, no telephone by the bedside, nothing that indicated it was a place of business.

I focused on the doors to the terrace where my uncle stood moments before. Palm trees swayed in the slight breeze as moonlight bathed the area in a soft ethereal glow.

"I can see again." Though I stated the obvious, wonder tinged my voice. And then tears of relief and joy clotted my throat.

"You can." He gave a nod and smiled, well pleased.

"Thank you," I whispered, trying like hell to maintain my composure.

It was more than getting my eyesight back, though. That just-hit-by-a-truck fatigue was gone, like he'd done more than heal my eyes. He healed *me* from the inside out. I squinted in the darkness as if that would help me focus on his face. From what I could tell, he was the archangel in my dream. Silvery shadows played upon his features.

"How did you do it?"

He started to answer but the door to my room burst open and yellow light spilled in from the hallway, splashing across the marble floor. Uncle Edward stood in the doorway, took a step into the room and then halted. The archangel rose from the bed and faced him. He was so tall, I had to tilt my head back to look up at him.

"Sariel." Edward did not sound happy to see the archangel. Recognition laced his voice even though the shadows blotted out his face. He had one hand on the knob and the other one clenched.

The archangel gave me one final glance. "Farewell, Anna."

"Wait—" I shoved the blankets off and jumped out of bed.

He disappeared. My shoulders drooped as I gaped at the space he occupied, now empty.

"He's gone." I blew out a frustrated breath.

"Are you all right?"

I spun to face Edward. "Who was he?"

He moved closer to me. "Your eyesight has returned?"

"Yes, he healed my eyes. Uncle, who was he?"

His jaw clenched so tight the muscles flexed along his jawline. "No one of consequence. Sleep, Anna. Tomorrow, we'll discuss our travel plans for Istanbul."

He left, closing the door softly behind him.

I sank to the edge of the bed, contemplating Edward's reaction upon seeing Sariel. It was clear he was familiar with him upon sight. The way he had his hand clenched told me he was ready to do battle with the archangel. What sort of history was between those two? All I had was the archangel's name, nothing more. I was visited by celestial beings before but this one stuck with me. It was different. My gut told me I needed to figure out who he was, how he knew me and my uncle. Edward wouldn't share that information with me, so I'd have to go about it a different way, but I didn't know how yet.

When the morning came, I shoved off the blankets and stumbled out of bed. In the light of day, I made out more details about the large room. The floor-to-ceiling windows overlooked a terrace cluttered with palm trees on one side. On the other, a clear view of the beach. The décor wasn't to my taste—sleek, elegant and modern—in black and white with accents of red and yellow here and there.

I made my way out of the room and paused. Stairs were off to one side. More rooms on the other side. Downstairs, the faint murmur of my uncle's voice wafted up to me.

I headed down to an open living and dining area. A table with enough seats for twenty dominated the dining area. A wall of windows adorned with gauzy curtains gave a spectacular view of the beach and the ocean beyond. The living area had a large white leather sectional, several no-back chairs, a charcoal gray shag rug on top of the white marble floor, an oversized marble and glass coffee table, more windows, an oversized bookshelf. Past the living room, another seating area that was smaller, cozier, with two love seats and another chair all in white leather.

I thought we were no longer in a hotel and I was right. My uncle was on the phone, pacing back and forcing along the rug. He hung up and then raked his hand through his hair. He dropped the phone on the marble table with a clatter. He startled at my sudden appearance but he quickly recovered.

"Anna, good morning. How do you feel?"

"Better. Like it never happened. It's strange, really."

I wasn't sure what Sariel did to heal me but whatever it was, it was nothing short of a miracle. Or maybe it was a miracle. He was an archangel, after all.

"Good. I booked us a flight to Istanbul." He said it so matter-of-factly, I blinked.

"We're flying commercial?" I asked.

"I called in every favor I could getting us out of Rio. Someone betrayed me that night. It's the only explanation for what happened." He clenched and unclenched his hands, his knuckles turning white the tighter he closed his fist. Anger radiated off him in waves. Surprise flickered through me. I'd never seen him like that. "I decided this would be the best course of action. Flying commercial is not my favorite way to travel but first class will have to do."

I couldn't argue with that logic.

He made first class sound like it wasn't any better than coach. For me, first class was better than being squished inside a tin can that was no better than a petri dish. I wasn't fond of flying commercial, either, after my private jet experience. I'd been spoiled.

"Okay."

"I took the liberty of ordering you new clothes. They'll be delivered within the hour."

I glanced down at what I wore. I had bloodstains on my shirt. Likely from the attack I suffered at the hands of the woman I suspected was my mother.

"Thanks," I said.

"You might want to get cleaned up. Your suite has its own private bath. There should be plenty of linens and toiletries for you. Our flight leaves in a few hours. Once your clothes are delivered, we'll be ready to leave."

I nodded. Uncle Edward was all business which was typical of his demeanor but seemed more direct and to the point than usual. More agitated and edgy. I wondered if the appearance of Sariel last night rattled him.

"Oh, and one more thing." He dug through a black duffle sitting on the sofa. I hadn't noticed it when I entered the room. He handed me a passport and new ID card. "For the trip."

I glanced down at the fake ID. The best money could buy. Better than the one I had made in the name of Zoe Cavanaugh. This one was for Summer Williams from Atlanta, Georgia.

"I took the liberty of picking a name for you. I'll be traveling as your father, Jacob Williams."

I flipped it closed. "Why the fake ID? Why not travel under our own names?"

He took a deep breath, blew it out. "I need to tell you something." He paused and my brows drew together. "Schneider sent the Knights of the Holy Lance after you. You're a target."

"That's not news. They found us at the airport and that woman tried to kill me."

"You don't understand. Schneider knows you're after the Spear of Destiny, too."

"How?"

He went back to the duffle and pulled out a piece of paper. He handed it over. "This is how."

I took it and read it over. It was a full account about me from someone named Natasha. It specifically named me a dream walker and Keeper of the Holy Relics and that I was on a quest to find them, specifically the Spear of Destiny. Natasha also knew I already found the Horn of Gabriel but it didn't say where it was. My head snapped up.

"Who's Natasha? How did she get this information?"

"Schneider's dream walker. The woman who attacked you at the bunker and on the tarmac. She got into your head, Anna. She found out everything about you and reported it back to Schneider."

"How did you get this?" I waved the paper at him.

"I have ways."

I gritted my teeth. "How, uncle?"

The evasive look on his face he didn't told me he didn't want to share. "I dream walked him."

I clutched the paper in my fist. "That doesn't explain how you got *this*."

He huffed out another breath. "Darius helped me."

My uncle was doing everything in his power to tell me nothing yet everything. "What's the whole story? Tell me everything after I was attacked to now."

"You know some already." He sighed. "I suppose I do owe you an explanation. When you were attacked and I saw you…bleeding, I thought for sure I'd lose you. If you were dead, then all hope would be lost. I couldn't allow that to happen. You were right. You did see me use a flaming sword that night. I tried to kill her but I failed. I used what little power I had to call Darius. All of that happened as I told you before. He brought you here."

"Where is here?" I asked.

He pressed his lips together as if the question was a difficult one to answer. "Anna, do you know there are other dream walkers all over the world? Other families who have the same ability as we do?"

Did I know that? I searched my memory banks. Isobel's husband was a dream walker, so did that mean…? My brain was fuzzy so it was hard to connect the dots. I shook my head.

"Luiz Santos is a friend of the family. He's traveling in Europe but allowed us to use his apartment. He lives here in Rio. He and his family are all dream walkers."

A throbbing started at the base of my skull and moved through to my forehead. I walked to the nearby sofa and sat. It was a lot of information for me to digest. In the past, I might have lost my temper and this conversation would end up with heated words between me and my uncle but I was determined to remain calm.

"Okay," I said slowly. "So, this is Santos' apartment. Darius brought me here. Keep going."

"Darius left with you but I was forced to fight the demons and Natasha. I thought she would try to get into my head, too, like she had yours but she had no interest in me. We fought. I was injured." He held up his bandaged arm. "By the time Darius returned for me, a group of Watchers had arrived to clean up the demon mess. As soon as Natasha saw them, she disappeared. Darius brought me here to you. While you were out, I tried to find out more about the woman, so I dream walked Schneider. Natasha recounted everything she learned about you. He's a big fan of making handwritten notes. When I discovered he had it, I asked Darius to steal it for me. I can't let your identity fall into anyone else's hands."

"But it's already too late, isn't it?" I asked. "Natasha knows who I am as does Schneider."

"Yes, and he's coming after you. I daresay we haven't seen the last of Natasha."

But her name wasn't Natasha. Her name was Annabelle Walker and she was my mother. Uncle Edward was in denial about her true identity. Natasha may be her new name and what she called herself these days but I knew the truth. Or I thought I did and was going to find out for sure.

Just as I was going to find out who Sariel, the archangel, was and why he healed me.

"Then what do I do? I can't hide. I have to find the Spear of Destiny."

"You search for it anyway and I'll keep you safe. We'll have to figure out some way to keep her out of your mind. If she finds you, I have no doubt she will try to kill you again."

"Let them try." I crumpled the paper in my fist and tossed it to the floor. "I'm not afraid."

As I said it, though, a lump of fear clotted my throat. I wasn't as a valiant as I tried to be, but the façade held and that was all that mattered.

"His followers are dangerous. He's brainwashed them. They'll do anything he asks without question. He wants you dead now that you're on the hunt for the spear, too. He won't stop until you are," he said. "You should be afraid."

Before I could reply, a knock sounded on the door.

"That will be your clothes. You should get cleaned up."

As he walked to the front door, I pushed off the sofa and made my way back to the stairs. A sense of foreboding came over me as I ascended and went back to my room. I suspected Edward was right. We hadn't seen the last of Natasha. But the next time could very well be the last time.

Chapter 15

I SHOWERED AND DRESSED in black cargo pants, black Henley, black boots. They weren't my signature pink but I'd live without them. I still had the jade-handled dagger but I wasn't sure how I was going to smuggle that through security. My uncle had even managed to produce a duffle for me to pack the rest of my clothes. His extensive wealth never ceased to amaze me.

I emerged from the bathroom, packed and ready to go and holding the dagger.

"What do I do with this? I'm not leaving it behind."

He contemplated the dagger. "I can place it somewhere safe."

I lifted an eyebrow. "Safe enough to get it through security at the airport? I'm not comfortable with it inside a checked bag."

"Neither am I, but I wasn't talking about putting it there." He held out his hand. "Trust me, Anna."

I placed the dagger in his palm. He closed his hand around it, scabbard and all, and then closed his eyes. It disappeared out of his hand.

"How did you do that?" I asked.

"I'll show you someday. For now, know that it's safe."

"Right along with your flaming sword, I'm sure," I said, deadpan.

He didn't respond but I had a sneaking suspicion I was right.

We left for the airport, made it through security and finally boarded the seventeen-plus hour flight. I was so not looking forward to that. It was reminiscent of the long flight I had to Hong Kong. Then I traveled with Lexi in coach. Now I traveled with my uncle in first class. I'd take the latter any day.

Finally, though, we were on our way to Istanbul and I was going to find the spear. With any luck, I'd still be able to find Kincade before Decker. Even though I had no idea how to find him or the realm Azriel held him. I was still determined to save him before the Fallen stole his soul forever.

I did a lot of internal contemplation on that flight from Rio to Istanbul. I thought a lot about what happened in Antarctica with Decker and the mystery woman I was convinced was my mother. I had to find the truth. I had to find out if it was her and I had to convince my uncle who she was. I wasn't sure how I would do that unless I proved it with a DNA test. Most of all, I had to find a way to bring her back from whatever hell Schneider put her in.

I still thought about Lexi. I was determined to take her out of Azriel's clutches, but I hadn't been able to return to that particular pursuit. I wanted to save her, but I also had to admit she may be too far gone.

Like my mother.

I had to find a way for both of them.

After a three-hour layover in Amsterdam, we were finally on the last leg of our trip. I was ready to be off the plane, in a hotel so I could take a hot shower and scrub off all the travel grit from every pore of my body.

We landed at the airport. I'd never been so happy to be on the ground anywhere before. We deboarded, headed through customs and made our way to ground transportation where my uncle had a car waiting for us. It was another one of those guys who reminded me of Secret Service and had the "don't fuck with me" expression.

Worked for me.

My uncle directed him to the Four Seasons Sultanahmet, no doubt another five-star hotel. I wondered how we were supposed to keep a low profile if we continued to live large.

At check-in, Edward got us a two-level suite decorated in a Turkish theme with neoclassic details. The main entrance led into a small area with chairs, a sofa, a couple of tables and several windows with pale yellow curtains giving the place a light and airy feel. It was far too cheery for my state of mind.

I dropped my duffle on the parquet floor. In the distance was the Blue Mosque awash in golden afternoon light giving it an ancient glow.

"Let's get started," my uncle said.

No rest for the weary. "I'd like to shower and maybe eat first."

"Time is of the essence—"

"Uncle, we've been traveling for nearly twenty hours. I'm tired, hungry and dirty. I doubt the spear is going anywhere. I have time for a shower and food."

He looked guilty at my chastising. "You're quite right, Anna. My apologies. Go clean up. I'll order room service and have food brought up straightaway. Then we'll discuss our plan for finding the spear. You still have the map and the postcard?"

Did I? I lost track of them both. "Uh…"

"You do, don't you?"

The last time I recalled seeing it was when Isobel, Kincade and I headed to the airport to start the journey. That was the day Azriel attacked and captured Kincade. The day he blew up the car, killing Raul and Isobel.

My luggage was in the back of that car that burned to a charred husk, but I gave my uncle the postcard and the note on Station 211 for safekeeping. He returned them after my little visit with Sebastian and company. I had them in my luggage after that but I couldn't quite recall what I'd done with them.

"Yes," I said with more conviction than I felt.

I'd worry about that after my shower. I snatched up the duffle and staggered my way to one of the bedrooms with an en suite. One thing was for sure, my uncle had great taste in hotels. The bedroom was large enough for a small chair between a window and the door to the terrace as well as a king size bed. A vase of happy purple flowers stood on a small round antique table. All I wanted to do was swipe it off to the floor and watch it crash. I was in a foul mood. I chunked the duffle on the bed and stared out the window at the view of the mosque.

This was it. I was here. I would finally be able to start my real search for the Spear of Destiny. I should be happy about that knowing I was one step closer. Instead, I had a horrible ball of dread tight in the pit of my stomach.

Things never went as planned. In Hong Kong, Lexi betrayed me and I nearly died. I didn't think my uncle would betray me here in Istanbul, but something was off since Rio. I didn't know what to think or do about it.

In a fit of aggravation, I closed the curtains over the window and terrace door plunging the room into semi-shadows.

I trudged to the bathroom, shedding clothes along the way. I turned on the hot water in the glass enclosed shower and stepped in, letting the hot spray hit me in the face. It felt good. My head fell forward and the water pounded the back of my neck.

I braced my hands on the wall and stood like that for what seemed an eternity. I didn't want to move. I didn't want to think.

And then the strangest sensation happened. Strong arms slid around my waist. A warm, wet body pressed against my back and heated breath tickled my ear. My pulse throbbed a wicked beat against my skin. Long, slow kisses pressed against the length of my neck. The distinct scent of cinnamon filled the small enclosure.

Terror sliced through me as I realized I wasn't dreaming. It was real. Someone was in the shower with me. A male someone. Revulsion cascaded through me.

"Let go, Azriel."

"Anna, how could you deny what we both want?" Azriel's breath tickled my skin.

I wanted to vomit. I grabbed his arms and gave him a shove. He released me and moved away. I refused to turn around and look at him because that's what he wanted. He wanted me to see him, wet and naked in all his glory. He wanted me to fall into his arms. He wanted me to succumb to his wicked seduction.

He'd tried to seduce me once before in my dreams. I managed to fend him off. I wasn't so sure I could do it now. Fatigue made me weak, made me drop my guard.

His hand ran down the length of my wet hair. His fingers trailed over my spine. "You don't remember, do you?"

I refused to take the bait. "Get out of my shower, you son of a bitch."

"It hurts to know you've forgotten all we were to each other."

His words were like little knives stabbing through me. I stepped closer into the hot spray, trying to huddle against the glass wall to put distance between us. I glanced up. His powerful body stood behind me in the reflection of the glass.

My breath caught in my throat. No one was more beautiful than him in that moment. His black hair was wet against his head. Water beaded his chiseled handsome face and his powerful shoulders. He licked his lips. His wings weren't visible but they were there, even if he had them hidden. My body responded in a way with such a violent scorching need, my knees threatened to buckle. My nipples hardened to tiny pink buds.

"Get. Out," I managed through gritted teeth.

"You'll remember someday. When you do, you'll come to me. You'll spread your legs for me and I'll fuck you hard until you beg me to stop." He leaned into me, his breath once again hot and damp on my ear. *"Chéri."*

And then he was gone.

How was he able to break through my uncle's protection and get inside my shower?

I crumpled into a tiny ball on the floor of the shower, the water pounding me, and wept. I cried out of frustration, exhaustion, annoyance, embarrassment, and everything in between. All the bath soap in the world couldn't scrub away Azriel touching or kissing me. I hated him. I wanted him dead. I hated he pushed all my hot buttons. His words burned through my mind. And, worst of all, the fiery need throbbing between my legs refused to stop.

Damn Azriel. I'd hate him until I died.

When my fingers were shriveled, I peeled myself off the floor of the shower, cut the water and stepped out, not even caring I dripped all over the floor. Barely toweled off, I stumbled out of the bathroom and collapsed on the king size bed, curled into a wet ball, and promptly fell asleep.

I dreamed of Kincade but I wasn't dream walking him. It was an actual dream. Or rather a memory. We were back in Dallas at my old apartment the night Ben was killed. I thought I managed to remove that ugliness from my mind, but it was still there in all its vivid glory.

Azriel held the knife at Ben's throat. Light glinted off the blade as he slashed from side to side and, in one last act of defiance and evil, he took Ben's soul.

I woke still wrapped in the damp towel with a scream gurgling in my throat. Uncle Edward burst into the room seconds later. He took in my disheveled appearance, my wet hair, the damp towel wrapped around me and realized I was alone. He sheathed the dagger he had in his hand.

"What happened?" he asked.

"Nightmare." I slid off the bed, clutching the towel. "Sorry."

"Nightmare?" His brows drew together. "You haven't had one of those in years."

I didn't want to tell him about my shower visitor. Thinking about him sent bile to my throat. I pawed through the duffle bag with shaking hands looking for clothes, trying to put the thoughts out of my head, trying to ignore my uncle's concern etching his face.

"It was nothing." I pulled out pants, a shirt, underwear. "I need to get dressed so we can talk."

"There's food when you're ready."

He left, closing the door behind him.

I sat on the floor, my back against the bed with the crumpled clothes in my lap. I was glad he didn't press me for details about the nightmare. I didn't want to talk about it. I dug deep for the motivation to put on clothes, go out there and pretend like everything was situation normal.

You'll spread your legs for me and I'll fuck you hard.

I squeezed my eyes shut, trying to block out the memory. For a reason I couldn't explain, thoughts of Kincade popped into my head. Where was he while Azriel was with me trying to taunt me, to tempt me? Was he still in that strange dungeon in a realm I couldn't reach?

An idea struck me. I knew what I had to do to save his life. That is, if Decker didn't find him first. If Azriel wanted me so bad, I'd use myself as bait. As soon as I had the spear, I'd call him, tell him to take me to Kincade, hand over the spear in exchange for his life while leading Azriel to believe I was willing to give myself over to him as well.

The mere thought made my stomach twist into a tight knot. I had no doubt, though, it would work. Azriel wanted me *and* the spear.

I dressed and pushed all thoughts of Azriel and Kincade out of my head. I had to focus now on the task at hand and that was finding the spear. I headed to the bathroom and dumped my wet towel on the floor. When I turned around, two documents were on the bed.

I moved closer to investigate. The Istanbul postcard and the map to the unnamed palace rested in the center of the mattress. Neither were there moments before. I didn't have them with me when we arrived here. I thought I lost them somewhere along the way and yet, here they were. Someone was helping me, maybe even guiding me to each relic.

I froze, staring at the postcard.

The picture was eerily familiar. I went to the window and shoved open the curtains. Holding up the postcard, I examined it and the Blue Mosque with it six minarets beyond. The picture on the postcard resembled the Blue Mosque outside my window.

My previous postcard of Hong Kong was of Two International Finance Centre. As it turned out, the Horn of Gabriel was hidden in an office of that building. If the

Istanbul clue was like the Hong Kong one, I assumed the spear was somewhere in the Blue Mosque.

Pinpricks of excitement burst along my arms. Indeed, I was closer than I ever imagined to finding the spear, which got me one step closer to Kincade.

I picked up the ancient map with a careful hand. The parchment was so delicate, I feared it would crumble any moment.

Finally, I made my way out of the bedroom. True to his word, my uncle had food on a tray by the seating area in the hotel room. He reclined on the sofa, holding a cup of tea in one hand while looking over the local newspaper. When I entered, he glanced up and noticed I held the postcard and map.

"You found it."

I nodded and handed it over. He took it, taking care with the delicate parchment and set it aside on the coffee table. He placed his cup on the nearby table and studied the postcard. I busied myself at the tray, trying to decide if I was as hungry as I thought. The escapade in the shower and subsequent dream had all but doused my appetite.

"This is of the Blue Mosque," he said, as though he was aware it for the first time.

"Yes, the mosque we can see from our hotel room." I gave him a pointed look. "Convenient. Did you plan that?"

"Not consciously." He flipped over the postcard, peering at the block handwriting with the words *Spear of Destiny*.

I shoved a piece of bread in my mouth and chewed. "I think the spear is there."

"What makes you think that?" he asked.

"When I got the postcard of Hong Kong it was of Two International Finance Centre. The horn was in that building.

If the same is true of this clue," I pointed to the postcard, "I assume the spear is in the mosque."

"Not necessarily. With this clue, you got a map. An ancient map."

"It could still be of the mosque," I said around a mouthful of more bread.

He dropped the postcard and reached for the map, taking care to unfold it. I poured a cup of coffee and headed over, taking a seat in the chair opposite him. I held the cup in my hands, enjoying the warmth radiating from the ceramic.

"Perhaps." He examined the faint lines. "It looks like a floor plan but nothing is marked."

"How are we going to figure out what it is?"

He tapped his index finger against his chin. "If memory serves, a Roman Catholic Church is somewhere in the city. I can't quite recall the name. Saint something."

"That narrows it down."

He flashed me a look of annoyance, unhappy with my quip. He grabbed his smartphone and tapped the screen. After several minutes of searching and staring at the small screen, he paused.

"No, I'm not remembering that right. It was once a Roman Catholic cathedral used in the Fourth Crusades for a time, but it was originally built as a Greek Orthodox Christian basilica back in the sixth century. Hagia Sophia." He turned the phone around to show me a picture. It had the same dome shape as the Blue Mosque, but four minarets rising on the sides. Not six like the Blue Mosque outside my window.

"And you think that has to do with the spear and the Blue Mosque?"

He snatched the postcard again and peered at it intently. "This isn't the Blue Mosque, though I daresay it looks much like it. I can see how you'd think so. This postcard is of the Hagia Sophia."

I took the postcard from him and tilted it into the light for a better look at it. I had never seen the Hagia Sophia, so I took his word for it.

"So, we have a starting point at least. What's next?"

"I examine the floor plan and try to figure out if it, too, is the church." He leaned back in the cushion of the sofa, laced his fingers and regarded me with a contemplative look. "First, though, I think we need to have another lesson in control."

I gripped the cup tighter in my hands, a slice of fear going through me as I held my breath. There was no way he discovered what happened with Azriel in the shower.

"After your experience in Antarctica and Rio, it's clear to me I failed in your teachings."

I blew out the breath through my nose. I stared at him, trying to decide what to say. It wasn't that he failed. It was that I was a crappy student and didn't take it as seriously as I should. I relied on my uncle being there to block out Azriel but it was clear he couldn't block him out all the time. If he was aware Azriel paid me a visit in the shower, he didn't say so. I knew he referred to my encounter with my mother.

"You didn't fail. I did," I said.

"It doesn't matter, does it? I need to teach you how to keep her out."

"And how do you propose to do that?"

"Put down your cup."

I placed it on the nearby table.

"Now stand up," he said.

I complied and he also got to his feet. He came around the table and stood in front of me. His gaze examined my face, as though searching for some sign of...what? He placed his hands on my cheeks, his fingers pressing lightly against my temples.

Then he was there, poking inside my mind.

"You sense me there, don't you?" he asked.

"Yes."

"Push me out."

"How?"

"Use your mind."

I tried, but nothing changed. I could still sense him. This time he pushed with more force, digging into the hidden recesses of my mind. I didn't like it. I pushed back but nothing happened.

"You're not trying hard enough, Anna."

"Yes, I am." Annoyance laced my words.

I tried again but he was stronger, more powerful than me. He pushed deeper and found my recent memories. I shuddered, trying to shield him from seeing Azriel in the shower with me. He jerked his hands back, his eyes wide, breaking the connection. His lips thinned into a straight line for a brief moment before he regained his composure.

"When?" he asked.

I knew to what he referred. "Earlier today."

"Is that why you had the nightmare?"

It surged to the forefront of my mind. The slash of the knife at Ben's throat. My scream. Kincade dragging me out of the apartment. I bit my lower lip and nodded.

"Why didn't you tell me?"

"Because I didn't want to worry you," I said. I wanted to reassure him, tell him I could handle Azriel but the truth was I couldn't. Azriel was a dark force I couldn't control…or resist. And that terrified me.

"But it worries you." He prowled the room, restless. "You should have told me. What did he want?"

"Me."

He halted, shock on his face. "Tell me everything, Anna."

I hesitated. I didn't want to tell him everything. He was my uncle. There were certain things we didn't talk about. This was private, personal. I hated I was weak and unable to fight back. I hated I had a sexual response to Azriel when he touched me, kissed me. I hated even more that he had managed to do it to me a second time.

It hurts to know you've forgotten all we were to each other.

"Tell me, Anna," he urged. "I can help you."

I clenched my jaw, trying to decide how to present it to him. My back teeth ached.

You'll remember someday. When you do, you'll come to me. You'll spread your legs for me and I'll fuck you hard until you beg me to stop.

"I'm not comfortable telling you this." I paused and bit my lower lip, trying to decide how to say it without using crass language like Azriel. "He keeps trying to seduce me. What I don't understand is why. He tried to kill me in Hell."

"He wants what he cannot have. You are special, Anna. He can't kill you because it will anger his Lord Master. If he can seduce you and bring you into his fold, he can use you to find the relics."

It made sense but I didn't want to believe it was true.

"He was unhappy I didn't remember him. He seems to think we used to know each other."

Edward's face blanched and he turned away quickly so I wouldn't see. But it was too late. I saw.

A sense of foreboding came over me. It was true. Azriel *did* know me and, somehow, I forgot. I reached for Edward, grabbed him by the arm and spun him to face me.

"Is it true?" I asked.

"We'll discuss later. Right now, we must return to your lesson." He started to reach for my face but I batted his hands away.

"No, I want the truth."

"There's no time for that, Anna. We will discuss it later."

That was always the way things were with him. He brushed me off, telling me all the time we'd discuss later. Someday later may not come.

"But—"

"If you'll listen and learn from me, I can teach you how to keep him out of your mind. This is the only way to keep him away from you." He paused, looking me over with that same contemplative look once again. "Shall we continue?"

I didn't like it but he was right. I had to learn to keep Azriel and my mother out of my head. I nodded and we resumed.

Chapter 16

WE WORKED TOGETHER FOR HOURS. By the time we finished, I finally learned to push Edward out of my mind and keep him out. I also learned how to keep the walls up and finally had a peaceful nights' sleep. It was the same trick Edward used, the one he extended when we were together so he could make sure I was protected. Now, I knew how to do it myself.

It took a lot of mental control. I hadn't prepared for that when I wandered out of the bedroom. I collapsed on my bed and slept for hours without fear Azriel or anyone else would interfere in my dreams. It was the best, most peaceful sleep I had in ages.

By the time I woke, another day had passed. It was another day lost to finding the spear and saving Kincade. After showering, I stumbled out of the bedroom to find Edward where I left him—sitting on the sofa looking at the map.

"Today we will explore Hagia Sophia," Edward said as though we hadn't been through the mental ringer. "I want to see if the floor plan resembles it."

"Fine."

I was still pissed he refused to answer my questions about Azriel. Pressing him about it would change nothing. Likely he sensed my level of anger but ignored it.

"It's a short walk from here."

"Great."

He tucked the ancient map carefully in his pocket. "You're angry with me—"

"It doesn't matter."

"It does matter and I promise you, I will tell you everything in time."

"When?" I pressed.

His lips thinned with that look that said he didn't want to answer but had to. "When the time is right. Now, we must find the spear."

"Uncle, the time is never right to tell me the truth. I came to you after Hong Kong because I wanted to do this thing I've been tasked to do. Yet whenever I try to ask you about my mother or the family history book, you brush me off. Tell me it's not the right time. I'm going to ask you again. When is the right time? And I want a definite answer." I put him on the spot but I had nothing to lose. Maybe he'd commit to giving me answers.

He ran a hand through his black hair, then popped it on his waist and blew out a heated breath. I'd never seen him do that and it almost seemed uncharacteristic. "All right. We'll visit Hagia Sophia and compare the floor plan to the museum. Afterward, we'll return here, order room service and I will answer all your questions. Is that satisfactory?"

I stared at him, wide-eyed, for a long moment before nodding. I hadn't expected a definite answer. He was always so evasive. Making a firm decision on when and where to talk about it was a huge victory for me.

"Yes, it is."

"Good. Let's go."

"I need my dagger."

He thin-lipped me but I gave him a non-negotiable stance. He gave a nod, then, and lifted his hand, palm open. The dagger appeared out of thin air. He handed it to me.

"You said you'd show me how to do that," I said, reminding him.

"Indeed, I will, but now is not the time."

"Of course, it's not." I didn't bother to hide the sour note in my voice.

We left the hotel and headed northwest on Tevkifhane toward Hagia Sophia. In the distance, its four minarets rose up, reaching for the sky. Even from this far away, the age of the building was apparent. The dome was one of the biggest I'd seen that wasn't a sports stadium of some kind. At the corner, we turned right onto Kabasakal. We both paused to take in the architecture of the ancient building. I didn't have much knowledge about the church but still appreciated it for what it was.

"One of the last standing Byzantine structures," my uncle said. "It's the only building in the world that's served three religions."

"Is that so?" I gazed at the building in wonder. It was truly beautiful with the enormous dome reaching for the heavens.

"There is a reason why the clue led us here," he said.

"Yeah, the spear is in there," I said, sounding certain. I tried hard not to roll my eyes.

"I hope so."

As we started for the main entrance, a sharp stabbing pain went through my head. I faltered, putting a hand to my head. It felt as though someone poked through my head. A warning niggled at the back of my mind.

"You all right?"

"There's something…"

I stopped as the stabbing pain hit me again. It was not unlike the feeling I had when I was attacked. I spun and gazed around the crowd looking for her. I had no doubt she was nearby.

I spotted her behind us at the corner. She saw me, too, and the stabbing pain shot through my head again. I immediately erected those mental walls and whipped out my dagger.

"How? How did she find us?" he asked.

"I have no idea."

She'd managed to track us. Or maybe she was tracking me.

Before I was attacked by demons in Hong Kong, a thin veil surrounded me. That same veil surrounded me and my uncle now. Shit was about to get real and fast. I gripped the dagger tighter in my hand until it cramped. Demons closed in, wafting their rotting stench.

"We're surrounded," he said.

"I'm aware." He didn't have to tell me. They came from every direction. "They aren't going to take me without a fight."

"We can't do that here on a public street."

"Oh, yes, we can." I had in Hong Kong. Istanbul was no different.

His flaming sword appeared in his hand. "Bring it on."

The woman flanked by two demons weaved her way through the crowd at a pace that said she had all the time in the world. They entered our little bubble. She halted in front of us. Her gaze landed on me. We sized each other up. She was the same height as me, still wearing the black catsuit, black gloves and boots.

Now that she was so close, it was clear she resembled the woman in the portrait in the manor. She *was* my mother. I was more convinced than ever.

"We do not need to fight," she said in that mellifluous voice of hers. "I've come for the girl."

When she spoke, Edward sucked in a sharp breath. Recognition flickered across his face before he masked it.

"You can't have her." Edward stepped in front of me, gripping his sword tighter in his hand, ready to attack.

Her purple gaze landed on him, looking him up and down with disdain. "You are nothing. You will die."

"Leave him out of this." I moved to stand between the two of them. "This fight is between you and me, Natasha."

One dark brow lifted. A smile tugged at the corners of her mouth. "You know my name. How clever you are. I want you to come with me. We will not harm you."

"Why should I come with you after you've tried to kill me twice?" I asked.

She regarded me with cool purple eyes. "I have been instructed not to kill you."

"By whom?" Edward asked.

"I think you know." Her reply was so cold, it sent a chill through me.

She referred to Schneider. He managed to track us down here in Istanbul because, like him, I searched for the spear. He wanted that spear about as bad as I did. I had a sneaking suspicion why he wanted me.

"If I come with you, will you let him live?" I asked.

"Anna, no—"

"Yes," she said, cutting Edward off. "You come with me, then no one gets hurt. Him or any other humans."

My heart rammed hard against my chest as fear poisoned my blood. The last thing I wanted was to go with her. She hunted me for a reason. I needed to find out what that reason was. Maybe I could find a way to reach her, figure out what

Schneider had done to her and return her to her former identity.

I started to reply, but Edward wrapped a hand around my elbow. He leaned close to me and whispered in my ear.

"You can't do this, Anna. You know what she's capable of, what she can do to you. If you go with her, you seal your fate."

"Perhaps not," I said. "I have an idea why she wants me to go with her."

His fingers tightened on my elbow, the tips digging into the fleshy part of my arm. "You cannot do this, Anna."

"I have to." I leveled my gaze with his. "To save you and her."

Disbelief entered his eyes but I didn't give him a chance to reply. I pulled my arm free, sheathed my dagger and moved to stand in front of her. "Then let's go."

I ignored Edward's objections to this plan. I was going if it was the last thing I did. I didn't look back as I followed her away from my uncle. I suspected he stared daggers at the back of my head. The only thing that gave me some comfort was he still had the map and the postcard. My hope was he would continue to search for the spear while I was off on this little venture.

I had no idea how it was going to turn out. I hadn't thought that far ahead.

Most of the demons drifted away, leaving the two flanking her. I followed her to the corner where we turned and went to the side of the Hagia Sophia. We headed past Prince Tomb to an entrance ignored by the general populace. She led me inside, the door slamming shut and sealing us in a chamber with a long stone hallway as ancient as the rest of the building. Someone installed fluorescent lighting but marks were still in the stone wall where there had once been torches.

The floor sloped downward leading into a tunnel darkened by shadows. I questioned my sanity by allowing her to capture me. Uncle Edward may have been right when he said I sealed my fate.

The tunnel narrowed some but her steps didn't falter. She had the path memorized. I was lost in all the twists and turns.

Another turn and the tunnel opened into a large cavern that had to be below the church. A large firepit hosted a roaring fire that lit up the place in an orange-yellow glow and threw flickering shadows along the walls and ceiling.

I expected Schneider and I was right.

I did not expect to see Decker barefoot and hog-tied with a gag in his mouth. He twisted his head to look at me as I approached and our eyes locked. How in the world did he end up here in their custody? Things were going from bad to worse.

"Ah, Fräulein Anna, welcome." Schneider lifted his arms in a gesture that indicated he was happy to see me. "Take her weapon."

Before I could react, two of his henchmen were on me. One to hold me and one to take away my jade-handled dagger. Hindsight told me I should have left it with my uncle. It was too late for that. The guy held it clasped in his hand and stepped away.

"You followed me to Istanbul?" I asked.

"Natasha is most adept at finding things I want. She tracked you for me." He motioned to my mother who stood next to me, unmoving. Then said to her, "Did you kill the man like I asked?"

She was quiet for a moment before she finally responded. "He's dead."

I forced myself to remain motionless. When we left him Edward was very much alive. Either she lied or she'd sent her demons back to kill him. I wanted to believe she lied because there were still remnants of my mother deep down in her psyche.

"Good." He gave her a satisfied grin. To me, he said, "I'm glad you joined us."

"What do you want?" I was never one to beat around the bush. I wanted to cut right to the chase.

He smiled. "You are not interested in small talk, I see. You and your companions stole something from me. I want it back." He motioned to Decker.

"I don't know what you're talking about." I played dumb because I knew damn well what he was after—the journal and the folder.

"Do not play coy with me, *fräulein*. You are aware of what you took. I want the journal back."

"I don't have it." It was the truth. I lost track of the journal after I was attacked in Rio. My uncle told me he had packed it, but I didn't know where it was now. Maybe in his secret realm hiding spot along with his flaming sword.

"But you can acquire it for me."

It was more of a suggestion than a question. I stared at him, unblinking. "Maybe. I don't know where it is."

He moved toward the fire pit, using a poker to rearrange some of the burning wood. "Perhaps you locate it for me."

I shrugged. "I don't know."

He lifted the poker out of the fire. It had some sort of emblem on the end. I realized then it wasn't a poker at all. It was a brand. He moved to Decker, the bright red iron inches away from the bottom of his bare foot. I had to hand it to Decker. He didn't flinch, wince or make any sort of noise.

"Your friend is a hard man to capture," Schneider said. "We found him in Caracas trying to make his way back to England."

Decker and I locked gazes again. I tried hard to read what was going on in that head of his, but I wasn't connected to him like I was Kincade. I suspected what Schneider told me was true. What I couldn't fathom was how he got caught. The man had the ability to teleport and turn invisible, for crying out loud. The only explanation was he was either caught by surprise or incapacitated.

"I need your agreement to bring me the journal, Fräulein Anna."

My mouth went bone dry as I watched the brand inch closer to his foot. I swallowed hard, trying to increase the saliva but doing no good. If he wanted the journal so bad, it must contain a vital piece of information not recorded anywhere else. A tickling sensation of fear prickled the back of my throat. I had to find that journal and read it. Maybe I'd find some piece of information I could use as leverage.

"I'll bring it," I said, my voice weak and raspy.

"Good."

"And then you'll release him," I said, my voice stronger as I nodded to Decker.

"I'm afraid not. He belongs to me now. I could use a man of his talent." With that, he shoved the brand against the bottom of Decker's foot.

I sucked in a sharp breath and took a step forward but Natasha grabbed my arm and held me in place. She shook her head to indicate not to interfere. Decker still didn't make a sound. I stared wide-eyed at him in utter horror. His eyes glazed over likely from the pain but it was clear he tried his damnedest to keep from crying out. I understood—he didn't want to give Schneider the satisfaction. Sweat beaded his forehead. Finally, Schneider removed the brand and placed it back in the fire.

"I won't bring you the journal unless you swear to release him," I said, my hands clenched into fists.

"Did you not understand when I said he belonged to me now? He's marked."

"I heard you loud and clear. I'm telling you I won't bring you the journal unless I have your word you'll release him."

He clucked his tongue. "Why must you be difficult when this could be so easy?" He gave a nod to Natasha.

That sharp stabbing pain was back. She tried to get into my head as she lifted her arms like she had back in the bunker. I put a hand to my temple, closing my eyes. I concentrated hard on the walls Edward taught me to erect but she was still poking, prodding me, trying hard to get inside my mind.

She whimpered frustration and doubled her efforts. She pushed against my mind. I pushed back more forcefully until she faltered.

"What are you waiting for? Do it!" he ordered.

"I am," she said in a breathy voice.

She pushed again. I pushed back. Concentration lines creased her sweat-dampened forehead. She was determined to get in my head but I was more determined to keep her out. I tried not to smile with victory as I shoved her out of my head. I gave her a pointed look. She met my gaze and shrunk backward a step.

"She is...stronger than before. She pushed me out of her mind."

Schneider's interest was piqued. He walked toward me, closing the gap until he stood right in front of me. As before, a dark and dangerous light flickered behind his eyes. I was almost certain a demon was in there, much like Chen was a demon. I inhaled a deep breath but couldn't smell a signature demon scent or otherwise. Who or what was he?

"Where did you learn to do that? You couldn't do that before."

"It doesn't matter," I said. No way was I telling him about my uncle. "I'll bring you the journal if you give me your word you'll release Decker."

His jaw clenched, the muscles flexing. "I will need more than the promise of the return of my journal."

I hesitated to ask. "What's that?"

"You search for the Spear of Destiny, yes?"

There it was. This is what I was waiting for since arriving. "Yes."

"Bring me the journal and the spear. I will release the man and let you live."

I almost snorted at his arrogance. As if he thought I was going to hand over the spear to him. I glanced from him to Decker to my mother, who had a stern look on her face. Like she knew I had to agree with him or else.

"How can I trust you to keep your word?" I asked.

He grinned. "You don't, now, do you? I suppose you'll have to take a leap of faith."

Not what I wanted to hear but I didn't have much choice. "That your final offer?"

"If you refuse me, you will never leave here. I could use another dream walker. This one failed to stop you at the bunker, forcing me to follow you halfway across the world." He motioned toward my mother.

Her eyes narrowed but she didn't move or make any response. I sensed irritation emanating off her in waves. My hands clenched. I resisted the urge to punch him in the face. That settled it. I'd come back with the spear and the journal and I'd release Decker and my mother.

And then I was going to kill Schneider.

"You have a deal."

And for the second time in my life, I made a deal with someone I shouldn't. My uncle would not be happy. Not one bit.

I glared at the guy who took my dagger. "I'm going to need my weapon back."

He gave a questioning glance to Schneider who gave a nod of approval. The guy handed me back the dagger. I was happy to have it back in my possession.

"You have forty-eight hours, *fräulein*."

"That wasn't part of the deal," I snapped. "You never mentioned a time limit."

He merely smiled. "If you wish to see your friend remain as he is, you'll agree to the terms."

Good grief. I couldn't say no. If I did, I'd seal Decker's fate to become one of Schneider's experiments. I couldn't let that happen. I had no idea how I was going to find the spear within forty-eight hours.

"And if I don't find the spear in the allotted time?"

"Then your friend works for me and you'll die. Natasha is quite an accomplished assassin."

Sounded like a challenge I had to accept. "Fine."

I'd bring him the spear, the journal, and then I'd definitely kill him.

Chapter 17

NATASHA LED ME OUT of the tunnel and back to the surface, to civilization. I was surprised I was able to get out of there alive. But I'd made promises I didn't intend to keep to save my skin. It was what I had to do to make sure I got out alive.

"Why did you tell Schneider Edward was dead?" I asked when we were a safe distance away from the German.

She was silent a moment before responding in a low voice as though she were concerned someone might overhear. "I cannot say." She paused, cut me a glance. "I cannot explain. Who are you?"

There were so many responses to that question. I could tell her I was the Keeper of the Holy Relics but I wasn't sure that would mean much to her. I could tell her I was a dream walker, like her, but that might spawn more questions I wasn't prepared to answer. I could tell her I was her daughter but I wasn't sure she would believe me.

"I'm no one of importance."

"I wish I believed you," she said.

We halted at the door leading outside. She turned to me, her gaze searching my face. In that moment, it was as though I peered at the portrait in the hallway at the manor. If this wasn't my mother, she was a clone. And if Schneider learned to clone, we had bigger problems.

I suspected, however, this woman was, in fact, the woman who gave birth to me.

"You are someone of importance if Schneider wants your help," she said.

I shrugged. "Just lucky I guess."

"What is this journal he wants?"

I shrugged again. "Beats me."

"But you have it?

"I do." Or I did. Really hoped I could get my hands on it.

"Do you know where this Spear of Destiny is located?"

"I have a good idea, yes. Are we going to play twenty questions all day or are you going to let me leave so I can find it?"

Annoyance flashed over her face, proving she was human and not some brainwashed automaton. A little glimmer of hope shimmered through me. She flung open the door and motioned me out. The veil still surrounded us though there were no demons in sight. I glanced at her, wondering if she had some magical way to hold the veil in place. Handy trick.

She gave me a nod of farewell. "We will meet again, Fräulein Anna."

"I'm sure we will." I gave her a jaunty wave as I headed out the door.

And next time I will find out who you really are.

Her voice drifted through my mind sending chills through me. The closing door behind me punctuated her words. I had no doubt she would know who and what I was by the time I returned with the journal and the spear.

I made my way down the street, ignoring the bustle of the crowd to get back to the hotel and hopefully find my uncle. As I rounded the corner back to the front of the building, he stood on the street, arms crossed looking rather unhappy. Relief went through me seeing him still among the living.

His expression didn't change when he made eye contact with me as I made my way to him. I halted in front of him. He didn't alter his stance. If anything, his body got more rigid with his anger.

"Do you realize what could have happened to you?"

"What do you mean? Die?"

"Anna, this is serious. You willingly put yourself in danger. You didn't think about the consequences—"

"I did. I knew what I was getting into. I'm not so inept to think I was walking into a tea party, uncle. I realized the gravity of the situation," I said.

"And yet you still went."

"I had to. She led me to Schneider. He captured Decker."

That got his attention. He relaxed his arms. "How?"

"I'm not sure. All he said was he found him in Caracas. I'm sure he used my mother to do it."

His lips thinned. "That woman is not your mother."

"Yes, she is. You saw her with your own eyes. It's *her*. It has to be. She looks exactly like the portrait hanging in your hallway."

He turned on the heel of his boot and headed away from the church, away from me. I was momentarily stunned before I finally was able to move. My uncle didn't walk away from anything, anyone. He did now because I was right and he didn't want to face the truth.

"Why don't you think it's her?" I demanded, hurrying to catch up. "Somehow Schneider captured her after I was born."

My breath see-sawed in and out of my chest, but he didn't slow his pace. I had to practically run to catch up to him. "Uncle—"

He reeled on me. "We will not have this discussion now."

"Oh, yes, we will. You can't keep avoiding it. I saw the vial of blood with the name A WALKER on it. If it wasn't hers, whose was it?"

He huffed out a breath and glanced around at the crowd flowing around us. "Let's go someplace and talk."

My heart rammed against my chest. It was the first time he willingly decided to give me information without me having to drag it out of him. I nodded agreement. He started walking again and I did my best to keep up. This wasn't like Marrakesh where I could easily get lost in the crowded streets. At least here, I followed him with ease.

We ended up at a Turkish barbecue joint with brightly colored umbrellas hanging along the front of the building above the entrance and patio seating. We were immediately greeted by a smiling gentleman who showed us to a tiny table in the back of the place. The tables had old tapestry-looking tablecloths with patterns reminding me of Santa Fe. Once we were seated in the rickety wicker chairs, I waited for my uncle to start talking.

He didn't.

I sighed.

We were going to play this game again. I waited, impatience crawling through my veins.

We ordered Turkish coffee. When it finally arrived, he took a sip and placed the espresso cup on the table.

"I have never spoken of this to anyone," he said at last. "You must understand that."

It sounded so ominous. I nodded.

"Annabelle was my youngest sister. Perhaps I was more protective of her than my other two sisters and that's what drove her away."

I wasn't sure I liked where this was going. I remained silent, determined to let him talk while I listened intently to every word.

"My father arranged her marriage to another dream walker in the Harred family. They were prestigious, wealthy and had ties to the royal family. But she wanted nothing to do with him. She would leave the estate on horseback almost daily for hours at a time. She was seeing someone in secret but I didn't know who. She was seventeen at the time, far too young to be serious about someone. Our family legacy was at stake."

A prickly eeriness went over me, through me, raising gooseflesh on my arms and the hair at the nape of my neck. This story was all too familiar and reminded me of my own history and sordid romance.

He paused, took another sip of his coffee. I waited for more details, salivating at the thought of gaining more knowledge of my mother and trying not to think how close our stories were. It was the most I'd ever been given about her.

"My father wanted me to find out who she was with and dispatch him. She was to marry the Harred boy and that was that."

"Weren't arranged marriages…" I paused, looking for the right way to phrase the question.

"Out of fashion?" He smiled understanding when I nodded. "We are dream walkers, Anna. We must find a way to keep our lines from dying out. That means we marry other dream walkers. Alexander Harred is from a strong line of dream walkers."

"I guess she didn't marry him." I took a sip of my coffee.

"She did not," he agreed. "When she discovered I was trying to break up her romance, she was furious. She disappeared the following morning. She left behind a note that said she'd left for America and she'd never return."

I stared, wide-eyed at him. It was not unlike what happened between me and Marcus when I was younger. I was certain Edward drove him off to keep me from seeing him. My mother's story ended in tragedy. Mine hadn't because Edward was a little more persistent and ruthless keeping me safe. I repaid him by running away from home.

But my story wasn't over yet. There were more questions about Azriel I needed answered. I understood a little more about why my uncle did the things he did—he wanted to protect me from Marcus, as he wanted to protect his sister. But I still didn't understand one thing.

"What does that have to do with Schneider?" I asked.

"She was pregnant with you when she left for America. I dream walked her and learned of her location, then followed her to the States to try to talk some sense into her. She told me to go home and leave her alone. When I confronted her about the pregnancy, she told me it was none of my business and she would raise the child in the States, not in that 'stuffy old manor.'"

He put air-quotes around the *stuffy old manor*. I almost giggled but managed to hold it in.

"What did you do?"

"I did as she asked. I left. I returned to England and I have regretted it ever since. I should have stayed, made her listen, made her come home. About a year later, I received word she died."

"You said she died in childbirth," I pointed out. Even I could see the error in the timeline. If she was pregnant when she left for the States, and Edward learned she died a year later, it didn't make sense she would have died giving birth to me.

"I did." He nodded slowly and didn't elaborate.

I stared at him, mute. The look on his face and the tone of his voice indicated something else happened. She hadn't died in childbirth. She died, allegedly, under other mysterious circumstances. Or there was more he wasn't willing to tell me. Some bit of truth he thought I wasn't ready to hear.

When all this started happening and I first returned to England, Edward told me he thought he suspected my father was an angel.

One of the passages in the family history book said the Keeper of the Holy Relics would be born of the Light on the Winter Solstice. Edward told me that was a clue to my father's identity and that he believed he was an angel.

"And what of my father? Did you ever find out who it was?" I asked him. I wanted to see if he remembered telling me and if he would elaborate.

His face was expressionless, impassive. "No."

"You said you thought he was an angel," I pointed out.

"I did."

Once again, he didn't elaborate. I suspected he was aware of the truth but didn't want to tell me for whatever secret reason he had. At times I thought Edward had an agenda all his own when it came to me and the Holy Relics. I could live with that for now.

"Do you suspect Schneider had something to do with her presumed death?" I asked, dropping the subject of my father and getting back to my mother.

"Then, no. I had no idea. I'd never heard of the Knights of the Holy Lance. Now, I'm not so sure. If that *is* her DNA in his lab, we have bigger problems than I realized."

"I agree. I think he's using it to make his own dream walkers."

"And we have to stop him. Anna, you asked me if I thought the clue to Antarctica led you there to find her." He paused again, running his finger around the rim of his small cup. He lifted his gaze, met mine. As always, he kept his thoughts shielded, his eyes guarded. I couldn't read into them even if I wanted to. "I didn't want to believe it but now I think you might be right. I think you were led there to find her."

I wanted to shout triumphant but couldn't. There was too much sadness in his voice, in his eyes, etched on his face. He still mourned the loss of his sister. Still thought she was dead. Maybe in a way she was and she would never be the woman he remembered. She would never truly be my mother.

"I never expected to see her again." He leaned forward and dropped his voice. "When I said to you that woman is not my sister, I meant it. She may look and sound like her but she has been altered. She can do things with her mind I don't understand and never could."

"Because Schneider altered her mind. He figured out what made her tick and exploited it. I intend to save her."

"You can't save her. No one can."

"I'm going to try," I said.

His brows drew together. "How?"

I shrugged. "Schneider wants me to bring him the journal and the spear in exchange for Decker's life."

"Why does he want the journal?"

"All I can figure is there's some bit of information in it not written down anywhere else. He needs it. Do you know where it is?" I hoped he still had it.

He nodded. "After the attack on you in Rio, I found it in your things and put it in my duffle for safekeeping. I have it back at the hotel. If you're right, we need to read that thing from cover to cover."

"Yes, I agree."

He tipped his head to the side in an inquisitive gesture. "You don't intend to give him the spear, do you?"

I shook my head. "I made a deal with him, though. He releases Decker if I bring him both. I intend to kill him."

Edward stared at me as though I'd grown a second head. I rushed on.

"I'll take him what he wants but I'm not going to let him have them. I'll save Decker and my mother and rid the world of that monster."

He continued to stare at me.

"Why are you looking at me like that?" I demanded.

"What exactly is your plan, Anna? You intend to waltz in there, hand over the journal and the spear while driving a dagger into his heart? We don't even have the spear."

"Yet. We don't have the spear *yet*."

He huffed out an exasperated breath. "You're determined to go through with it?"

"Yes," I said, emphatically.

He pressed his lips together in that look I recognized as annoyance. "If you're determined to go through with this, at least let me help you."

I couldn't contain the broad smile that erupted. "You mean it?"

"Sadly, yes. Perhaps this little venture will turn out a tad better than our foray into Hell."

I giggled. Our foray, as he called it, had nearly got us both killed.

"Let's go read the journal." He tossed money on the table to pay for the coffee.

I couldn't wait to see what was in it.

Chapter 18

THINGS WERE NEVER EASY. When I thought we were going to catch a break, I was wrong. As we walked back to the hotel, we spotted several demons tailing us. I placed my hand on the hilt of my dagger, ready to do battle.

"I see them, too," Edward said in a low voice. "They don't appear to be making any threatening moves, so we should keep moving and return to the hotel as quickly as possible. Fighting isn't an option."

But I was spoiling for a fight. First Kincade was lost to me and now Decker. I wanted to take it out on someone. Plus, stabbing demons and seeing them turn to ash gave me a rush and made me feel better about the world in general.

"Fighting is always an option," I said.

"Not here on the street. Not where humans can see."

Edward stepped up his pace. I had no choice but to follow suit.

I had slaughtered demons on the streets of Hong Kong. Looking back, I wondered if the Watchers sent in a clean-up crew in the wake of my killing spree. I wasn't aware at the time, but likely they came in behind me and cleaned up the mess after my cousin's rooftop betrayal.

I wondered what Genghis and his crew were up to, if they were still fighting demons and fallen angels in Hong Kong. I hoped they were. The world needed more like him.

Humans didn't realize demons walked among us. Humans also didn't realize guardian angels walked among us. My uncle and I both could see them. I was so used to them being a part of everyday life, I hadn't noticed they were there anymore.

But today, fewer walked the streets with their respective humans than what I took note of in Hong Kong. I wondered if Azriel was still killing guardian angels to take human souls.

I hadn't mentioned seeing fewer guardian angels to my uncle but it occurred to me perhaps I should. My uncle was like this all-seeing eye. Even though he raised me from the time I was thirteen, I didn't *know* him. The man was an enigma. Like the way he hid away the flaming sword and my dagger.

As we hurried along the street, it happened. The pace of the humans moved into slow-motion. Edward halted so abruptly I nearly ran into the back of him. I skidded to a halt, my hand still on the hilt of my dagger. Around us, the opaque veil descended as several demons closed in. We would be forced to fight even though Edward didn't want to. I was almost giddy with excitement.

"Get ready," he said.

I unsheathed the dagger. He lifted his hand, palm open, and the flaming sword appeared. I loved that cool-as-shit trick.

Two demons ran in a sort of limping-lumbering jog toward us. One had pointed teeth, weird eyes like a serpent, and a giant red horn protruding from his forehead. The other had arms that were longer than normal, claws for hands and a hunchback. We went into action. Edward killed the one with the horn. I stabbed the one with claw hands. It turned to ash.

A scuffle behind us made us turn in unison like a well-choreographed dance. Two more demons headed our direction. These two were as ugly as the ones we took out. Edward and I went into action and killed them with ease.

A growl to my left and I spun to face the newest attacker. He was nothing but a minion and I was stabbed him, turning him to ash. Edward killed another one with his flaming sword by cutting off its head.

"I don't get it," I said over my shoulder.

"What?"

"This was far too easy," I said. "They're not trying that hard to kill us."

"You noticed that, too?"

We were on the same page at least. If they weren't trying to kill us, what was going on?

I got my answer a second later. Azriel appeared holding a badly beaten Kincade. His face was black and blue. One eye was swollen shut. Blood stained his shirt. His hands were shackled together in front of him, his wrists raw. Yet even through all that, he was well and truly pissed off. I darted forward but Edward stopped me by throwing out his free hand.

"*Chérie*, I thought you'd like to see how your lover fares." He gave me that all-too-familiar wolf smile. "Not so well."

Don't listen to him, Anna. He's a fuck.

Kincade's voice exploded into my mind. At least Kincade was still Kincade. Our eyes met from across the short distance. Life sparked in those depths and, despite his outward appearance, he still had fight left in him. But for how much longer?

"Do you have the spear?" Azriel's lascivious gaze raked over me. I had the instant urge to cover myself even though I was fully clothed.

Edward moved between us, still holding that flaming sword. "These things take time, Azriel."

The Fallen turned his cold, dark gaze on my uncle. "I wasn't speaking to you, *my lord*."

Surprise flickered through me at the way he addressed my uncle. I never heard anyone call him that except Piers. It seemed odd Azriel would call him that. I gave him a sideways glance, but he refused to meet my gaze. He kept his eyes pinned on Azriel as anger burned high in his cheeks. The Fallen turned his lethal gaze back on me.

"Do you have it?"

"My uncle is right. These things take time. I've had delays—"

"I do not wish to discuss your perceived delays." Azriel pressed his palm on Kincade's chest. "The *gardien*'s soul will soon belong to me. I look forward to controlling him."

Kincade cut him a glance that was so imperceptible, it would have gone undetected had I not been looking at him. That one look said so much, too. He was annoyed by the fallen angel as much as me. I was glad Kincade was still in there somewhere.

"I'll find it," I said.

"You said that before."

"The spear is here in this city. I need more time."

"Time is a luxury you do not have, *chéri*."

He pulled away his hand, pulling a little bit of the light from Kincade and taking another piece of his soul. Kincade emitted that deep guttural growl low in his throat that haunted me. He slumped forward, his shoulders drooping.

"Continue to disappoint me and he *will* belong to my Lord Master. Time is running out."

"You bastard—"

I took a step toward him, the dagger raised, but my uncle stopped me. He likely understood what would happen if I charged the fallen angel. But all I imagined was sticking him in the throat with the blade. I wondered what would happen to him if I did. Would he turn to ash, too? Or would he bleed? I wanted to find out. My palm itched with the need to kill.

Azriel chuckled. "Until we meet again. But before I leave, I wish to bestow upon you a gift."

He blew me a kiss before they disappeared, back to whatever realm they'd come from.

"A gift?" Edward asked.

"That's what scares me." I did a three-sixty-turn but the veil remained.

I never knew with Azriel what was coming next. He was a bastard, that was for sure. And he was killing Kincade. My to-do list had grown exponentially since arriving in Istanbul. I had to double my efforts to find the spear so I could kill Schneider, save Decker and my mother, find the realm where Azriel held Kincade and take him out of there before the fallen angel stole more of his soul.

I needed more hours in the day.

And likely a miracle.

I still hadn't decided if I was truly going to hand over the spear to Azriel, but I'd cross that particular bridge when I got to it.

"Anna?"

Edward's query got my attention. I followed his gaze to the demon approaching our veiled existence. My breath caught in my throat. My heart stopped. My knees turned to water and threatened to buckle. I blinked, rubbed my eyes with my free hand and blinked again.

Surely, I was seeing things. Right?

Or was I?

"Who is it, Anna?"

I had the answer but my mind wouldn't work. My mouth wouldn't form words. My eyes clouded with sudden tears.

The dagger went slack in my hand. I lost my breath like someone had punched me hard in the gut.

"Anna?" Edward's urgent voice was in my ear but I ignored him.

The demon walking toward me had dark wavy hair and the darkest, depthless blue eyes I'd ever seen. Blue eyes I once loved and got lost in. Blue eyes I wanted to love forever.

He also had a long menacing scar across his throat.

"Ben."

My whispered voice warbled with tears. Astonishment punched me hard in the chest as he walked toward me. Azriel was a master at manipulation and knew *exactly* where to hit me. Damn him.

Edward's head snapped in his direction seconds before he charged Ben, flaming sword held high. I sucked in a sharp breath as comprehension shattered through my disbelief. He intended to chop his head off like he had the other demons, killing him for good.

"No! Uncle, don't! Don't kill him!"

I surged into action, reaching Edward. My hand grazed his shoulder, narrowly missing him. He halted and gave me a heated glare.

Ben stopped, his blue-eyed curious gaze on me.

"Anna, he's a demon. He is not the man you remember. That man is no more."

I didn't care. I brushed past my uncle moving to stand in front of Ben and sheathed the dagger. We stared at each other a long, desperate silent moment. My heart flipped. My stomach turned into knots. He may be a demon but it didn't stop me from wanting to hug him, from the guilt that swarmed through me over his death.

"I know your face," demon-Ben hissed.

I nodded. "And I know yours."

He lifted his hand to my face. Even though Edward was behind me, likely on high alert, he didn't interfere. I stood my ground, waiting for what would happen next. This was Ben. He wouldn't hurt me. He couldn't hurt me.

As he lifted his hand, I realized his fingers were now claws. His skin had turned from that delicious golden color to a ruddy hue, as though he'd had way too much exposure to the summer sun. The sleeves of his shirt were rolled to his elbows, revealing the branding along his skin going up both arms. They were symbols I recognized as demonic. It sent a sharp pain to my chest.

His cold hand landed on my cheek, the pads of his fingers pressed into my skin. Deep. His claws dug in as he dragged his hand down my cheek. He left a trail of blood behind but I didn't care. His blue-eyed gaze turned red moments before his hand landed on my throat. Before I could react, he squeezed.

I coughed, trying hard to push air into my lungs.

Edward shouted behind me. A flash of flame sparked as his sword came down, slicing through Ben's arm, severing it at the wrist. He released me with a hiss and stumbled backward. I crumbled to the ground.

My uncle cut his connection to me to save my life. Demon-Ben held his injured arm by the elbow as he stepped away. Then the veil was lifted and he was gone.

I lost had for the second time.

My uncle helped me to my feet. He produced a handkerchief and pressed it against my cheek to stop the bleeding. Passersby took note of my disheveled appearance and gawked. Edward wrapped his hand around my elbow and led me away from the street. He hid his sword so quickly I hadn't seen.

We arrived back at our hotel room without incident. He sat me down on one of the chairs and went to work cleaning the claw marks.

Emotion fled. A cold numbness settled over me while he bandaged my cheek.

"It wasn't him," Edward said.

"It was."

"No, Anna. The man you knew as Ben is dead. He's a demon now. He belongs to Azriel."

"I have to find him."

"Anna." His voice was low, soft as he stopped moving and focused on my face. He shook his head. "*He's a demon. You cannot save him.*"

"I know what he is!" The words exploded from me in a rage. "I watched Azriel slice his throat and take his soul. I was there when it happened. I saw the whole thing. He died because of me. Because I was too damned stubborn to do what Azriel wanted."

Edward stared at me with sympathy etched all over his face. I never told him the whole story because Kincade beat me to it. By then, I had no reason to talk about it to Edward. No reason to dredge up those feelings again. Yet they kept coming back to the surface no matter how hard I tried to push them away, to forget.

Kincade knew. Because he was there, too.

"I'm sorry, Anna." Genuine remorse was in his tone.

"So am I." I pressed cold fingertips to my lips to keep from weeping.

He finished bandaging my cheek then stood and walked away. I heard him on the phone calling for room service. My stomach grumbled but I didn't feel much like eating. Edward returned with a highball glass in hand and gave it to me.

It smelled like whisky.

I took it, downed it. It lessened the pain.

"Why?" I asked though I likely had the answer.

"He wants to torture you. Sending Ben would hurt you."

I held out my empty glass for a refill. He obliged without question. I downed the drink again. Drinking whisky reminded me too much of the night Ben was killed. Kincade plied me with the booze then, too.

But I wasn't going to curl into the fetal position and cry. Not this time. I pulled myself together. I set the empty glass aside, cracked my knuckles and gave my uncle a pointed look.

"Let's find that spear."

We spent the entire night looking at the map of the palace and researching. Edward was convinced it was part of the Hagia Sophia. He surprised me again by showing off his incredible searching and hacking skills. I had no idea he was so computer savvy. The man was magical. While he hacked into historical archives all over the world, I had my own little research project. I started reading Schneider's journal from cover to cover.

I paged past what I'd already seen—pictures of the spear followed by the detailed plan of the Knights of the Holy Lance. Past the page of the drawing with the double helix. I turned the page and a loose sheet of paper folded in half slipped out. Upon opening it, a sense of familiarity went over me. I recognized was the ripped-out page from the family history book. Edward must have found it in the folder and stuck it in the journal for safekeeping. I glanced at him, but he intently stared at his laptop screen, the wash of light from the monitor lit up his face in a garish glow.

Deep down, I suspected Edward was a sentimental sort. He was protective of the family history book. Perhaps the missing page was why he kept it under lock and key for so long. Only once during my childhood did I find the book lying open on his desk. I stuck the paper back in the book and turned the page.

The following handwritten passage was all about comparing DNA strands from a donor Schneider had acquired. Odd phrasing. He listed each volunteer's name with a description of how it matched up with what he called the donor's DNA. Following that was a lengthy in-depth description of how the nanobots were implanted into the neocortex.

Once the nanobots were implanted into the brain, they controlled it while the body was asleep to allow a patient with vivid dreams to first control them and, eventually, step into the dreams of others. But, as I'd seen with Sofia, that patient had to be touching the other person to make the connection.

Natasha and I did it without touching another person.

Schneider and his doctor figured out that part of my mother's brain, inserted the nanobots to let them do their thing, and gave her super mind powers. She was the prototype. He'd figured out how to make the others like her by using the nanobots to inject a drug derived from her blood into their brains. Following that was a detailed description of the drug, what it was, how it was derived including the chemical makeup, and how it was injected using the tiny machines.

No wonder he was hot to retrieve the journal.

The vial in the lab with the name A WALKER could not have been the first or last one. He had to have been doing this experiment for years.

I flipped back to the front of the book where he talked about first acquiring the donor. I wasn't sure what I was looking for but I would recognize it when I saw it. There was no information about the donor. As I scrutinized the page, I spotted a number written in faded pencil in the top right-hand corner. I peered at it closer and realized it was a date.

21/6/2010

So, June 21, 2010, which was six months to the day after I was born.

I stared at that page for a long time with wide eyes. My heart pummeled my breastbone.

If the donor was my mother and he acquired her six months after I was born, that meant she didn't die in childbirth like I long believed. She had lived and Schneider captured her and held her against her will.

"Uncle, I think I know why he wants the journal." I turned back to the page detailing the use of the nanobots and my mother as the prototype. I handed him the book.

He read over the page, then glanced up. "You said you saw a vial of blood in the lab."

I nodded, biting my lower lip. "He wants the journal because it details exactly how to make the drug and inject it with the nanobots into the subject's brain. And there's more." I took the book from his hands, flipped back to the page with the date. "Schneider writes on this page he managed to acquire a donor and look here." I held it out to him, pointing at the date.

He narrowed his eyes as he tried to make out the faint number. "It looks like a date."

"Yes," I said, nodding vigorously.

"June 21, 2010."

"Right."

He met my gaze. "So?"

"So, that's exactly six months after I was born. It proves my mother is alive. It proves Natasha is my mother."

His face leeched of color as he sat back in the cushions of the sofa. "It proves nothing." He said it in that dismissive tone indicating he wasn't interested in continuing with the line of conversation.

Aggravation clawed through me. I wasn't going to let it go. "What's it going to take for you to believe? A DNA test?"

"Yes," he said it so matter-of-factly I blinked. He turned back to his laptop, dismissing the journal.

Frustration clawed through me. Ok, fine. I'd get a lock of hair, a cheek swab, *something* from her. Somehow. Someway. I had to prove this woman was my mother and make him believe.

"I found something, too. The footprint of this map matches the Hagia Sophia but I don't think it's of the actual church." He tapped away on the computer and then spun the laptop in my direction. As if we hadn't just been discussing my presumed dead mother.

"Where'd you get a laptop?" I asked.

"I had Piers overnight it to me."

Good old Piers.

He had two images on the screen. One was a scanned version of the map. The other was of the floor plan of the church. Sure enough. They matched.

"It looks the same to me. Why do you think the map isn't the floor plan?" I asked.

"You said tunnels are underneath the church?" he countered.

I nodded. When we got back to the hotel room and I had a couple of shots of whisky, I told him all about the tunnels Natasha took me through to meet with Schneider.

He tapped his forefinger against his chin. "We need inside. Do you remember the door she took you to?"

"Yes. It's on the side out of view."

"We need to reach those tunnels."

"You think that map is of the tunnels?"

"I'm not sure. It's merely a hunch but, yes, I do."

Edward's hunches were usually right. Anticipation shuddered through me. One more step closer. "When do we go?"

"It would be better under the cover of darkness. That gives me a few hours to plan." He folded the map with a careful hand and slipped it in his shirt pocket. "When I return, we can head to the church."

"The sooner the better. I'm on a deadline."

"I'll be gone a while to gather supplies. I suppose you can stay out of trouble while I'm gone?"

I wanted to laugh except he was right. I did tend to get myself into trouble. "I'll behave."

"You better." He gave me a nod and then headed out the door.

I wondered how he survived on so little sleep. I was exhausted. I yawned, stretched, and headed to bed. It didn't take me long to fall asleep and start dreaming immediately. I realized too late I'd forgotten to put up my mental walls when Azriel stepped into my dream.

We were back in my apartment in Dallas, back to the place where Ben was murdered. Why did I continue to dream about this place? It held nothing but bad memories.

As soon as I saw him, I realized I was no longer in control of my dream. He used his wicked magic to control me, to keep me in place so he could do whatever he wanted with me. To me. But I still had my wits.

"Get out of here, Azriel."

"Did you enjoy my gift?" He gave me that grin I so despised. The one that made me want to punch him in the mouth.

"You call that a gift?"

"I thought you would be pleased your darling Ben is not lost. Though I have to admit I didn't appreciate the damage Edward did to him."

In the dream, I regained some control and moved away from him, out of the bedroom and into the tiny living area. There was no furniture, nothing. He followed me, crowding me against a wall. Pinning me with his lethal black glaze. The scent of cinnamon emanated off his skin. He leaned into me, his face a breath away from mine. Much to my dismay, my heart raced. My pulse quickened with his nearness. He wound his forefinger around a lock of my hair.

I wanted to bat his hand away, but I was paralyzed again.

"One day, we will be together again. All you have to do is admit how much you want me."

"I don't want you," I said, my words a raspy whisper. "I want nothing to do with you."

He leaned in for a kiss but I turned my head. His breath tickled my earlobe, my neck. His hand slipped around the back of my head as he cradled the nape of my neck. His lips landed on my cheek, leaving his hot brand.

"You wish to kiss me back, Anna, don't you?"

"No."

Yes, I did. I wanted him. I fought the urge to turn my head, to press my mouth against his and drink him in. Taste him. Let his tongue do a sinful oral duel with mine. My breath shuddered between my lips as he continued the onslaught of my neck.

"You lie, *chéri.*"

My nipples hardened as he spoke against my skin. Warmth spread between my legs. Involuntary responses to his kisses and his demon magic. Ones that revolted me and yet I could do nothing to stop it. My resolve weakened. I wanted to turn into his arms and let him have his way with me. His words from the shower haunted me. A flash of an image of our naked, entwined bodies came and went. He wanted to me to show me what we could do to each other.

He flew back away from me. The spell was lifted. Surprise flickered through me and I was able to move again.

"Stay away from her, you fucking animal."

Kincade snarled the words at Azriel. I blinked surprise, trying to comprehend. He held the Fallen against a wall, his forearm pressing into his throat. Confusion set in as I watched the two of them in my dream.

A dream I didn't control because Azriel controlled it. And Kincade was in it. How?

"Do you intend to kill me?" Azriel asked. "If so, get on with it. But know this, *gardien*. If you kill me here, now, you will die in that dungeon a long, slow death. My Lord Master will still take your soul and you will still become one of us."

Kincade didn't move. He clenched his jaw, the muscles ticking along the edge. I would have missed it if I wasn't watching him so intently. He pulled his arm away and stepped back.

"A wise choice," the fallen angel said. Then to me, "A pity I will have to punish him for his act of defiance."

"What do you mean?" I asked, finally finding my voice.

"I think you know."

Fear snapped through me, hot and wild. "You said I could bring you the spear. You said you'd trade his life for the spear."

"And yet you haven't. You continue to fail me, Anna. How can I continue to let the Watcher live if you cannot bring me one simple relic?"

Frustration lanced through me. Kincade met my gaze, his green-gold eyes burned bright as they fixed on me.

Don't listen to him, Anna. Kincade's voice whispered through my mind. *He wants the spear. He'll wait for you to bring it to him but don't you dare give it to him.*

"I'll have the spear tomorrow." It was a promise I wasn't sure I could keep but I was going to damn well try.

"And then?" Azriel lifted one eyebrow in question.

"I'll bring it to you. I swear it."

He was satisfied with that answer. "Very well."

The dream was over. I snapped awake with a gasp, beads of sweat on my face and forehead. My legs twisted in the covers as I struggled to untangle myself, kicking and crying out with my frustration. Out of the blankets at last, I stumbled to the bathroom and splashed cold water on my face.

Azriel was going to continue to torture Kincade and there wasn't a damn thing I could do about it.

I wondered though. Can Kincade dream walk? It was clear I didn't control the dream. Somehow Kincade invaded the dream. And it wasn't the first time. It made me wonder about the dream I had of Kincade when he came to me, kissed me, when I was in control of that dream, yet wasn't at the same time. It was a weird sensation. And later in the hospital in Hong Kong, he asked me if someone "not of our line" could dream walk.

The conclusion I came to was he was able to do it, too.

Everything I learned about my mother and Kincade had me shaking with rage, disbelief and a thousand other emotions I couldn't identify. Did Edward know Watchers dream walked? If he did, why hadn't he told me? I was restless and prowled the room, cracking my knuckles. I couldn't sit here and wait for Edward to return. I was spoiling for a fight. I had to expend all this excess energy.

Still dressed, I snatched my jade-handled dagger and headed to the streets to find and kill some demons.

Chapter 19

NIGHTLIFE IN ISTANBUL was in full swing. There were lots of partygoers and revelers out for an evening of fun, food and drinking, while I was spoiling for a fight. I kept the dagger hidden at my waist in its sheath until I was ready to use it.

There wasn't a lot of demon action going on but I definitely saw the guardian angels shadowing their human counterparts. For a moment, I thought all was right with the world, that maybe all my pent-up rage was self-inflicted and I should go back to the hotel and sleep it off.

Across the street from me, I recognized the Fallen from his expansive black wings. He attacked an unsuspecting guardian angel, ripping out his wings. I reacted too slow as I bolted into a run. I didn't make it to them in time before the Fallen stole the soul of the guardian's unsuspecting human and disappeared in the blink of an eye.

I skittered to a halt, looking down at the girl who fell dead on the sidewalk. Shrieks went up around me as others called for help. I took a step back, glancing around the crowd.

There. I spotted the Fallen stalking another guardian angel. The cacophony of noise erupted around me as first responders came on the scene and people gathered around the dead girl. I kept my eye on the target. I sprinted toward them, unsheathing my dagger and palming it, ready to plunge it into my prey.

A blonde girl moved into my line of sight with a shimmering sword in her hand. She swung it in one arcing swoop and chopped off the head of the Fallen before he killed the guardian angel and stole the human's soul.

I halted on the edge of the sidewalk and stared, mouth agape. The Fallen's headless body tumbled to the ground, blood oozing from it. She had a look of self-satisfaction on her pretty face as she sheathed her shimmering sword.

She made eye contact with me, gave me a nod before spinning on her boot heel and heading back up the street. I stood rooted in place watching her go, trying to make my feet move. Moments later, Watchers showed up to clean the mess she left behind. Almost as though they were waiting for her next kill.

I had to find out who she was. Obviously, she could see the Fallen and the guardian angels. I needed more information. I hurried after her, trying to catch up. I called out but she kept walking at a quick pace, her blonde curls bouncing up and down her back.

She rounded a corner and I lost her. I halted, looking up and down the street, wondering where she went. Then a cold, sharp blade was at my throat.

"Who are you and why are you following me?" the girl asked.

I lifted my hands in surrender. "My name is Anna. I mean you no harm. I saw what you did back there."

"What did I do?" Suspicion laced her every word.

"You killed that Fallen before he could kill the guardian angel and steal the human's soul."

She stiffened, her hand going rigid against my throat and for a moment, I thought she might slice open my neck.

"I promise I'm not here to hurt you," I said.

She inhaled a deep breath, exhaled and released me.

"It's not safe to talk here. Follow me."

I spun and followed her through the crowd, down an alleyway where she knocked in a weird pattern on a couple of bricks. A door slid open and she ushered me inside. I followed without considering the ramifications and the door slid shut behind me, sealing me inside a small room that had once been a storage room in the back of some merchant's ancient shop. We were alone.

She turned to me. I got a good look at her face. She had a girl-next-door look about her and curly blonde hair that hung down to her shoulders. Her nose and cheeks were dotted with freckles. She dressed in all black. The sword she carried was strapped to her back. She had a dagger strapped to one thigh which rested above knee-high black boots.

"You can see them?" she asked, getting to the point.

"I can."

Her eyes narrowed. "How?"

I shrugged. "I just can. What's your name?"

She didn't answer as she gave me a once-over, her gaze pausing on the jade-handled dagger at my waist. "Nice dagger."

"Nice sword," I said.

"Where'd you get it?" she asked.

I pulled it out of its sheath. "It was given to me by a merchant in Hong Kong."

She dragged her lower lip through her teeth. "Li Mei?"

I stifled a gasp. "Yes. You know her?"

She pulled the shimmering sword from the scabbard and held it aloft. "She gave me this. It kills the Fallen."

I blinked, staring at it with wonder. I held up my dagger. "This kills demons."

She eyed it with a curious gaze, then sheathed her sword and held out her hand. "May I?"

I placed the blade on her palm. She examined the handle with a critical eye, then moved under a fluorescent light. She ran her thumb over the handle. She glanced back at me and gave me a "come closer" nod. I moved next to her as she turned the blade into the light, running the pad of her thumb over it once more. Letters were carved into the jade. For the first time, I noticed the A and the weird open-bottomed O carved into the handle of the dagger.

$$A\Omega$$

She pointed to it. "See that?"

I knew those symbols as much as my own name, but my brain was failing to come up with what they were. She pulled out her sword and showed me the same symbols carved on the ivory handle of her weapon.

"Alpha and omega. First and last letters of the Greek alphabet," she supplied without me having to ask. "*I am Alpha and Omega, the beginning and the ending.*"

Chills skittered up my spine as the dawning of realization hit me. She quoted Revelation. I understood why I could kill demons with the dagger and why she could kill Fallen with the sword. They were heavenly weapons.

Who exactly was Li Mei? An agent of God?

"I'm Ophelia." She smiled and stuck out her hand. "Ophelia Duffy."

"Anna Walker." We shook.

"Nice to meet you."

"How long have you been doing this?" I asked.

"Killing Fallen?" She shrugged. "A while, I guess. I met Li Mei about a year ago in Shanghai. That was shortly after I was—" She halted pressing her lips together.

"After you were what?"

She peered at me with an intense gaze, one eye narrowed in mistrust. Likewise, I wasn't sure I could trust her, either. She was a virtual stranger I met sixty seconds ago. I didn't want to tell her my life's story. I didn't want to tell her I was Keeper of the Holy Relics.

"Who are you?" Her tone was suspicious.

"I told you. Anna Walker."

She shook her head. "No, who are you *really*? Why do you have that dagger? Li Mei wouldn't have given it to you if you weren't someone important."

I wondered if her having the shimmering sword meant she was someone important.

"I've been tasked with finding five Holy Relics." It was the most information I was willing to give her without giving too much away.

"Holy Relics?" A pale bow lifted. She sounded impressed. "Who gave you this task?"

"Does it matter?"

"Somewhat."

"I can't tell you. It's confidential."

"Bullshit."

"Tell me who you are," I challenged. "How did you get that sword?"

"I told you. Li Mei gave it to me."

"And?" I prompted.

"And nothing."

"Bullshit," I countered.

She huffed out a breath. "I'm part of a task force to hunt and bring down the Fallen killing guardian angels and stealing souls."

Why was I always the last to know the cool shit? I thought of Kincade and how he'd told me he was trying to catch Azriel. "Do you work with the Watchers?"

"You could say that. I kill Fallen. They come behind me and clean them up. Win-win."

Another little informative nugget I filed away. It was good someone else was on the job of killing Fallen.

"My task force leader disappeared. The others sort of gave up because no one knows where he is. I've been going it alone."

I wanted to ask who her task force leader was, but I bit off the question.

"I'm sorry about that." Silence descended between us for a long moment. "A Fallen murdered my boyfriend."

I wasn't sure why I told her but it seemed like the natural thing to do. As I said it aloud, the sadness punched through me. It still hurt to talk about.

She pressed her fingers against her mouth in horror. "How awful. Did you…see it happen?"

I nodded, reliving the horrible day once again. It haunted me. "And he took his soul."

"Anna, I'm so sorry."

"Why do they take them?" I asked suddenly. "Do you know?"

She shifted from one foot to the other looking as though she didn't want to tell me. "They're building an army of demons for Lucifer. The task force wants to take them out to save innocent humans and stop the army from growing."

I pressed cold fingertips to my lips as I turned away from her thinking of Ben. He'd been taken from me and turned into a demon and now he was going to fight in Lucifer's army. I hated the thought. It twisted my gut into a knot.

"You didn't know?" she asked.

I shook my head. "I suspected but I wasn't sure."

"I know what would make you feel better," she said.

"And what's that?" I glanced back at her.

"Let's kill some demons and Fallen. You want to?" She flashed a smile.

Did I ever. "You bet I do."

We left the weird alleyway behind and headed into the night. Ophelia was good at finding Fallen and killing them. The Fallen used demons to sniff out the weakest prey. We teamed up. I could scent demons and kill them with my dagger while she chased down the Fallen and used her sword to behead them.

There were more demons than Fallen lurking in the city but she was okay with that. She killed her fair share of demons. To say we had fun doing it felt wrong. I couldn't help but think I made a new BFF because we became a great team in a short amount of time. She was a badass with her sword.

Like previous times, we moved behind an opaque veil to stay out of sight of the humans. I wasn't sure how it worked but I guessed it was some form of magic demons used when they spotted their prey.

"There's one." Ophelia pointed to the Fallen stalking a woman in a burka and her guardian angel.

She took off after them before I could respond. Several demons blocked my path between us. I took the first one out with ease. The second one was a gruesome looking fellow with yellow serpentine eyes and a forked tongue. He dodged my thrusts as he anticipated my moves.

He lunged but I was too slow. He clamped his clawed hand around my throat, pulling me close to him. The tips pierced my skin. He smiled, showing off a mouthful of sharp pointy teeth.

"Now you die," he said with a hissing breath.

I fumbled with my dagger, but managed to stick him in the gut. He turned to ash at my feet. As demon remnants fluttered to the ground, Ophelia skittered to a halt across from me.

"I was coming to help," she said on a pant. "Looks like you handled him."

Before I could reply, the ground rumbled. The veil we hid behind as we took out demons and Fallen dissipated. Humans detected the strange rumble and glanced around, looking confused. Some went about their business as if it was the most natural thing in the world. Others were on the verge of panic.

A yawning black chasm opened in the middle of the street. A giant of a demon stepped out seconds later. It was huge with black leathery wings, a sort of scaly armor, standing on back legs that ended in cloven hooves. It merely had two holes for a nose and black eyes sunken into its misshapen head. Two giant horns curled around its face out of its forehead. It held a giant black axe. It pinpointed the two of us with its demon eyes. When it opened its mouth to growl, it glowed with a bright fire.

Humans shrieked and scattered like mice.

"Oh, shit," I whispered. My heart kicked into high gear. Whatever it was, this was not going to go well. We ran out of luck.

"What is that?" Ophelia moved closer to me, her voice shaky.

"I have no idea."

It took a step toward us, two, the ground shaking with every one of them, and bent down with a menacing growl. Heat emanated off its body. The smell of sulfur accosted my nose.

"What do we do?" Her voice pitched with her panic.

"Um...run."

We turned and bolted up the sidewalk along with the other humans scattering and trying to save their own skins. The thing followed us, much to my dismay. Its heavy footsteps rocked the ground behind us. The black axe landed next to Ophelia, missing her by a few inches. She squealed, jumping out of the way and crashed into me making me stumble. We collided with some poor guy trying to save himself as concrete debris rained down around us.

The thing pulled the axe out of the street and tried again. I shoved Ophelia out of the way and jumped backward as the axe landed right in front of me, the ground cracking all around the blade and causing more destruction. I was pretty sure the dagger would not turn this thing to ash but I had to try.

As it tried to remove the axe from the ground, I dove and plunged the blade in the back of the thing's hand. It did not approve and shrieked. It was so angry, it spit fire. Balls of flame rained down. I jerked backward, taking the dagger with me, and stumbled out of the way.

It got the axe out of the street, turning its head and looking right at me with those beady black eyes. Ophelia leaped in front of me, holding her shimming sword aloft and waving it back and forth like a crazy person.

"Back! Get back, you beast!"

It didn't like the shimmering sword and squealed as it staggered away from us both.

"It doesn't like the light," I said. "Keep doing that!"

"I can't keep it up forever," she said. "How are we going to get rid of this thing?"

I had no idea. I frantically glanced around at the chaos we'd managed to cause in the city. All because we wanted to take out some demons and Fallen. I doubted fire would make it go away. It appeared to be partially made of fire.

A tourist with a fancy camera took a picture of the damn thing. When the flash went off, it blinded the beast. It emitted a horrifying screech and put its hand in front of its face as if to ward off the light. The tourist ran away in fright.

It was a start.

How could I get a brighter flash of light?

"Anna!" she shouted, still swinging her sword at the thing. "What the hell are you doing?"

"I have an idea." I bolted into a run for the tourist who snapped the picture running in the opposite direction.

"Where are you going, Anna?" she shouted after me.

I didn't answer. I was too busy trying to run down the tourist with the fancy camera. I needed that flash.

A hulking object smashed into me, knocking the wind from my lungs. I crashed to the ground, my elbows and knees smacking the concrete with a sickening crunch. I smelled the demon before I saw it. It grabbed a handful of my hair and pulled me up, nearly yanking it all out by the roots.

This was going from bad to worse.

Nearby was a familiar high-pitched squeal. I cringed in anticipation of what came next. I squeezed my eyes shut as the demon exploded. Guts splattered me from head to toe. Somehow, I always ended up with demon guts on me at some point.

A Watcher saved my ass. I turned to find him standing nearby as he lowered his smoking gun. A gun similar to the one Kincade carried.

"You all right?" he asked.

He gave me a cursory glance before bolting away, not waiting for an answer.

"I'm fine, thanks," I said, a sour note in my voice and followed.

He joined two more Watchers, all armed. They positioned between Ophelia and the giant demon, pointing their guns at the thing and firing at the same time. It took several seconds of continuous firing but the thing finally crumpled to the ground, dead.

One of the Watchers pulled a pin out of a hand grenade and tossed it at the demon. They all turned and ran.

"You'll want to run," he said as he passed me.

Ophelia and I followed, my heart in my throat, as we ran behind the three Watchers. Seconds later, the thing blew up in a flash of light. It reminded me much of the night Ben died. I glanced over my shoulder in time to watch the light fade. Nothing but black ash was left.

We all stopped running. I bent over, my hands on my knees as I tried to catch my breath.

"Thanks," I said on a pant.

"Anna, what the *bloody hell* is going on here?" a familiar voice said.

Oh, great. My uncle stood several feet away, his flaming sword in one hand and anger etched all over his face. He was well and thoroughly pissed.

"Yes, Anna, tell us what the bloody hell is going on here," the Watcher who saved me said.

"Um..." I implored Ophelia for help with all the facial expressions I managed to convey but she shrugged. So much for that.

"How did that demon get here?" Edward hid his flaming sword as he approached.

"That's what we'd like to know." The Watcher crossed his arms over his chest and glared at the two of us like we had all the answers.

I straightened and glared right back at him. "We were killing demons and Fallen—"

"I told you to stay out of trouble," Edward said to me. "For once in your life, couldn't you do as I ask?"

My head snapped in his direction. "Don't lecture me, uncle. I'm not a child."

"Fight about that later," the Watcher said. "We are aware you were killing demons and Fallen. We've been cleaning up your messes all night."

"Killing Fallen is kind of my job," Ophelia said, finally breaking her silence. Kudos to her for sounding completely annoyed.

Watcher dude pinpointed her with his angry glare. "And you are?"

"Ophelia Duffy. I'm part of the task force assigned to rid the place of Fallen killing guardian angels. And *you*?"

"Task force, huh. I've heard of it. I'm Leo. This is Rogan and Axel. And you?"

"Anna Walker. This is my uncle, Edward Walker."

He stared at me a long, quiet moment. The three Watchers exchanged glances.

"Keeper of the Holy Relics," Leo said. "We heard about you."

I frowned. "Yay?"

"*You're* the Keeper?" Ophelia's eyes widened with shock. She said it with some reverence. Like I was special. "Why didn't you tell me?"

"We are all forgetting what occurred here," Edward said, impatience lacing his tone. "Where did that demon come from?"

"Conjured most likely," Leo said. "Maybe from one of the Fallen before she killed him. The real problem is the mass hysteria this is going to cause with the humans." He glanced around the mostly deserted city. A few brave humans lingered to see what was going to happen next.

"Can't you do something about that?" Edward asked.

"Not without causing more problems." This from Axel. "Sebastian will be unhappy."

"We'll clean up the demon mess," Leo said. "But there's not much we can do about that." He waved toward the destroyed street and sidewalk.

"Do what you can," Edward said. "Sebastian will have to be notified. The sooner the better."

"With a mess like this," Leo thumbed behind him to the pile of ashes, "we have no choice. We have to notify Sebastian. Axel's right. He'll be pretty unhappy."

"Damage control." Edward spoke with some authority to the Watchers which puzzled me. He had nothing to do with them yet he talked to them like he was in charge of everything. "Anna, come. We need to return to the hotel and prepare."

His hand wrapped around my upper arm. He pulled me away as though I were an errant child.

"What about me?" Ophelia jogged next to us to keep up with my uncle's quick pace.

"What about you?" Edward asked. "Go back to wherever you came from."

"Uncle, that's not nice."

He halted, turned to her. "I mean no disrespect, miss, but my niece and I have a lot to do in the next few hours. We don't need any more help or anyone else getting in the way."

"I can help you. My task force disbanded because of our missing leader. I need a new assignment."

Edward lifted an eyebrow. "Apologies, miss, but I am not in charge of giving you a new assignment."

"She has a shimmering sword," I said. "It has the same symbols on it as my dagger."

I pulled it out and showed him the Alpha and Omega. Likewise, she pulled out her sword and showed him the ivory handle. Edward peered at both of them and then met her gaze.

"You said your name was Ophelia?" he asked. She nodded. He sighed. "Fine. Meet us at the Hagia Sophia midnight tomorrow. Not before."

"Cool." She flashed a smile. "Thanks."

"And stay out of trouble. No more killing Fallen."

"Yes, sir. See you then."

"And what are we going to do until then?" I asked.

"You're going to wash that demon mess off you and put on clean clothes. Then we will discuss the plan," he said.

And that was that. I gave Ophelia a jaunty wave as we headed back to the hotel.

Chapter 20

I WAS RELIEVED to be back at the hotel, showered and in fresh clothes. Demon guts smelled worse than a sewer. I never enjoyed the experience and yet it continued to happen to me.

My uncle managed to gather supplies for our late-night run to the church. He had rope, flashlights, flares, a backpack with rations—how long did he expect us to be down there?—and water. After my shower, I joined him in the small living area. He had the fragile map open and spread out on the coffee table. Next to it were blueprints of the church. I idly wondered how he managed to acquire those, but he was a mastermind when it came to stuff like that. He waved me to a chair.

"I'm almost positive this ancient map is of the tunnels under the church. It matches the footprint," he said. "However, the map is more detailed and has what appears to be numerous tunnels going off one main chamber." He nudged them toward me to examine. "Do you remember where you met Schneider?"

I glanced between the blueprint and the map. I definitely saw the correlation between the two. I pointed to the side of the church.

"We went in through this door," I said. "She took me through a series of tunnels with twists and turns. I don't remember them all. This chamber is bigger than the one I was in." I pointed to the large space on the map. "There was another one I think."

An antechamber maybe? I couldn't tell but it wasn't the same one as where I met Schneider.

"How are we going to find the spear?" I asked.

"We? Not we, my dear. You. I'll lead you there and you're doing the rest is up to you."

Great. I had no clues other than I thought the spear might be somewhere in that church. That was based on the postcard clue that mysteriously appeared.

"All right," I said. "Then we need to figure out how to get here." I pointed to the larger chamber, the one that was on the map. "This is where I think we should start."

When I was in Hong Kong, I met Chen. As we shook hands, I had a flash of an image of the horn and suspected he was the one who had it. So far, here in Istanbul, I wasn't so lucky. No stranger came up to me to shake my hand and give me hints about the location of the spear. Kind of a bummer but I guess everything wasn't so easy.

"I can get you there," Edward said, sounding confident. "Anna, can you trust this Ophelia person?"

I considered. All I knew was she was gifted the sword by Li Mei. "She has that sword. Li Mei gave it to her. She's the one that pointed out the Alpha and Omega to me on the handle."

"The same person that gave you the dagger?" he asked.

I nodded.

"Hm," was all he said.

"She was after Fallen and she *did* say she was part of a task force. Leo agreed he heard of it. And she's heard of me, so though I didn't know her, she must be somewhat trustworthy," I said. "And, really, uncle, we could use more allies."

While our list of enemies grew long, our list of allies was short. Kincade and Decker were currently compromised. The other Watchers were iffy. I wasn't sure if they were truly our allies or an interested third party.

"Agreed," he said. "I think she can help us. But, more importantly, I think she can help you. I'll find out exactly who she is."

My brow furrowed. "How?"

"I have connections."

Of course, he did. He had associations and acquaintances with people all over the world. I sort of admired how he had all these contacts and knew stuff about people, places and things. I aspired to be like him.

"Like Sebastian?" I asked.

"Yes." He eyed me, as though waiting for another question. "Why do you sound suspicious?"

"Because you were ordering the Watchers around like you were some sort of authority figure."

He laced his fingers and sat back in the cushions of the sofa. "I merely expressed to Leo the importance of notifying Sebastian of the issues you and Ophelia caused in the city."

Guilt swept through me for a brief moment before I got it under control. "That wasn't my fault."

He lifted a brow. "Was it hers?"

I shrugged with my innocence. "What are they going to do?"

"They can help the humans forget what they saw. The destruction of the city can be easily explained away."

The way he said it, it was like this was a common occurrence. I had to wonder if the Watchers were like *Men in Black* who ran around with a flashy-thingy erasing memories.

"Why did you leave the hotel?" he asked.

Oh, I hated when he asked me point blank questions like that. Usually when he did, he already had the answer.

I shifted in the seat, uncomfortable. "I needed some air."

"And you took your dagger and decided to cause mayhem?"

"Not exactly. That wasn't my plan." My plan was to kill a few demons because they crawled all over the city.

"Anna, I know you better than you realize. Were you spoiling for a fight?"

I huffed out a breath. "Look, I needed some air. I ran into Ophelia and we teamed up."

"You needed some air because what happened? Another nightmare?"

The truth was I didn't want to tell him about the dream with Azriel and Kincade. I hadn't had time to process it myself or come to grips with the fact Kincade was possibly a dream walker.

"You did, didn't you," he said, though it wasn't posed as a question.

I ignored his response and moved on to a question of my own. "Uncle, can Watchers dream walk?" I peered at him closely as I waited for a response.

A muscle ticked in his cheek. "No. Why?"

"Because I think they can."

"You have proof of this?" he asked.

"No, but I have a suspicion."

His brows knit. "One of them dream walked you?"

"Yes," I said.

He paused as he swallowed hard. "Kincade?"

My throat went dry. "Yes." The word came out an icy whisper.

Again, a muscle ticked in his cheek. "An interesting turn of events, to be sure."

"You didn't know?"

"Despite what you think, I do not have an inherent knowledge of all things," he countered. He ran his hand over his chin. "I told you before he took an interest in you. Now it makes more sense."

"You did tell me that," I agreed with a nod. "I'm not sure he realized that's what he was doing, though." I didn't want to tell my uncle the details of the dream. I was still trying to forget them myself.

"And you did?"

"Yes."

He didn't respond as he gave me a thoughtful look, then reached for the blueprints and the map. "You better rest. Tomorrow will be a long night."

A typical Edward dismissal. Without responding, I rose and went to bed.

I was running out of time. Schneider gave me forty-eight hours and I was on the downward slope of that and hadn't laid eyes on the spear. But I was closer than I was and that was good news. I hoped.

The next day dragged on. Edward wouldn't let me leave the hotel room for fear I would manage to drum up more trouble. Leo reported back and was the bearer of bad news—they couldn't do any more damage control than they already did. Sebastian was less than happy about that.

We got the local morning paper and realized the gravity of the situation. The tourist who snapped a picture of the demon sold the picture, allowing it to be printed on the front page with the headline *Are We Doomed?*

"This is bad, Anna. Humans will not understand what's happening," he chastised.

"I don't even understand what's happening," I countered.

He frowned. "This is serious business. If the humans realize supernatural elements are around them, it could cause mass hysteria."

"I'm sorry, uncle. I never meant for any of that to happen."

He sighed and nodded understanding. "Let's get to the church tonight and find the spear before you manage to cause more chaos."

I ignored the jab. "What did you find out about Ophelia?"

"Her story checked out."

"You trust her now?"

"Until she gives me a reason not to, yes."

Good enough for me.

Night fell. We dressed as though we were going on a combat mission. I wore black cargo pants, shirt and boots as I headed out with my uncle. My dagger was strapped to my side.

The nightlife was booming as it always was except there was a different vibe. More people were out partying than ever before. I also noted an uptick in the number of demons roaming the city. I wondered if that was due to my and Ophelia's previous night's activities.

Ophelia was supposed to meet us outside the church but so far, she was a no-show. I paced in front of the building, scanning the faces of the crowds trying to find her. But she was nowhere in sight and I worried something happened to her. Edward played it cool and hung back in the shadows, leaning against a planter.

"Come, Anna. We cannot wait here all night. We have a job to do."

"Just a few more minutes."

I continued to pace, looking for her. Not finding her. Wondering where she was and what could have happened to her. I chewed my lower lip. I glanced at my watch. Ten minutes, twenty had passed and still no Ophelia.

"Anna, you're starting to draw attention with your pacing. Perhaps she decided not to come after all."

I didn't buy it but nodded anyway. She was too excited to want to help us, so it didn't make sense she'd stand us up. Edward led us to the side door on the church I used with Natasha.

"Was it locked?" he asked.

"No, she went through with no problems."

He tried the handle. It turned with ease. We exchanged looks of surprise. He pulled out a flashlight and handed it to me, then pulled out another one for himself.

"Stick close." He started through the door and I followed.

"Do you know where you're going?" I asked.

"Yes."

He stared at the map long and hard enough to memorize it while I merely glanced at it. I followed him down the tunnel. It was reminiscent of the trip I took with Natasha except darker and a little scarier. I didn't want to run into Schneider down here.

Edward paused at the end of the tunnel. The choices were to go right or left. If I recalled, Natasha led me to the right. Edward glanced both directions before turning left. He acted like he knew where he was headed so I continued to follow. We ended up at a dead end.

"This can't be right," he said. "It's not a dead end on the map."

"Can I see the map?"

He pulled it from his shirt pocket and handed it to me. I tucked the flashlight under my arm in such a way I could read the map in the half light. He pointed to our location.

"We're here."

He was right. According to the map, there should have been a continual tunnel. I examined the wall closely. I handed him back the map. Holding the flashlight aloft, I ran my hand over the stones in front and the ones on either side of us.

"This is new construction," I said. "This wall in front was put here and not that long ago."

"How can you tell?"

I shone my light around the small chamber. "This stone feels older. It crumbles easily when I touch it." I pointed to the ones on either side of us, then the one in front of us. "This wall is smooth. Like the brick is new."

He ran his hand over the walls and nodded. "Quite right, Anna."

He dropped the backpack, rummaged through it for a minute and brought out a small sledgehammer. I had no idea what possessed him to bring a sledgehammer but was glad he did.

"You might want to stand back," he said.

I watched, awe struck, as he swung the sledgehammer several times until he at last broke through the wall with ease. The stone crumbled with every hit. Minutes later, an opening large enough for the two of us appeared.

Despite reservations, I followed him through the opening and into the next chamber. Two tunnels were in front of us angling off in different directions. Edward consulted the map, despite his boast he had it memorized, and chose the tunnel on the left. I managed to keep my sarcasm to myself though I wanted to retort with a smart-aleck remark.

The air temperature dropped as the walkway sloped downward. Cobwebs hung from corners. The place had a damp and dirty smell to it. The only thing that would make this anymore creepy was if we held torches instead of flashlights.

He paused again, his light shining in an arc in the small walkway. The bright beam lit up the place. On the opposite side of the walkway was another opening in the wall. He started toward it.

"Are you sure you know where you're going?" I asked as I followed.

"It's this way."

"What is?"

"The large chamber on the map."

I followed him through the opening in the wall. He stopped so abruptly, I nearly ran into the back of him. He sucked in a sharp breath. I peered over his shoulder. The slanting beam from the flashlight glittered off gold and jewels.

"What..." but the question died on my lips.

"Hold this."

He handed me his flashlight, then went about digging in the pack. He brought out a box of matches, then took the light from me, shining it over the walls. Several old torches rested in ancient brackets on the walls covered in dust and cobwebs. His stoic face broke into a giant grin.

It wasn't often my uncle grinned about anything but it was kinda fun to see him giddy about lighting torches. He lit the first one with several matches. With that one, he lit subsequent ones until the entire chamber glowed in yellow-orange torchlight.

When he finished, he clicked off his flashlight. I did the same. And the two of us stood side by side staring at the vast treasure hidden underneath the Hagia Sophia. Right away, I spotted gold candelabras, an ancient Egyptian sarcophagus, a number of paintings worth millions, jewels of all kinds, a treasure chest with the ultimate pirate booty.

"Uncle, what are we going to do now?"

"We're going to look for the spear," he said, matter-of-factly.

"In this?" I pointed to the disorderly mess.

"It has to be here."

"What makes you think so?" I asked.

He slipped the ancient map out of his pocket and handed it to me without a word. I inferred I was supposed to look at it so I unfolded it with a careful hand. I squinted at it.

"What am I looking for?"

"We're in the large chamber directly under the center of the church," he said. "Hold it up to the firelight and look at the notation."

I barely made out the world *mizrak*. I never noticed the word before but perhaps it could only be seen with the aid of firelight.

"*Mizrak*. What does that mean?"

He gave me a pointed look. "Turkish for spear."

My little heart skipped a beat as I turned back to the chaos of treasure. If the notation on that map was correct, it was in this chamber. Within reach. I folded the map and handed it back to him, excitement bubbling through me.

"All right. I better get busy."

I snatched a torch off the wall and started my trek through the chamber.

Chapter 21

MY EXCITEMENT QUICKLY WANED, replaced instead by an overwhelming sense of despondency. How was I ever going to find the spear in this hodgepodge cache? I wasn't interested in the treasure. All I wanted was the spear.

Edward left me to my own devices while he did whatever Edward did in places like this. He made it clear finding the spear was all me and he wasn't going to lift a finger to help. So be it. I didn't need his help anyway. But as I moved through rows and rows of glittering jewels and golden everything, I couldn't help but think about how hopeless this task was. I dropped to the dusty floor and stared at my warped reflection in a gold platter.

In the flickering light and wavering reflection, I saw dirt smudged on my face. My hands were filthy from touching and moving stuff. Dust coated my pants and cobwebs clung to my shirt. I was annoyed with the whole process.

Finding the Horn of Gabriel had not been this difficult. Maybe it was too easy for me. It practically fell in my lap. The spear, not so much. I leaned my head back and peered at the ceiling imagining all those celestial beings that liked to harass me having a good laugh over my lack of location skills.

"Would it kill ya to give me a sign?" I whispered.

"Hello, Anna."

I nearly jumped out of my skin at the sound of the voice coming out of the darkness. I scrambled to my feet, bobbling the torch in the process. Stepping out of the shadows was the archangel, Sariel. I pressed a hand against my fluttering heart and took a deep breath.

"You scared the life out of me," I said.

"Apologies." He gave me a sheepish grin. "I came to help."

"To help? Find the spear?"

He nodded.

I glanced around the area. "Am I warm at least?"

"Warm?" His brows knit in confusion. "I wouldn't know about your body temperature."

"No, I mean…warm as in am I close to the spear?"

"Ah, of course. Perhaps you follow me?" He beckoned me closer and stepped into shadows.

What did I have to lose?

I followed Sariel, the flicker from my torch casting a circle of light. I made out the outline of his giant wings as he moved deeper and deeper into the chamber. My heart moved into my throat. My stomach twisted into a knot. I wasn't sure if this was the right thing to do or not but I had to trust him. I hoped he wasn't leading me into a trap. I didn't know him all that well. Even if he did return my eyesight.

He paused at the end of the row near the back wall of the chamber and motioned to his right. All I saw in that direction was a pile of junk.

"Okay so? What about it?"

"You asked for a sign. I gave you one."

I moved closer for a better look. Wooden boxes were stacked on top of each other. Some so old, they were ready to crumble any second. One had jewels encrusted on the top. Another had chunky iron hinges with a lock that appeared to have been made in the first century. I paused on that one, my heart clotting my throat.

"That's it."

I reached for it, pulling it from the heap. I needed two hands to open it which meant I had to ditch the torch.

"Can you hold this, Sariel?"

No response.

I turned to hand him the torch, but he was gone.

Weird. I guess he poofed in to help me and poofed out.

I had to figure out another way open it. I knelt on the floor, placing the box in front of me. Holding the torch in one hand, I flipped up the latch and opened the box.

And gasped.

It was nothing more than a rudimentary looking spear tip lying haphazardly in the box. There was a fragment of wood sticking out of the bottom like the spear had been broken off from the main handle. It was nowhere close to the fake we acquired in Antarctica. That one had some sort of gold filament wrapped around the center of the ten-inch tip. This was nothing like that. While it was the same length, it had no gold.

I knew what I had to do. I had to touch it, like I had the Horn of Gabriel. I had to see if it was truly the Spear of Destiny.

I reached for it and paused. My fingers curled closed as my heart drummed a wild beat. I swallowed, my throat dry and scratchy. I wanted to know if this was it but at the same time, I was terrified.

I took a deep breath. "You got this."

And placed my fingertips on the spear.

The history of the spear flashed through my mind from the time it was placed in the box all the way backward, to the time of Christ when Longinus pierced the side of Jesus as he hung on the cross, to even before that when the spearhead was forged and attached to the wood. In between was a long kaleidoscope of jumbled images smudged together. I pulled my hand away and stared at the unassuming little artifact for several heartbeats.

"*One of the soldiers pierced his side with a lance, and immediately there came out blood and water.* I found it," I said to no one in particular. I glanced up at the ceiling. "Thank you, Sariel."

I closed the box, scooped it up and turned back to the front of the chamber to find my uncle. As I made my way out, unease pressed into me. I was so sure of my path before I found the spear, now I wasn't so sure. Before, I had every intention of giving the spear to Azriel. Now, maybe I reconsidered that idea.

All I was sure about was I had a date to keep with Schneider. But I wasn't going to let him get his grimy hands on this spear.

Plus, I still intended to kill him for what he did to my mother and Decker. What he tried to do to me. To all those women who were back in Antarctica being brainwashed into thinking they were doing their country a fine service.

It was time to serve some justice.

"There you are. I've been wondering where you—" My uncle halted as he focused on the box cradled in my arm. "You found it."

I nodded. "The history of the spear flashed through my mind."

His eyes widened for a moment before he regained composure. "What did you see?"

"Everything. Too much to comprehend. It was mostly a jumbled mess. Someone put the spear in this box but it was unclear who. Then more images before Longinus pierced Jesus' side with the spear."

"May I?" He held his hands out.

I gave him the box. He opened the lid and gazed down at the relic with all the reverence it deserved.

"This is much different from the fake, isn't it? It looks ancient. Like I thought it would." He closed the box and handed it back to me. "Well done, Anna."

"You're not going to touch it?"

"No," he said with a shake of his head. "The spear is a powerful relic. I fear what it can do to me if I try to wield it."

"What do you think it'll do?"

"It can bend the destiny of the world...and the bearer."

I eyed the box with a suspicious glance. If I intended to hand this spear over to Azriel for Kincade's life, what would happen? Would he be able to use it for his nefarious deeds? Was I *sure* I wanted to do that?

"Did you pick it up?" he asked.

"No."

"Good. Don't. I'm not sure what it will do to you."

Well, that was ominous. "We need to get out of here. I have a date with Schneider."

"Right. Come."

He turned toward the opening and headed out. I snuffed out the torch and placed it back in the bracket on my way out. As I did, my senses suddenly went on high alert.

"Uncle, stop."

He halted with my sharp command, turned to look at me with a questioning glance. "What is it?"

"There's...something..."

I sniffed the dank air but there was nothing out of the ordinary. Unease pressed through me. I inhaled one last time and that's when I caught a whiff. Pungent scents of nutmeg and allspice. The sickly-sweet scent overpowered me. I put a hand to my head and groaned. Edward was at my side in an instant.

"Tell me."

"Don't you smell it?" I asked.

"No. What is it?" Worry creased his face.

In the shadowy tunnel I made out the vague outline of someone approaching. I thought it strange the Fallen's scent was that of the tang of spices. Azriel smelled like cinnamon. But demons like sulfur and death.

"Fallen."

Edward's flaming sword materialized in his hand. I cradled the box against my chest and wielded my dagger. We were both ready and spoiling for a fight.

Two of them moved down the tunnel toward us and stopped, staring at us with their black wings spread wide and their feet shoulder-width apart. We stared at each other, no one saying anything. Edward stood still, his sword held aloft and the two Fallen eyeing it. The shadows concealed their features but I made out one was a woman and one was a man.

Finally, the man put up his hands as if in surrender. "Put down the flaming sword."

"No." Edward's tone left no room for negotiation.

"All we want is the girl," the woman said.

"You can't have her," he said.

"We've been sent to retrieve her," the man said, looking at me with his baleful dark eyes.

"Who sent you?" I asked.

"Chancellor Schneider wishes us to tell you time is up," the woman said. "And you're to come with us."

"How did you find us?" I asked.

"You think you're so mysterious," the man said. "You are not. We have followed your every move since you left his Excellency's presence."

Edward and I exchanged a glance as worry clawed through me. Schneider didn't trust me. He sent these two Fallen to keep tabs on me these last two days.

"There is no need for violence," the man said.

Yet. There was no need for violence *yet*. I glanced at Edward who glared daggers at the two, then gave me the side eye.

"You will come with us now and bring the relic." The man nodded to the box in my arms.

"I'm coming with you," Edward said.

He stashed his flaming sword. Again, his tone left no room for negotiation. I understood why he wanted to come. Neither one of us wanted to let the spear out of our sight. Likely, Edward had some plan in mind to keep the spear out of Schneider's hands altogether. I wasn't going to argue the point and make Edward stay behind. I'd seen him in action. He fought with a serious attitude. I wanted him on my side.

"You were not part of the deal," the woman said. "The chancellor will be displeased with your presence."

"I don't give a toss if he's displeased or not. I'm coming."

Silence stretched between us, my stomach twisting into various knots. I wasn't prepared to face Schneider yet. I thought I'd have time to mentally prepare for the coming battle but it didn't look like that was going to happen. I was going into this thing head first and not looking back.

Finally, the man nodded. "Come."

It turned out we weren't far from Schneider. He was still hiding out in the same chamber where he was previously under the church. The two Fallen took us through the twisting tunnels almost back to where we started and led us through more twists and turns that were vaguely familiar from my first jaunt through the underground passageways.

When we arrived at the chamber with Schneider, he still had the bonfire going. My mother stood to one side of him. Decker on the other. He was no longer bound and gagged which was, at least, a good sign.

Several of Schneider's solders lined the wall behind him and a few more demons and Fallen were scattered about. They had captured Ophelia. Her hands were bound and a knife was at her throat.

Schneider didn't bother to hid his self-satisfaction as he gloated over having captured two of my allies. I wanted to kill him all the more.

"I hope you bring good tidings, Anna," he said, a smile on his face.

Ophelia stood rooted in place with a sort of calm I wouldn't be able to display. There was a fierce glint in her eyes. If push came to shove, she wasn't going down without a fight. Decker's face was impassive and impossible to read.

And then my mother. Her gloved hands were clenched into fists at her sides.

"And who is this?" Schneider asked.

"He refused to stay behind," the man who brought us said.

"He's my uncle," I said.

Schneider gave Edward a look of distaste, then glared at Natasha.

"You told me he was dead," he said.

"An oversight by your minions," she replied.

"I'll deal with your betrayal later. You should have killed him when you had the chance." He turned back to me and eyed the box. "Where is my journal?"

"In a safe place." Truthfully, I had no idea where the journal ended up, nor did I care. I wasn't particularly interested in giving it back to him. Last time I saw it, it was in the hotel room.

"You didn't bring it with you?"

"No, because you kinda kidnapped me and didn't give me a chance to retrieve it. You should know that, though, since you had me followed." I cut a glance at the two who brought us.

He still eyed the box. "Do you have the spear?"

Geeze, this guy had a one-track mind.

"Again, I assume you already know the answer to that question since you sent your lackeys to fetch me."

Schneider's jaw clenched, the muscles ticking along the edge as his lips thinned into a straight line. He didn't care for my witty response at all. His eyes narrowed. "Give me the box and we will call it even."

"Release my friends first."

"Your friends?" He snorted as if I told a great joke, then motioned to Decker. "I've branded him. He belongs to me. The girl is expendable and Natasha has more use left in her."

My mother shot him a glare, but he didn't notice. Decker's face remained impressively impassive.

"You gave me your word," I said.

"And you yours. Yet you come without my journal." He held out his hand. "Give me the box. The journal no longer matters."

"Why?" I asked.

"Because if you give me the spear, I don't *need* the journal."

Yeah. He wouldn't need the journal when he was dead, either.

"Ophelia, Natasha and Decker go free," I said. "*First.*"

"Or what? You'll kill me?" He laughed. "You haven't a chance here, *fräulein*. If you try, my men will be on you before you know what happened."

Edward chose that moment to wield his flaming sword. "If you touch my niece, I'll kill you myself. Do as she says."

Schneider stared at the flaming sword, his eyes wide with surprise. "Who are you?"

"As she said. Her uncle."

While he was impressed with the flaming sword, he didn't believe Edward was my uncle.

He snapped his fingers at the one holding Ophelia. He removed the knife from her throat. She didn't mask the annoyed anger one bit. I didn't see the sword on her. Certainly, they would have disarmed her when they captured her. She didn't make a move to leave. Likewise, Decker and Natasha remained at his side.

"You see? They wish to remain here with me in my service." He gave me a thin lipped smiled as he extended his hand to me. "Now, give me the spear."

"Anna?"

Edward queried my name. He didn't want me to hand it over any more than I did. I was so not good at thinking on my feet. I had no idea what to do because I hadn't had time to think about this scenario and obsess over it like I usually did.

"All right," I said, my words slow and emphatic. "I'll give you the spear, provided they all tell me they don't wish to leave your employ. I want to hear it from their lips."

He huffed. "Why do you make things so difficult, Anna? All I have to do is give the order and you will be dead in an instant. But you know this, don't you?"

"Decker, tell me the truth," I said, ignoring Schneider. "Do you want to stay here?"

Decker cut the man a surreptitious sideways glance. "I'm staying."

Disappointment flickered through me. I looked at Natasha. "And you, too?"

"I must remain," she said.

Crestfallen, I nodded as I fought back the sting of tears. I never did like being wrong. Ophelia was my last hope.

"Ophelia?"

Her fingers twitched as she met my gaze, then glanced around the room. She gave me a faint smirk. "Oh, I'm staying but not for the reason you think."

She moved so fast it was hard to see her. She spun toward the soldier who held her at knifepoint and whipped her sword from where he had it tied to his waist. With a flash of the shimmering blade, she cut the guy down. He didn't have a chance to defend himself.

"Don't give it to him, Anna!" she shouted as she flew into action.

I cradled the box against my chest and wielded my dagger. My uncle went to work with his flaming sword cutting down everyone who came at him. Schneider emitted a growl of frustration and charged me, but Decker grabbed him from behind and threw him to the ground. I thought for sure every bone in his body cracked but the man managed to climb to his feet and turned toward me.

Natasha went to work raising her arms as she did before when she attacked me. Schneider screamed, putting his hands to the side of his head. Blood streamed from both nostrils, from his ears and down the side of his face. Bloody tears leaked from his eyes. He coughed and blood spewed out.

All of this chaos reigned around me as I stood rooted and frozen in place cradling the box and the dagger unable to move. I didn't know why. It wasn't like I was under a spell. It was more like I couldn't force myself into the fray.

And seeing Schneider with blood coming out of his face was horrifying. I imagined the terror my uncle felt when he watched it happen to me.

I snapped out of it finally. I couldn't let Schneider die that way. After all, he was mine to kill.

"Natasha, stop!"

Her head snapped in my direction as her arms dropped. Schneider crumbled to the ground in a heap. Our eyes met. Determination etched in the lines along her face.

"Farewell."

She whispered the word before she bolted from the chamber and back to the tunnel leading out. I couldn't stop her, dammit. All I wanted to do was save her from Schneider. Perhaps I had, but I envisioned a different outcome. One that involved her coming back to the hotel with me and my uncle for a mini family reunion. I was fooling myself to think that was going to happen.

"Anna, behind you!"

Ophelia's shout sent me into action but too late. Someone smacked the back of my head with a blunt object and I went down. Pain exploded behind my eyes and through my head. Stars sparkled through my vision. The dagger fell out of my hand, clattering on the stone floor. The box landed and shattered into a thousand toothpicks in front of me, leaving nothing but the spear on the debris.

As I tried to regain my composure, Schneider realized the spear was on the ground between us. He had enough clarity to come after it while I tried to clear the brilliant sparkles from my vision.

"Get the spear, Anna," someone said—Decker, I think.

But I couldn't move. I watched through my hazy vision as Schneider clawed and crawled his way to the spear. I had to *move* and now. I pushed my leaden limbs into action as the man reached the spear and clamped his hand around it. He pulled it to his chest.

At that moment, all was lost. I lost the Spear of Destiny.

"Anna!" Edward shouted.

My head hurt. I couldn't focus. I blinked my heavy lids. My vision blurred but I was able to make out Schneider climbing to his feet, holding the spear by the short stick. He held it aloft and shouted triumphant in German.

Decker launched at the wanna-be chancellor, tackling him like a linebacker sacking the quarterback. They collided with the hard ground and the spear bounced out of his hand and skittered across the floor. It reminded me of the fake spear skittering across the frozen lake back in Antarctica. It was enough to spur me into action.

I dove and wrapped my hand around the spear, bringing it close to me.

A sense of strangeness overwhelmed me. The spear vibrated through my hand and entire body. Like a wave rippling through me and then I was in control of everything and nothing. Strange yet new and exciting thoughts filtered through my now cleared head as I got to my feet.

I can change my destiny. I can be someone other than the Keeper of the Holy Relics. My life is my own. I can command and control all those who would follow me.

"Anna, drop that spear." Edward's stern voice drifted to me. Though I heard him, I couldn't comply nor did I want to drop the spear. I clutched it tighter in my hand.

"*Now*," he added.

"No." I cradled it like a newborn babe. "It's mine. And I can do with it what I wish. I can control things. People." I pointed it at him. "You, uncle. You no longer hold sway over me."

I pointed it at him, thinking how much I despised the way he controlled me. How he ruined my life when I was a teen. How he took away the man I loved. I wanted to free myself from him and this whole Keeper nonsense.

"Anna..." His voice drifted away as he fell to his knees.

"You will release me of my vow to be Keeper of the Holy Relics," I said.

"I...release...you..." Edward said.

Satisfaction oozed from every pour of my body. "I will leave this place and never come back."

"Anna, there is one person who can release you from the vow," Decker said. He left Schneider on the ground and stood in front of me. His big hulking body blocked out everything and everyone. "And it's not Edward."

I blinked, focused on him, pointed the spear at him. "Get out of my way."

"It doesn't work on me," he said. "Give me the spear. It's corrupting your mind."

Don't listen to him. He's trying to trick you. He wants the spear for himself. He wants to take it from you. He wants to control the world with it. He wants to control you.

"You can't have it." My voice hitched at the end.

He wrapped his hand around my wrist. With his other hand, he uncurled my fingers one by one. "Don't listen to it, Anna. It wants to control you but your mind is stronger than that. You are stronger than that. I've seen it. Not even a super dream walker destroyed you. Don't let the spear."

He wants it for himself! Don't you see that? Don't be a weak-minded fool. Don't give it to him! He'll take it. He'll wield it. He'll destroy the world! Only you know the way. The right way.

I came back to myself. My true thoughts drifted in. Decker was right. The spear was controlling. Much like when Azriel controlled my dreams.

"But...I..."

I struggled to erect the mental walls. The influence of the spear was greater than my power.

"Anna, listen to my voice. The spear is turning you against it. Release it. It wants to control you, to make you do things that aren't you."

"No."

Yes. Give him the spear.

I pushed those walls up, up, up.

"Yes. Give it to me, Anna," Decker said.

The spear lay against my palm. My mind was fuzzy, like I was swimming through cotton. But the haze started to clear.

"I don't..."

"Here, use this to wrap it in." That was Ophelia's voice.

Before I closed my hand around the spear again, Decker snatched it away and held it out to her. And everything was right with the world. I shook my head, my senses coming back. Ophelia wrapped a white scarf around the spear, taking pains not to touch it.

"What happened?"

"It tried to control you," Edward said. He put away his flaming sword. "I warned you it was powerful and something like that would happen."

Bodies littered the chamber. Ophelia and my uncle did a number on the poor unsuspecting demons and Fallen and killed them all.

All except Schneider who still writhed on the floor in pain.

"It was supposed to be mine." He spit out a mouthful of blood.

"Yeah? Well, now it's mine." I retrieved my dagger and knelt to his level. "I'd like to say it pains me to do this, but it doesn't."

I stabbed him in the heart. He shrieked a hideous high-pitched scream. Red flared through his pupils. For a moment, clarity came into his eyes and the black oily shadow lifted out of him. It glared at me with those red eyes before taking off and disappearing through the roof.

Schneider gasped one final breath. Confusion etched across his face as he peered up at me. And then the light disappeared from his eyes as death claimed him, though I suspected it was not the end of the Knights of the Holy Lance or the red-eyed demon that possessed him.

I glanced at Ophelia. "Are you all right?"

She nodded. "I was ambushed at the entrance of the church. They were waiting for me. Almost like they knew I was coming."

"They did," Decker said, confirming it. "They were following both of you. You shouldn't have come back for me."

"I had to," I said and left it at that.

My only regret was my mother. In the chaos, Natasha had escaped. I hadn't a clue where she'd go or if I'd see her again. I failed.

Ophelia extended the spear to me wrapped in her scarf. "I'm glad you found it."

I hesitated before taking it from her. Thankfully, the material between my hand and the relic kept it from overtaking my mind again. "Me, too." I glanced at Decker. "Now, let's get your brother back."

Chapter 22

"HOW DO YOU INTEND TO DO IT?"

It was a question my uncle posed after we all returned to the hotel. Ophelia and Decker joined us in the small living area. I sat in one of the chairs holding a cup of steaming tea. The spear, still wrapped in Ophelia's scarf, rested in the center of the coffee table.

I caught Ophelia up to speed on the situation with Kincade. Anger vibrated through her. She was ready to go after the Fallen herself with her shimmering sword.

"I haven't decided yet," I lied.

If Kincade was here, he'd point it out since he had an internal lie detector. My plan was to lure Azriel with the spear and sex. Though I wouldn't willingly go through with it, the thought revolted me. I was aware the plan could easily backfire. All that mattered was getting Kincade back in one piece with his soul intact.

Decker brooded and was silent since leaving the church. He didn't want me to go after Kincade. I waited for him to talk me out of it but so far, he remained quiet.

I had questions for him, too. Like why he hadn't turned invisible and teleported out. He stayed with Schneider and I didn't know why.

"I'm not sure how to reach this mysterious realm." Yet another lie. If I lured Azriel out of hiding, he would take me to Kincade. It wasn't a foolproof plan, but it was a plan.

"You can't." Decker broke his silence and pinpointed me with his lethal gaze. "I'm not going to let you."

I wanted to laugh. Like he had a choice. Like he controlled me. "I'm going. I don't care what it takes. I *will* find Kincade."

"It's not that easy, Anna," he said.

"I have the spear. That's what he wants. You're not going to bully me into staying away from Kincade." If I had to give up the spear for his life, so be it.

Decker wasn't backing down. "And I'm not going to let you interfere with him."

"You mean you're not going to let him give up his position." I sounded so bitter I tasted the acidity in my own words.

"Anna, enough," Edward said.

"Why didn't you use your abilities to flash away from Schneider?" I asked, ignoring my uncle.

Decker's face flushed with color and his jaw flexed. "The brand on the bottom of my foot suppresses them. Either the fire or the iron did it but I'm not sure which. I couldn't get to the realm where Azriel is holding Kincade if I wanted."

I stared at him with wide eyes, my heart picking up speed. "How were you planning to rescue him?"

He leaned back in the cushions of his chair and blew out a breath. Defeat was written all over his features. "I was going to ask Sebastian for help."

Decker and I both knew Sebastian wasn't going to lend aid to save Kincade. He'd already written him off. Decker came to me wanting help freeing his brother in the first place. It was clear what I had to do. I was the last one left to save Kincade.

Now it was all up to me.

My uncle's expression told me all I needed as he slowly shook his head.

"Whatever you're thinking, Anna, stop."

"If I don't find a way, no one will," I said. "And I have to find a way." My gaze fixed on the spear in the center of the table.

"You can't possibly think to give the spear to Azriel," Edward said.

"I don't want to, but if that's what I have to do to save him, I will." I stood and reached for it. My uncle clamped a hand around my wrist.

"Anna, don't do it. Remember what it did to you when you had it. Imagine what it will do to Azriel or—God forbid—Lucifer," he said.

I shuddered at the thought. He was right. But Kincade's soul was in jeopardy. That drove me to press forward. "I'm aware." The words came out a whisper. "But I have to try."

His fingers uncurled from my wrist, releasing me. He sat back in the sofa. "What's your plan?"

I picked up the spear. "I'm going to give Azriel what he wants." I swallowed, my throat dry and scratchy.

"And what is that?" Decker asked.

"Me."

"Have you lost your bloody mind?" Edward asked. "How can you be sure you'll be able to break free of him? He could hurt you in ways you cannot begin to comprehend."

"I'm aware of the risks, uncle, but there's no other way he'll take me to Kincade."

"Then what? I don't like this plan at all."

I shrugged. "I'll play it by ear." I headed toward my bedroom.

"Where are you going?" Edward called after me.

"To call Azriel. May as well get this over with."

I didn't wait for a response as I went into the small room and shut the door. I gazed down at the spear wrapped in the gauzy material. My stomach was in a tight knot. I wouldn't doubt this would go horribly awry. Nothing in my world went right. Why should this be any different?

A knock sounded on my door. I cracked it open to see Ophelia standing on the other side. She pushed her way in and shut the door, leaning against it.

"Take me with you," she said.

"Ophelia, no."

"Yes. Your uncle is right to be concerned about you. I can help you. I have the sword and mad fighting skills. And a complete and utter dislike for the Fallen."

She had me there. She was right—she did have mad fighting skills. She also had more than an utter dislike for the Fallen. She downright detested them. She'd killed enough of them the other night to prove that to me without a shadow of a doubt.

"I can't guarantee the outcome will be good," I said. "Azriel could still kill Kincade even if I give him the spear."

"I understand and am willing to risk it," she said with a nod. "I *want* to help you, Anna. Let me."

I reminded myself Ophelia was not my cousin, Lexi, who had betrayed me with Azriel. True, we weren't well acquainted, but after our night of demon and Fallen hunting, she proved a worthy ally. And, as I thought before, I needed allies.

I also needed Kincade safe.

Finally, I nodded. "All right. You can come."

She laced her fingers and cracked her knuckles. "Good. Bring on this Azriel."

The pommel of her sword stuck up over her shoulder and I nodded to it. "You better leave that behind."

"No way."

"Ophelia—"

"You're not leaving yours behind. Why should I?" She indicated the dagger strapped to my waist.

She had a point. I nodded and took a deep breath.

I came this far. Everything I did headed to this point. So why was I nervous? Because Azriel could disarm us immediately, take the spea0072, kill us all. A lot was at stake and I was taking a huge chance.

I clutched the spear in my hand and closed my eyes, thinking of Azriel. Why was it he would pop in when I least expected it, when I didn't want him? And when I *did* want him to appear, he didn't.

"Azriel," I whispered his name. "I'm ready. I have the spear. Come and get me."

"Come and get me? Seriously?"

My eyes popped open and I glared at Ophelia. "Hey, don't heckle me. It's all I got."

"There has to be another way," she said.

"You got a better idea?"

"Well…no."

"Okay. Let me try again."

I closed my eyes again and envisioned the fallen angel. His tall, muscular physique, his expansive dark wings, his scent of cinnamon. And then the warm aroma of cinnamon enveloped me.

"Holy shit," Ophelia whispered.

When I opened my eyes, he stood on the other side of the room. He glanced between the two of us and finally his gaze landed on me.

"I cannot be conjured, Anna, like some djinn."

"Yet you came when I called," I pointed out. "That has to account for something."

His face darkened with his annoyance. Score one for me. "I am not here to grant three wishes, *chéri.*" Again, he looked at Ophelia. "Though I would not be opposed to a ménage."

"Gross." Ophelia scowled.

That did nothing but piss Azriel off. He stalked toward her, stopping inches from her. "Who are you, little girl? Are you the one I've heard about? The one who kills Fallen?"

"Forget her for a second, Azriel." I tried to put things back on track. I pushed my way between them and held up the relic. "I found the Spear of Destiny."

He reached for it but I snatched it away, holding it behind my back. When I did, Ophelia slipped it out my hands. I didn't fight her, nor did I react. I kept my gaze on Azriel.

"Not so fast, hot rod," I said. "Kincade's life for the spear. That was the deal."

He glowered. "You still insist on saving the *gardien*, I see." His eyes narrowed. "I will need more than merely the spear for the *gardien's* life, *chéri*. I thought you knew this."

Heat flashed through me. I licked my dry lips. All of his filthy advances made sense. He was aware his powers of seduction worked on me almost too well. I didn't want to admit to him I allowed him to think he was seducing me.

"If you release him, I will give you the spear and…me."

His brows rose. "Have you remembered?"

I nodded though I had no idea what he was talking about. It was better to bluff and dupe him into taking me to Kincade. He smiled…actually smiled. Not the wolfish grin he always gave me but a more real, more genuine one. A smile lighting up his dark eyes.

And it triggered an overwhelming sense of familiarity deep inside me. A long-buried memory, perhaps one wanting to surface. I had seen his smile before. But where? When?

It shook me to the core.

"The things we will be able to do together..."

A breath shuddered out of him. I mentally filled in the blanks and didn't like it. He clamped a hand around my upper arm.

"Now!"

At my exclamation, Ophelia wrapped her arms around my upper body as Azriel flashed us away to the dungeon in the mystery realm. Kincade was still shackled to the wall by his wrists. He was worse than last time. His face was a bloody pulp. He had two black, swollen eyes. Blood was on his chin and matted his hair. His shirt was nothing but tatters. Seeing him like that sent a knife right through my heart. Ophelia audibly gasped behind me.

"You've seen him. Now hand over the spear." Azriel moved to Kincade's side, open hand ready to take whatever remained of his soul.

So far, he appeared not to notice Ophelia had her sword and I had my dagger. I hoped it stayed that way.

"It's not going to be that easy, bud," I said, sounding braver than I felt. "Release him first."

"If I do, are you prepared to give yourself to me?" he asked. "Here? Now? In front of your lover?"

Ophelia sucked in a sharp breath through her nose. Imperceptible, but because she stood close to me, I heard it. Kincade's head twitched ever so slightly. I would have missed it had I not been looking at him.

"Yes." The word was like acid on my tongue.

What the fuck are you doing?

Kincade's thunderous voice burst into my mind. *Chill out. I know what I'm doing.*

Have you lost your mind, Anna? I have everything under control here.

Oh, do you? You're the one in shackles. Not me. Let me handle this, Kincade.

Azriel's wolf smile returned. I understood now. It was a smile of triumph. That smile I hated with every piece of my being. Ophelia standing behind me with her Fallen-killing shimmering sword strapped to her back gave me comfort. I hoped Azriel wasn't aware of the weapon, but he was smart and clever and likely already was by the tell-tale sign of the scabbard peeking over her shoulder.

Balls.

"I'm glad you finally remembered, *chéri*." He forgot about Kincade as he moved to me. He twined a lock of my dark hair around his forefinger. Kincade growled like a feral junkyard dog and rattled his chains as he fought against them. We both ignored him. "You and I are going to be invincible."

Don't let that filthy animal touch you, Anna.

"We are," I said in my breathiest, sexiest voice.

Unless he was dead. I was going to smile when I turned him into a corpse.

The fallen angel went back to Kincade and unlocked one wrist. I sensed Ophelia's restlessness behind me. She was dying to pull out her sword. I gave her a quick glance over my shoulder and a sharp one-shake of my head. She shifted from foot to foot and dragged her lower lip through her teeth.

Don't do this, Anna. I'm not worth it. Let me die here.

Azriel, slow as he ever was, unlocked Kincade's second wrist.

I hated hearing Kincade like that. It both scared and infuriated me. *Shut up, will you? I'm working here.*

Maybe he got it. Maybe he didn't. Either way, he stopped projecting his voice into my head. And that was fine by me.

The fallen angel bent and unlocked both ankles. Kincade was upright so long, he crumbled to the ground. He crashed against the stone floor without a grunt. I wanted to run to him, to pull him into my arms and cradle him against me. Instead, I forced myself to stand stone still as Azriel turned to me. The pulse in his neck throbbed with anticipation.

Revulsion rippled through me.

I didn't want this. I didn't want him. I swallowed hard.

Azriel held out his hand. "The spear."

I took a deep breath and nodded. "Ophelia has it."

I stepped aside and nodded to her. Her eyes were wide and shone with the fear sliding through her. I thought I'd shake with my own fear but I wasn't. I put a hand on her shoulder.

"A tagalong?" Azriel asked, amused. "When I'm done with you, she and I will become acquainted."

Ophelia stiffened with her revulsion.

"You'll keep your damn hands off her," I said.

"Because you want me for yourself." A lecherous glint twinkled in his dark eyes. "Now, the spear." He held out his hand.

"Give it to him," I said, my voice strong and sure.

She hesitated. She didn't want to give it to him anymore than I wanted him to have it. But a deal was a deal.

I had no idea what was going to go down once Ophelia handed the spear to Azriel. I didn't have a plan. But maybe for once in my life I would be good at improv.

Maybe.

She clutched the spear still swathed in her scarf, glanced down at it, then Azriel, then me. I gave her the go-ahead nod. She handed it to Azriel who took it, licked his lips and unwound the scarf from around it. I watched with wide-eyes, my heart pounding a hard beat in my chest. When the last of the material had unfurled, a glint of gold wrapped around the tip glimmered in the light. Surprise flooded me. My head snapped in her direction.

Ophelia flashed me a smug smile before she contained it.

She and my uncle had pulled a fast one. How had they managed to switch the real spear for the fake? Edward was determined to keep the real relic out of the fallen angel's hands by any means necessary. Including fooling me.

Azriel didn't notice it was the fake spear.

"At last, I have it in my possession. The fabled Spear of Destiny." He pointed it at me. "Now, you will disrobe for me."

Ah, so that's how it worked. He figured he could use the spear to bend my will to his. I didn't move.

"Do it."

"You have the spear. Isn't that enough?" I asked.

A dark glower came over his face. "Are you taking back your promise, Anna?"

Ophelia's eyes were as round as saucers. "Anna...?"

I met her gaze and swallowed hard. "A deal is a deal. And I never go back on my word."

I eyed the pommel of her sword sticking out of the scabbard over her shoulder. She gave me an imperceptible nod. I reached for my shirt, unbuttoned the top two buttons and started to pull it off.

Ophelia wielded her sword and put it against Azriel's neck. His hand clamped around her wrist so tight, his knuckles turned white. She inhaled a sharp breath. At the same time,

Kincade unfolded his broken body from the floor and moved so fast, he was nothing more than a blur. He shoved me against the wall, covering me with his big body. Heat radiated from him into me. My breath caught in my throat.

"Trickery," Azriel said on a forced smile that said he was not amused. "So, the *gardien* was not as injured as he appeared."

"I'm a fast healer," he said.

Hearing his gruff voice rumble against me was music to my ears. I wanted to wrap my arms around him and hug him, hard.

"And you, little one. You *are* the one who's been killing my fellow Fallen."

Azriel dug his nails into the fleshy part of her wrist. To her credit, she didn't even wince.

"Someone's gotta do it," she said and flashed a smile.

"Indeed." One brow lifted. "And today your killing spree ends."

The glint of the blade was in his hand seconds before he plunged it into Ophelia's side. He stabbed her with the fake spear. I screamed her name. Kincade lunged and caught her before she hit the ground. The sword tumbled from her hand, clattering on the stone next to her.

Azriel snatched the shimmering sword before any of us could grab it. Ophelia emitted a strangled gasp seeing her beloved sword swiped.

"Damn you, Azriel!" I said.

He threw the fake spear at me. It landed at my feet. "What sort of fool do you take me for? Where is the real spear?"

"I...I don't know." And that was the truth. I had no idea where it was.

"Someplace you'll never find," Ophelia said.

"Tell me now and the little one can live. If you don't, she dies along with your lover."

Kincade shot daggers from his eyes. If looks killed, his would. He gave Azriel the evil eye but the Fallen was focused solely on me. He moved toward me, taking slow deliberate steps. I pushed against the wall, wanting out of his path, knowing I couldn't.

"I ought to kill you now."

"But you can't," I taunted. He already tried—and failed. I was secure in the knowledge I was safe from him but Kincade and Ophelia weren't.

"You had no intention of giving yourself to me, did you? What was your plan, *chéri?*"

My plan was I didn't have a plan which was a mistake. But there was no going back. I was stuck here with Kincade and an injured Ophelia.

"Fine. They die and you will remain my prisoner."

He disappeared in a flash. I pounded the back of my fist against the wall.

"What are you doing here, Ophelia?" Kincade asked.

"I didn't know you were here."

Surprise flickered through me. "You know each other?"

"I need something to stop the bleeding," Kincade said, ignoring my question. "Now, Anna."

I frantically glanced around but found nothing. I whisked my shirt off and tossed it to him. He gave me a quick cursory glance to see I'd at least had the forethought to put on a sleeveless undershirt. He ripped my shirt in half and pressed a small section against her side.

"It's not bad," she said.

"No, you're lucky. The wound isn't deep. Good thing that spear was dull."

I tried again. "How do you know each other?"

"He's my task force leader. The one that disappeared," she said. Then to Kincade, "I had no idea Azriel captured you."

"I couldn't get a message to you," he said. "What about the others?"

She gave a shrug. "They quit. But I didn't."

Kincade tried hard to hide the grin pulling up the corner of his mouth but it was there. He turned his attention to me. "You lied about giving yourself to Azriel. *That* was your grand plan?"

"It was all I had," I said, defensive. "It worked."

Of course, Kincade knew I lied but it gave me comfort to know he knew.

"Where did you find the fake?"

"Long story." I didn't want to rehash the whole Antarctica thing. Which reminded me. "Ophelia, how did you switch the real spear for the fake?"

She gave me the same smug smile she emitted when Azriel unwrapped the fake. "Sleight of hand."

My eyes narrowed. "No. How? Did my uncle have something to do with it?"

"Of course, he did. When we left the church, you walked ahead of us. You didn't see Edward and I switch them. He didn't want you to give it up."

"You were going to trade the Spear of Destiny for my life?" Kincade scrutinized me closely with death-ray eyes. It took all my self-control not to squirm.

I ignored him. "Where's the real one?"

"Edward still has it. Likely on his person," she said.

I scowled. Annoyance flickered through me at Edward's mistrust of my handling the spear. I didn't want to admit he had a valid point in keeping it out of my hands, but I hadn't expected him to go to such lengths. I planned to take it up with my uncle when we got out of here. *If* we ever got out of here.

"We have to find a way out," I said.

"Yeah, we do, but you managed to trap us here. Way to go. I told you I had everything under control," Kincade said.

"How was I supposed to know you're like Superman? I thought you were nearly dead."

I didn't point out his face still looked like someone had used it to practice martial arts. I had a lot of questions about what he thought he was going to do and how he was going to do it, but I didn't say any of them. If he had a plan, why didn't he (a) tell me and (b) implement that plan?

"Because I was waiting for the right time," he said.

"Huh?" Ophelia blinked up at him, confusion etched on her face.

"Stop doing that." I glared at him.

"Doing what?" she asked, glancing at me and then Kincade.

"He's reading my mind," I said. To him, "And stay out of my head."

He ignored me. "You all right, Ophelia?"

When she nodded, he eased her to the floor, then got to his feet and wobbled. I reached for him, grabbed his arm and steadied him. The flash of fire in his gaze told me he didn't want help but I wasn't backing off. He wasn't as strong as he pretended to be which told me a lot. He was hurting but he was too damn stubborn to admit it. I wondered how much damage Azriel actually did to him. Worry gnawed through me.

"I'm *fine*," he said through clenched teeth.

"I told you to stop."

Our gazes locked for a couple of heartbeats. I could fall right into those alluring green-gold eyes of his. Sometimes, they sparked a predatory glint. Other times, they were gentle. Calm. I couldn't stop thinking about what my uncle said, that we were connected. Azriel had called him *gardien*. Decker didn't want him to give up his position for me. All I knew was he *was* my guardian. Mine. He'd chosen me for some reason and it made my stupid heart skip a stupid beat.

Ophelia didn't miss it as she scooted her way to the wall and sat upright, still holding my torn shirt against her side. "When you two stop mooning at each other, maybe we can figure a way out of here?"

Heat flashed through me and made a direct route to my cheeks. I released him, cleared my throat, and took an interest in the surrounding room. There was one door—a cell door—looking out into the hallway. Light flickered along the smooth stone floor from torches in metal brackets lining the wall.

"There's no way out," Kincade said. "There are wards and all kinds of magical barricades keeping us in. No one is going to find us here. No one unless Azriel wants them to find us."

"Where is here?" I asked.

"One of the Nine Realms of Hell."

"You mean one of the circles?"

He nodded. "The Second Circle, I think."

My uncle and I were in the First Circle not so long ago when I recovered the Horn of Gabriel. Darius helped us get there and got us out when things went awry. I doubted Darius would help me, Kincade and Ophelia out of this one.

There was one other option. I dream walk my uncle, tell him where I was and hope he found us. Since Decker had no teleportation skills anymore, I wasn't sure how he was going to achieve that. Still, it was worth a shot.

"What are we going to do?" Ophelia asked.

"I have an idea." I slid down the wall and sat, drawing up my knees and closing my eyes.

"You're going to take a nap?" Annoyance laced her words.

"No," Kincade said. "She's going to dream walk. Your uncle?"

"Yes. Maybe he can help us."

"What does that mean? Dream walk?"

"I'll explain later," I said. "Now, shh. I need to concentrate."

It didn't take long to step into that dreamy world between awake and asleep. I found my uncle's consciousness right away. He wasn't sleeping, either. He was pacing. And he was pissed.

"Anna, where the devil are you? I've been trying to find you for hours."

"Azriel has us trapped in the Second Circle. Ophelia and Kincade are injured. We need help."

He spread his hands, looking helpless. "I have no idea where you are. I need more information."

"It's some kind of prison cell. It smells like death and rot."

He scowled. "That's not enough for me to go on."

"Ask Decker," I urged. "Maybe he can help."

"Even if he can tell me where you are, he can't take me there," Edward said.

He was right. But it still didn't stop me from trying. "There has to be some way."

He was silent a long moment as he continued to pace. He halted, his hands behind his back. "I'll think of something."

He was gone in a blink. Like he'd hung up from talking to me. It was typical Edward. He hadn't given me an answer but somehow that still gave me comfort.

"Well?" Kincade asked when I opened my eyes.

"He's working on it. In the meantime, we sit tight."

A rumbling sounded somewhere nearby. We all looked at each other.

"You sure about that?" Ophelia asked.

Nope. I wasn't sure about anything at all.

Chapter 23

THE RUMBLING HAPPENED a second time. It sounded more like a low growl than anything else which made me wonder if there was a creature in the cell next to us.

"What's that sound?" Ophelia whispered.

"It doesn't sound friendly whatever it is," I said.

"What did Azriel mean when he said you finally remembered?"

Kincade's sudden question threw me. A question to which I had no answer. I shrugged. "I have no idea."

He peered at me with narrowed eyes. "That was the truth at least."

Good to know some things didn't change with him and he was still using his lie detector on me.

But Azriel's elated exclamation didn't sit well with me. What *did* he mean by that? I confronted my uncle about it before but he was cagey at best about the answer. Azriel indicated we had a history which disturbed me. I'd never met him until that day I dream walked Emma and he was in her dreams. I was a little offended at the suggestion I lied about it to Kincade.

"Why would I lie about that?"

"Because you don't want me to know the truth. Because you know I want Azriel dead. Because you have some secret crush on him."

I scoffed. "Are you serious? I have nothing but revulsion for him. He murdered Ben in front of me. He nearly beat me to death in the First Circle. Or did you forget that?" I put my hands on my hips, the anger searing through me. Guardian or no, he was pissing me off.

"I forget nothing."

His searing gaze never left me and somewhere in the depths I knew he meant it. When I first told Kincade I nearly died at Azriel's hands, he was in the hospital in Hong Kong. I still remembered his hands curling into fists, skin leeching of color as he crushed the hospital bedding in his palms.

He told me he'd make sure Azriel never put another hand on me. I heard him say it as if he said it again, right now, in my head. Yet he hadn't been there when Azriel accosted me in the shower or all those other times when the fallen angel tried to seduce me.

"Tap the brakes, you two," Ophelia said. "You staring at each other like that makes me a little uncomfortable."

"Like what?"

We said it in unison and looked at her at the same time.

"Like you need to get a room and get it over with."

I flushed again, the heat pressing into my cheeks. He flashed Ophelia a heated glare before moving to the other side of the room and lowering his aching body to the floor with a grunt. We both understood what she insinuated but I refused to entertain the idea.

Finally, I said, "I want Azriel dead, too, but he conveniently disappeared."

"And took my damn sword," Ophelia said. "We have to get it back."

"We will." I sounded more confident than I felt.

"How?"

"I'm working on it." It was my turn to pace the length of the small cell.

I cut a glance at Kincade. He had raw marks on his wrists. He needed medical attention. I doubted he would admit it, though.

"Well, this is fun," Ophelia said. "So, what exactly is dream walking?"

I continued to pace. "I can see and enter people's dreams."

She stared at me for a long moment with wide-eyed admiration. "You can? Do they know you're there?"

"Sometimes. Sometimes not. My uncle and I can interact that way." And Kincade, though I wasn't sure if he realized that. I refused to look at him for fear my facial expression would give away any hidden thoughts. He was pretty good at reading me.

"Why would you want to do that?" she asked.

She was an inquisitive one. "I used to work in a hospital. A lot of patients arrived in a catatonic state. I thought I could help them."

I left it at that but knew she was going to have more questions.

"Could you help them?"

I stopped pacing, ran my hands through my hair. "No."

"You tried," Kincade said.

"Yes, I tried. And failed." Then to Ophelia, I said, "Azriel can dream walk, too. In a dream, he killed a woman's guardian angel and took her soul. When I woke up, it was too late for her. She was dead."

Understanding came over her features. "That's how the Fallen are collecting souls."

"Yeah, they can do it in dreams as well as real life," Kincade said. "I've been tracking Azriel for a long time."

"I should have killed him when I had the chance," she said. "When I still had the sword."

She was upset about losing the sword. I made a mental note to add its retrieval from Azriel on my to do list.

The low growl sounded again. This time it was right outside our cell door. We all looked that direction in time to see a hairy, disgusting beast lumber by.

"Guard," Kincade said. "It won't bother us if we don't bother it."

I watched as it moved on down the corridor.

"Nothing but trouble there, Anna," he said.

But I was still armed with the dagger. I wondered if I could get its attention—

"Don't even think it," Kincade said. "You can't get through the bars anyway."

It irked me he read my mind so thoroughly. I considered the bars and bit my lip. I couldn't get through, huh? I reached for them. The second my hand touched them a bolt of lightning zapped through me. I flew back, hit the wall and crashed to the floor. Ophelia gasped as Kincade rushed to my side. He scooped me off the floor. I was limp in his arms.

"I tried to warn you," he said.

I shook my head to keep from seeing stars. I blinked, trying hard to regain my bearings. I was acutely aware of the way his arms encircled me and helped me to a sitting position. I wasn't going to complain about that one bit. Nor was I going to complain about the way he gazed at me with those sexy green-gold eyes.

I had to stop looking into those eyes of his. They were starting to make me weak in the knees. I did *not* need to be weak in the knees for Kincade.

"Seriously. You two need to get a room."

He dropped me like a hot potato and moved away. I crashed once again to the floor but not as hard this time. I managed to scoot toward the wall, resting my back against the cold stones.

"So, I guess we're stuck here," I said.

"Unless your uncle can pull off a miracle, yes," Kincade said.

I leaned my head back and stared up at the dark ceiling of stone. I sent up a silent prayer, hoping Edward would come to the rescue.

I lost track of time. It felt like an eternity. My stomach growled and so did Ophelia's. She moved next to me and rested her head on my shoulder. Her wound stopped bleeding at last but she still needed medical attention.

Where the hell was Edward?

Across the room, Kincade sat against the wall with his long legs outstretched and crossed at the ankles. A lock of hair had fallen over his forehead. His poor beat-up face was at rest. The bruising had turned from dark black and purple to more of a yellow-green in places. He was kind of handsome with his hard-sculpted face, broad shoulders and wide chest. The well-defined muscles of his biceps were evident through the tattered clothes. I was glad he rested and hoped that would help him heal faster.

Next to me, Ophelia yawned, then straightened. She grunted as she stretched her neck.

"Did you have a nice nap?" I asked.

"Fair," she said. She stretched her arms, lacing her fingers and cracking her knuckles. "Can I ask a personal question?"

"Sure."

"Is he your boyfriend?"

"No." I said it almost too quickly.

"Azriel thinks so."

"Azriel is a lunatic."

She peered at Kincade's sleeping form. "What is he to you?"

That was a great question and one I didn't want to ponder too much. "We're...allies." Because I didn't know what else to call him.

"Sure looks like more than allies to me." She waggled her eyebrows.

"What's that supposed to mean?" It was a dumb question. I had the answer.

"The way you look at each other says a lot."

"And how is that?" Another dumb question but I wanted her perspective.

"Like you want to rip each other's clothes off."

I snorted. "Hardly."

I couldn't help it. I glanced his way again. His arms crossed over his chest as he slept. It gave me plenty of time to examine the way that one vein popped out of his left upper arm. I tried hard to ignore that. I also tried hard to ignore the way his handsome face was at peace. Okay, so, I entertained the thought but I wasn't sure I was over Ben yet. And Kincade was...well, *Kincade*.

"Whatever you say." She rolled her eyes.

The cell door opened and in stepped Azriel with several of his crony demons. We all got to our feet. He gave Kincade a cursory glance, then paused on Ophelia.

"Still alive, I see." The fallen angel sounded disappointed but dismissed her as he pinpointed me with his dark gaze. "You said you remembered what we'd been to each other."

I shook my head. "I didn't. You merely assumed that."

He snarled, baring his teeth. "Then perhaps, *chéri*, you need help remembering."

I didn't like that sound of that. My gut clenched. Kincade moved closer, pushing his way between the two of us.

"You'll keep your hands off her."

The fallen angel's dark, demented gaze flickered to him. "You have no say in the matter." He snapped his fingers.

The two he'd brought with him went into action. They grabbed Kincade before he reacted and pushed him back to the wall, shackling his wrists once again. One went to Ophelia and restrained her by holding her arms against her side. My heart jangled in my chest. I didn't like where this was going.

"What are you going to do, Azriel? Torture me?" The sarcastic tone hid my fear.

Block him, Anna. Don't let him in your mind.

Kincade was right. I put up my mental walls.

"Torture? Call it what you will, *chéri*. I call it enlightenment. You left me no other choice."

Shit.

Fuck.

That's what I liked about Kincade. He never minced words.

The second demon working with Azriel wrapped his burly arms around my upper torso and held me in place though I struggled against him. He reeked of that horrible demon odor, invading my nose as Azriel smiled his famous smile. He pressed his hands on either side of my face doing a weird imitation of the Vulcan mind meld. My head exploded in pain as I winced with the throbbing behind my eyes.

"It's time I help you remember everything."

My knees buckled. The only reason I remained upright was because the demon held me. Azriel held fast and kept my head from dropping to my chest. Behind me, Kincade rattled his chains.

"You will look at me while you remember. I want to see the clarity in your eyes."

This time, I couldn't resist or block him no matter what I tried. His dark demon magic was too strong for me and rendered my body motionless, much like he did when he dream walked me. Memories exploded into my mind of a time long ago when I was young and innocent and stupid.

It was when I lived with my uncle. I was seventeen and late for my riding lesson and there in the stable was a new worker. He was tall and gorgeous with dark eyes and hair black as the night. That first day when we met, he helped me with the saddle. He flirted with me, made me feel special, wanted, needed.

Days passed into months and we struck up a friendship, then a romance. His name was Marcus. We spent a fair amount of time in the stables where we kissed a lot, touched each other a lot. It was one of those days he'd snipped a lock of hair from the nape of my neck. He kissed it, wrapped it in a pale blue ribbon as a keepsake. He told me how much he loved me. How much he wanted me to be his. He romanced me, seduced me. He was my everything. The sun rose and set with Marcus. We made plans to run away together, to marry.

But my uncle discovered our affair, sent him away. I never saw him again.

"You received a note, left on your dresser, inviting you to the stables. Do you remember now, *chéri?*"

There was more. Something I was missing. Something I didn't understand. Yes, I remembered a note left on my dresser inviting me to meet the stable boy. Marcus Davenport was his name. I had a crush on him and pined for him and—

*The stable boy...*Oh, God.

I blinked as I focused on Azriel's face. His dark eyes. The dark hair. I always sensed a familiarity about him but I never placed it.

He held up his hand. Resting in the palm was the lock of my black hair wrapped in the pale blue ribbon.

The sharp scream ripped from my lungs as I realized the horror of it all. Marcus was Azriel in disguise. He seduced me then as he tried to seduce me now. Kincade shouted a lethal obscenity, his chains rattling against the wall with the same fury boiling through me.

"You would have given yourself to me had it not been for your uncle and a meddling angel. They destroyed our happiness, our love. But we are still connected, you and I. You know it as well as I do." Azriel's dark gaze pressed deep into my soul, searching for the light that it was.

Yes, I knew it. Another memory flooded through me. Of his doing or mine, I wasn't sure which. I envisioned the small tattoo on the back of my left shoulder, the tiny blue butterfly. The one Azriel masquerading as Marcus inked there.

It was how he marked me. How he managed to keep track of all my movements.

What a weak fool I was to let him do those things to me. To think he loved me for me.

"You are special, Anna. So special. I've wanted you for so long. I've dreamed of it. Haven't you?"

His fingers tangled in my long hair. He gripped the hair at the nape of my neck where he'd snipped a lock so long ago. I could no more stop him than I could a freight train.

Azriel stripped me of everything as though he stripped me of my clothes, laid me bare and vulnerable for all to see. My head tilted back as he slanted his mouth over mine and kissed me with such fervor and lust, I was powerless to resist. His tongue shoved into my mouth, bumping against mine. The scent of cinnamon filled my nose as did the taste. Still holding my head with one hand, he groped me with the other.

Time slowed and it was as though I moved into a tunnel. In the distance, Kincade's angry voice shouted. Ophelia whimpered her disgust. Inside my mind I shouted for him to stop. I couldn't react with my body even if I wanted to because I was still paralyzed. Desire and need burned through me, leaving an ache so agonizing I wanted Azriel to satisfy it.

"How does it feel to have your lover watch while I take you?" he whispered against my mouth. Then licked my top lip.

Bile rose to my throat. Tears leaked from the corners of my eyes. He kissed my forehead, his heated lips pressing against my skin. My mind clouded with thoughts of fucking Azriel. The sane part of me tried desperately to claw my way out of this hell, while the other part of me controlled by Azriel wanted to succumb.

"Admit you want me, Anna, as you did once long ago." His mouth left a scorching trail down my neck. He nibbled my earlobe.

"Accept me. Give me the relics. Help me find the rest. Together, we will rule side by side."

Yes, I will.

I warred with myself while he poked around my head, fondled me, kissed me, seduced me, tempted me.

Fight him, dammit, Anna!

Kincade's thunderous voice burst through my mind, snapping me back to my senses.

I had to fight him with everything I had.

I would never help Azriel. I would never give him the relics. He could dark magic me six ways until Sunday and still I would not bend. He would have to do more than control me with his magic. He would have to control my mind.

The realization hit me hard. That was exactly his plan. Seduce me. Brainwash me. Make me follow him. It was not unlike what Schneider did to my mother. Not unlike what Azriel did to Lexi.

"Anna, resist him," Kincade said.

"Shut him up." Azriel's angry words rumbled through his chest.

I squeezed my eyes shut, unable to respond. All I could see in my mind's eye was Azriel with the face of the man I once loved. The carefully constructed walls I put up to keep him out crumbled. Oh, how I hated he was in my mind manipulating me, tempting me, making me want him. It was a waking nightmare and, in that nightmare, I reached for him. His arms slid around my waist as he pulled me close. It was worse than him touching me, kissing me. I couldn't push him out of my thoughts no matter how hard I tried.

Kincade was there in a flash of power, dominance, control. In the dream state, he was fully healed and functional. He forced his way between us, shoved Azriel backward until he released me. Azriel retaliated by swinging his fist and punching him on the jaw. Kincade kicked him in the chest so hard the fallen angel stumbled backward.

The demon magic slowly dissipated, giving me back my senses. While the heat and need still pumped through me, I was able to regain control of my mind. I shook out of the waking dream to find Azriel still standing close enough to kiss me. Kincade was still shackled to the wall and Ophelia remained a prisoner of one of the demons.

"Impressive how you manage to control your thoughts," Azriel said. "Even more impressive how you managed to have the *gardien* come to your rescue."

"She had nothing to do with that. It was all me."

Kincade's low victorious voice rumbled out of his chest and through me, breaking the spell Azriel had over me. A breath shuddered out between my lips. Not from the lust and desire for Azriel. A sudden...swooniness swept over me at Kincade's response and all I wanted to do was throw my arms around his neck and hug him, *hard.*

Azriel's head snapped in his direction. He moved away from me, fire flashing deep in his dark eyes as he glowered at Kincade and realized the same thing. The Watcher was more powerful than we'd known.

"You can dream walk."

I knew it! Kincade could dream walk. My suspicions were finally confirmed.

Azriel's eyes narrowed as he moved closer to Kincade. "You are more of a threat than I realized. Your soul will make a wonderful addition to our demon high lords."

Oh, God, no. He was going to kill Kincade and take his soul for good. I tried to move but my limbs were still numb from the fallen angel's magic.

"Anna!" Ophelia's high-pitched voice practically shattered my eardrums.

I still couldn't move. I couldn't talk. It was like my tongue had frozen. Yet I was aware of everything happening around me. Azriel moved toward Kincade who struggled against his shackles.

"Anna, do something!" she shouted.

I wanted to but, despite my brain's insistence, my body wouldn't move. My neck muscles twitched. It wasn't much but I at least turned my head. Great. I had a front row seat to Kincade's demise. Azriel opened his hand and placed it on Kincade's chest over his heart.

In the previous times Azriel did this to him, Kincade never fought. Now, in his weakened state, his face contorted as though he were in massive pain. He writhed, trying to escape from the fallen angel, yanking against the shackles and ripping more skin from his already raw wrists.

Ophelia was right. I needed to act and now. I closed my eyes again and concentrated hard on moving my limbs. The demon holding me was distracted by the show. I sensed he delighted in watching the fallen angel steal souls.

Azriel wasn't going to steal Kincade's. Not today.

A power deep within surged through me. Adrenaline maybe. Or the shear fight to save Kincade. My fists clenched into balls. All my muscles stiffened. In one move, I shoved the demon off me, snatched my dagger from my waist and stabbed him. He turned to ash.

I moved with as much speed as I could muster. In the small space, I was on Azriel before he realized what happened and plunged the dagger deep into his side. All the way to the hilt. But he didn't turn to ash.

He cried out as he released Kincade who slumped over, unconscious. I drew Azriel closer, peered deep into his eyes.

"You aren't going to win today, Azriel."

He smiled that wolf smile. The one I hated so much. "*Touché, chéri.*"

I was left holding a bloody dagger as he disappeared.

Chapter 24

I HOLSTERED THE DAGGER and rushed to Kincade's side. "Help me get him out of these."

"Is he still alive? Where are the keys?"

"Find them."

I pressed my hands against his cheeks and gently lifted his head. Beneath the bruises, his skin was pale. His breathing was shallow. I worried about how much damage Azriel managed to do to him. Ophelia found the keys in the ashes of the dead demon. She unlocked one wrist. I tucked my body under his arm and shouldered his weight as she unlocked his other wrist. She did the same and together we lowered him to the floor. He slumped against the wall. I pressed two fingers against his neck. His weak pulse fluttered.

"He's still alive."

"What are we going to do?" At least she didn't sound hysterical when she asked. It was clear, though, it was an effort for her to keep her voice calm. She was as scared as me.

But it was a question to which I didn't have an answer because we were still stuck in the damn cell in the Second Circle. Where the bloody hell was Edward?

I shook my head slowly. "I have no idea."

We lapsed into silence. I sat on the floor next to Kincade holding his hand. Ophelia was across from me trying her hardest not to look forlorn.

"What did he do to you, Anna?"

"What do you mean?" I tried to sound casual but my voice sounded like nothing but a scratchy whisper. I was stalling for time to come up with an answer that wasn't an answer.

"After Azriel..." Her words trailed off.

I swallowed the lump of bile that rose in my throat. I didn't want to relive it. I didn't want to think about it. I knew what he tried to do, what he almost succeeded in doing. Nothing made me feel better than plunging that dagger into his side, knowing I wounded him as he wounded me.

"It doesn't matter."

"But you...and Kincade..." She huffed out a heated breath. "I don't understand."

"He was in my mind." I paused, then added, "They both were."

Kincade tried to save me from him. Tried and succeeded enough for me to regain some of my senses. More questions etched on her face but I wasn't prepared to answer them. Not now. Maybe not ever. I never wanted to experience that again.

The memory was still fuzzy. Like it was shrouded behind a fog I was unable to pierce. It didn't change, though, the reality of what he did to me.

And Azriel would pay.

The real question was how much of Kincade's soul had he taken?

I pressed my hand against his cheek and wished his gruff voice would burst into my mind. I worried my lower lip. Maybe I could dream walk him like I had the two patients back in the hospital in Dallas.

I closed my eyes and concentrated and a second later I was in his mind. We stood in the center of the godforsaken cell. But the lighting was different. Shadows pressed all around us as a circle of white light illuminated us. While his face wasn't bruised and his body wasn't damaged, he had dark circles under his eyes.

"You can't save me, Anna."

Hot tears burned the backs of my eyes like acid. "Don't say that."

"He took too much. There's nothing you can do."

I refused to believe him and shook my head. "I will find a way."

In the shadowy darkness, he stepped closer. He cupped my face with warm, soft hands. My heart tripped over itself as appreciation flickered in those green-gold eyes.

"It means a lot you tried." His thumb swept over my cheekbone. "Let me go."

"You can't leave me like this." My words cracked on my hitched breath. "You can't leave me, Kincade."

"You have your uncle."

"No—"

Anna. Anna!

In the distance, someone called my name. It sounded like my uncle. Kincade dropped his hands and stepped back into the circle of light. Someone gave me a shake and then I was awake and peering at Edward. How had he managed to get into the cell past the wards?

"Anna, come on. We haven't much time."

"How did you find me?"

"Let's call it divine intervention." He wrapped his hand around my upper arm and helped me to my feet. "Let's go."

"I can't leave him. I won't." I glanced down at Kincade whose breathing turned shallow. He was giving up. I wasn't.

"I brought someone to help," Edward said.

He stepped aside. Darius stood behind him. My heart sank to my toes. He already came to our rescue once in the First Circle. Now he was here in the Second Circle. What would happen to him this time? How would he be punished? I pressed cold shaking fingertips to my lips.

"Darius, no."

He ignored me and hefted Kincade over his shoulder as though he weighed nothing. He gave me a cursory glance as he moved past to the open cell door. Ophelia fell in step behind him. Edward took my arm again and tugged me along.

I stumbled behind him. An odd object on the floor caught my eye. I bent to pick up the lock of hair in a blue ribbon. Recognition punched me in the gut. I crushed it in my fist before shoving it in my pocket. My uncle saw but didn't question. Likely he already knew what it was.

"Come, Anna."

"Why? Why did you bring Darius? You *know* he'll be punished for coming here."

"He wanted to come. I couldn't stop him."

The cell door was busted as though someone used a battering ram. I wondered if that was my uncle or Darius. We were in the corridor with the flickering torches, splashing yellow-gold-red light along the walls and floor.

"Wait here. I will return," Darius said.

"No—" He disappeared before I finished telling him not to come back. I reeled on my uncle. "You should have talked him out of it."

"Anna, he's too far gone. Nothing short of a miracle can save him."

"What about Decker?" I demanded.

"He still can't teleport. After you contacted me, I started looking for you. I contacted everyone I could trying to find you. Darius said he knew where you were. He said you were in danger," Edward said. "You and the others. He told me he could get you out."

Darius popped back in, cutting off my response. Edward turned to him and gave a nod to Ophelia. "Take her next."

The girl gawked at him, her lashes fluttering as her cheeks flushed pink. He either didn't notice or ignored her reaction as he wrapped his arms around her and disappeared.

"What is this trip to the Second Circle going to do to him?" I asked.

"I cannot say. You must believe me when I tell you I tried hard to talk him out of it. He wouldn't listen. He insisted on coming after you."

My stomach twisted in a knot. I thought I might be sick. Darius returned, though, and I pulled myself together, suppressing my emotions.

"Anna next," Edward said. "I'll wait here until you return."

Darius nodded. I didn't object though I wanted to. The warrior angel wrapped his arms around me. I rested my cheek against his chest as we poofed away. It always made me sick to travel like that and this time was no exception. We landed in the library of my uncle's manor a second later.

Overcome with dizziness, I grasped the edge of his desk to steady myself and keep from passing out. The warrior angel put his hand on my shoulder to steady me.

"Darius, why did you come?"

"You know why."

I looked up at him. More black and gray feathers took over his once snowy white ones. "No."

He searched for the words before he finally answered.

"Since the trip to the First Circle, I gained certain abilities. One of them is the ability to track you. Edward came to me and asked for help finding you." I started to respond, but he placed a finger over my lips to silence me. "Anna, before I return for your uncle, there is something I must return to you. That's why I brought you here away from the others."

I swallowed hard. "The horn?"

He nodded. He produced it out of thin air, much like when my uncle produced his flaming sword. He ran a hand over the shiny surface in reverence, gazing down at it for the last time.

"It means much you entrusted me with it. However, I can no longer be trusted." He lifted his gaze to mine. "Whatever is happening to me will accelerate now. But I'm glad I helped you one last time."

All because he entered the Second Circle. Because he entered Hell. Because of me.

"Darius..." Tears clouded my vision. I blinked them away. He extended the horn. I slipped it out of his grasp and clutched it to my chest. "Thank you for coming for me."

"Your guardian is safe now but Azriel controls much of his soul."

"How do I get it back?" I asked.

He shook his head. "You don't."

I refused to believe that as I refused to believe Darius could not be healed. I would find a way for both him and Kincade.

"I will retrieve your uncle. We will not meet again." He kissed my forehead, then whispered, "Farewell, Anna."

He was gone before I could tell him good-bye.

Still clutching the horn, I sprinted out of the library and up the stairs to find Kincade. My legs burned by the time I reached the floor with the bedrooms. Ophelia loitered outside one of the rooms.

"There you are. He's in here."

She ushered me inside the guest room. Decker hovered at the foot of the bed while a strange man stood next to Kincade, his hand on his heart, eyes closed.

"Who the hell is that?" I demanded.

"One of our healers," Decker said. "This is Samuel."

"How did he get here so fast?"

"He arrived before Darius retrieved you," he replied.

Hope soared through me. Kincade's face was far too pale and had a sickly pallor to it. I hoped this healer was able to help him. Samuel opened his eyes and removed his hand. He looked at the three of us and slowly shook his head.

"What does that mean?" I demanded.

"He's not going to make it," Decker clarified.

Those hot tears were back and burning the back of my throat, my eyes. "No. He has to live. You have to help him." My hysteria started to bubble up.

"Nothing can be done, Keeper. Kincade is trying to fight back, but he's not strong enough. Too much of his soul was taken. It is inevitable he will succumb," Samuel said.

I clutched the horn tighter in my arms. I finally figured out Kincade was a dream walker and possibly my guardian and now he was dying.

Decker put a hand on my shoulder and pushed me out of the room into the hallway. Ophelia followed. If I was holding anything but the Horn of Gabriel, I'd have thrown it out of shear frustration.

My uncle trudged up the stairs and halted at the end of the landing. Our eyes met, mine full of accusations and anger. His full of empathy and regret.

"Come, Ophelia. Let's tend your wound." Decker led her back inside the room and closed the door.

Wise move. They didn't need to be a witness to me throwing a fit. I stomped down the hallway and halted in front of my uncle.

"He's going to die."

"I am sorry, Anna."

I wanted to say a lot of things, but didn't. *Why didn't you let me give Azriel the spear? How could you let him die? This is all your fault. I could have saved him.*

Maybe it was my fault. Maybe it was no one's fault. Maybe this was the way things were supposed to be. I didn't know anymore. It didn't change the fact Kincade was going to die. I wanted to yell, scream, fling myself to the floor and pound it with my fists.

But I didn't. Instead, I stood there holding the horn trying not shake with rage.

"Darius gave you back the horn, I see."

"He did. He doesn't think he can be trusted." All the more reason to find a way to reverse whatever was happening to him. "Will it be safe here from Azriel?"

He was silent a moment before he finally nodded. "Yes. Come with me."

Edward waved for me to follow him down the stairs to his library. Once inside, he closed the door and locked it. He moved to the far wall of shelves behind the desk and stood there, peering at the books. He ran his finger down the aged spines of several first edition volumes before pausing and slipping one out of its spot. The shelf hissed, clicked and came open.

He pulled the shelf aside to reveal a steel door with a massive lock on it. He turned a dial, spun the wheel and gave it a tug and pulled open the vault door.

I stared, dumbfounded, at the opening.

All the years I lived in this manor I had no idea the vault was there.

He motioned for me to enter. Hesitant, I finally moved to it and stepped inside the vault. The huge room felt like stepping into a bank vault. It was sterile, not a speck of dust anywhere. In the center of the room was a small conference table and eight leather chairs. On the left side of the room, shelves that contained ancient artifacts. On the right side of the room, more shelves with all kinds of artwork that included oil paintings, sculptures, more first edition books.

One particular painting caught my eye. Fourteen people on a boat on a stormy sea. I stared at it a long moment, wondering where I'd seen it before.

I was aware my uncle was rolling in the dough but I had no idea the endless depths of his wealth. The man had more collectible art in one place than the Louvre, more collectible books than the Library of Congress, more holy artifacts than the Vatican. Nails from the Holy Cross. A box labeled the Shroud of Turin. Another boxed identified as the Crown of Thorns. I wanted to stop and examine every single one of them, but my uncle had other plans.

"The horn will be safe in here." He motioned toward an empty shelf ready to be the new horn's new home. "The stainless-steel walls are lead-lined."

Edward picked up a box lined with a garnet velvet material that was custom made for the horn. He opened it, held it out to me.

"Where did you get that?" I asked.

"I had it made."

Of course, he did.

I placed the horn inside the box. He closed it. I watched him walk to the side of the room with all the art. There was one empty shelf as though he cleared it in preparation for the

Holy Relics. I scanned the room but didn't spot the Spear of Destiny anywhere.

"You were prepared," I said.

"I'll share the combination with you on the condition you keep the relics here. That includes the Spear of Destiny." He gave me a pointed look, almost as though he read my mind. "Can you do that?"

I gritted my teeth, thinking of Kincade upstairs dying because I couldn't give Azriel the real Spear of Destiny. Maybe my uncle was right. Maybe I shouldn't give him the spear.

But if it'd save Kincade's life...

Finally, I nodded agreement.

He pulled the spear out of one of the pockets on his cargo pants. It was still wrapped in the gauzy white material of Ophelia's scarf.

"I switched the spear without telling you," he said as he placed it on the shelf next to the box with the horn. "But I had to protect the relic."

"I understand," I said, my voice weak.

"Do you?"

I bit my lip. Nodded. I understood why he did it. I did. But I was frustrated at the hopeless situation.

"Good. I'm glad, Anna. You must take your job as Keeper of the Holy Relics seriously." He headed for the door of the vault.

I huffed and followed him out.

"I do take it seriously." Now more than ever. Now because Kincade's life was hanging by a thread.

Edward locked the vault behind us and closed the shelf, hiding it. He started for the door in the library but I still had a couple of bones to pick with him.

"We need to talk about Marcus, uncle."

That halted him in his tracks. He turned back to me, his brows knit with question. "I thought we put that subject to rest."

"No, the subject is not at rest. There's more to the story you never told me. But you're going to tell me today. Right now."

His face turned impassive. It was that look he gave me when he didn't want to talk about a particular subject. "What am I supposed to tell you?"

"For starters, why my memories were concealed." I folded my arms over my chest, defensive.

"Don't be ridiculous." He waved a hand of dismissal and started for the door.

"I know the truth," I called after him. He stopped but didn't turn around. "Azriel used his demon magic to help me remember."

He turned to me. His face drained of color. "What did he do to you, Anna?"

"He tried to rape me. If it hadn't been for Kincade, he would have. But it was nothing compared to what he did to my mind." My words hitched at the end, my throat clotting with tears. I wasn't ready to talk about it with anyone, much less my uncle.

He clenched a fist, his knuckles leeching of color. "Perhaps we should sit. You must tell me everything. I'll ring for tea."

"I don't want bloody tea! I want answers, dammit."

For the first time, defeat creased Edward's features. He took a deep breath, exhaled and moved to the seating area and sat. He motioned for me to do the same. It took a lot of courage to sit across from him in the same chair I occupied when I first returned, when I'd been called to become the

Keeper of the Holy Relics. While I wanted to know the truth, I was terrified of it as well.

"Tell me what you know," he said.

"Marcus was Azriel in disguise."

He swallowed hard, then stood and walked to the wet bar. He poured two whiskies and returned, handing one to me. I downed it before he sat again. He watched me with one dark brow lifted in awe, then did the same. He returned to the wet bar, grabbed the decanter and refilled our glasses.

"So, it's true," I said.

"Yes." He lowered into the chair, placing the decanter on the table next to him. "I'm sorry you learned it that way. I should have told you."

I nodded. "Yes, you should have. The memory is still fuzzy. I need to know what truly happened to me."

He took a deep breath, nodded. "Back then, I wasn't aware of who—or what—Marcus was. Not at first. He came to me from a friend. A friend I no longer trust. I had no idea who he truly was until…" He paused, searching for the right words.

"Until what, uncle?"

"Sariel came for a visit."

He cut me a glance, as though waiting for me to react. When Sariel came to heal my blindness in Rio, it was obvious he and Edward were well acquainted. When I didn't react, he continued.

"He saw through Azriel's glamour and flew into a rage. When he found you together outside the stables, he went after Azriel. He tried to kill him, but you stopped him. Do you remember?"

I flushed hot as I turned my thoughts inward, piecing together what I recalled. The fog lifted and it came back to me in a flash. I recalled Sariel nearly killing Azriel and I, being a lovesick child, threw myself in between them. Begged the archangel not to kill the man I loved. Yes, I remembered what Sariel said to me that day.

Can you not see what he truly is, Anna? Do not look with your eyes, child. Look with your heart, with all your senses.

But my heart thought it was in love and my senses were muddied because, by then, Azriel had tattooed his demon magic into my skin. Sariel emitted a sound of frustration. He stepped behind me, put his hands on my shoulders and gave me a gentle shake.

Look, Anna. Look at him. See him for what he truly is.

I saw then and was horrified. I felt then as I did now. Sickened to the point I wanted to hurl. I managed to keep myself in check, though.

"Sariel banished him and placed protection over Walker Manor." I blinked, the clouds clearing as I focused on Edward.

"Yes. At that point, I hadn't told you about the prophecy or anything related to the Holy Relics. Sariel and I agreed it would be best to block your memories and suppress your abilities to dream walk. All you'd recall was I sent away the man you thought you loved."

And by doing so, taking the blame.

There was a space in time I didn't remember much about Marcus leaving and what had happened to him. All I recalled was being incredibly angry with Edward he drove him away. I resented him for it. It was why I left England and returned to America to make my own way.

"Azriel was determined to turn you against me, against the prophecy. He would have succeeded, too, had Sariel not intervened." He took a swig from his glass, refilled it. "Azriel damaged you, though. He marked you. I tried hard to protect you but I failed you, Anna."

I swallowed hard as I ran my fingertip around the rim of the glass. "No, uncle."

I wondered what would have happened had I succumbed to Azriel's charms, had I allowed him to take my innocence. I'd been lucky when Sariel and my uncle intervened. I shuddered with revulsion and downed the drink, letting the burn of alcohol sear away the agony.

In a way, my uncle and I failed each other. I failed him when I refused to return home and let him train me. He failed me when he couldn't protect me from Azriel/Marcus. I wondered, though, if he *could have* protected me from him. I recalled being completely enamored and head over heels in love with Marcus. I never felt that way with Ben.

"You didn't fail me," I said at last, my voice thick with tears. "I failed myself."

We gazed at each other with silent understanding. He almost smiled. Relief sputtered through me. The war between us was over and done. We would never fight about this particular subject again and for that I was glad. It was as though a great albatross was removed from around my neck.

"I wanted you to stay to help you," Edward said.

"But I didn't." He was right. I was a petulant child.

"No. I let you go. I learned my lesson with your mother." He heaved a sigh. "In hindsight, it might have been the best thing for you. Azriel could no longer find you until you dream walked the wrong person."

But Emma wasn't the wrong person. She was my friend.

"You said Sariel suppressed my ability to dream walk. If that's true, why was I able to do it with Emma that day?"

"Perhaps the suppression he placed on you ended. Or perhaps your need to help that woman superseded it and you broke through of your own accord."

I thought of Emma, the first patient I dream walked in a long while back in Dallas. That's when I first met Azriel. That one little act was the catalyst setting everything into motion. I wondered if I never dream walked her or anyone else, would I be on this journey? Would Ben still be alive? Would I still live in Dallas working at the hospital as a phlebotomy tech?

Did it matter? I couldn't change the past. I'd drive myself crazy trying to figure it all out.

I downed the whisky. Likewise, Edward emptied his glass. It was therapeutic getting drunk with him. Like we were finally one-hundred-percent on the same side.

"I should have told you sooner," he said.

"No, uncle. Things happen for a reason, I think."

We lapsed into silence and continued to drink whisky. I would never doubt my uncle again. He truly did have my best interests at heart. He was someone I trusted and counted on no matter what. I was a total shit to him and he still helped me, guided me, taught me.

I would never forget.

Chapter 25

BEFORE WE BROKE FOR THE NIGHT, a little drunker than I intended, Edward decided to trust me with the combination for the vault. I staggered up the stairs, halting at Kincade's room to look in on him. Decker had propped himself in a chair near the bed. His head leaned back on the wall as he dozed. Kincade was still unconscious, still had shallow breathing, still had that sickly pallor to his skin, still had bruising on his face and jaw.

The healer had wrapped his raw wrists in gauze. I recalled seeing the skin flayed and torn and was glad they had given him some medical attention. Somewhere along the way he'd lost his shirt. The blankets were tucked under his arms. A dusting of dark hair sprinkled across his broad muscled chest.

I thought about everything that had happened between us. From the first day we met to the way he held my face in his hands in the dream and told me to let him go. There was a flurry of activity deep in my gut. I didn't want to let him go, damn it.

It hurt me to see him like that. It hurt me to know I had the power to save what was left of his soul. I leaned against the doorframe and watched him sleep, thinking of the combination of the vault and knowing the spear lay within reach.

I'll share the combination with you on the condition that you keep the relics here. That includes the Spear of Destiny. Can you do that?

Technically, I hadn't promised I'd keep the Spear of Destiny in the vault. Had I? I never verbalized it. All I did was nod my head. It would be so easy to skip downstairs, open the vault, take the spear and give it to Azriel in exchange for Kincade's soul. If I did that, though, I risked my uncle's wrath not to mention the fact I betrayed his trust.

But I couldn't let Kincade die, either.

I straightened in the doorway, smoothed my hands down the front of my pants and whispered, "Fuck it."

I hurried down the stairs, keeping my steps as light as possible. All the lights were off as everyone in the household had finally gone to bed except me. I wasn't going to sleep anyway. Not with my adrenaline running high and my nerves on red alert. I pulled open the door to the library. Our dirty glasses were still on the table along with the empty decanter. Guilt swept through me before I quickly brushed it away.

I was doing this. I had to.

With my pulse pounding a wicked tattoo in my throat, I made my way to the shelf, pulled the specified volume to open the secret door and pushed it wide. I stared at the vault door, getting the nerve up to open the door.

As I reached for the combination lock, my hand shook. I clenched my fist to stop the shaking long enough to open the lock. A second later, the door opened and I stood there looking at the artifacts my uncle had managed to collect over the years. The Spear of Destiny rested on the shelf still wrapped in Ophelia's scarf next to the box with the Horn of Gabriel.

I didn't question my actions when I rushed into the room, snatched the spear from the shelf and tucked it into the waistband of my pants. I hurried out of the vault, closed it, locked it, closed the hidden door.

And stood in the dark with my heart hammering in my chest, my breathing labored as it see-sawed in and out.

"I'm sorry, uncle. But I have to."

I had no idea how I was going to get Azriel's attention. After our last few encounters, I doubted he'd come when I called.

This was my Hail Mary pass. If this desperate attempt didn't work, then the clock had run out and the game was over.

I went to the gardens outside where Edward, Decker and I had discussed saving Kincade not so long ago. Where we'd planned our trip to Antarctica. Moonlight splashed over the flagstone walkway and bathed the plants in that blue-white glow. It was a cool evening. The wind rustled my hair and made goosebumps spring along my naked arms.

"Are you sure you want to do this, Anna?"

The familiar voice floated through the air but I didn't immediately recognize who it was. Standing next to one of the antique rosebushes was the angel. As he moved near, I recognized Sariel.

"I can't let him die," I said.

"It's your choice, of course, but Edward is right. Giving Azriel the spear is dangerous."

"Azriel wants it. I want Kincade alive," I countered.

"You're right, *chérie*. I do want it."

Behind me, Azriel had arrived. I spun to face him. He sat at the small café table with his feet propped up on the top. He looked the same as always—dark and lethal.

"How romantic you wish to save the *gardien's* life with an act that will destroy what little trust you have with your uncle." He sounded smug.

I tamped down the anger that wanted to punch him in the face and tugged the spear out of my waistband. I held it in my palm. "I will hand it over on two conditions."

His eyes narrowed. "I restore your lover's soul, I presume, is one of them. Yes?"

"Yes, and you give me back Ophelia's sword."

His face remained impassive at my request. "No."

"Then no deal."

He stared at me with such hate filled eyes, I wanted to cower. Sariel put his hand in the middle of my back between my shoulder blades as if to bolster me and give me the confidence I needed. I lifted my chin a little higher.

"Those are the conditions for possession of the spear. The girl's sword and Kincade's life," I said.

Azriel dropped his feet and unfolded his tall, muscular body from the table. He strolled toward me as if he had all the time in the world. Sariel moved to stand next to me, as though to protect me. His presence gave me comfort. The fallen angel gave the archangel a look of disdain.

"Sariel, I thought never to see you again."

"Nor I you," Sariel said. "I'm here for Anna. If you try to harm her, I will not hesitate to kill you."

Azriel blinked. I'd never seen him look so taken aback by such a casual threat. He usually took it all in stride. With his gaze still on Sariel, he held out his hand.

"Give me the spear and I will be on my way."

I closed my hand around the material-wrapped spear, hesitating. I shouldn't do this, but I had to. For him. For Kincade. "The sword and Kincade's soul first and it's all yours."

He glowered. "You swear you will hand it to me if I do as you wish?"

"I swear. No backsies."

He sighed and produced the Ophelia's shimmering sword out of thin air. He held it out to me. I grasped the pommel and took it from him. The thing was heavier than I expected.

"To restore his soul, I will need to be with him."

I glanced up at Sariel with the unspoken question. He nodded confirmation.

"Fine, let's go," I said.

We trudged back inside the manor, up the stairs. I paused at Ophelia's room and leaned the sword against the wall next to her door, then moved on to Kincade's room. I pushed open the door and led them both inside. Decker woke as the door banged open and jumped to his feet, immediately on the defensive the second he laid eyes on Azriel.

"What is he doing here?"

"I brought him to heal Kincade," I said.

Decker's eyes narrowed at Azriel, then at me. He noticed the spear in my hand. Surprise flickered over his face. He opened his mouth to respond when I gave a sharp shake of my head.

"Stand aside, Watcher, if you wish for me to save the *gardien*."

They had a silent standoff until finally Decker moved away from the side of the bed giving Azriel access to Kincade. The fallen angel moved to his side, looking down at him for a quiet moment before he placed his hands on his chest. He closed his eyes. Almost immediately his hands lit up in a blue glow as he transferred what he had of Kincade's soul back into his body. Kincade sucked in a sharp breath, his eyes opening, searching the room, falling on me for several long seconds and closing again. Azriel removed his hands and turned to me.

"Now, the spear," he said.

I didn't hesitate when I handed it to him. He unwound the scarf, careful to keep the material between his hand and the spear. "This better not be a trick as before."

"No trick. This is the real deal," I said.

He examined it closely. Satisfied, he wrapped it up again. He gave me a farewell nod and disappeared.

It was done.

"You idiot," Decker said through clenched teeth. "Why did you give him the relic?"

"Anna did what she felt she had to," Sariel said before I could reply.

"And doomed us all," Decker said. "Edward will not be pleased."

"Go ahead and tell him. I don't care," I snapped. "He'll find out sooner or later anyway."

I never took my eyes off Kincade. His breathing had returned to normal and color was finally coming back into his face. Azriel had done what he promised. He'd returned his soul. I did what I promised. I gave him the spear.

Decker stomped out past me. His heavy footsteps thumped on each step as he went down the stairs.

"Did I do the right thing?" It was a question I didn't expect an answer to but the archangel answered anyway.

"You made a decision to save his life. You followed through with it and you did the what you knew to do." He placed a hand on my shoulder. "It was a difficult decision."

"Decker is right, though. Edward may never speak to me again when he finds out what I did."

"It was a risk you took. Now, you will have to face the consequences."

I nodded understanding. I would prepare myself for Edward's wrath.

"Why does Azriel call him *gardien*? Is he my guardian angel?" I looked up at Sariel. He was a head taller than me and I had to tilt my head back to look at him. "Do you know?"

He glanced from me to Kincade, a contemplative look on his face. "I don't believe it was intended for him to be your guardian, but he has made it his mission to become that. And that decision has consequences, too."

I understood it meant he would be removed from his group in the Brotherhood of Watchers. I didn't know much more than that but maybe Kincade would share the rest of the story with me someday. Maybe he would tell me why he chose me.

I couldn't decide how I felt about that.

"I must take my leave of you, Anna." He squeezed my shoulder before releasing it and turning toward the door.

"Thank you, Sariel, for coming to protect me from Azriel."

He paused in the doorway. "There are people who want you to succeed, Anna. You have the strength and the gifts to do so. Don't let anyone stand in your way."

My brows drew together in question. I had no idea what that meant. He disappeared before I had a chance to ask him.

Such was the way with these angels, Fallen and otherwise. They poofed in and out at will.

From the bed, Kincade emitted a soft groan. I went to his bedside, pulled the chair closer and sat and waited. He took a deep breath and finally opened his eyes. He blinked several times as our eyes met. My heart did this funny twitter in my chest and my stomach did a weird swooping thing. He was silent which was terrifying. His booming voice didn't burst through my mind berating me for handing the spear to Azriel and that scared me, too.

"Hi," I said finally.

He blinked but still said nothing. Had he lost his powers of speech? Was he super pissed at me for doing what I did? Did he know what I did for his soul? He must because that was my intention all along in the Second Circle. He was against it then. He would be against it now.

I bit my lip and shifted in the chair, uncomfortable under his scrutiny.

"Okay, well, are you going to say something or what?"

He didn't look away but he didn't respond either which was maddening.

"I did what I had to do. I'm not proud of it but…" I pressed my lips together in a thin line to stop blabbing.

"You found a way. Like you said." His voice was gruff, like he woke up from a long nap.

I flushed. I said a lot in that moment of desperation when we were in each other's minds. I didn't want to admit how bereft the thought of losing him left me, though I never appreciated it to begin with. He was an annoyance that followed me everywhere. We'd been at odds since the moment we met.

"I did." I nodded. "I'm sure my uncle will be unhappy about that."

"You gave up the spear?"

"Yes."

"For me."

"Yes."

He focused his gaze on an object across the room. "You shouldn't have done that."

No, I shouldn't have. Sariel was right. I would have to live with whatever consequences befell me now. And I was okay with that. I'd done what I set out to do. I'd saved Kincade from a fate as a Fallen high lord. It was more than I could do for Darius. It was more than I could do for Ben who was now in demon form.

He turned his head to look at me once more. "I'm glad you did."

He said it so softly, I almost missed it. Blood drained from my head in a whoosh, leaving me lightheaded and dizzy. Was that almost a thank you? I couldn't fathom that from him. This man who had saved my ass from demons and from Azriel. Tears pricked the backs of my eyes and I swallowed hard to keep them at bay. I had to escape this room. Flee from the way Kincade peered at me with those intense green-gold eyes. I couldn't breathe. I couldn't think. I shot to my feet.

"Well, I should let you get some rest."

I hurried to the door, my feet silent on the rug as I made my hasty retreat.

"Anna..." I paused, glancing at him over my shoulder. "See you later?"

Now I knew I was going to cry. I nodded and fled.

Chapter 26

I CLOSED HIS DOOR behind me and leaned against it. Silence descended in the dead of night. The only sound was the giant grandfather clock at the end of the stairs with a quiet tick-tock and occasional bong signaling the top of the hour or the half hour.

I wondered what Azriel would do with the spear now that he had it. Since I touched it, I had the power to find out.

With heavy steps, I trudged to my room at the end of the hall. As I headed to the bathroom, I stripped off my shirt. A part of me didn't want to believe the tattoo was there though I knew, without a doubt, it was. Still, I wanted to see it again. To remind myself it was there and it was part of me. I turned my back to the mirror and peered over my shoulder. Sure enough. On my left shoulder was the small blue butterfly inked with demon magic into my skin.

If I was into symbolism, I'd note the butterfly represented freedom and transformation. Kinda ironic it was put there by a fallen angel.

With a huff, I pulled my shirt back on and staggered into the room. I flung myself on the bed. As I laid there staring up at the ceiling, I kicked off my shoes and thought of the spear. My eyes drifted closed. It took my tired mind a few minutes to tap into the ability to seek and find the relic but I found it still wrapped in Ophelia's scarf as Azriel carried it through the realms of Hell. The scenery went by in a flash, past those writhing in pain, past twisted, naked bodies in an orgy, past a putrid slush where a foul, icy rain poured as gluttons squirmed in the mire. Past all the circles until he reached the center of Hell to what appeared to be a tomb. Someone was hunched on the tomb. From my vantage point, it appeared to be a black blob.

Here he paused and held the spear in his outstretched palm. The black blob uncurled its body. Every bone in the spine straightened one by one under the leathery onyx skin. Six giant wings resembling a dragon's unfurled from his back. A breath shuddered out of me, turning immediately to smoke in the icy wind from the beast's wings.

As the beast cast his red eyes on Azriel, the fallen angel dropped to one knee, bowed his head yet still held the spear out to him.

"Lord Master, I've brought one of the relics you seek," Azriel said.

"Only one?" His dark voice reverberated throughout the chamber.

"One for now, Lord Master."

The beast eyed the spear but didn't take it from Azriel's hand. Instead, he asked, "What of the woman?"

"She has one other and knows where to find the remaining relics."

I pressed a hand against my mouth to keep the gasp from escaping.

"Did you succeed in bringing her into the fold?"

"No, Lord Master. Not yet. But there is still time."

The beast growled, a low guttural sound deep in its throat. "You fool. You couldn't break through the protection surrounding her, could you? Just as you couldn't break through the last time when she was but a girl. Now she grows stronger."

"I tried."

"And failed not once but twice."

"I will try again."

The beast was silent for a moment. "I will give you one last chance."

"As you wish, Lord Master."

The beast stepped down from his tomb. "Rise and look at me."

Azriel did as he was commanded.

"Take away the relic. It's useless to me until I have all five and the woman. I cannot use them without her. Bring all to me and you shall be rewarded."

"All I want is the woman and her powers."

I pressed my hand harder against my mouth to keep from crying out. I didn't want to alert either of them to my presence. I didn't know if they sensed me, but I didn't want to risk it.

"And you shall have her to do with as you please…after you bring her to me and she gives us what we want."

I pulled myself out of there. I didn't need or want to hear anymore. It sickened me. The beast, Lucifer, wanted me and all five relics. He wanted to use me and the relics to destroy mankind and become their king. *Our* king. An unholy king.

My stomach twisted in a tight knot as terror slashed through me. I had no idea the danger I was up against. Everyone kept warning me and I kept blowing them off. Now, I understood. The beast said Azriel couldn't break through "her protection." What did that mean?

I was an idiot. Handing over the spear to Azriel was a huge error in judgement. At least, though, he hadn't given it to Lucifer yet. Or, rather, Lucifer wasn't interested in the spear until he had all the remaining relics.

And me.

The gravity of the situation hit me hard and fast. I was running around as though none of this mattered but now I got it. I truly was the Keeper of the Holy Relics. What price would I have to pay for handing over the spear?

I didn't want to think about that now. Now, I needed to scrub away everything that had happened in the last hours.

I slid off the bed and stomped to the bathroom, shedding clothes as I went. I took a scorching hot shower, standing under the spray and scrubbing with soap until my skin was red and raw. No amount of washing would remove the remnants of Azriel in my mind or seeing him in Hell with Lucifer. Those images would forever be burned into my mind. I would have to live with them.

But I didn't have to let them control me. I was stronger than that. I was going to defeat the fallen angel bastard if it was the last thing I did.

I dressed as the sun came up and my stomach rumbled. I couldn't remember the last time I had a meal. If I went downstairs, I'd see my uncle. The thought twisted my gut but I'd have to face him eventually.

May as well get it over with.

I trudged down the stairs, preparing to face the firing squad. I resisted the impulse to stop and peek in on Kincade. I wasn't ready for that either. Idly, I wondered where Decker had ended up. If he left or if he was still wandering around the manor somewhere. And Ophelia. Where was she?

In the dining room, Edward was already sitting in his usual spot at the head of the table spreading orange jam on a piece of wheat toast and drinking coffee with the morning paper. He was dressed in a three-piece suit looking like someone out of a time and place that didn't exist anymore and it gave me pause. I felt wildly under-dressed in black cargo pants, black Henley and my pink combat boots. I halted in the doorway, afraid to take one more step, afraid he would pinpoint me with those cold blue eyes. I braced myself for the wrath.

"Good morning, Anna," he said without looking up. "Sleep well?"

I didn't move. The question was almost like he knew I didn't sleep at all. He folded the paper, running his finger down the crisp edge, and took a sip of coffee. He waved me to a nearby chair.

"Have a seat. Let's talk."

That didn't bode well. I fervently wished a black hole would open in the floor and swallow me whole. Since it didn't, I took the seat next to him. He poured coffee into the delicate china cup resting on the saucer in front of me. I took a deep breath.

"I have a confession," I blurted. I hadn't intended to tell him right away. No use in delaying the inevitable, though.

"I know." He sounded calm, cool. Not at all like the response I expected.

"You know?" I splashed cream in the cup, stirred until the black turned taupe.

He sipped his coffee, took a bite of toast, chewed thoughtfully. "There was no way I would be able to stop you from giving the spear to Azriel. You understand I had to try."

I met his cool blue gaze, understanding dawning. "You left the spear there on purpose, didn't you?"

"I dangled the carrot, yes. You took the bait. You are not so enshrouded in mystery as you might think, my dear."

I frowned. I wasn't trying to be mysterious. I was trying to save a life.

"You and Kincade are connected. I suspected before but now I know for sure."

"How can you be so sure?"

"He gave up his place in the Brotherhood of Watchers for you. You gave up the spear for him."

I stared at him, wide-eyed and fighting those damn tears again. When he put it that way, it sounded like we'd both made a sacrifice for each other. It sounded like we were more than allies or friends. I didn't understand what motivated me to do it anymore than I understood what motivated Kincade to give up his place in the Watchers.

Icy pinpricks danced down the back of my neck and spine. What the hell were we doing with each other?

"You both made a conscious decision," he continued. "I find that admirable."

My hand shook as I reached for the cup and sipped, trying to hide my quivering lip. The hot coffee burned my tongue and the back of my throat. My uncle kept talking.

"Anna, you had a guardian angel once, but I believe Azriel killed her when you were a child."

"Her?" My voice cracked.

He smiled. "Guardian angels can be male or female." He placed his cup back in the saucer. "When I found you in America at last and brought you here, I made sure you were well protected."

My brows knit. "How?"

"I have ways."

Always cagey, this one.

"My protection, though, was only good for so long." He gave me a pointed look. The tattoo on my shoulder tingled.

"Because Azriel marked me," I said, not really wanting to voice the thing.

He nodded. "Kincade took it upon himself to become your new guardian. That's why I allowed you to take the spear to Azriel. You cannot do this alone. And I cannot help you as much I want. I have duties here."

"Duties?"

I was only able to form one-word responses. My uncle's verbosity this morning stunned me out of my shoes.

"Yes, duties befitting someone with the title of the 13th Baron of Cannington." He gave me a lopsided grin that was totally out of character.

I almost snorted. When I moved here as a nosy thirteen-year-old girl, I learned the truth about Edward of his royal lineage. I never really gave it much thought. But, of course, his lineage was the reason why he had unlimited wealth. That and maybe he was really good at the stock market.

I assumed part of his duties were to attend Parliament as a member of the House of Lords, but I honestly didn't have a clue. He'd never been forthright with me about anything related to him. He kept information locked up tight in that brain of his which was an impregnable vault. No one was as good at keeping secrets as Edward. He shared when he deemed it important.

"Since I have no children, and since the barony can be inherited by the female line, I intend to make you my heir."

I stared at him as though he had grown a second head.

"Huh?" This was all too much. I came downstairs expecting him to skewer me for giving Azriel the Spear of Destiny and here my uncle tells me I was heir. What the actual fuck was happening?

"I have business to attend to in London. You'll want to stay here, naturally, to keep an eye on Kincade. I'll be gone a few days, so I leave you in charge."

I stared at him as the blood whooshed out of my head. Tiny pinpricks danced in my vision. I didn't understand any of this. No, that wasn't true. I *understood* it but I had a difficult time comprehending it.

"So...you're not mad about the spear?" It was the only question I managed to come up with and actually voice. I had many others.

"On the contrary. You did what I expected. As I recall, we discussed this previously. I told you if it came to that, we'd find a way to take it back. And we will. Or, you will, rather." He dabbed the corners of his mouth with his napkin, then placed it on the table beside his plate. "Now, if you'll excuse me, I need to prepare for my trip."

As he walked by, he kissed me on the top of the head like a father would his daughter.

I watched him leave wondering what was in the whisky last night and if he'd lost his mind. Or maybe I'd fallen into the Twilight Zone sometime during the night when I touched the spear while it was in Azriel's presence. Whatever happened, it was freaky.

I hadn't told him about what I discovered about Azriel and Lucifer. Mostly, I shoved it to the back of my mind because it was too terrifying to think about. I stared at the coffee in the cup wondering what I was supposed to do next when Ophelia bounced into the dining room. She had a jovial spring in her step.

"Anna! How did you do it?"

I blinked to clear my head. "Do what?"

"You got my sword back. How?"

"I asked Azriel and he gave it to me."

A look of disbelief crossed her face as she plopped down across from me and poured a cup of coffee. "Well, thank you. I'm glad to have it back." She paused, her brows knitting with concern. "You okay, Anna? You look shell shocked."

I was shell shocked. Like Edward dropped a bomb on me and skipped out as though there was nothing awry.

"I have no idea." Because I truly didn't.

I took a sip of coffee and managed to focus on the platter in the center of the table heaped with bacon and sausage. My stomach rumbled, letting me know the bacon and sausage needed to be on my plate. I reached for it.

"How's Kincade?" Her voice was tentative, as though she was scared to ask.

"Better."

"Better? I thought…" Her voice trailed off.

We reached for the same piece of bacon and our eyes met. Hers full of question and confusion. I swallowed.

"I did what I had to do to save him," I said. "He will recover."

"Oh." She dropped the bacon and reached for her cup. "I see."

Understanding was written all over her face. We didn't discuss it further. Her response indicated to me she likely knew what I did. Since she didn't have a stake in the matter, likely she didn't have an opinion. Or maybe she didn't want to voice her opinion. Either way, it didn't matter. It was done and there was no going back.

"Where's Decker?" I asked.

She shrugged. "The last time I saw him he was with Kincade."

He stomped out last night. I thought about his motivations, though. At first it was like he wanted me to save Kincade from Azriel and, somewhere along the way, he changed his mind. Maybe he knew something I didn't. Maybe Kincade conveyed to him his decision to leave the Watchers and become my official guardian.

More questions. No answers.

Such was the way of things in my life.

"I hope you don't mind me staying here," she said with a mouthful of bacon. "I've lost my task force so I need a new purpose."

I peered at her from across the table. Yes, that was true. Kincade left the Watchers and that was mostly my fault. Why shouldn't she stay here?

"Ophelia, you're welcome here for as long as you want."

She smiled. "I'm glad you said that. Because I want in."

"In what?"

"In on a piece of the action. You're the Keeper of the Holy Relics. I'm out of job and I need one. What do you say?"

I considered. She could fight. She could also kill the Fallen with her shimmering sword. Likely she'd be a good asset. But I wondered…if she had the sword and she was on a task force with Kincade, did that make her…a Watcher? My eyes narrowed.

"Who are you?" I asked.

She flushed. "I thought that was obvious."

"If you were on a task force with Kincade, are you part of the Watchers?"

"No." She shook her head. "I'm human like you. Li Mei gave me the sword fair and square. When the Watchers got wind of what I could do with it, they came to me and asked me to help hunt the Fallen."

I couldn't help my inherent mistrust of others after everything I'd been through. I wished Kincade was there so he could confirm her story. Not that I thought she was lying because what did she have to gain?

"All right. You're in."

She grinned and clapped her hands. "This is so exciting!"

"Don't get overly excited yet. I don't have my next move planned, yet."

"You go after the next relic," she said. "When do we start?"

"It's not that easy."

"Why not? Don't you know where to look?"

That was the real trick, wasn't it? The truth was, no, I didn't because I hadn't received one of those mysterious postcards with the name of a city. Hopefully one would magically appear sooner rather than later.

"Not yet but I will." I pushed back from the table. "There's a workout room in one of the buildings on the north end of the estate if you're interested. I'm sure the trainers, Gilli and Gideon, will be happy to kick your ass like they did mine. I'm going to check on Kincade."

I left the dining room and headed back up the stairs past the gallery of paintings where I paused to admire the one of my mother. I wondered where the woman who called herself Natasha was now. I hadn't seen her since leaving the tunnels under the church when she bid me farewell and disappeared. As I peered up at the portrait, I was convinced her true self was buried deep in in her Natasha personage.

"You favor her."

Kincade's deep rumbling voice startled me and I jumped. I pressed a hand against my racing heart. Why did people insist on sneaking up on me?

"You scared me."

He stood at the end of the hallway barefoot wearing blue pajama pants and a blanket from his bed wrapped around his shoulders showing off his muscled chest with a dusting of dark hair. His wrists were bandaged. A wicked silvery scar went down the left side of his chest almost to his navel. I hadn't noticed before. I wondered how he got it. His hair was disheveled and he had that just-woke-up rumpled, sexy look about him. Green-gold eyes scrutinized me in a way that made me shift from one foot to the other. The bruising on his face had faded and he was looking more like himself.

More like the detective with the criminal good looks when we first met and less like a punching bag.

Swift heat pumped through me. My mouth went bone dry. I remembered the way his hands cupped my face, his thumb grazing my cheekbone, as he told me to let him go. His palms were soft and warm against my face. I wondered if they truly felt that way or if it was merely a figment of the dream walk we shared. I forced my gaze away from him and back to the portrait of my mother.

"My mother…she's alive."

He moved to stand next to me, his body heat radiating over me. I wanted to close my eyes and bask in its glory, but I forced myself to remain neutral.

"Are you certain?" He stood so incredibly close to me when he spoke, his deep voice rumbled through me.

I nodded. "She was in Antarctica." I didn't elaborate.

Silence filled in between us. I was aware he had questions about the fake spear, Antarctica and my mother. I wanted to tell him everything that happened since he was captured by Azriel in the limo, but now wasn't the right time for that.

"I thought she died when you were born."

"I thought that, too, once." I heaved a sigh. "It's a long story."

"Maybe you'll tell me that story. When you're ready."

I appreciated how he didn't want to push me into talking about it. I had so many close calls with death and evil and general shit, I wouldn't know where to begin. In some ways, it seemed as through an eternity had passed since that ill-fated limo ride. The reality was only a few weeks had gone by.

"I have to find her, Kincade."

He didn't say anything for a long, quiet moment. Finally, he nodded. "I'll help you find her."

The way he said it twisted my gut into a tight knot. When was he going to come right out and tell me what he was to me? Or would he ever tell me? Was I supposed to acknowledge it or not? Or was I supposed to pretend we were situation normal and nothing had changed between us?

A hell of a lot had changed. I was no longer the same person I was back in Dallas. Neither was he for that matter. He'd nearly died at the hands of a Fallen. I'd nearly been raped at the hands of a Fallen in front of him. I hated what we both went through.

At any rate, I was glad we were going to fight this fight together. It gave me comfort he had my back. And when I was ready to talk about all the other shit, I'd tell him about my mother nearly killing me with her mind, and Azriel and Lucifer, too.

Until then, it was okay by me to stand there together in mutual silence and look at the portrait of my mother.

"Should you be out of bed?" I tried hard not to look at him again.

"No."

I sensed he wanted to say more, like an innuendo inviting me to hang out with him there. He didn't.

"Why are you?"

"I sensed you were near."

"You did?"

My stomach fluttered. Despite my best effort not to, I met his gaze. The air crackled between us with a fiery electricity I never experienced before. My pulse did double-time, drumming through me and sending heat to my cheeks. I didn't want to feel that way with Kincade. It shook me to the core so much I took a step back away from him.

"I did."

He took a step toward me, closing the gap between us. Like before, his body heat radiated over me and I had a sudden thought he was going to kiss me.

Like for real this time.

My mouth went dry. Did I *want* him to kiss me? He breathed in deeply, closing his eyes as though he inhaled something truly decadent. When he opened them, his pupils dilated to wide dark circles.

"You smell like honey."

I swallowed hard as the blood rushed out of my head in an abrupt *whoosh* making little pinpricks of light dance in my vision. Azriel told me that once. That he smelled my honey scent on Kincade.

"Do I?" My voice cracked on a raspy whisper.

We stared at each other for another heartbeat. A rush of heat went through me. He moved a step closer, crowding me, filling up the space around me. His gaze drifted from my eyes to my mouth and back again. I couldn't help but notice his pulse beating a rapid throb in his neck.

I was unprepared for this reaction in me, in him.

I licked my lips. His eyes landed there a moment more before meeting my gaze again. A breath shuddered out of me. While angels had a decidedly spicy scent, Kincade had a heady masculine scent. I detected exotic hints of patchouli and sandalwood.

He turned and padded back to his room, closing the door softly behind him. The spell was broken. Disappointment flooded me and I sagged against the nearby wall.

I blew out a breath as I found myself navigating uncharted waters where Kincade was concerned. And here I thought things were getting back to normal. Fat chance of that happening. I pushed off the wall and clutched my elbows as I headed back to my own room, thankfully on the other end of the hallway away from Kincade. As I closed the door behind me, I spotted a plain white envelope on the bed. My gut twisted into a tight knot.

I picked it up, opened the flap and pulled out a postcard of the ancient city of Acre, Israel. I flipped it over. On the back, written in that familiar blocky handwriting, were the words *Staff of Moses*.

I knew where I was headed next.

###

Find out how the dream walkers began in *Provenance, Dream Walker: Origins*

Dream Walker: Origins is an origin story to enrich your reading experience for Call of the Dark, Book 1 in the Dream Walker series. Find it at your favorite retailer.

In 1147 England, John of Yorkshire is ushered to his mother's side as she lay dying. When she tells him the secret she's harbored his entire life, it alters his destiny forever. He sails for the Holy Land on a quest to find his absent father. But the ship is pushed off course due to bad weather forcing them to port in Lisbon, Portugal. There, he reluctantly enters a fight to return the city to Christian rule only to discover something more divine awaits him.

Watch for more Dream Walker: Origins at
www.MichelleMiles.net

Next in the series:
Flame and Fury

Anna Walker's quest for the Holy Relics has been far from easy. Her ill-fated choices have turned things into unmitigated disaster. As she decides how to proceed, she is visited by the Prince of Greed who's come to collect his debt—destroy her uncle or hand over her soul.

But Anna refuses to do his bidding and instead turns her attention to the Staff of Moses, the fabled staff of miracles. Teaming up with Kincade, the two begin the search only to be hindered by an ancient sorcerer sent by Lucifer hellbent on thwarting their quest. When Anna is cursed by the darkest of forces to turn away from the Light and embrace evil, she is weakened by the black magic. Now Kincade must find a way to save her before it's too late for her and her soul.

Turn the page to get a sneak preview of the next book in the series!

Early December, Somerset, England

Christmastime at Walker Manor had never been as festive as it was with Ophelia Duffy in residence. She was like a Christmas fairy with her decorating skills and insisted decking the halls from top to bottom, inside and out. She somehow had convinced my stoic uncle to hire a crew to hang white outdoor lights around every inch of the manor giving it a festive luminosity I was sure they could see from the International Space Station.

Perhaps she was a Christmas elf in disguise who'd come to shower all us Scrooge's in Walker Manor with good tidings and cheer.

When I lived in Walker Manor as a teen, I couldn't recall a time where there was anything more than a modest decorated tree in the parlor. Nothing like what Ophelia had managed to accomplish in less than a week. Beribboned and lit garland wound down the banister. Mistletoe hung in the entryway to the library. I made a concerted effort to steer way clear of that in light of recent events with Kincade.

A Christmas tree was in the parlor and the library. The fireplace in the library was decked out in garland and lights and decorated with stocking hangers that spelled out the words JOY and NOEL. She'd even managed to make red and white stockings with all our names on them and hung them. I was baffled as I peered at them wondering how she managed to pull that off. There was one for Edward, Ophelia, me, Kincade, Gideon, Gilli. Even Piers, the butler, had a stocking.

Three miniature trees adorned with gold ribbon and twinkle lights dominated the entryway. The plain white tablecloth on the dining table had been replaced by a festive green and red plaid one. Gold placemats were positioned at every place setting. She'd even found a red and white sleigh and made it a centerpiece with a gorgeous winter-themed flower arrangement.

Christmas was everywhere.

I stood in the foyer at the foot of the stairs looking at all the trimmings wondering how she'd managed to sweet talk Edward into letting her decorate with reckless abandon when I spied the tiny bunch of mistletoe with a red bow hanging from the middle of the parlor doorway.

She was a sneaky one.

What was next? Carols, eggnog and gay apparel?

"Isn't it great?"

Ophelia bounded down the stairs and halted next to me to admire her handiwork. Her face beamed so bright with joy it was hard not to smile in return.

"It's nice."

"Nice?" She huffed. "That's all I get for my efforts? *Nice?*"

I peered at the Christmas tree in the parlor with its twinkle lights happily flashing. It was decorated in blue and silver complete with a blue velvet tree skirt.

"I don't know how you managed to talk Edward into paying for it all."

She blinked surprise. "Are you kidding? All the decorations were in the attic. I made the stockings." She beamed with pride.

Now it was my turn to blink surprise. "In the attic? Since when do you go nosing around the attic?"

"Since Gideon kicked my ass and I needed a break from training." She rolled her left shoulder. "I'm still sore."

I could relate. Gideon was the on-site trainer with his twin sister, Gilli. I steered clear of them since my return from Istanbul because I wasn't a glutton for punishment.

"Anyway, I found all these decorations in tubs up there. Someone took great care in organizing them and labeling everything. Someone who loved Christmas," she said.

"Huh."

That someone couldn't be Edward. I'd never seen most of this stuff. I moved here when I was thirteen and we had modest Christmas celebrations. Usually, it had been just me and Uncle Edward. Sometimes a few other family members would make an appearance but really, there was never a houseful of people and Christmas morning was low key.

There was no Christmas magic. No leaving cookies and waiting up for Santa because I knew he didn't exist from the time I was young.

Maybe that's what I needed. What *we* needed. A little Christmas magic and belief in Santa.

"Well, it's lovely. You did a great job." I looked at her, smiled.

"You really like it? Even the mistletoe?" She batted her long dark lashes and gave me a mischievous grin.

I narrowed my gaze. "What are you trying to pull here?"

She put on her best innocent look. "Oh, nothing. Just trying to help things along."

"What things?" My voice was laced with suspicion.

"You know. *Things*." She shrugged.

I knew what she was getting at and I didn't like it. She saw me and Kincade together far too much. She inferred the two of us were a thing. It was so far from the truth.

Kincade and I were...well, I didn't know what we were but we certainly weren't a *thing*.

It had taken me weeks to get the image of him with nothing but blue pajama pants and a blanket around his naked upper torso out of my head. That and the way he looked at me as though he wanted to devour me. I still hadn't quite put it out of my mind and sometimes the memory would hit me when I least expected it.

Like now.

Sure, I could admit Kincade was hot. Tall, broad-shouldered, overly muscled with green-gold eyes that were hard to resist. I only recently discovered he was part of the Brotherhood of Watchers who gave up his place to help me, something he hadn't admitted to me. I knew because my uncle told me. At any rate, he was so not the guy for me.

"I also understand someone has a birthday coming up."

My head snapped in her direction. "Who told you that?"

"A little birdie."

I scowled. I imagined that little birdie was named Edward. "I am not interested in celebrating my birthday."

"Why not?" She looked hurt.

"Because it's four days before Christmas and it doesn't matter anyway." I waved it away, trying to make sure she understood my birthday was nothing special.

"Anna, don't be that way. It's your special day."

I snorted. That's another thing. No one had ever made a fuss over me for my birthday since it was so close to Christmas. Oh, sure, Edward gave me the obligatory card, cake and present. I'd never had a party. I'd never gone to Chuck E Cheese. I never had a bounce castle in my backyard. Or friends. Or party favors. Or party hats.

And I was okay with that. It wasn't a big deal and I was making a valiant effort to forget I'd be turning twenty-nine. The last year had been hell enough. I didn't want to know what another year of life would bring me.

Likely more heartache and heartburn.

And hell.

"I don't need a special day." I could tell she wanted to say something else when I cut her off. "I'm going to work out. I think today is a good day for Gideon to give me a good ass-kicking."

"We're not done talking about this, Anna."

"Sure, we are." I flashed a grin as I walked away.

It infuriated her but I didn't care. I didn't want to talk about my birthday or Christmas. I left the main house and walked across the lawn in the chilly afternoon air. A cold soft rain started to fall, giving my exposed arms goosebumps and making me shiver.

I arrived at the workout room and came to an abrupt halt.

Kincade was already there lifting weights on the bench press.

I couldn't catch a break.

He dropped the weight and sat up. Our eyes met. We stared at each other in silence and I got a tingling sensation in the pit of my gut.

"Where's Gideon?" I asked.

"Not here."

He pushed off the bench and stood, reaching for a towel and wiped his face. He wore a sweat-dampened gray workout shirt that clung to his muscular torso, black workout pants and shoes. I could see faint scars on his wrists from his previous experience in the Second Circle of Hell when Azriel had imprisoned him. It'd taken him a while to heal. Our paths hadn't crossed much in the last few weeks while he convalesced. Mostly because I was avoiding him like he had a communicable disease.

"Oh, well, I'll come back later then." I started to leave.

"You can work out with me."

His deep inviting voice made me halt mid-reach for the door. I peered over my shoulder at him to see if he was kidding or not. His face was serious. His eyes hard and piercing. If I agreed, it would be the closest we'd been since that day in front of my mother's portrait when I was certain he wanted to kiss me and didn't.

"Oh, it's okay. I'll—"

"What are you afraid of, Miss Walker?"

That tingling sensation was back, prickling all the way up my spine to the nape of my neck. He hadn't called me that in a while. Here I thought we were on a first name basis. "I'm not afraid of anything."

"You sure?" He tilted his head to the side in a challenge.

Kincade had this weird internal lie detector, so he probably knew I lied to cover my feelings. He could have pointed out I was afraid of a lot of things but he didn't. He could have told me he knew I didn't want to get that close to him. But he didn't. He could have told me I was a coward for wanting to put as much distance as possible between us.

But he didn't.

I thought when he was all the way healed he would move on and go back to wherever he went. He had stayed. He told my uncle once he could do better training me than those "two idiots" Gideon and Gilli. I wondered how true that was and couldn't resist the invitation.

I matched his head tilt. "All right. You're on."

He tossed the towel to the floor then cracked his knuckles. "Let's see what you got."

We approached the workout mat on opposite sides, like I had before with Gideon. Kincade placed his feet shoulder-width apart and flexed his fingers. I stood there like a dummy trying to decide my next move.

"Come at me." He waved his hands in invitation.

I hesitated so I stalled. "I don't want to hurt you."

He looked bored and annoyed. He cracked his knuckles once more and then charged. He moved so fast I didn't have time to brace myself or react. The next thing I knew I was flat on my back staring up at the florescent lighting.

"Sarcasm will not save you, Miss Walker." He stood next to me looking down.

Maybe not but it was the only armor I'd ever had. There was something intimidating about his six-foot-plus frame standing over me. His thigh muscles were the size of my waist. There was no doubt in my mind he was a big guy that dwarfed my not-so-petite stature.

He held a hand down to help me up. I grasped it and he tugged, pulling me with ease to my feet.

I don't know what came over me. I dropped my head and charged, hitting him square in the chest and driving him back. He hadn't expected it and stumbled, losing his footing. As he started to fall, he wrapped his arms around me. I crashed against him as he thudded on the mat.

Strange how in that one moment all I could think about was how nice and perfect I fit against him. He gave me that same electrifying look as he did that day in front of my mother's portrait.

I shivered and shoved away but he held fast.

"What are you afraid of?" His deep voice was low, rumbling against my chest.

"Nothing."

"You're trembling."

"I'm not."

"You are. Is it because we're close? You don't want to be close to me?"

He'd know if I lied so I had to go with the truth. "I don't."

"Why not?" His gaze lingered on my lips. Damn if I couldn't help but lick them.

I was terrified of the emotions slicing through me when I was near him but I didn't want to say that.

"I think you know why."

His warm hand cradled the nape of my neck and held me in place. My pulse beat so hard I could hear it throbbing in my ears. The blood drained from my head leaving those pinpricks of light dancing in my vision. I didn't know if I wanted him to kiss me or not. I was terrified what it would do to me.

His other arm tightened around my waist. He rolled and pinned me underneath him, laying half on and half off me. I gasped.

"Now try to get free," he said.

"What?"

"You heard me, Miss Walker."

"But you're bigger and stronger than me."

An eyebrow lifted. "And you're holding back. Afraid you're going to hurt my feelings?"

I laughed. And then brought my knee up to his groin. He grunted, his grip slacked enough for me to squirm free and get to my feet. I spun and kicked him in the side. He swiped his arm and knocked me off my feet. I went down on the mat, landing on my left side, jarring my shoulder.

"That's better." I could hear a smile in his voice but I knew he wasn't smiling.

"You are so twisted." I dragged my body to all fours and looked at him.

He sat on the mat with one knee up and his forearm resting on top as though we were having a picnic in the park.

"You like twisted."

"Do I? I don't think so."

He shoved to his feet then held his hand down to me again. I eyed it with suspicion.

"Let me help you," he said.

I grasped his hand. He hauled me up with a wild jerk that made me stumble into him. I swear he did it on purpose.

"Stop that."

"Stop what?"

Deep in his green-gold eyes I could see mirth and something akin to desire burning there. It shook me to the core.

"You know what you're doing."

"Do I?" He paused and once again his gaze lingered on my lips. "Do you?"

I swallowed hard. I could read between the lines. I wasn't oblivious.

I tried to decide if I liked where this was going. I could easily be swayed by Kincade's charms, rough as they were. We'd dream walked each other and I'd seen a softer side of him he didn't publicly display.

"What are you not telling me, Miss Walker?"

The abrupt change in subject made me blink. "What do you mean?"

"You know what I mean. No sense playing dumb."

There was a lot I hadn't told him. Like how my mother was still alive and had become an agent for the Knights of the Holy Lance. Or that Lucifer wanted me all to himself. Or that other thing about Azriel I tried to bury.

"There's nothing to talk about."

I stalked toward the door. He grabbed my arm and spun me to face him. Fury creased his face.

"Don't walk away from me."

Praise for Call of the Dark
Dream Walker, Book 1

"I loved this book! It's a great start to a new adventure series. It reminds me of a mashup of urban fantasy and the Indiana Jones movies with angels and demons thrown in." —5 stars, Amazon Reviewer

"I literally inhaled the book in just an afternoon! I can't wait for the next installment!!!" —5 stars, Goodreads Reviewer

"...action packed with a heroine to cheer for...I will be eagerly awaiting the next book." —5 stars, Goodreads Reviewer

"One nail-biting rollercoaster!" —5 stars, Amazon Reviewer

"Powerful...an adventure of a lifetime...I can't wait to see what happens next."—5 stars, Bookbub Reviewer

"Loved it!" —5 stars, Goodreads Reviewer

"Great characters and amazing storylines. A must read." —5 stars, Amazon Reviewer

Praise for the Adventures of Ransom & Fortune

Highland Fling, Volume 1

A girl, a hit man and a time machine may be more than Dane Fortune can handle.

"…characters with real chemistry and a rip-roaring adventure." —5 stars, Amazon Reviewer

"…a fun twist to time travel…" —4 stars, Amazon Reviewer

"Dane Fortune is a delicious blend of everything you want in a hero." —4 stars, BookBub Reviewer

"I liked the set up for this book. It's pretty exciting and I didn't want to put it down." —5 stars, Amazon Reviewer

Dead of Winter, Volume 2

At the mercy of a faulty time machine, will Skye and Dane be able to make it home alive?

"…heart-stopping…full of anxiety-inducing moments and nail-biting suspense." —5 stars, BookBub Reviewer

"…a fun adventure that will leave [you] wanting more Ransom and Fortune." —4 stars, Amazon Reviewer

"…you'll want book 1 first so you can join in the wild ride from the beginning." —5 stars, BookBub Reviewer

"Adding the element of time travel to a book already rife with fantastical events—the story's endless possibilities are spellbinding." —Fort Worth Magazine

The Citadel, Volume 3

Still lost in time, Skye and Dane face their most dangerous enemy yet.

"What an amazing and addicting series!" —5 stars, Amazon Reviewer

"... plenty of action and a great storyline kept me reading until I finished it!" —5 stars, Amazon Reviewer

"Can't wait for the next one!" —5 stars, Amazon Reviewer

Lord of the Underworld, Volume 4

This title has never been published before and is a brand new adventure!

"This was a fast paced read…" —4 stars, Amazon Reviewer

"…a fast paced time travel adventure that is such a fun and easy read." —5 stars, Amazon Reviewer

"…a well written story that kept me turning pages, I want to read the next book." —4 stars, BookBub Reviewer

Watch for more adventures with Skye and Dane!
www.MichelleMiles.net

Praise for the Dragon Protectors

Desiring the Dragon Lord, Book 1

"Michelle Miles kicks off her new Dragon Protectors series with a bang…" —4 stars, Amazon Reviewer

"I read this book in just a couple of days. I couldn't put it down!" —5 stars, Amazon Reviewer

"…a wonderful book full of strong minded characters." —5 stars, Amazon Reviewer

Seducing the Dragon Knight, Book 2

"From the start this book has danger and a bit of mystery." —4 stars, Amazon Reviewer

"I love this author and this genre. A must read." —5 stars, Booksprout Reviewer

"I was half in love with Rafe when we met him in Desiring the Dragon Lord, but oh get me a fan and a cool drink, because his hot factor increased 100-fold in the second installment." —4 stars, Amazon Reviewer

Tempting Her Dragon Bodyguard, Book 3

"I loved reading this book and hope there are more to come." —5 stars, Amazon Reviewer

"Book three in the Dragon Protectors series is a well written story that kept me turning pages. I had to know what was going to happen." —5 stars, Amazon Reviewer

"…a captivating storyline…" —4 stars, Amazon Reviewer

Praise for Age of Wizards

In the Tower of the Wizard King, Book 1

"The book has a very strong and intriguing plotline as well as unforgettable characters. I liked the parallel narration of the present and the past as it made the story both more complicated and more involving…" —5 stars, Amazon Reviewer

"The mix of past and present stories brings the reader full circle and will keep you engrossed in the story. Beware though, you may not want to put the book down! …two thumbs up…!" —5 stars, Goodreads Reviewer

"Michelle Miles brilliantly weaves twists and turns, love stories both past and present, secrets, betrayal and revenge, with multi-dimensional characters, two different timelines and two different worlds." —5 stars, Amazon Reviewer

"I thoroughly enjoyed every aspect of this book, and highly recommend it. Filled with fantasy and three dimensional characters I couldn't put it down." —5 stars, Amazon Reviewer

On the Hunt for the Wizard King, Book 2

"We really got to watch all of the characters grow and change throughout the book. No one was what you expected. Miles did a great job of keeping you guessing and wondering what was around the next corner." —5 stars, Amazon Reviewer

"Wow! This story is so full of magic with action and adventure I could not put it down. The land of fae is an exciting magical world where anything can happen, and I definitely was not expecting some of the twist and turns that transpired." —5 stars, Amazon Reviewer

Also by Michelle Miles

Dream Walker
Call of the Dark
Blood and Bone

Age of Wizards
In the Tower of the Wizard King
On the Hunt for the Wizard King

A Ransom & Fortune Adventure
Highland Fling, Vol 1
Dead of Winter, Vol 2
The Citadel, Vol 3
Lord of the Underworld, Vol 4

Dragon Protectors
Desiring the Dragon Lord
Seducing the Dragon Knight
Tempting Her Dragon Bodyguard

Realm of Honor
One Knight Only
Only for a Knight
A Knight to Remember
A Knight Like No Other
Shadows of the Knight

Guardians of Atlantis
Tempting Eden
Seducing Eve
Ravishing Helene
Guardians of Atlantis Box Set

Coffee House Chronicles
Talk Dirty to Me
Nice Girls Do
Have Yourself a Merry Little Latte
Take Me I'm Yours
Sex, Lust & Martinis

Forever Yours
A Little Taste of Heaven

Shorts and Anthologies
A Dance Among the Faeries, Short Story
Eorwulf, Short Story
The Soul of Sharah, Short Story
Sinfully Sweet, Short Story
Flights of Fantasy: A Collection of Short Stories

Watch for more at www.MichelleMiles.net

About the Author

Michelle Miles believes in fairy tales, true love and magic. She is the award-winning author of the epic fantasy, IN THE TOWER OF THE WIZARD KING, as well as the fantasy romance series, REALM OF HONOR, featuring knights and their ladies fair, and the paranormal dragon-shifter romance series, DRAGON PROTECTORS.

In her spare time, she enjoys listening to music, reading, cross-stitching and watching movies. Even though she's a native Texan, she loves castles, dragons, fairies and elves and is an avid Game of Thrones fan. She can be found online at Facebook, Twitter, Instagram, Pinterest, and Goodreads.

CPSIA information can be obtained
at www.ICGtesting.com
Printed in the USA
BVHW041148300920
589971BV00013B/327